P9-DCV-701

AFRAID OF THE DARK

ALSO BY JAMES GRIPPANDO

Money to Burn
Intent to Kill
*Born to Run**
*Last Call**
Lying with Strangers
*When Darkness Falls**†
*Got the Look**
*Hear No Evil**
*Last to Die**
*Beyond Suspicion**
A King's Ransom
Under Cover of Darkness‡
Found Money
The Abduction
The Informant
*The Pardon**

And for young adults
Leapholes

*A Jack Swyteck Novel
†Vincent Paulo's debut
‡FBI agent Andie Henning's debut

AFRAID OF THE DARK

James Grippando

HARPER
An Imprint of HarperCollins*Publishers*

 For information, address HarperCollins Publishers, 10 East 53rd Street, New York, NY 10022.

ISBN: 978-0-06-184028-9

4 Tiffany
FWIW . . . 143

AFRAID OF THE DARK

Chapter One

KUTGW.

Sergeant Vince Paulo stared at the text message on his smart phone and didn't have a clue.

In many respects, Vince was at the top of his game. Good looking and full of confidence, he'd come to the city of Miami police force straight out of the marines after a tour of duty in the Gulf War. He was born to be a cop, and a college degree in psychology combined with his battle-tested coolness under pressure made him a natural for crisis management. Five years as lead negotiator had earned him the reputation of a risk taker who didn't always follow the conventional wisdom of other trained negotiators. His critics said that his unorthodox style would eventually catch up with him. The prediction only made Vince bolder.

But this texting bullshit made him feel impotent. New acronyms popped up every hour. The coffeehouse had free Wi-Fi, so Vince put down his latte and Googled the definition of "KUTGW."

Keep up the good work.

Benign enough, especially from a sixteen-year-old girl.

Intercepting text messages between teenagers wasn't Vince's regular duty, but there was little he wouldn't do for his best friend, Chuck Mays. For years now, Chuck had partnered with Vince on a number of high-tech law enforcement projects. He was currently in Asia looking to outsource the collection of personal information on millions of consumers and globalize his company's data mining services. His wife Shada and their daughter McKenna had stayed behind in Miami. It was an important trip, but Chuck had almost canceled it. Shada was *that* concerned about their daughter's ex-boyfriend. It was while Vince was giving his friend a lift to the airport that Chuck had flashed a deadly serious expression and uttered the ominous words that Vince would never forget:

"I don't know the whole story, but I'm telling you, Vince: Shada is convinced that the son of a bitch is going to hurt McKenna if she doesn't stay away from him."

As a cop, Vince had seen plenty of restraining orders ignored, so he didn't even suggest that the Mays family seek one. McKenna wasn't exactly cooperative anyway. She refused to let her parents monitor her cell or computer, and to Chuck's dismay, her mother had sided with McKenna. Chuck was standing on the curb outside the international terminal, two hours away from boarding the Miami-London leg of his flight to Mumbai, when he persuaded Vince that this was a potential safety issue that transcended teen privacy concerns. But he didn't want "just anybody" looking over McKenna's shoulder. Chuck provided the spy software—rudimentary stuff for a self-taught computer genius who was pioneering the personal information business. Vince agreed to review McKenna's text messages from three P.M. to nine P.M. Eastern time, hours that Chuck spent sleeping on the other side of the world. Chuck would cover the rest of the day.

Vince removed the plastic lid from his tall paper cup and grimaced. More foam than fuel. That would teach him to order something other than his usual straight cup of joe. No wonder customers felt entitled to monopolize a table for hours on end—just them, their laptops, and five-dollar cups of no coffee.

TFANC. Time for a new coffeehouse.

Vince spooned away the foam as McKenna's text messages continued to load on his smart phone. The wireless transfer from

McKenna's memory card to his occurred in seconds, no way for McKenna to know what had hit her. Message after message, line after line, nothing but teenage babble. Vince was actually feeling pretty fortunate to be single.

How do parents keep up with this insanity?

Vince scrolled through McKenna's messages, coffee in one hand and his cell in the other. Reading this stuff was downright painful. OMG. LOL. CU L8R. It was the endless electronic version of Exhibit A in the case against the existence of intelligent life on Earth. One last swig of coffee—and then he froze. The most recent message hit him like a 5 iron to the forehead. It was thirty-five minutes old. McKenna had sent it to Jamal—the ex-boyfriend.

FMLTWIA.

It was alphabet soup to just about anyone who wasn't in high school, but Vince had seen the Miami Police Department's crib sheet on teenage sex and texting—"sexting." FMLTWIA had stuck in his mind only because it was among the most vulgar. He had known and loved McKenna since she was a ponytailed little girl with half of her teeth missing, so it shocked him that she would even know what it meant. The thought of her actually sending such a message to her ex—*supposedly* ex—boyfriend made him sick to his stomach. Vince suddenly felt an avuncular need to intercede, to step in where his friend Chuck would if he weren't eight thousand miles away.

Vince dialed McKenna's cell. There was no answer, but Chuck's spyware also had GPS tracking ability. A simple punch of a button on Vince's cell would reveal the exact location of McKenna's phone, which 99.9 percent of the time meant the exact location of McKenna. It wasn't something he did lightly, but this kind of sexting wasn't just the high-tech version of the "truth or dare" games that kids used to play when Vince was in school. The on-screen coordinates told him that McKenna was at home. Vince dialed the landline for the Mays residence. No answer, which didn't mean that McKenna wasn't there—but it *did* mean that McKenna's mother wasn't. McKenna was home alone. Alone with Jamal.

FMLTWIA. Fuck Me Like the Whore I Am.

Vince didn't shock easily; and yes, it was a different world now. But if Chuck was right—if seeing Jamal was playing with fire—then this was gasoline. His hand was shaking as he dialed McKenna's mother on her cell.

Shada didn't answer. *Now what?*

Vince had no specific instructions from Chuck on what to do if Jamal came around while Dad was out of the country. But his friend's words came back to Vince—*that son of a bitch is going to hurt McKenna*—and the FMLTWIA text message hardly bespoke a teenage girl with healthy self-esteem. He knew he had to do something—fast.

Vince bolted from his chair, hurried to his car, and burned rubber out of the parking lot. Steering through traffic with one hand, he speed-dialed McKenna again and again. He could tell that her phone was powered on—it took five rings before going to voice mail, not the instant transfer that indicated a cell was off—but she didn't answer. Another call to her mother also went unanswered. He dialed Chuck in Mumbai, even though it was four A.M. there. The call immediately went to voice mail, and Vince stammered at the beep, not sure what to say. He settled on something vague but urgent.

"Chuck, we've got a bit of a situation here. Call me immediately."

One hell of a message to wake up to.

Vince put the cell in the console and focused on driving. It was early evening, but it felt much later. Sunset came early in January, and the junglelike canopy over Coconut Grove blocked the famous Miami moonlight, making for dark residential streets. Cyclists and joggers were out with their blinking safety lights and reflective tape. Vince was careful to avoid them as he overtook slower moving vehicles, his car racing well above the twenty-five-mile-per-hour limit on the winding two-lane road to the Mays house. He pulled into the driveway and stopped so quickly that the front bumper nearly kissed the Chicago bricks. There wasn't even time to slam the car door shut as he sprinted up the walkway to the front door.

He rang the bell and waited, catching his breath as he surveyed things with a cop's eye. McKenna's car was parked in the driveway. No others were in sight, except for Vince's. Jamal's could have been in the garage, he supposed, beside Chuck's.

He rang the doorbell again, then stepped back for a broader view of the house. As best he could tell, no lights were on inside. But that didn't mean anything. It was a two-story house, the biggest on the block. Plenty of bedrooms and back rooms.

FMLTWIA.

"McKenna!" he shouted, giving the solid mahogany door three firm knocks.

Again he waited, but with each passing second his pulse quickened. Vince had excellent cop instincts, and his gut was telling him that something was wrong, that inside the house it wasn't just a couple of high-school sweethearts discovering themselves.

"I'm telling you, Vince: Shada is convinced that the son of a bitch is going to hurt McKenna."

Vince dialed her cell one last time, gripping his phone tightly as it rang once, twice—and then the ringing stopped.

"McKenna?"

No answer. But someone had picked up, he was sure of it.

"McKenna, is that you?"

The voice on the line was weak, but the words were unmistakable.

"Help . . . me."

Vince leaped into action, kicking the front door open and drawing his firearm as he burst into the foyer.

"Police!" he shouted. "McKenna! Where are you?"

He switched on the lights. The stairway brightened, and Vince immediately spotted drops of blood on the beige runner. He charged up the steps with his pistol drawn, the cell to his ear as he identified himself and called for backup.

"Possible sexual assault," he told the dispatcher. "Ambulance needed!"

The upstairs hallway was dark, except at the very end. Outside the third bedroom on the left, the faint glow of a lamp shone through the open doorway and hovered like a ghost in the black corridor. Vince planted his back to the wall, eager to find McKenna but cautious of a possible confrontation with her attacker.

"Miami police!" he shouted again. "McKenna, are you up here?"

No response. Vince moved a few steps closer to the lighted bedroom and halted. More drops of blood in the hallway. They led like a crimson trail to the doorway. From this angle, he could see partially into the room. On the rug was a pool of blood.

Dear God.

Vince jumped into the open doorway, feet spread in the marksman's crouch, pistol aimed at any possible perp.

"Freeze!" he shouted, but even that single word caught in his throat. McKenna was naked on the floor, her twisted body covered with her own blood.

"McKenna!"

Vince went to her, knelt at her side, and raised her head from the floor. He saw no weapon in the immediate area, but the defensive wounds on her hands—her left thumb was hanging by a thread—ruled out any possibility of self-inflicted injuries. The largest wound was to her rib cage, a gaping hole that was spewing bloody foam and almost certainly indicated a punctured lung—a sucking chest wound. The internal bleeding had to be massive, but most of the blood on the floor was from the slash across the left side of her neck. A direct hit to the carotid artery would have been fatal long before, but hers had at least been nicked. Blood everywhere, so much blood, more than any human being could lose and live to tell about. Vince checked for a pulse. Weak. Almost nonexistent.

"McKenna?" he said, his voice rising.

Her eyes blinked open.

"Hold on, baby," he said.

McKenna's body was going cold, so Vince pulled a blanket from the bed and covered her. He tore the top sheet into bandages. He wrapped a long strip around her chest, and he took it as a bad sign that she didn't writhe in pain; she was barely conscious. The other strip he folded into a square and applied pressure to the neck wound, careful not to obstruct her airway. Neither was much help. The blood kept coming, the noisy wound in her chest kept spewing red foam. In complete frustration, he dialed the police dispatcher again.

"Where the hell is the ambulance?" he shouted. "I need one, *now*!"

"It's on its way."

Two squad cars to patrol all of Coconut Grove just weren't enough, but Vince was all too aware of the department's economic reality.

"I have a sixteen-year-old white female, multiple stab wounds. Get me a doctor on the line. I need someone to tell me how to help her!"

"Keep her warm to prevent shock."

"Already did that," said Vince.

"Apply pressure to the wounds to slow the bleeding."

"I'm doing that, but she's got a sucking chest wound and possible damage to the carotid artery. We need help!"

"ETA is three minutes," said the dispatcher.

McKenna was trying to speak. Vince added one last plea for the dispatcher to hurry, and then he disconnected, putting his ear to McKenna's breath.

"Am I . . ."

"McKenna?" he said, as if to help her finish her thought.

". . . gonna die?" she asked.

Blood was coming from her mouth.

Holy shit!

A huge part of him wanted to think only of that healthy and determined little girl he used to watch on the soccer field, the beautiful and intelligent young woman who had survived the social horrors of middle school. But as he looked into her eyes, he saw past his own denial and found himself staring into two darkening pools of the obvious and inevitable. Vince had seen that same look in the eyes of a fallen soldier in combat, in the eyes of his father in hospice care. McKenna was not long for this earth—he was almost certain of it.

Cop instincts took over. He wasn't giving up all hope, but if the worst happened, Vince wanted to make damn sure that the lowlife bastard would pay for what he'd done to McKenna. He grabbed his phone, dialed his home number, and waited for his answering machine to pick up. From that point forward, all words—his and McKenna's—would be spoken directly into his cell and recorded onto his machine.

Vince put the phone to McKenna's lips. She seemed scared, so helpless, as she looked up at him.

"Tell me," she whispered. "Am I dying?"

Blood had soaked all the way through the blanket. The folded square of torn bedsheet on her neck was completely red. But Vince couldn't be that brutally honest.

"No, sweetheart. You're gonna be just fine."

"Really?"

"Who did this to you?"

"Am I going to die?"

"No, McKenna. You're going to be fine. Who did this?"

"You really think I'm going to be okay?"

"Yes, it's not your time. I saw much worse than this in Iraq, and they're all fine. Tell me who did this to you."

She was fading. Vince tried again.

"Who did this to you?"

She coughed on the blood in the back of her throat. Vince checked the chest wound beneath the blanket. Even with the makeshift bandage, the foam oozing from the slit between her ribs emitted a gurgling noise. That hole in her chest was literally sucking the life out of her.

"McKenna, tell me who did this to you."

He put the cell to her mouth, and her eyes closed. It was too much effort to keep them open and speak at the same time. "Jamal," she whispered.

"Your boyfriend?"

She tried to nod but couldn't. "My first," she said, her voice barely audible.

The gurgling noise from her chest gave way to sudden silence. McKenna's eyelids stopped quivering. Vince dropped the phone, threw his leg over her body, and jumped into CPR mode.

"Come on, McKenna!" he said as he pushed against her rib cage. Frothy blood squirted from her chest wound like seawater from a blowhole, and Vince froze, not sure what to do. He tried mouth to mouth, but he was breathing into a pool of blood that had risen up in her throat. He checked her pulse. There was none. Her body was motionless. Vince tried one last series of chest compressions, and more blood shot from the blowhole. Vince fell forward, pounding the floor with his clenched fist.

"Son of a bitch!"

He slid his hands behind her head and supported the back of the neck. McKenna's beautiful face was deadweight in his hands. Tears filled his eyes as he took her in his arms, the blood-soaked blanket turning his shirt bright red.

Sirens blared from somewhere down the block.

Too late was Vince's first thought, but deep inside he knew he didn't mean the ambulance and police backup. If only he had checked those text messages twenty minutes sooner.

I was too late.

Then he heard a noise downstairs.

Jamal?

He kissed McKenna's forehead, quickly pulled the blanket up over her face, and jumped to his feet. In a matter of seconds he was down the hall and at the top of the stairs. The sirens were getting closer. There was another noise. It was coming from the garage.

He's still here!

Vince flew down the stairs, ran through the living room, and stopped at the kitchen counter. He'd visited the Mays house many times before, and he knew that the pockmarked, pecky-cypress door on the other side of the kitchen led to the three-car garage.

The sirens were loud now, just outside the house. Vince could have—should have—waited for backup. But a complicated mix of emotions took over. Anger. Guilt. Grief. More anger. His pistol firmly in hand, he hurried across the kitchen and pushed open the door.

"Freeze!" he shouted, but even he couldn't hear his command. The mere act of opening the door had triggered a noise that was deafening. The heat overwhelmed him. The flash blinded him. For a split second—it seemed much longer—it felt as if someone were pushing his eyes out the back of his skull, as his head snapped back with the force of a mule kick.

And then all was black.

Three years later
January

Chapter Two

It was Jack Swyteck's second trip to Cuba in the past three weeks. He had yet to meet a Cuban.

Miami was his home, and while it was true that Miami was closer to Havana than to Orlando, Jack's flight to the Oriente Province at the southeastern tip of the island was over four hundred air miles. His personal escorts from the naval airstrip to the detention facility were two U.S. marines, a blue-eyed farm boy from Kansas and a first-generation Mexican-American from Los Angeles. His co-counsel, a JAG lawyer assigned to the case despite her client's obvious discomfort with a female attorney, was from the South Side of Chicago. The civilian translator from Mogadishu was delivering Jack's words in Somali and, occasionally, Arabic. Jack's client was from East Africa. A spinmaster might have made the argument that the U.S. Naval Base in Guantánamo was just as much a melting pot as the nation that ran it. To Jack, the whole place felt more like a ticking time bomb.

"I'm not a government interrogator," said Jack, but he was essentially talking to the walls. Four of them, to be exact, an eight-by-ten steel-and-concrete shed, with a separate holding cell and bunk to the left.

Jack's client said nothing. It was playing out exactly the way Jack's first visit to Guantánamo had—the lawyer talking, the client too distrustful to acknowledge his existence.

The briefing material estimated that Prisoner No. 977 was

in his mid-twenties, but three years of confinement and various forms of government "enhanced interrogation" tactics had aged him beyond his years. His thin, dark face was dull and weary. His long black beard was gnarled, his fingernails brittle and yellowed. His first language was officially listed as Somali, but no one seemed to know for certain. There were no confirmed reports of his ever having uttered a word to anyone at Gitmo.

"Maybe he speaks Pashto or Farsi," said Jack. "Can we try another language?"

"Only if you get another translator," the interpreter said.

There was no time for that. In sixteen hours Jack was scheduled to be in federal court in Washington arguing for the prisoner's release. As habeas corpus proceedings went, this one was in a class by itself, but Jack had the pedigree to handle it. Some fifteen years ago, a four-year stint with the Freedom Institute had been Jack's first job out of law school. His father was the governor of Florida at the time, a man who'd campaigned on a strong pro–death-penalty platform. Jack was hardly the perfect fit for a ragtag group of former hippies who worked only capital cases, but he and his old boss Neil Goderich had remained close over the years. It was Neil who'd asked Jack to take the case of Prisoner No. 977. Jack had no illusions of selling his friends and family on the everybody-deserves-a-lawyer argument. It was a huge pro bono undertaking for a sole practitioner, but Jack kept his involvement quiet—until it came time for the government to clear his visit to Gitmo, and the FBI background check left his neighbors wondering if he was a mob lawyer on the verge of indictment. Finally, he had to come clean. The reactions were pretty uniform.

Are you kidding me?

You're defending a terrorist?

His best friend, Theo Knight—a death row inmate until Jack and a DNA test had proved his innocence more than a decade ago—was the only one to shrug it off: "Dude, know what GITMO stands for? *Giving Interrogation Teams More Options.*"

Funny, kind of—if you were pounding back beers at one of Theo's bars in Miami. But once the airplane landed at Gitmo, there wasn't a lot of laughter. Jack had read the report from the former prosecutor, who had resigned from the case in disgust. Prisoner No. 977 had been rounded up by Ethiopian troops from a suspected al-Qaeda safe house in southern Somalia. He was accused of sheltering Fazul Abdullah Mohammed, al-Qaeda's operations chief, who was responsible for planning the 1998 bombings of the U.S. embassies in Kenya and Tanzania, as well as the 2002 car-bombing attack in Kenya and missile attack on an Israeli airliner. A handwritten confession was the centerpiece of the case against him. He didn't write it. The one-page document was handed to him for his signature after several days of beatings, forced administration of drugs, and threats against his family. It was written in a language (Amharic) that he didn't speak, and he signed with his thumbprint, which was consistent with reports that he was completely illiterate. The Ethiopians turned him over to the Americans, to whom he refused to speak. Prison logs reflected that Prisoner No. 977 attempted to kill himself eleven hours after arriving at Gitmo. Eight weeks later he was on the so-called "frequent flier" program, where, in a two-week period, he was moved to a new cell 112 times—an average of every three hours—in order to ensure he was sleep deprived and disoriented. Over the three years at Guantánamo, he was repeatedly subjected to extreme cold, bright lights, and various stress positions, and he was often kept in solitary confinement.

Still, he refused to speak to anyone—even to his lawyer.

"I'm here to help you," said Jack, almost pleading now. "You have no way of knowing this, but in twenty-eight of the thirty-three detainee cases heard since last January, federal judges in my country have found insufficient evidence to support keeping them in prison. Many of those men were held without charges far longer than you."

The prisoner's gaze drifted away. He looked at the prayer mat rolled neatly and resting atop his bunk, then up at the large clock on the wall, then back out to nothing. There was no reason for him to trust Jack. None.

Fifteen minutes passed, Jack's words meeting with silence. Even on death row, Jack never had a client ignore him like this.

What now?

Jack glanced at the JAG lawyer to his right, then looked at the prisoner, who was now leaning back in his chair. This was going nowhere. It was absurd, really—the Yale-educated attorney sitting at a card table in a dank shed trying to explain habeas corpus to an illiterate peasant who was chained to the floor. Jack was running out of time, and becoming anxious was not going to help. He considered his next move, then completely shifted gears.

"My mother and grandmother were actually born in Cuba," Jack said.

Jack paused for the translator. He knew very little about the man in shackles before him. But he knew that he must have family. Maybe they could connect on that level. The prisoner hadn't seen or spoken to his loved ones in years. With a deep breath, Jack pushed forward with his last chance at a breakthrough.

"My mother left the island when she was seventeen, a couple years after Fidel Castro came into power. Her name was Anna. My grandmother put her on an airplane alone and sent her to live with relatives in Tampa. I can't even imagine how painful it must have been to watch her daughter go, but Abuela refused to let her child live under a dictator. She hoped to get off the island and reunite in a few months. It took much longer. She missed my mother's wedding. She missed the birth of her only grandchild—that would be me. It took forty years for my grandmother to finally get out of Cuba. By then, I was in my thirties, and my mother was long gone. Doctors didn't know much about preeclampsia back then. She died soon after I was born."

The translation brought no reaction. Forget *"I'm sorry."* Jack didn't tell that story often, but it was the first time in his life that he'd told it without drawing so much as a blink of the eye.

"What I'm trying to say is that I know what it must be like to be separated from your family," Jack said, and then he waited.

The prisoner looked up, impassive, his demeanor unchanged.

Time was running out. Jack could feel his heart beating faster, the prospect of failure strangling him. He struggled to maintain an even tone as he spoke.

"I also know what it's like to be accused of something you didn't do."

Jack told him about his friend Theo Knight—arrested as a teenager, an innocent man who had wasted four years of his youth on death row, twice having come so close to the electric chair that he'd eaten his last meal and had his head and ankles shaved for placement of the electrodes. It was hard not to get energized when talking about Theo, and Jack's words were coming so fast that the translator was having trouble keeping up.

"Four years," said Jack. "That's even longer than you've been here. Now Theo is a free man. My best friend. He owns two bars in Miami, plays the saxophone every Saturday night at a joint he calls Cy's Place in honor of his great-uncle. Everybody wants to be Theo."

Jack didn't mention that all of his other clients from those days were either dead or still on death row. He just let the thought of Theo and his newfound freedom hang in the gulf between them. But the prisoner was unmoved.

Family. Get back to family.

Jack was about to start talking again, then stopped, deciding to steer clear of his famous father. Tales of the former cop who had signed more death warrants than any other governor in Florida's history probably wouldn't endear Jack to a man in shackles. Jack was running out of angles. He was down to Grandpa Swyteck—his father's eighty-seven-year-old father.

"I visited him in the nursing home a few weeks ago," said Jack. "He has Alzheimer's."

Jack stopped. The prisoner looked at him curiously, as if—perhaps—he had been listening with interest to Jack's stories about his grandmother and Theo and was expecting Jack to say more about his grandfather. But Jack wasn't sure what to say next. It suddenly occurred to him how little he knew about the old man. A momentary sense of sadness came over him.

"He was born in the Czech Republic," Jack said. "Czechoslovakia, it was called then."

Finally a reaction—though Jack wasn't sure what had triggered it. He simply watched as the prisoner sat up, rested his forearms atop the card table, and looked Jack in the eye. There was another long stretch of silence, and then finally, in a moment that nearly blew away Jack and everyone else in the room, the man's lips moved.

"I have been there," he said. "In Prague."

The JAG lawyer looked at Jack, then at the prisoner, then back again. "He speaks," she said in disbelief.

Jack took one more long look around the room, at the cell and the steel bunk and the steel toilet and the O-ring drilled into the floor attached to the man's ankles. Then he leaned forward in his chair, looking straight at the man in front of him.

"Yeah, how 'bout that," said Jack. "In perfect English."

Chapter Three

It was a ten-hour car ride from Miami to Pensacola, like going to Alabama. The flight in Chuck Mays' new Cessna took a little over two hours. Vince practically kissed the ground upon landing, thanking God that Chuck hadn't suffered a midair heart attack that would have left Vince at the controls. At the terminal they piled into a rental car—Chuck, Vince, and Sam. Sam was Vince's golden retriever.

His guide dog.

Since losing his sight, Vince had heard all the amazing stories. The guy who blew his nose so violently that his eye popped out. The firefighter whose eye was left hanging by the optic nerve after a blast from a fire hose. The child who ruptured her eye on a bedpost while bouncing on the mattress. What made these cases remarkable was that in each instance the ultimate visual impairment was nonexistent or negligible, or so the tales of medical miracles went. On the other side of the coin were patients who seemed to suffer only minor ocular trauma, the globe still intact, but whose vision was lost forever. They were the unlucky ones, the Vince Paulos of the world.

"You are going to be amazed by this technology," said Chuck as he steered into the parking lot.

Vince heard him, but he didn't answer right away. All this talk about some kind of military gadget that could effectively restore his vision had him drifting back to the day he'd lost his sight—to that pockmarked door again, the opening to his personal and permanent tunnel of darkness.

"Vince?"

"Yeah, sorry. I was just thinking for a minute." It was a lie, of course, at least the part about "a minute." Vince had done far better than anyone had expected over the past three years, staying on as a full-time instructor with the police force and occasionally serving active duty as a negotiator, providing for himself, leading a surprisingly normal and enjoyable life without sight. Even so, a man couldn't help thinking and rethinking from time to time, imagining how different things might have been if he just hadn't pushed open that door.

The car stopped, and Chuck shut off the engine. "We're here," said Chuck.

Here was the Institute for Human and Machine Cognition (IHMC), a not-for-profit research institute where Chuck had some contacts. Vince had never heard of the place, but IHMC research partners included everyone from NASA and the Defense Advanced Research Projects Agency (DARPA) to IBM and Boeing. They don't just think outside the box, Chuck had told him, these guys are reinventing the box. The idea was to fit human and machine components together in ways that exploited their respective strengths and mitigated their respective weaknesses. For Vince, that meant the possibility of a whole new door to walk through.

"This way, Deacon Blues," said Chuck.

Vince smiled as he and Sam climbed out of the car. Chuck had been playing "Deacon Blues" and other old Steely Dan songs on the car stereo ever since telling Vince that one of the board members at IMHC was Jeff "Skunk" Baxter, a self-taught specialist in terrorism, missile defense, and chemical and biological warfare who was better known as a guitarist with Steely Dan and the Doobie Brothers. Skunk was one of those reinventing-the-box guys who worked alongside retired army generals, scientists, cognitive psychologists, neuroscientists, physicians, philosophers, engineers, and social scientists of various stripes.

They got a name for the winners in the world . . . call me Vincent Paulo.

Vince was trying not to get too excited, but if this new technology for the blind did everything Chuck said it could, Vince would literally be looking at life through a new porthole.

Fuck that door.

Sam stopped, and so did Vince. They were at the entrance. Chuck pushed the intercom button and announced their arrival. The receptionist's voice crackled over the speaker, a buzzer sounded, and Chuck opened the door. Vince stopped him before entering.

"Hey, I want to thank you," said Vince.

"No need, dude."

"Just . . . really. Thank you."

"I haven't done anything yet."

Nothing could have been further from the truth. The only man who had lost more than Vince in that explosion had been Chuck. McKenna's body had been consumed in the blaze. Two months later Chuck's wife was gone. Police had found Shada's overturned kayak floating in a section of the Florida Everglades that was crawling with pythons and alligators. An empty bottle of Valium and a suicide note were in her car. Her body was never recovered. Not once had Chuck even hinted that Vince had dropped the ball while he was out of the country, that Vince could have done anything to prevent the tragedy. Indeed, watching Chuck rebound through his work had been a real source of inspiration for Vince. Eleven months after McKenna's death, the fledgling data-mining company that had been sucking cash out of the Mays family was turning a profit. Six months ago, Chuck sold out to a media conglomerate for eight figures and formed a new venture—MLFC Inc.—which to most folks was an acronym for Mays Laser Fast Computers. It was over beers that Chuck and

Vince had come up with the name My Last Fucking Company.

"You're a good friend," said Vince. "I mean that."

Chuck sniffed the air like a golden retriever, then did his baritone Sam-the-dog voice. "Hmm, the shit's really gettin' deep here. Can I go inside and wipe my paws?"

The receptionist greeted them in the lobby and took them to the computer lab. It was a room like any other to Vince. He heard the hum of fluorescent lighting overhead. He felt the cool draft from an AC duct on the wall. It was actually *too* cool—a sign of how many computers they were trying to keep from overheating—yet Vince was perspiring with anticipation. Finally, Dr. Adam Feldman joined them. Feldman had a PhD in neuroscience, hours of experience with a device called Brainport, and the good sense to cut the small talk short. He quickly launched into business.

"The basic premise here," said Feldman, "is that you see with your brain, not with your eyes."

"Which means I've seen a lot of the inside of my skull over the past three years," said Vince.

"I meant that *all* sighted species see with their brains," said Feldman. "All the brain needs is the input. In your case, the eyes can no longer transmit. That's where Brainport comes in. Could you remove your sunglasses, please?"

Vince always wore them. To the office, at the beach, inside the house. He even wore them on his rock-climbing vacation last August. He heard a panting noise as he tucked the sunglasses into his coat pocket.

"Is that Sam or me?" asked Vince.

Dr. Feldman chuckled. Vince figured he wasn't the first blind man to get a little giddy over this device.

Feldman described what he was doing each step of the way, partly to educate Vince, partly to help him relax.

"These special eyeglasses I'm putting on you have a small video camera mounted on the nose bridge. The camera acts as the eyes to gather visual information. The images are transmitted wirelessly in black, gray, and white to this handheld computer," he said as he slid the device into Vince's hand.

It felt slightly larger than an iPod. "Okay. But I'm not seeing anything."

"Hold your horses there, cowboy," said Feldman. "The computer will translate the visual information into electrical signals. Let's turn it on."

Feldman guided Vince's thumb to the switch. Vince pressed it and waited. "I'm still not seeing anything."

"Vince," said Chuck, "One step at a time, all right?"

The anticipation was even beyond his first step onto a battleground as a marine, at least a million times greater than his first time with a woman. Well, maybe not a million. He took a breath and said, "Sorry, guys."

"No problem," said Feldman. "Just to give you some idea of what's going on, Brainport is built on the concept of sensory substitution, which means that when one sense malfunctions, another sense can compensate, serving as a stand-in. Even a blind person walking down the street with a cane is basically using a form of sensory substitution."

"Been there, done that," said Vince. He reached down and patted Sam on the withers. "Don't worry, buddy. I'm keeping you."

"You raise a good point," said Feldman. "I don't want to overstate the device. It's meant to supplement the cane and the guide dog. The idea is to help you perform everyday tasks that may seem simple to the sighted, such as reading street signs and searching for empty seats on a bus. A little additional information will make your life easier and safer."

"Tell him how you're studying it here at the institute," said Chuck.

Vince couldn't see him, but somehow he knew Feldman was smiling. "Again," he said, "we're talking about sensory substitution. Imagine a Navy SEAL with superhuman senses similar to those of owls or snakes."

"Are you saying I have to walk around sticking my tongue out at people?"

"No. But you're on the right track. The tongue ultimately replaces the eyes in transmitting visual input to the brain. That camera mounted on your glasses acts as your eyes, the visual images go to the little computer in your hand, and the computer translates the visual information into electrical signals. Those signals are transformed into gentle electrical impulses that end up on your tongue."

"How?"

"The lollipop," said Feldman.

"The what?"

"It's an electrode that you hold in your mouth to receive the electrical signal. The white portions of images become strong impulses, the gray become medium impulses, and the black result in no impulses. The tongue sends these impulses to the brain, where they are interpreted as sensory information that substitutes for vision. The whole process works in much the same way that the optic nerve in the eye transmits visual information to the brain."

"That's great if it works. What do you think about that, Sam?"

The bushy tail brushed Vince's ankle as it wagged.

"You ready?" asked Feldman.

"Beyond ready," said Vince. "Bring on the lollipop."

Chapter Four

At noon the following day Jack was having lunch near the federal courthouse at a Japanese restaurant called Sue-Him, Sue-Her, Su-shi—truly the kind of place that could whet the appetite of Washington lawyers, as long as the waiters avoided the obvious jokes about sharks eating raw fish.

The case of *Khaled al-Jawar v. The President of the United States of America* was heard in the same courthouse opposite the National Gallery of Art where, in that other world before 9/11, a grand jury had heard the sordid details of the Monica Lewinsky affair and Judge John Sirica had sorted out the Watergate scandal. Jack had elected not to have his client testify via secure video feed from Guantánamo, arguing that it was the government's burden to justify the detention. By eleven thirty, the hearing had ended and the judge had issued her ruling from the bench.

Neil Goderich was on his third cup of sake, furiously drafting a press release.

"How's this?" asked Neil, trying to make sense of his own scribble on the yellow legal pad. " 'Today, yet another Guantánamo detainee—Khaled al-Jawar from Somalia—was ordered released by a federal judge in Washington on the ground that there was insufficient evidence to justify his detention. While this is not the first detainee proceeding in which release has been ordered, the case of al-Jawar is particularly striking. He was just a teenager when he was shipped to Guantánamo three years ago, unquestionably tortured, never accused of being a member of either al-Qaeda or the Taliban, barely saved after a suicide attempt upon his arrival at Gitmo, and then locked in a cage indefinitely with no charges against him. The case completely unraveled after al-Jawar's lawyer—Jack Swyteck, son of former Florida governor Harry Swyteck—presented long-concealed evidence that his client 'confessed' to sheltering al-Qaeda operatives in East Africa only after Ethiopian troops threatened and drugged him into submission. So unpersuasive was the government's evidence against him that the judge excoriated the Justice Department in an unusually strident and hostile tone for attempting to continue his detention.' "

He paused, looked up, and frowned at Jack's reaction. "What's wrong?"

"Too much," said Jack.

Neil took another hit of sake. "All right, I'll leave your father out of it."

"It's not that. I just don't like it."

"But it's all true."

Jack put his chopsticks aside and leaned forward, his expression very serious. "What if he blows up a building tomorrow?"

"Then the government should have built a stronger case to keep him locked up. That's their job."

Suddenly, it was like old times. Most people thought Jack had left the Freedom Institute because he was nothing like the other lawyers: Eve, the only woman Jack had ever known to smoke a pipe; Brian, the gay surfer dude; and Neil, the ponytailed genius who had survived Woodstock. In truth, Jack considered all of them friends. They'd even shown up for his surprise fortieth birthday party. What had made Jack feel like such a misfit was the way they celebrated their victories. Forcing the government to prove its case was enough for Jack. Getting another guilty man released didn't make him want to throw a party. Or issue a press release.

"Al-Jawar should never have been locked up," said Neil.

"How do you know that?" asked Jack. "For that matter, how do you even know his name is al-Jawar?"

"Because he told us."

"Yeah, in English. A language no one even knew he spoke until yesterday."

"Whatever his name is, he's not guilty of anything but wearing a Casio watch," said Neil.

It was a reference to the fact that more than a dozen Gitmo detainees were cited for owning cheap digital watches, particularly the infamous Casio F914 watch, the type used by al-Qaeda members for bomb detonators.

Jack selected a pod of edamame from the bowl and brushed away the excess sea salt. "It bothers me that it never came out in court that he speaks English."

"That wasn't relevant. The confession they forced him to sign wasn't written in English—or in any other language that he speaks."

"I don't believe his story about being from Somalia. I think he's American."

"So what?

"He's hiding something."

Neil shrugged and turned his attention back to his press release. "Al-Jawar is actually one of the lucky ones," he said, speaking his edits aloud. "According to a report issued by *Human Rights First*, at least one hundred detainees in U.S. custody have died since 2002, many suffering gruesome deaths."

Jack was about to reel in the polemic, but a woman seated on the other side of the restaurant caught his attention. It was Sylvia Gonzalez, the Justice Department lawyer who had argued the government's case against his client.

"Don't look now," Jack started to say, but of course Neil did. He recognized Gonzalez instantly, as well as the man she was with.

"How fitting," Neil said, as if spitting out the bad taste in his mouth. "She's with Sid Littleton."

"Who's he?"

"Founder and CEO of Black Ice, the go-to private military firm for the Department of Defense. Surely you've heard of them. They're the independent contractors that the military hires to do things the military can't do, like shooting unarmed Iraqi civilians."

It was the editorial spin of a former hippie, but just as Jack was about to goad him into saying something really entertaining, the prosecutor spotted them.

"Woops, here she comes," said Jack. "Be nice."

"Congratulations," Gonzalez said as she offered her hand. Jack shook it. "You did a heck of a job," she added.

The conciliatory tone and gesture put him off balance. It was extremely professional of her. *All the more reason not to issue that stinging press release.*

"Thank you," said Jack.

He quickly introduced Neil, who remained in his chair, acknowledging her only with a weak wave of the hand. For Neil, anyone who lunched with the likes of Sid Littleton and Black Ice was the enemy, and there was never any fraternizing with the enemy.

"I was just putting the finishing touches on our press release," said Neil.

Jack sighed, wishing he hadn't mentioned it.

"You may want to hear what I have to say first," said Gonzalez.

Neil chuckled, but Jack wasn't sure why.

Gonzalez said, "I apologize for interrupting your lunch, but I'd rather not put this in an e-mail, and I think it's only fair to give you a heads-up on some last-minute developments in the al-Jawar matter. Your client is on a flight to Miami as we speak."

Jack bristled. *I knew he was American.* "Why?"

"Custody is being transferred to the Florida Department of Law Enforcement."

Neil popped from his chair, unable to contain himself. "What do you mean *transferred*? The judge ordered his release."

"He is being referred to the Miami-Dade state attorney for prosecution on criminal charges unrelated to terrorism."

"What—jaywalking?" said Neil, his neck swelling. "This is ridiculous."

"Easy, Neil," said Jack.

"No, this infuriates me," said Neil. "Every time a judge rules for a detainee, the DOJ tries to save face with vague references to some new evidence collected by the task force on detention that may lead to a criminal indictment. It's sleazy. This is another example of the administration's defiance of a court order and its refusal to admit that there was never any legal basis to detain these prisoners."

"This morning a grand jury indicted your client on one count of first degree murder and one count of attempted murder," said Gonzalez.

Neil fell silent.

Jack did a double take. "And you say this is unrelated to terrorism?"

"It's purely a local law enforcement matter," she said. "Your client is from Miami. His real name is Jamal Wakefield. And three years ago he killed a girl named McKenna Mays. Stabbed her to death."

Jack gave it a moment to sink in. Then he looked at his old boss and said, "Let's hold off on the press release, Neil."

Chapter Five

Jack was back in Miami by nightfall. He was wandering around lost in the airport's Flamingo Garage when he finally remembered that his car was in the Dolphin Garage. To a Floridian, parking garages named Dolphin and Flamingo were like identical twins named Frick and Frack. All that was missing was cousin Royal Palm. A ridiculously long moving sidewalk connected the two garages, and Jack's cell rang as he stepped onto it. The display read SUNNY GARDENS OF DORAL. It was his grandfather's nursing home.

"He's being combative again," the nurse said.

Jack got these calls about once a week. The usual scenario was that Grandpa was sleeping peacefully when the night nurse barged into the room, overpowered him with the health-care equivalent of waterboarding, and forced an unwanted and probably unnecessary medication down his throat fast enough to land her in the *Guinness Book of World Records, Nursing Edition.*

Who wouldn't be combative?

Jack was tired of the arguments, and the sound of his grandfather ranting senselessly against the post office in the background was breaking his heart.

"P.O., no, no," the old man shouted. "P.O., no, no!"

"Put him on the phone," said Jack.

"I can't. We're restraining him."

"*What?* I'll be there in twenty minutes."

He hung up and ran to his car. He was speeding down the ramps from the roof of the garage when his phone rang again. This time, however, the word PRIVATE appeared on the caller-ID display, and the timing brought a much needed sense of calm.

"Andie?" he said, answering.

"Hi, babe," she said.

Andie Henning was Jack's fiancée. He'd popped the question at the surprise birthday party she'd thrown for him last month. Andie had accepted on the spot—and disappeared eight days later. When people asked him what it felt like to be engaged, Jack honestly couldn't tell them. He didn't know where Andie was, didn't know when she was coming back, and had no idea when she would call next. She made him promise not to come looking for her, refused to share her new cell number, and wouldn't tell him who she was living with. He didn't know what she looked like anymore, though he was certain that the gorgeous long hair that had once splayed across his pillow had changed entirely. Jack didn't even know her new name.

Andie was unlike any woman Jack had ever known—and not just because she was an FBI agent who worked undercover. Jack loved that she wasn't afraid to cave dive in Florida's aquifers, that in her training at the FBI Academy she'd nailed a perfect score on one of the toughest shooting ranges in the world, that as a teenager she'd been a Junior Olympic mogul skier—something Jack didn't even know about her until she rolled him out of bed one hot August morning and said, "Let's go skiing in Argentina." He loved the green eyes she'd gotten from her Anglo father and the raven-black hair from her Native American mother, a mix that made for such exotic beauty.

He hated being away from her.

"When are you coming back?" he asked.

"You know I can't answer that," she said.

He knew. But on days like today, he couldn't help but ask. Funny, he'd been divorced for years, perfectly fine with living alone. But Andie's enthusiastic "yes" had been like the flip of an emotional light switch. The thought of being away from her tonight was almost too painful.

"I can't talk long," she said. "Just wanted to check in, say I love you."

"Love you, too."

"And Jack?"

"Yeah?"

"I'm not at liberty to say much about this, especially over the phone. But . . ."

He waited, then prodded. "But what?"

"Do yourself a favor," she said. "Stay away from the Jamal Wakefield murder case."

Jack gripped the phone. It had been one of their express understandings—a solemn pact to ensure a happy marriage between a criminal defense lawyer and an FBI agent. He didn't tell her how to do her job—whether to take this undercover assignment or that one—and she didn't tell him what cases to handle. He knew it wasn't a rule she would have broken lightly.

"I'll keep that in mind," he said.

"Good," she said. "I'll call again when I can."

One more "I love you," and she hung up.

Jack tucked the phone away and stopped the car to pay the teller at the exit to the Flipper-flamingo, string-bikini, piña-colada—*whatever*—garage. He tried to take Andie's advice in the spirit in which it had been given. It was eating at him so badly, however, that he almost missed his exit for the Dolphin—what else?—Expressway. A cabdriver gave him the horn and the finger as Jack cut across two lanes. His train of thought switched to his grandfather shouting out random letters while trying to break out of the Alzheimer's bed restraints, but he was also thinking about Andie's advice. Warning. Whatever it was.

"Stay away from the Jamal Wakefield murder case."

He knew her concern had nothing to do with the fact that

the accused was a former Gitmo detainee, or that the victim was a sixteen-year-old girl. It wasn't even the fact that the attempted murder charge involved the blinding of a cop named Vincent Paulo. It was the fact that Jack *knew* Vince. Not only knew him, but owed him. He and Theo both were indebted to Sergeant Paulo, big time. And now Jack represented Jamal Wakefield of Miami, Florida, aka Khaled al-Jawar of Somalia.

Sorry, Andie. Sorry, Vince.

P.O., no no.

Coming, Grandpa.

Why is nothing ever simple?

Chapter Six

I should have held at sixteen," said Vince.

He was back at home in the comfort of his bed. Sam lay quietly on the rug beside the dresser. His wife was at his side, still awake.

"What did you say, honey?" asked Alicia.

"In Dr. Feldman's office today," he said. "I was sitting on a king and the six of clubs, and like an idiot, I say, *Hit me.* Of course I busted. He dealt me a seven."

Vince felt the gentle caress of her hand at his chin, then the warmth of her kiss at the side of his mouth.

"I'm so happy for you," she whispered.

Vince smiled as she rolled back to her side of the mattress. It was late and he needed rest after such a full day, but he was too excited to sleep.

The Brainport session had lasted two hours. The first hurdle was to understand that it wasn't like seeing with your eyes. "It's more akin to a language in that you develop a skill," Dr. Feldman had told him. After five minutes he was able to operate the device. Within an hour he was recognizing sensations on his tongue and reaching out for a ball as it rolled in front of him. By the end of the session he was playing blackjack—not with Braille cards, but with regular ones. The next goal was to get him through an obstacle course, and from there the sky was the limit. Unfortunately, he couldn't take it home. Brainport was experimental. But it gave him hope. Today had been a great day, and nothing was going to spoil it.

Not even Jamal Wakefield.

"Vince?" asked Alicia. "Do you think . . . Will you have to testify at the trial?"

Jamal Wakefield, the three-year-old unsolved murder of McKenna Mays, and "the horrible price Miami police officer Vincent Paulo paid trying to bring the alleged killer to justice," had been the lead story on the local evening news. Vince had received a heads-up that morning from the assistant state attorney. He and Alicia had skirted the topic all night long, talking nonstop about Brainport. It had become the elephant in the room.

"I'm meeting with the assistant state attorney tomorrow. It'll be fine. Don't worry about it."

Vince peeled back the bedsheet to feel the night air on his chest. All of Florida was basking in glorious January weather, perfect for sleeping with the window open. Then, slowly but surely, Vince could almost feel a 101-degree cloud coming over him—a cloud so noxious that it probably violated several articles of the Geneva Conventions. Sam was a terror when there was fallen fruit in the backyard.

"Damn, Sammy," he said as he pulled the sheet up over his head. "Can you lay off the avocados?"

The cloud evaporated, cool air rustled the window sheers—and Vince could all but hear the wheels still turning in Alicia's head.

"Vince?" she asked in a tentative voice. "What do you think the prosecutor will tell you tomorrow?"

He lowered the bedsheet and sighed. Even after three years, it wasn't easy to talk about it. "I'm sure I'll have to testify."

"But they didn't call you before the grand jury."

"They used the written affidavit I signed three years ago. Not that they even needed it. All they had to do was play the recording of McKenna naming her boyfriend as the killer. The trial will be a different story. I was the only one there when McKenna died. I was holding the cell phone to her mouth when she identified her killer."

Vince could feel his wife rise up on her elbow, her concern palpable. "I'm scared," she said.

Those words hit him hard; Alicia didn't scare easily. They'd met on the force, when Alicia's father had been Miami's mayor, and she'd risen to become one of the top young cops in the department. "There's nothing to be afraid of," said Vince.

"I mean I'm afraid for us," she said. "I don't want this to take us back to the bad old days."

She was talking about a stretch of time before they were married, a few weeks after he became a hero, soon after the doctors removed the bandages—when Vince came to the frightening realization that he would never again see her smile, never look into those eyes as her heart pounded against his chest, never see the expression on her face when she was happy or sad or just plain bored. That was the same day he'd told her it would be best to stop seeing each other, and the unintended pun had made them both cry.

Vince held her tight. "That's not going to happen."

She unwound from his embrace and pressed her forehead against his, as if willing him to look her in the eye.

"Do you promise?"

It gave him goose bumps, this latest confirmation of how foolish he had been to push Alicia away, assuming as he had that it was only a matter of time before a beautiful young woman fell out of love with a blind man.

"Yes," he said. "I promise."

A strange noise reverberated near the dresser. They froze, each one processing it in a separate darkness, and then shared a laugh as they dove beneath the sheets.

"Sam!"

Chapter Seven

On Thursday morning, two hours before the scheduled arraignment of Jamal Wakefield in Miami-Dade County circuit court, Jack went to the Pretrial Detention Center with just one objective:

"I'm withdrawing as counsel," he told Neil.

The long prison corridor was lined with iron bars, and Neil had been waiting for Jack outside one of the attorney-client conference rooms. Charged with a capital offense, Jamal was held in a safety cell, away from the drunk drivers and petty thieves, which meant that he was allowed just two "under glass" visits per week. Inmates were allowed to meet and talk privately with their lawyers, however, and Jamal Wakefield was waiting on the other side of the locked door. Jack blurted out the words before Neil could even say hello.

"I'm sorry," said Jack. "I'll do whatever I can today to transfer the case to you. But I'm out."

Neil just smiled, completely unfazed. "Like old times, isn't it?"

It was indeed déjà vu. Jack had probably resigned a dozen times from the institute before actually packing up and leaving. It wasn't just the emotional drain of defending the guilty. As he'd told Neil more than ten years ago, he probably could have stuck it out if he had met just one guy on death row who was genuinely sorry for what he'd done. But those weren't the kind of cases that the institute handled.

"Give me one chance to change your mind," said Neil.

"It won't work."

"I'll cut off my ponytail if it doesn't."

Whoa. That was serious. "You're on," said Jack.

The guard unlocked the door from the inside, and the two lawyers entered.

"I'll be back in thirty minutes," the guard said, and then he closed the door.

The fluorescent lights overhead were so bright that Jack almost needed sunglasses. The floor was bare concrete, and the cinder-block walls were pale yellow with no windows. Seated at the Formica-topped table was Jamal Wakefield. The transformation since Gitmo was startling. A shave and a haircut alone made him look years younger, and even after three years of incarceration, it was easy to see how handsome McKenna's boyfriend had once been. Jack truly didn't recognize him.

The silver-haired man seated beside Jamal, however, was another story.

"Long time no see," said Peter Swenson.

In a classic case of overcorrection, Jack had literally switched sides after leaving the institute, spending the next two years of his career as a federal prosecutor. As Neil knew well, Swenson was the polygraph examiner that Jack had used regularly to test his informants.

"With my ponytail on the line, I wanted Jamal to be examined by someone you trust," said Neil.

"All right," said Jack. "You got my attention."

Advance clearance was required to administer a polygraph in jail, but Neil had taken care of that, and Swenson's equipment was ready to go. Two fingers on Jamal's left hand were wired to electrodes. Pneumograph tubes wrapped his chest and abdomen. An inflatable rubber bladder rested on the seat of the hard wooden chair beneath him, and another was behind his back. A blood pressure cuff squeezed his right bicep.

"Time's a-wastin'," said Neil. "Let's roll."

Swenson turned his attention to his cardio amplifier and galvanic skin monitor atop the table. The paper scroll was rolling as the needle inked out a pulsating line.

"All set," he said.

Jack knew the drill, and Swenson had taken care of the preliminaries before his arrival. The first task was to put the subject at ease. He started with questions that would make Jamal feel comfortable with him as an interrogator. Do you like music? Have you ever owned a car? Is your hair purple? They seemed innocuous, but with each answer Swenson was monitoring the subject's physiological response to establish the lower parameters of his blood pressure, respiration, and perspiration. It was almost a game of cat and mouse. The examiner needed to quiet him down, then catch him in a small lie that would serve as a baseline reading for a falsehood. The standard technique—Jack had seen it unfold many times—was to ask something even a truthful person might lie about.

"Have you thought about sex in the last ten minutes?"

"Uh, no."

Jamal blinked about five times. It wasn't something that men necessarily liked to admit—especially when charged with the obsession-driven murder of their girlfriend—but it was a scientific fact that anyone with a Y chromosome thought about sex every three minutes. The room fell silent as the examiner focused on his readings. He appeared satisfied. He knew what it looked like on the polygraph when Jamal lied. Now he could test his truth telling on the questions that really mattered.

"Is your name Jamal Wakefield?"

"Yes."

"Are we in Miami, Florida?"

"Yes."

Jamal seemed almost robotic in his responses—and rather than staring off blankly at the wall or the ceiling, he was looking straight at Jack, fully aware of the man he needed to convince.

"Is today Sunday?"

"No."

"Are you fluent in Chinese?"

"No."

"Did you kill McKenna Mays?"

"No."

"Have you ever climbed Mount Everest?"

"No."

"Are you a man?"

"Yes."

"Are you sitting in a chair?"

"Yes."

"Do you know who killed McKenna Mays?"

"No."

Not a flinch. It was making Jack uncomfortable, the way Jamal had locked eyes with him, but Jack wasn't going to be the one to back down.

"Do you wear eyeglasses?"

"No."

"Are you in jail?"

"Yes."

"Is your prison jumpsuit orange?"

"Yes."

"Were you in the United States at the time of McKenna Mays'death?"

"No."

"Are you glad this test is over?"

Jamal almost answered, then realized that he was being toyed with. He almost seemed to smile as his gaze slowly shifted from Jack to the examiner.

"I guess so," he said.

Swenson disconnected the monitors. "I'll need a few minutes to interpret the results," he said as he packed up the equipment.

Neil summoned the guard. The door opened, Swenson left the room, and the lawyers were alone with their client.

Jack looked at Neil and said, "If that test shows any signs of deception, I'm out."

"Understood," said Neil.

"Even if the test is clean, I'm probably still out."

Jamal spoke up. "I didn't kill McKenna."

Jack glanced over. "You shouldn't have waited until today to tell me that."

"Last time we talked, I hadn't been charged with anything."

"The guy has a point," said Neil.

Jack and Jamal had locked eyes again. "You don't deny the fact that you were McKenna's boyfriend, do you?"

"I don't deny that."

"So you knew you were the prime suspect in McKenna's murder."

"Yes," Jamal said. "I knew."

"And that never once came up in our conversation at Gitmo, even after we switched to English."

Jamal paused, then said, "That wasn't my fault."

"Whose fault was it?"

"Yours."

"Mine?" said Jack, incredulous.

Jamal's expression was completely serious. "I thought if I started speaking English to you that it would help build trust between us. The opposite happened. The way you reacted, you just shut me down."

Jack replayed the moment in his mind. The English had definitely come as a surprise, and in hindsight Jack probably could have handled it better.

"I don't remember shutting you down," said Jack.

"I'm not saying you did it intentionally. That's just the way it played out. You mentioned your grandfather was from the Czech Republic, and I told you I'd been there."

"You told me in *English*," said Jack.

"And from that point on, the whole conversation was all about my native tongue. We never followed up about Prague."

"What was there to follow up about?"

Jamal gave him an assessing look. "That's where I was when McKenna was murdered."

The words came over Jack like an arctic front. Before he could speak, there was a knock at the door. Neil opened it, and Swenson entered the room. The lawyers and their client looked at him with anticipation, and Swenson delivered the news without delay.

"The test shows no signs of deception in any of the three areas of examination," said Swenson.

Neil was openly smug about it, and he couldn't help summarizing: "He didn't kill McKenna, he doesn't know who did, and he was outside the country when it happened."

It was a bit of theater orchestrated by his old boss, but Jack had to admit that it was pretty effective.

The examiner's work was finished. Neil thanked him, and Jack did likewise, and when the door closed, Jack's gaze shifted back to the young man seated at the table before him. There were definitely still signs of prolonged incarceration—the thin face, the skin tone a bit off, the unhealthy fingernails. But Jamal was becoming more of an enigma with each passing minute.

"Something is missing here," said Jack. "The police have a recording of the victim saying in her dying breath that you killed her, but you were in Prague?"

"That's right," said Jamal.

"Am I to believe that this case is as open and shut as handing over your passport to the state attorney?"

"My passport won't show that I went anywhere."

"Were you traveling illegally?"

"You could say that."

"What about an airline ticket?"

"I can't help you there."

"Credit card statements or cell phone records?"

"Nothing like that."

"Any photographs of you out of the country?"

"No."

"Travel records of any kind?"

"Unfortunately, no."

Jack puzzled for a moment, then asked, "Were you traveling with someone?"

"Yes."

"Who?"

"That's not really clear."

"Are you being a smart-ass?"

"Not at all."

"How did you get there?"

Jamal glanced at Neil, apparently seeking a green light—as if to ask, *Do you think Swyteck is ready for this?* Jack followed the prisoner's gaze toward Neil, who simply pulled up a chair for his co-counsel.

"It's a long story," said Neil.

Jack didn't move. Then finally, he came to the table and took a seat.

"All right," he told his client, "let's start at the beginning."

Chapter Eight

I was born in Somalia," said Jamal, "my father's homeland. My mother is a U.S. citizen, so I am, too. She and my father never married, and she took me to Minneapolis when I was a baby. Lots of Somali immigrants there."

"I didn't know that," said Jack.

"Somalis, Scandinavians—who can tell the difference?"

A sense of humor. *That's new.*

"My father still lives in Mogadishu," said Jamal, "so I speak Somali as well as English. I lived with my mother until I dropped out of high school and got the hell out of the freezer. I hopped on a bus to Florida and took an apartment in Miami Beach. I waited tables for about a year, then finally got a job with Mr. Mays."

"I presume that's how you met McKenna," said Jack.

"Yup. He's a self-taught computer whiz who never finished high school. Just like me. We hit it off. He introduced me to his daughter. I was nineteen. She was sixteen—but very mature for her age."

Neil popped open his briefcase. "I have pictures," he said as he laid them out on the table.

The difference between Jamal's appearance then versus now was not as dramatic as Jamal-the-client versus Jamal-the-Gitmo-detainee, but it was striking nonetheless. Not so long ago, Jamal had sported nothing short of movie-star good looks. Even so, one's eyes naturally gravitated toward McKenna.

"Pretty girl," said Jack.

"Beautiful," said Jamal. "I used to kid her that she was the perfect blend of obnoxious blond father and stunning Bahamian mother that modeling agencies looked for."

Jack held his next question, choosing instead to observe for a moment. Jamal was unable to look away from the photograph, his eyes moistening. It was the first real show of emotion Jack had seen from his client.

If it was real.

"Did you get along with her mother?"

"It's funny. I thought we were going to get on just fine. McKenna told me that her grandfather was Muslim, like me. But I guess her mother had rejected Islam."

"Did she reject you?"

"It wasn't anything specific. I just got a vibe that she wasn't nuts about me."

Jack checked his watch. The arraignment was less than an hour away, and he needed to speed things up.

"Let's fast-forward a bit," said Jack, "to the time before McKenna's death. Tell me how you came to leave the country."

"I was abducted."

"Abducted?"

"Yes," he said with a straight face.

"By whom?"

"I don't know for sure. But I believe it was the U.S. government."

"Okay, I'm outta here," said Jack as he pushed away from the table.

"No, no, listen," said Neil.

Jack shook his head. "I took this case pro bono because you were right, Neil: Everybody deserves a lawyer. But I'm a sole practitioner, and I don't have time to talk spy novels to a circuit court judge."

"My father is a recruiter for al-Shabaab," said Jamal, "the Mujahideen Youth Movement."

That got Jack's attention. While preparing for the trip to Gitmo, he had heard of al-Shabaab. Officially designated a terrorist organization by the United States in March 2008, it had been waging a war against Somalia's government to implement sharia—a stricter interprentation of Islamic law.

"Yesterday I stood before a federal judge and assured him that there was no basis to detain you at Gitmo," Jack said, his eyes narrowing. "*Now* you're telling me that you were an al-Shabaab recruit?"

"I have nothing to do with them," said Jamal, "but they definitely tapped into my old neighborhood in Minneapolis."

Neil added, "Ethiopia invaded Somalia in December 2006 to push the Islamists out of Mogadishu. It was an outrage to most Somalis, which made it an easy rallying cry for al-Shabaab. Ever since then, they have been reaching out to young Somalis all over the world, recruiting them to fight."

"At least two of my friends from high school ended up dead in Somalia," said Jamal.

Jack settled back into his chair, willing to listen a little longer. "What does any of this have to do with your being abducted?"

"Two high-school friends of mine were killed fighting in Somalia. My father was a recruiter in Mogadishu. Obviously, my name landed on somebody's list of suspected terrorists."

Things were slowly starting to sound more plausible. Jack checked his watch again. Time was short. "Tell me what happened. The short version."

"Like I said, I was working for McKenna's father in Miami. He did a lot of secret projects, some for the government, some for private industry. I never knew who the clients were, never got the details. But he had this one called Project Round Up, and I knew it was big."

"Big in what way?"

"The supercomputer ability, the amount of data being gathered, the data-mining capabilities—everything was out of this world."

"What part of the project were you involved with?"

"Encryption," said Jamal.

"How to encrypt your own data, or how to read through someone else's encryption?"

"At the time I was abducted, I was doing both."

"Let's get back to that. When you say you were abducted . . ."

"I mean exactly that," said Jamal. "Some goons came into my apartment in the middle of the night, threw me on the floor, put a hood over my head, stuck me in the ass with a syringe . . . and then it was lights-out."

"Did you get a look at them?"

"No way."

"Then what happened?"

"I woke up in a dark room strapped to a table. And from then on, it was like a scene out of *24*."

"What to you mean?"

"Bright lights, then total darkness. Loud calypso music, then total silence. Exteme cold temperature, then hot. Every time I fell asleep, a sprinkler in the ceiling squirted me with ice-cold water. The only time I wasn't shackled to the floor was when they put a hood over my head, so I kept walking into the walls. They wouldn't let me use the bathroom when I needed to, didn't feed me until I was starving, and then after I finally got something to eat they served me another three meals ten minutes apart. All of this was obviously designed to disorient me. Then the interrogation started."

"What did they ask you about?"

"Project Round Up. I told them everything I knew about the encryption, but they insisted that I knew more than I was telling them."

"And all of this happened in Prague?"

"I had no idea where it was. Until they let me go."

"They just turned you loose?"

"They gave me another injection to knock me out. I woke up on a bench near a bridge. As soon as I figured out where I was, I ran to a pay phone and called my mother in Minneapolis. That was when I found out that McKenna had been murdered and that the cops were looking for me."

"How long had you been out of the country at this point?"

"I had no idea, until my mother told me what day it was. It was even longer than I'd thought: seventeen days."

"Did she believe you?"

"Of course. The last time we'd talked on the phone was ten days before McKenna was killed. I used to talk to her every day. She knew something had happened to me."

"Did you talk about coming home?"

"Are you kidding? She said I would be handing myself over to a lynch mob. A cop was blinded, CNN aired a tape recording of McKenna naming me as the killer, my picture was all over the news, and every cop in America was on the lookout for me."

"What did you do?"

"I headed for Somalia to hide with my father."

"The terrorist recruiter?"

"At the time, I didn't know he was involved with all of that. He was just my father, and I needed help."

"Did you stay with him?"

"For about a week. He got me a fake passport to turn me into Khaled al-Jawar, which is the name you knew me by."

"Was that a real person or a made-up name?"

"I have no idea, and I was so scared that I didn't care. This was at the height of the Ethiopian invasion. I could hear the gunfighting in the city, especially after dark. Then one night the troops busted down the door to my father's apartment, and they took me away. You know the rest of the story. It was exactly what you told the judge in Washington. The Ethiopians forced me to confess that I was sheltering al-Qaeda operatives, and then they handed me over to the CIA."

"Probably for some amount of bounty money," said Neil.

"I'm sure," said Jamal. "Next thing I knew, I was on my way to Gitmo."

"And you didn't bother telling them who you really were."

"Well, *duh*. I would have been sent to Miami on murder charges. I figured that if I kept quiet—if I could play the part of a Somali peasant named Khaled al-Jawar—the Americans would have to release me sooner or later."

"So no one at Gitmo ever accused you of being Jamal Wakefield?"

"Nope."

Jack looked at Neil. "They must have known. Fingerprints or something."

Jamal glared, as if he resented having to repeat himself: "They never said anything about it," said Jamal, his voice taking on an edge.

Jack said, "Obviously the interrogators in Prague knew your true identity, right?"

"Oh, they knew everything about me there. And they used it, too."

"In what way?"

"Threats, mainly."

"They threatened you?"

"All the time. It started mostly with threats against my mother—the things they were going to enjoy doing to her if I refused to talk about Project Round Up."

"Any other threats?"

"Yeah. Including one that they kept."

"Tell me."

Jamal's expression turned very serious. "They said if I didn't give them the information they wanted, they would kill McKenna."

His words hung in the air, as if her violent death had taken a whole new turn.

There was a knock on the door, and the door opened.

"Showtime," the guard said.

Jamal's arraignment was scheduled for eleven A.M., and there was just enough time to get the prisoner downstairs for a court "appearance" via closed-circuit television from the jailhouse.

"So," asked Neil, "does this mean I get to keep my ponytail?"

Jack had almost forgotten that Neil had bet his precious locks that Jack would stay on the case after hearing Jamal's story. But it didn't take the smartest lawyer in the world to see the problems in Jamal's case—even if he was telling the truth.

"For now," he said. "But keep your scissors handy."

Chapter Nine

It was 11:04 P.M. when Jack finally got home from the office. When it came to pro bono cases, the well-established rule that "no good deed goes unpunished" seemed to have an exponential ripple effect, as if every hour spent working for free put you three hours behind on billable files. He walked through his front door and plopped on the couch just in time for the tail end of the lead story on the late local news.

"Wakefield was denied bail," said the anchorwoman. "A trial date has not yet been set."

Trial. The very thought made Jack shudder. Neil had offered to pay him out of the Freedom Institute's operating budget, but Jack knew how that would play out. Jack would present a bill, and Neil would wax on about all the schoolchildren who would have to go without textbooks because there was no money to sue the mayor for paying six-figure salaries to his chauffeur, his barber, and a nineteen-year-old waitress at Hooters who was also his "secretary."

Jack switched off the TV, changed into jogging shorts and a T-shirt (his standard sleepwear), and headed to the bathroom to brush his teeth.

He'd been too busy all day to think much about Jamal Wakefield, but, naturally, bedtime brought the nagging questions to the fore. Had Jamal been out of the country when McKenna was murdered, or did he go on the run after she was killed? Was he telling the truth about the first round of secret interrogation, or was he making up an alibi? The polygraph examination was clear enough: no signs of deception. But that had absolutely no bearing on what was perhaps the biggest question of all.

"Why in the hell are you even doing this?" he asked his reflection in the mirror.

It sure wasn't for the pat on the back from friends and family. Grandpa Swyteck had seemed to sum up the absurdity of it all. It had taken Jack two hours to calm him down from his "combative" episode, and it had been hard to tell if Grandpa was grasping any of the things Jack was telling him about his day. Finally, he'd leveled off at a semilucid level—or so Jack had thought.

"My grandson defending terrorists," he'd said bitterly.

Apparently he'd absorbed plenty. "Accused terrorists, Grandpa."

"That's a hell of a job for a Jew."

Jack had blinked hard, not comprehending. "A lot of the lawyers representing the detainees are Jewish, actually."

The ceiling tiles had suddenly caught Grandpa's attention, and he was swatting at dust floaters like a man catching flies. Jack needed to reel him back in before the nurse returned to chart him as "combative."

"Grandpa, you know we're not Jewish, right?"

"What do you mean we're *not Jewish*?"

In truth, Jack had never known his grandfather to be of any faith, but the angry glare had taken Jack aback. "You were born in Bohemia in what used to be Czechoslovakia. We're Czech."

"Yes, Czech *Jews*."

Jack could have spent the next ten minutes trying to explain that even though Grandpa had never been a churchgoing man, his son—Jack's father—had gone to Mass every Sunday, married a Catholic girl from Cuba, and even taken communion from the pope during his second term as governor. But Grandpa had dozed off, exhausted from his earlier struggle with the nurse.

"Getting old sucks," Jack said to the forty-year-old man in the mirror.

Jack heard a car door slam. He returned his toothbrush to the rack and peered out the bathroom window, but overgrown palm fronds blocked his view of the driveway. He listened.

Footsteps.

Someone was definitely out there. Key Biscayne was safe by Miami standards, but the last time anyone had shown up unexpectedly at his house after midnight, a couple of pissed-off Colombians had decided to express their displeasure with his courtroom performance by turning his 1966 Mustang into a charred hunk of metal. Jack went down the hall to the living room and waited. It was dark, lighted only in places by the dim glow of an outdoor porch lamp that shined through the open slats in the draperies. He listened, hearing nothing. But something—a sixth sense—told him that someone was on the other side of that door.

"Who's there?" he asked.

There was no answer, but as he started forward, the knock startled him. It had the familiar rhythm:

DUH, duh-duh-duh-duh, DUH. . .

He stood in silence, waiting for the final *DUH, DUH*. Instead, there was the voice he knew well:

"I'm *baaaaack*," said Andie.

She couldn't carry personal items—including a house key—when she was working undercover. Jack smiled as he hurried to turn the deadbolt and open the door. He barely got a look at her face before she burst across the threshold, threw her arms around his neck, and planted her lips on his. The passion was contagious, but finally she stopped for air.

"You're blond," he said.

"You like it?"

He wasn't sure—but he was glad the FBI hadn't forced her to cut her hair for her assignment. "Looks great." He laced his fingers with hers and noticed she was not wearing the engagement ring he'd given her.

"Sorry," she said, attuned to his discovery. "I love my diamond, but it doesn't fit the undercover role."

It was the most she'd told him about her assignment to date. "Are you going to tell what role that is?"

"If I told you . . ."

"I know, I know: You'd have to kill me."

"That's the bad news," she said, smiling coyly. "The good news is: Wait until I show you my preferred method of execution."

"So you *are* going to tell me?"

"No. In your case, I punish the ignorant."

"You mean innocent."

"Keep arguing, Counselor, and you're going to end up with a suspended sentence." She closed the door with a hind kick, her eyes never leaving his. "I have to be back at noon."

Jack glanced toward the bedroom, then back. "That doesn't give us much time."

"I'm going to take a quick shower," she said. "How about you join me?"

"Hmm. Very tempting, honey. But there's absolutely no way we'll get out of there without having sex, and sex in that teeny-tiny shower stall rates right up there with sex on a coffee table. Alluring in theory, but what the hell's the point when there's a perfectly good mattress twenty feet away?"

"You're such a putz."

"It's a gift. I'll open some wine."

She kissed him and went off to the bedroom. Jack found a bottle of red in the wine chiller. His collection was comprised mostly of gifts from clients, and this bottle of Betts & Scholl Hermitage Rouge was from Mr. Scholler himself—an old friend who'd had the good sense to listen to his wife and buy up declining apartment buildings on Miami Beach right before *Miami Vice* made art deco cool again. Timing was everything in life.

"Jack," Andie sang out from the shower, "naked, sex-starved woman wants her wine."

Luck didn't hurt, either.

"Coming," he said, a glass in each hand.

Theirs was not the perfect engagement, but Jack had given up on perfect long ago, right about the time he'd discovered that his first marriage was the perfect storm. A man didn't ask an FBI agent to marry him and then tell her not to do her job. No more than Andie would tell Jack not to do his—with the exception of Jamal Wakefield. Andie had made it her business to tell Jack to stay away from him. More than anything else—more than the grief he'd caught for defending an accused terrorist, more than the emotional burden of a murder case involving a blind cop and a dead teenager—Andie's decision to step on his wing tips was eating at Jack.

A billow of steam moistened his face as he entered the bathroom.

"Here you go," he said as he opened the shower door. She was gorgeous even when shaving her legs.

Andie gave him a kiss, took a long sip of wine, and handed the glass back to him. Jack leaned against the wall, keeping an eye on the blurred beauty behind the foggy shower door. And he was still thinking about Jamal Wakefield. He just couldn't let it go.

"So you really don't want me to take that case, huh?"

The shower door opened a crack. She had shampoo in her hair and a look of incredulity on her face. "You want to talk about that *now*?"

She disappeared back into the shower, and Jack tasted the wine from his friend's vineyard. Timing was everything, it reminded him, but for Jack, "no time like the present" was the general rule.

Probably why the wine is Betts & Scholl, not Betts & Swyteck.

"It just took me by surprise," said Jack. "You've never tried to steer me away from a case before."

The shower stopped. Jack handed her a bath towel, and Andie

stepped out, wrapped in terry cloth. She towel-dried her newly blond hair and then stood before the mirror, speaking as she combed through the snarls.

"Jamal Wakefield is bad news," she said.

"Well, what does that mean?" asked Jack.

"It means you should stay away from him."

"That's your opinion."

"I'm trying to help you, Jack."

"Help me what?"

She put down the comb, a little flabbergasted. "Okay, if you were to take this case, you'd find this out anyway. So let me tell you now. After McKenna Mays was murdered, the police got a warrant and seized her boyfriend's computer."

"What did they find?"

"Encrypted files."

"So what?"

"Encrypted files from known terrorist organizations," said Andie.

"And you know this because . . . ?"

"Because I have friends who don't want to see you embarrass yourself."

"You mean embarrass you."

"This isn't about me."

"It's not? Really?"

Andie glared but said nothing. She grabbed her wineglass and walked out. Jack followed her to the bedroom.

"Look, I'm sorry, okay?" said Jack. "But none of this makes sense to me."

"Well, exactly how much of my duty of confidentiality and loyalty to the FBI do you expect me to breach in order to keep you from making a huge mistake?"

"I don't expect anything. I never asked your opinion."

Her mouth fell open, and her chuckle of disbelief spoke more than words.

Jack said, "I didn't mean that the way it sounded. It's not that I don't value your opinion."

"Can we drop this, please?"

Jack breathed in and out. "I wish I could. But now I'm more confused than ever. This kid spent three years at Gitmo. They fingerprinted him there. Surely they ran his prints through every conceivable database and discovered that he was really Jamal Wakefield. Now you're telling me that the FBI found encrypted files on his computer with links to terrorism. But no one at Gitmo ever asked him if his name was Jamal Wakefield. And at the habeas corpus hearing two days ago, the Justice Department let him walk for lack of evidence. I just don't get it."

"They didn't let him walk," said Andie. "They played their ace in the hole: They got the state attorney to indict him for murder."

"Why play that ace? Why not just have the Justice Department tell the judge about his computer and keep him locked up on terrorism charges?"

"Because if you tell the judge about the computer, someone might want to see what's in the files."

"Someone like me?" asked Jack.

"Like any defense lawyer," said Andie.

"Would that be the end of the world—if someone wanted to find out what was in Jamal's encrypted files?"

"I don't know," said Andie. "But why risk letting that kind of information go public when you can keep an accused terrorist locked up for the rest of his life on a murder charge?"

"It's all in the interest of national security—is that what you're saying?"

"Yes."

Jack suddenly recalled what Jamal had told him about the interrogators' threats against McKenna in Prague.

"And what if Jamal didn't kill McKenna? Would it still be in the interest of national security to keep him locked up for the rest of his life and keep his encrypted files secret?"

"What are you talking about?"

Jack took a long breath, then shook it off. "Nothing," he said.

They stood in silence for a minute. Finally, Andie dimmed the light and turned on some music. The mood slowly changed. Andie walked toward the bed, and Jack ogled her like a sailor on shore leave as her towel dropped to the floor and she slid beneath the sheet. Andie had a telltale way of arching one eyebrow, and it always got Jack's motor running.

"Are we going to talk all night?" she asked, peering across the room at him.

Jack swallowed the rest of his wine, then smiled.

"God, I hope not."

Chapter Ten

Andie was gone by Friday at noon. Jack barely had time to ponder where her undercover assignment might have taken her. At three P.M. he was in Courtroom 2 of the Richard E. Gerstein Justice Building.

The media seemed to hover perpetually around the criminal courthouse, poised to capture the arraignment of a federal prosecutor caught biting a stripper, the verdict on a high-priced call girl who claimed that "nymphomania made me do it," or some other "trial of the century"—Miami style. At the government's request, however, Judge Flint had closed his courtroom to the public. The prosecution sat at the mahogany table to Jack's left, closer to the empty jury box. Neil Goderich was at Jack's side. Together, the defense had almost fifty years of trial experience, and greener lawyers surely would have felt outgunned by such an unusual pairing of government lawyers.

"William McCue on behalf of the state of Florida," the assistant state attorney said, announcing his appearance for the record. "With me today, for purposes of this emergency motion only, is Sylvia Gonzalez of the United States Department of Justice, National Security Division."

The judge peered out over the top of his reading glasses. "I must say it isn't every day that I see a lawyer from the NSD's Counterterrorism Section in my courtroom."

Gonzalez rose to address the court. "This case presents special circumstances, Your Honor."

" 'Special circumstances'?" said Neil, rising. "Gee, and I thought 'enhanced interrogation' was the government's only euphemism for 'torture.' "

Beneath the table, Jack ground his heel into his partner's big toe, and Neil struggled not to yelp. Gonzalez had been a consummate professional at the habeas proceeding in Washington, and Jack shot his cocounsel a look that said, *Tone it down.*

"Neil Goderich of the Freedom Institute on behalf of the defendant," he announced. "With me is Jack Swyteck, who has yet to decide if he has the set of you-know-what to take this case to trial, but he has agreed to assist me at this emergency hearing."

Not sure what to do with Neil's remark, the judge simply cleared his throat and moved on.

"I have before me the government's emergency motion to prevent the defense from pursuing a frivolous alibi—specifically the defendant's claim that at the time of the commission of the crime, he was held by the U.S. government in a secret interrogation site in the Czech Republic prior to his transfer to Guantánamo Bay, Cuba."

Neil rose, eager to speak, even if he was out of turn. "Before we proceed, I have to say that this motion seems highly premature. We have not even informed the government that my client intends to pursue an alibi defense, and under the rules we are not required to do so until ten days before trial."

"Does that mean you're *not* going to assert an alibi defense?" asked the judge.

"They most definitely will," said the prosecutor.

Neil smiled thinly, as if the prosecution had stepped into his trap. "I'm not sure how the government would know that, since Mr. Wakefield has never before stated publicly that he was detained in the Czech Republic. Unless, of course, the government knows from its own records that my client was, in fact, held at such a site."

"We know because the defendant called the victim's father from jail last night and told him," said the prosecutor. "Mr. Wakefield dated McKenna Mays, and now that he has been indicted, it has apparently become important for him to convince Mr. Mays of his innocence."

That took the wind out of Neil's sails, and Jack felt his pain. A client who did something stupid from jail and then neglected to tell his lawyer about it was routine at the institute.

The judge said, "Given the national security issues raised by the alibi defense, I don't see the motion as premature. Ms. Gonzalez, proceed."

The Justice Department lawyer went to the lectern. It was almost taller than she was, and rather than disappear behind it, she stepped to one side to address the court.

"Judge, as anyone who reads the newspapers knows, the United States has acknowledged the existence of a limited number of so-called black sites—facilities at which enemy combatants were detained and interrogated prior to, or in lieu of, their transfer to Gitmo. As early as 2005, reports circulated about such sites in Afghanistan and at other locations in the Middle East. Later, however, unfounded rumors emerged about a possible site in an Eastern European country—perhaps in Poland, Romania, or the Czech Republic.

"Here, Mr. Wakefield claims that he was held in a secret facility in Prague. It is important for this court to understand that no one has *ever* produced a shred of evidence that a black site existed in the Czech Republic. The United States denies it. The Czech Republic has asserted that such reports are libelous.

"The Department of Justice has asked the state of Florida to file this motion because we anticipate that Mr. Wakefield's attorneys will subpoena intelligence officers and demand classified documents to establish his alibi. If that happens, the Justice Department will file an action in federal court under the Confidential Information Protection Act to quash those subpoenas. That will only delay the trial, and we are sensitive to the fact that Mr. Mays, who lost his daughter, and Officer Paulo, who lost his eyesight, have already waited long enough for justice. Granting this motion would avoid further delay. Denial of this motion and allowing the defendant to pursue this alleged alibi would be tantamount to turning NASA upside down to show that he was abducted by aliens and taken to another galaxy."

Neil rose, again a little too eager. "Judge, that is simply not true. Although the government refuses to admit it, there have been numerous reports about sites in Eastern Europe."

"Rumors," said the prosecutor. "No proof."

The judge raised a hand, putting an end to the cross-debating. "Let me ask you this, Mr. Goderich. Is it true, as you just stated, that your client has never stated publicly that he was detained in Prague before going to Gitmo?"

"Well, yes. That is true," said Neil.

"So am I to infer that Mr. Wakefield never told anyone that he was held in a secret detention facility until he spoke with the victim's father last night—until *after* he was indicted for murder?"

Neil froze, seeing where the judge was headed. "I can't answer that question without breaching the attorney-client privilege," he said.

Jack did a double take. The implication was clear, and Jack didn't think Neil really wanted to go down that road.

The judge leaned forward, as if he were cross-examining Neil. "Are you affirmatively representing to this court that prior to his indictment Mr. Wakefield told you that he was detained in Prague?"

Neil paused, and Jack could almost hear him tap dancing.

"I'm simply saying that I am unable to give a yes-or-no answer to that question without breaching the attorney-client privilege."

"That's nonsense," the prosecutor said. "Mr. Goderich filed a detailed memorandum in federal court setting forth the entire history of his client's detention. He wrote in detail about his apprehension by Ethiopian troops in Somalia and his alleged forced confession. He wrote in detail about his transfer to and detention at Gitmo. In fact, Mr. Wakefield pretended to speak only Somali for his entire three years in captivity, until he was charged with murder. If Mr. Wakefield had been detained in Prague, we would have heard of it by now."

Neil fell silent, realizing his mistake.

Jack rose. "Judge, may I speak?"

"No. I've heard enough."

"Shit," Neil said under his breath. "I pissed him off with that attorney-client smoke screen."

"The government's motion is granted," the judge said. "The defendant will be allowed to testify at trial about his alibi if he so chooses. But until you show me more than Mr. Wakefield's own belated claims of a secret facility in Prague, the defense will not have the subpoena power of this court to compel government officials to testify or to produce records about an alleged secret facility."

"But—"

"That's my ruling," the judge said with a bang of the gavel.

"All rise!" said the bailiff.

Jack and Neil climbed to their feet as the judge made his way to his chambers. The side door opened, the judge disappeared into his chambers, and the lawyers gathered their papers. Neil looked as if he'd just been shot in the chest—or worse, as if he'd shot himself in the foot.

"I'm sorry," he said. "I've never dropped the ball like that in my life. What in the hell was I thinking?"

Jack wasn't one to judge, especially when it was someone as talented and ethical as Neil. Besides, Jack suspected that something else was at work—something much bigger than a misstep by his co-counsel.

"No worries," said Jack.

"Swyteck," said the prosecutor, "may I talk to you privately for a minute?"

Jack and Neil exchanged glances. "I'll meet you downstairs," said Neil. He closed up his briefcase and headed for the exit, leaving Jack alone with the prosecutor.

"Here's the deal," said McCue. "Wakefield pleads guilty to both counts—first degree murder and attempted murder—and I won't seek the death penalty. Life without parole."

"That's not much of a deal."

"We're talking about a teenage girl brutally murdered and a cop who was blinded trying to save her."

"You should be pitching this deal to Neil Goderich."

"I'm not offering it to him. In fact, I'm only giving it to you because—"

The stop was abrupt, and as the silence lingered, the reality washed over Jack, making his blood boil. "Because my fiancée asked you to?"

McCue didn't answer, and his body language was anything but a denial. Jack glanced across the courtroom toward the lawyer for the Department of Justice—the same agency that Andie worked for. She averted her eyes.

"I'll give you until Monday," said McCue. "After that, it's the death penalty. No more deals. No more favors."

Jack took a deep breath as he stood and watched the prosecutors leave the courtroom, and he wasn't sure who made him more angry: the arrogant assistant state attorney with his Washington ringer or the meddlesome new blonde who had stopped wearing her engagement ring.

Chapter Eleven

On Saturday morning Jack found himself surrounded by a sea of spandex. Headed for CocoPlum, one of south Florida's tony waterfront communities, he was stuck behind hundreds of cyclists—a side-by-side wall that stretched across three lanes and moved at the mind-numbing speed of eleven miles per hour. Cartegena Circle—a suburban south-Florida version of the vehicular insanity surrounding the Arc de Triomphe—was not just the meeting place of choice for weekend warriors on wheels. It was quite possibly the world's greatest concentration of bulging blobs of jelly who had absolutely no business wearing form-fitting clothing.

Jack was inching around the circle in his ten-year-old Saab convertible with the ragtop down, practically riding on the rear bumper of a new Maserati—so new, in fact, that it had a temporary tag. Bullet gray with dark tinted windows. Chrome wheels so shiny that they couldn't have left the showroom floor more than two hours ago. Jack wondered how anyone could plunk down a quarter-mill on a new Maserati in the post–hold-on-to-your-ass-cuz-I-just-lost-mine economy. The answer was splashed across the back window in block white letters: FLORIDAFORECLOSURES.COM.

Talk about a sign of the times.

Jack steered into CocoPlum, stopped at the guard house, and

rolled down the window. "I'm headed to the Mays residence," he said.

The guard jotted down his license plate number and offered quick directions. Jack followed the line of tall royal palms toward the water.

Last night's phone call had come as a total shock. Jack still hadn't decided to try the case. Even if he had, never in a million years would he have guessed that his first interview would be the victim's father. Then again, never in a *billion* years would Jack have thought that Chuck Mays would call and insist on meeting him—alone. Jack was fully prepared for an angry lecture on why he shouldn't stoop to defending the man who had murdered McKenna Mays.

Jack pulled into the driveway of a tri-level Mediterranean-style mansion. The new Mays residence was far more impressive and in a much pricier neighborhood than the one that had burned to the ground. The eight-bedroom waterfront estate hadn't risen from the ashes with just insurance proceeds. In the past three years, Chuck Mays had made a pot of money in the data-broker business with a service that delivered billions of dossiers to police, private investigators, lawyers, reporters, and insurance companies. Success was relative, however. He now lived alone.

Jack was walking up the driveway when that new Maserati came flying around the corner, tires squealing as it pulled into the driveway behind him. A muscle-bound man with a surfer's suntan and shoulder-length blond hair stepped toward him.

"Chuck Mays," he said, shaking Jack's hand. He was wearing nylon shorts and a sleeveless work-out shirt, the "V" of sweat on his chest suggesting that he'd just come from the gym.

"Nice car," said Jack.

"Not my style. Got it on the cheap, but I'll probably sell it. Basically for guys with little dicks."

"You own a foreclosure company?"

"You mean that sign in the back window? Fuck no. Mr.

Foreclosures-dot-com got foreclosed on, and I snatched up his wheels. Ain't that fucking great?"

Jack had come expecting to meet the still-grieving father of a teenage girl. Instead, he found Hulk Hogan's younger clone, who dropped the F-word like a carpet bomber. But Jack wasn't fooled. "Chuck Mays could be the most intelligent human being you will ever meet," Neil had told him at dinner the night before.

"So," said Jack. "You wanted to talk?"

"Yeah." He pressed the keyless alarm, and the Maserati chirped. "Follow me." He led Jack up the walkway and into the house. It had all the charm of an unfurnished hotel lobby: twenty-foot ceilings, enormous crown moldings, bare marble floors, and naked white walls—not a rug, painting, or framed photograph anywhere. The chandelier in the foyer still had the price tag hanging from it.

"How long have you lived here?" asked Jack.

"Moved in after Shada passed away," Mays said.

Jack had, of course, heard about his wife's suicide. Lose a daughter, then a wife, and who could give a rat's ass about decorating a new house?

Jack followed him toward the kitchen. Mays offered him a barstool at the granite counter and went to the refrigerator.

"You want a beer?"

It was not yet noon, but pointing that out to a guy like Mays would have probably earned Jack a major wedgie.

"Sure," he said.

Mays popped open two cans and put one in front of Jack. "Cheers," he said, and then he guzzled down most of it. Jack half expected him to start burping out the entire Mays alphabet: *fucking-A, fucking-B. . .*

"I didn't used to drink, you know," said Mays.

Jack knew what he was saying. "I hear you."

Mays had a little beer foam on his mustache. He took care of it with a backhand swipe of the wristband.

"Your client called me from jail the other night," said Mays.

"I heard about that in court yesterday," said Jack.

"Told me where he was when McKenna was murdered."

Jack wasn't sure how to respond, so he let Mays keep talking.

"I've been giving his story a lot of thought," said Mays.

"I know it must sound hard to believe," said Jack.

Mays locked eyes with him, and for a moment Jack wondered if he was going to reach over the counter and slug him. Finally, Mays stepped away, took a file from a stack of papers on the kitchen table, and laid it on the countertop in front of Jack.

"What's this?" asked Jack.

"Payroll records for my company. It's from three years ago, when Jamal worked for me."

Jack opened the file and found his client's name on the list of employees.

Mays said, "We had automatic deposit for Jamal's paychecks to go to his bank every week."

Jack glanced at the transaction dates on the ledger. "So is it a coincidence that he was off the payroll for the two pay periods before your daughter was murdered?"

"Jamal stopped showing up for work. So I stopped paying him. Tried calling him, got no answer. Went to his apartment. Nobody there. Called his mother in Minnesota. No idea where he was. She even filed a missing person report."

Jack looked at him, confused. "All that actually *supports* Jamal's claim that he was abducted before the crime."

"I realize that," he said.

Jack studied his expression. The guy was no easy read. "Why would you help me defend the man accused of killing your daughter?"

Mays drained the last of his beer, then crushed the empty aluminum can in his bare hand. "Jamal Wakefield was sitting in Gitmo for three years."

"Well, nominally at least it was Khaled al-Jawar."

"That's exactly my problem," said Mays. "Those fuckers knew they had Jamal. But no one told me. They just let me go on thinking for three years that the man who killed my daughter was still on the loose, never going to be brought to justice."

"I can see where you'd be angry."

"This isn't about anger. I'm just saying they have a different agenda, and I understand that. They think Jamal's a terrorist, and they want to keep him locked up."

"The Justice Department did take an unusual position in court yesterday," said Jack.

"What do you mean?"

"Normally, when a criminal defendant wants access to classified information, the feds make him jump through all the hoops under the Confidential Information Protection Act. The government doesn't care how long it takes. But in Jamal's case, they're suddenly all concerned about the swift administration of justice."

"You see what I'm saying?" said Mays. "It doesn't really matter if he killed McKenna. So long as he ends up behind bars, it works out either way for them."

"But it matters for you."

"I just want the truth. I think you do, too, which is why you're on the fence about taking this case to trial."

"Who told you that I was on the fence?"

He shook his head, as if Jack were naïve. "My supercomputers can search eight billion files in an instant, tell me where you lived when you were in college, and pull up the Social Security number of every man, woman, and child who ever lived in the same zip code. Give me another minute and I can do the same thing for two hundred seventy million other folks, and not a single one will have the slightest idea that he was being checked out. Then, if you like, we can compile a complete personal dossier for every high-school graduate who earns six figures, smokes Marlboros, uses the name of his childhood pet as his preferred online password, and has a landlord named Bob."

Jack hesitated, but he knew Mays wasn't kidding. "You can't click a mouse and know how I feel about a case."

"No, I'm not quite there . . . yet," Mays said with a smile. Then he turned serious. "But I do know this: You wouldn't be anywhere near this case if something wasn't telling you that Jamal is innocent."

Jack didn't respond.

"Vince Paulo is a friend of mine," said Mays. "I know he's one of your personal heroes. And why shouldn't he be? He was the lead hostage negotiator who stopped a raving lunatic from killing your best friend."

Jack couldn't deny the facts.

Mays said, "You'd have to be one incredibly cold and ungrateful son of a bitch to defend the guy who blinded him."

"It's a tough one," said Jack.

"Damn right it is. But we both know one thing."

"What?"

"If Jamal is innocent, that means the man who murdered my daughter and took Paulo's eyesight is still out there, a free man. That's why you're on this case, isn't it?"

"I'm not comfortable having this conversation," said Jack.

Mays grabbed him by the wrist, his move lightning quick. "I couldn't care less about your comfort."

"Let go of my arm."

Mays squeezed harder, his bicep bulging. "I need to know if they've got the wrong guy. I have *the right* to know."

"Mr. Mays, let go of my arm."

"Tell me the truth. Would you be in this case if you really thought Jamal did it?"

They were locked in a stare down. Mays' eyes were like lasers, but it was the kind of question Jack would never answer.

"I'm giving you one last chance," said Jack. "Let go of my arm. *Now.*"

Mays had the grip of a mountain climber, not a computer

genius. His eyes narrowed with anger and then, finally, he released Jack.

"Get out of my house," said Mays.

Jack flexed his wrist, got the blood flowing, then walked straight to the foyer and opened the front door.

"Swyteck," Mays called out, his voice booming down the hallway.

Jack stopped in the open doorway, but he didn't answer. He didn't even glance back.

"Defend him if you want," said Mays. "But if he's guilty and you get him off, I'll kill you. That's not a threat. That's just the way it is."

Jack stepped out. Behind him the door closed with an echo that traveled beyond the bare walls of the big, empty house.

Chapter Twelve

"P.O., no, no!"

Jack recognized his grandfather's shouting the moment he entered the Alzheimer's wing. It was coming from inside his room at the end of the hallway—that same pointless rant against the post office that Jack had heard many times before.

"P.O., NO, NO!"

The thought of his grandfather swatting at nothing and shouting nonsense made Jack want to rush to his side, but Saturday lunch was a peak visiting hour at Sunny Gardens. The hallway was clogged with clusters of residents and guests, many using wheelchairs or walkers. Merely the wind from his sprint could have knocked over most of them, and Jack had more sense than to run through an Alzheimer's nursing home anyway. He hurried as quickly and as safely as he could to the open doorway.

"It's okay, Grandpa," he said as he entered the room.

His grandfather didn't seem to notice him, but thankfully the shouting had ceased. He was sitting up in the mechanical bed, quietly staring up at an elderly woman who was standing at his bedside.

"That's my bubbala," she said in a soft voice of praise. She was holding his hand and stroking his forehead. Jack didn't recognize her, and instead of the blue uniform of a Sunny Gardens employee, she was wearing a green cotton dress with a thin white sweater. Her hair was done in the classic style of a fading generation that went to the beauty parlor every Saturday morning. Jack wasn't sure if Grandpa recognized her either, but she had an undeniably calming effect on him. They couldn't seem to take their eyes off each other.

"Who are you?" asked Jack.

Her gaze remained fixed on the older Swyteck, and she answered in the same soothing tone. "Who am I?" she asked, smiling at Jack's grandfather. "I'm Ruth, of course. Bubbala's main squeeze."

Grandpa has a girlfriend?

Jack watched them. Ruth was singing to him now, too soft for Jack to hear the words, but the tune was familiar and pleasant enough, even if it was in an older voice that cracked now and then. Grandpa's eyes were closing, and in a matter of minutes, he was sound asleep. Ruth kissed him gently on the forehead.

"I love you," she whispered, and then she stepped away from the safety rail.

Jack tried not to appear too shocked. His grandfather had been a widower for twenty years, and Jack had no idea that he'd even dated since.

"I'm Ruth Rosenstein," she said, offering her hand.

Jack shook it and started to introduce himself.

"You're Jack, I know," she said. "Bubbala's told me all about you before . . ." She glanced toward the bed and smiled sadly. "Well, before."

"How long have you two you known each other?"

"Oh, it's been about five years now."

Jack suddenly felt small. He was in his thirties when his maternal grandmother had finally come over from Cuba, and he'd spent countless hours building a relationship with her, making up for lost time. Grandpa Swyteck had lived most of his life just a plane ride away in Chicago, yet Jack knew so little about his father's father. Jack saw him on holidays and at important family events, but the relationship was never deep. It was more like the obligatory grandson visits, even after he retired to Florida. Even after he went into the facility.

"Do you have time for a cup of coffee with me in the cafeteria?"

"I'd like that," said Jack.

An old Irving Berlin tune—"I'll Be Loving You . . . Always"—played softly over the intercom system as they walked together down the hallway and found a table by the window. The coffee wasn't good, but Jack didn't really notice as Ruth told him how she'd met his grandfather, the kind of things they used to do together, the close relationship they had forged.

"Last year at Passover he even joined me at the seder," she said, suddenly wistful. "That was one of his last really good days."

Jack smiled a little. "He thinks we're Jewish, you know."

She drank from her cup, and then her expression turned very serious. "What do you think, Jack?"

Her response was not at all what Jack had expected. "Excuse me?"

"Oh, never mind."

"No, please don't say 'never mind.' Did my grandfather tell you something I should know?"

She measured her words and said, "I think the best way to put it is that there is some confusion about that."

"With Alzheimer's there's confusion about everything."

"True," she said. She put her cup and saucer aside. "Let me just share one little story with you."

She was using that very calm tone again, but it made Jack's heart race. "All right," he said.

"Two years ago your grandfather and I went to see a play called *Edgardo Mine.* It's a true story about a little boy named Edgardo Mortara. Do you know it?"

"Mmm, no."

"Edgardo was the son of a Jewish merchant in Bologna, one of eight children raised in an observant Jewish home in the 1850s. When he was an infant, he was very sick with fever, and the family's Catholic serving girl secretly baptized him because she didn't want him to be excluded from heaven. Happily, Edgardo survived his illness."

"Something tells me there's not a happy ending."

"Hardly," said Ruth. "Nineteenth-century Bologna was part of the Papal States. Under church law, a child who was baptized could not reside in a Jewish home. It's not clear how, but whispers about Edgardo's secret reached all the way to the pope. One night the constabulary showed up at the Mortara house and took him away."

"This is a true story?"

"Absolutely. The church's position was that Edgardo could return to his parents if they converted to Christianity. Needless to say, Edgardo never came home. It was a huge international incident, but the pope wouldn't budge. The boy even lived with him in the Vatican for a while. Edgardo ended up a Catholic priest, one of the protégés of Pio Nono."

"Pio Nono?"

"That was the Italian name for Pope Pius IX."

"That's what Grandpa shouts from his bed. I thought he was railing against the post office."

"Pio Nono is actually the main character in the play. Your grandfather was very moved by the story."

"Who wouldn't be?"

"I mean it really impacted him," she said. "Much more than I expected."

Jack waited for her to say more, but she fell silent. "Because . . . he's Jewish?"

"Honestly? I don't know. Maybe something inside me made me want to think he was. Look at me," she said, laughing at herself, "I'm eighty-three years old and still trying to please my mother. Oy vey."

Jack smiled. It was easy to see how his grandfather had enjoyed her company.

His cell phone rang. Jack didn't recognize the number, so he didn't answer.

"I'm not saying it's so," said Ruth, "and the last thing I want to do is create an identity crisis for you. But I have heard of people literally on their deathbed, telling their children or grandchildren the truth about their ancestry. And you can't always dismiss as crazy everything that comes out of the mouth of someone with Alzheimer's."

Jack's phone chimed with an incoming text message. He glanced at it, then froze.

"It's Pio Nono," it read. "*Call me. NOW!"*

"Is something wrong?" asked Ruth.

Jack shook off the chills. "Will you excuse me one minute?"

Ruth seemed concerned, as if she might have said something to anger him, but Jack had no time to explain.

He hurried out of the cafeteria and found a quiet place to return the call from a dead pope.

Chapter Thirteen

Jack ran to his grandfather's room.

It was creepy the way the message had referenced Pio Nono, and Jack feared it was a threat—aimed not just at him, but also at the man who had been shouting those words at the top of his voice.

"Are you okay?" he asked as he rushed toward the bed.

Grandpa was breathing but was out like a light, his mouth wide open. Ativan, Jack presumed—one of the anti-anxiety medications made famous by the Michael Jackson homicide, better known in nursing homes as the day-shift relief drug: Load up the patient at lunchtime, chart him as "nonresponsive" through sunset, and let the night shift deal with him. Jack would have a word with the prescribing doctor later.

He pulled up a chair beside the bed, retrieved the number from his cell history, and returned the call. After two rings there was a voice on the line.

"Got your attention, I see."

"Who is this?" asked Jack.

"Someone you need to talk to."

"How did you know I was in the middle of a conversation about Pio Nono when you texted me?"

"I heard you," the man said, his scoff crackling over the line. "Is there any other way?"

For all the concern over confused residents wandering out of the building, Sunny Gardens wasn't nearly vigilant enough about checking visitors. "Are you in the building?"

"That's enough questions. Just shut up, relax, and listen. I'm not calling to threaten you or blackmail you. I'm calling to help."

"Help me what?"

"Defend Jamal Wakefield."

An aide knocked and entered to clear away Grandpa's lunch tray, making enough noise to wake anyone who wasn't overmedicated. Jack stepped into the bathroom for privacy, closed the door, and turned on the exhaust fan to cover his voice.

"How are you going to help?" asked Jack.

"I know things."

"What kind of things?"

The man paused, then said, "I know where Jamal was when McKenna Mays was murdered."

Jack gripped the phone even tighter. "Where?"

"Exactly where he said he was."

Yesterday's court hearing had been closed, so the alleged black site in the Czech Republic was not yet public information. Jack wasn't going to supply the answer for him. "And where would that be?" he asked.

"Prague," the man said. "In a warehouse two kilometers from the airport, to be exact."

It was the kind of detail that added credibility; not even Jamal had known the exact location. "Are you telling me that my client was in a detention facility at the time of the murder?"

Silence. But Jack could tell that he was still there. "How do you know where Jamal was?" asked Jack.

There was another stretch of silence, and Jack wasn't sure if he had a liar, a crank, or just a reluctant witness.

"How do you *know*?" said Jack.

Finally, an answer: "I'm the guy who took him there."

Jack's heart nearly skipped a beat. "Listen, we need to meet. If you're still anywhere near this building, I can do it now."

"Now is not good."

"I'll come to you," said Jack.

"Not now."

"Don't play games."

"It's not a game. Problem is, I don't have the photographs with me. You're definitely gonna want them."

"You have actual pictures that show where Jamal was?"

"What do you think, Abu Ghraib is the only place they had a camera?"

This was starting to sound too good to be true. Then again, it wasn't so long ago that photographs of naked prisoners stacked into human pyramids, men on dog leashes, and other forms of abuse at Abu Ghraib prison in Iraq would have seemed unimaginable.

"You name the time and place," said Jack. "I'll be there."

"Tonight. Eight o'clock. Go to any of the cafés by the Lincoln Theatre and sit outside on the mall. When I'm convinced that you came alone, I'll find you."

"See you then," said Jack, but the caller was already gone.

Chapter Fourteen

"He wants money," said Theo.

Jack was riding shotgun in Theo's car, cruising toward Lincoln Road Mall on Miami Beach. Theo Knight was six feet three and 250 pounds of badass, which made him Jack's go-to guy when strangers called out of the blue and said, "Let's meet—*alone*." Theo was Jack's investigator, bodyguard, bartender, best friend, and confidant, none of which had seemed possible when Jack had represented the only teenager on Florida's death row. It took years of legal maneuvering and last-minute appeals, but Jack finally proved Theo's innocence. The new Theo had spent the last decade making up for lost time, pushing life to the edge, as if to prove that he was only as "innocent" as a former gangbanger from the Grove ghetto could be.

"I'm not going to pay anyone to testify," said Jack.

"Then there's no point in going," said Theo. "People don't get involved unless there's something in it for them."

"Not everyone is you," said Jack.

"The guy called and texted you on a pirated cell phone so that you couldn't trace it back to him. He's going to ask for money."

Theo had checked out the number at Jack's request, and it was hard to argue with Theo's interpretation of the results. "Just drive," said Jack.

Theo cranked up the radio. Jack immediately reached over and turned it down. It was the kind of music that made him feel old. He just didn't see the poetry in it, even if it was on some level remarkable that so many words could actually be rhymed with *suck* and *bitch.*

"Just trying to get you into the South Beach state of mind," said Theo.

Jack glanced out the passenger's-side window. The real crowds wouldn't show up until after midnight, but the sidewalks were beginning to bulge with the usual mix: the obvious tourists and a few couples, but mostly twentysomethings who had largely ditched the art of normal face-to-face conversation and preferred to hook up for sex via text messaging. Even just a year ago, it might have made Jack wonder if he'd been born twenty years too soon. Now he just felt glad to be engaged.

Good God, I really am forty.

"Let me out here," said Jack.

"Dude, all right already. I'll put on some jazz."

"It's not the music. The caller said to come alone. Just park."

The only option was valet, and Theo steered toward the curb. Reaching into his wallet, Jack did some quick math and figured that the hourly parking rate added up to $18,000 a month. He was suddenly thinking of his old friend Scholl again—mystery solved as to how he'd built a world-class art collection and a wine-making empire.

"Wait here for two minutes," said Jack, "then find a place on the mall to hang out where you can watch me. If the guy turns out to be some kind of nut job, I want you close by."

"Got it, chief."

"And wish me luck," said Jack as he started away.

"Dude," said Theo.

Jack stopped and looked back.

"That client of yours—Jamal what's-his-name."

"What about him?"

"He probably dreams about strapping on a vest and blowing up Lincoln Road Mall."

Jack paused. For a time, the one person who had seemed to shrug off Jack's representation of a Gitmo detainee was Theo. But when push came to shove, even the kid from Liberty City—an innocent man pulled from the electric chair—had the same reservations as everyone else.

Jack had them, too.

"That's the buzzkill," Jack said. "But my money still says he didn't kill McKenna Mays."

Jack headed up the sidewalk toward the mall, leaving Theo behind in the crowd.

From a wooden bench near the illuminated public fountain, a man wearing a stylish Italian suit and hiding behind sunglasses watched with the intensity of a trained professional. It was a cool night, but he was sweating profusely. His eyes were tiring, and forcing himself to stay so focused was giving him a headache. Jet lag, he figured. Flying from Europe to the States was easier than going the other way, but with the plane change in Paris, it was still a fourteen-hour flight from Prague.

Lincoln Road Mall is an outdoor collection of shops, cafés, and restaurants that stretch for several blocks of pedestrian traffic only. The Lincoln Theatre, home to the New World Symphony, is a historic art deco–style building at the east end of the mall. It's a curvy restored jewel, right down to the original cinema marquee and floral relief on its coral pink facade. That night, against a dark purple sky and in the glow of soft evening light, it looked like the postcards commemorating one of the many movie premieres that defined the theater's early years.

The mall was buzzing with activity, and the man in the dark Italian suit was well aware that his target could have chosen any number of nearby cafés to sit and wait. Designer shades were stylish even after dark, but his were no fashion statement. His eyes revealed nothing as he watched Jack Swyteck take a table beside a potted palm directly across from the theater.

Sweat gathered on his brow. His heart was racing. This wasn't normal. He wasn't even nervous. He removed his jacket and laid it on the bench beside him. He was still roasting. He hoped he wasn't catching the flu.

Damn airplanes are like a germ factory.

The crowd flowed in both directions, two endless streams that checked each other out and occasionally swirled away into little eddies of conversation. Some were dressed to kill. Others were barely dressed. They were all under his surveillance, his eyes and mind working together and processing each passing image like the superfast, superpowered face-recognition software that never seemed to work for him the way it worked on television dramas. Reject after reject, his eyes darted left to right, east to west, and back again. Hundreds and hundreds of passersby without a match.

His throat tightened. His left foot was starting to tingle. More like his entire left side. The foot—no, the leg all the way up to the knee—was actually numb. This was no mere adrenaline rush.

What the hell is going on?

He wanted to rise, but his body refused. With a wobbly push he forced himself up from the bench, and it gave him a head rush. The flow of pedestrians through the mall was starting to blur. The glow of streetlights, landscape illumination, and colored neon had blended into a ghostly fog. He removed his sunglasses and strained to focus. His gaze tightened, and for a split second things came clear to him. He'd seen them before, just an hour earlier—another pair of eyes hiding behind sunglasses after dark—and his mind replayed the brief and seemingly meaningless encounter. It wasn't so much the face he remembered as that long, white mobility cane approaching at a surprisingly fast clip. It was a needlelike missile that had emerged from the crowd, guided by the hand without sight, and no matter which way he turned, he couldn't get out of the way. He jerked one way, the stick followed, and in the ensuing head-on collision, that mobility stick had jabbed into his ankle like a jousting stick.

I can't feel my foot.

He glanced back at the café table by the potted palm across from the theater. Swyteck had no idea who he was even looking for—no reason to know what was happening to the man he was supposed to meet.

His gaze shifted back toward the white walking stick in the crowd, but it was gone. Or maybe it was still there and the image wasn't registering.

I can't see—can't . . . breathe!

He wanted to scream. No voice. He tried to run, but he felt nothing from the chest down. His arms, too, failed him, refusing to break the fall. He felt only the wind on his face as he dropped to the sidewalk. His chin slammed against the concrete, and as darkness took over, he noticed that he couldn't taste the blood.

Then the silence turned black.

Chapter Fifteen

A woman screamed, and Jack jumped to his feet.

Just a few doors down, a crowd was gathering near the illuminated fountain. Through the growing forest of onlookers, Jack saw a man lying flat on the pavers with people around him speaking in short bursts of panic and waving their arms in frantic gestures. He threw a ten-dollar bill on the table to cover his sparkling water and sprinted toward the commotion. By the time Jack got there, an older gentleman had already rolled the fallen man onto his back, ripped open his shirt, and started chest compressions. An elderly woman was shouting into her cell phone.

"My husband's a retired physician and is trying CPR," she said, "but the man's not breathing, and there's no pulse!"

Another woman came forward, opened her purse, and said, "I have an aspirin."

"Can't," said the doctor, waving her off. "He's unconscious."

"Looks more dead than unconscious," said one of the on-lookers.

"Did anyone see him collapse?" asked the doctor.

A waiter spoke up. "I did."

"How long ago?"

"Five minutes or so."

"Be exact."

The waiter checked his watch. "I'd say more like seven."

"Tell them they've got sixty seconds!" the doctor shouted to his wife.

She repeated the message to the 911 operator, but Jack heard no approaching ambulances in the neighborhood. The doctor kept at his work, a hundred compressions per minute, desperately trying to revive him. He looked exhausted. Jack stepped in to relieve him.

"I got it," said the doctor. "I need an automated external defibrillator. Check the theater."

The symphony drew an older crowd—apart from the cocaine addicts, they were South Beach's most likely demographic for cardiac arrest. *Good call, Doc.*

Jack ran. The doors were open, and Jack burst into the lobby. It took him ten seconds to shout out his needs to the woman at the will-call window. It took her an ungodly long time to bring him the emergency kit. Jack grabbed it and raced back to the mall. Paramedics were finally on the scene. They had already administered the three stacked shocks that Jack had seen a hundred times on television dramas—200, 300, 360—and an IV was in place. One of the EMTs was struggling to intubate, but he couldn't force the airway.

"Forget it, let's roll!" he shouted.

The man looked utterly lifeless as the team lifted him onto the gurney. The crowd parted as paramedics whisked him down the mall to the ambulance at the corner. Jack took it as a bad sign that they didn't even bother to turn on the sirens as the ambulance pulled away.

"He's not going to make it, is he," said Jack.

The doctor was standing beside his wife, his shirt soaked with sweat.

"Completely asystolic. Poor guy was at least twelve minutes into cardiac arrest by the time emergency arrived. Almost twenty by the time they pulled away. Once you get beyond six, at most eight minutes . . ." His voice trailed away, as if he were too tired to verbalize the obvious. His wife squeezed his hand and assured him he'd done the best he could.

Two police officers were on the scene to secure the area around the fountain with yellow police tape.

"Please, folks, step back," said the cop.

Jack noticed a third officer near the bench. The man's suit jacket had been left behind, and the cop was fishing out a wallet, presumably for a driver's license—something to reveal the identity of this well-dressed man who'd apparently come alone to the mall. Or come to meet someone.

Jack was suddenly thinking again of his scheduled meeting with his informant.

"Is this being treated as a crime scene?" Jack asked him.

"Back away, please. Let us do our job."

The crowd began to disperse, people returning to their café tables to find melted ice cream or cold plates of linguine with clam sauce.

Jack turned his attention back toward the police. The yellow plastic tape was in place, but two men and a woman ducked under it. The crime scene investigation team had its job to do, which was the protocol for an unwitnessed death in a public place. But for an apparent heart attack, it seemed to Jack that they'd arrived in quite the hurry. Jack walked around to the other side of the fountain and approached the doctor again.

"Excuse me, but did anything about this seem suspicious to you?" Jack asked him.

The doctor shrugged. "Not really. Other than the fact that he was in his late twenties, maybe thirty. Pretty young to have a heart attack. I'd be surprised if the toxicology report doesn't show something."

Jack thought back to the earlier phone conversation in his grandfather's bathroom. The voice on the line had definitely not been an older man's.

"Yeah," said Jack. "Something."

Jack checked his watch: 8:10 P.M. The meeting time was to have been eight o'clock. Jack took one more look at the busy crime scene, then walked away and returned to his table at the café. The fizz had gone out of his sparkling water, but it couldn't hurt to sit and wait a little longer. Deep down, however, he knew that his informant would be a no-show.

A quick glance at the napkin confirmed it, and Jack felt chills.

On the white paper napkin beneath his water glass was a handwritten note—and Jack was certain that it hadn't been there before. With a CSI team nearby, Jack had the presence of mind not to touch the napkin or the glass. Condensation from the melted ice had blurred one of the words, and the penmanship wasn't that good to begin with, but he was still able to read the entire message:

Are you afraid of The Dark?

"Is everything okay?" asked the waiter.

Jack was still staring at the napkin, absorbing the final two words of warning: *Back off.*

"Sir? Is everything okay?"

Jack glanced toward the crime scene, then back at the waiter. "Did you see anyone come by this table while I was away?"

"No, but to be honest, I was off watching the paramedics, just like everyone else."

"Almost everyone else," said Jack, his gaze returning to the napkin. Part of him wanted to get up and scour the mall for clues, but he would make it his job to protect this message from contamination until it could be properly collected and checked for fingerprints and forensic analysis.

"Do me a favor," he told the waiter. "Ask one of those cops to come over here. And tell him to bring an evidence bag."

Chapter Sixteen

Vincent Paulo hated Sunday nights. Always had. It was the thought of Monday morning that dragged him down. Tonight, however, the culprit was Saturday night—the fallout from what had happened yesterday evening at Lincoln Road Mall, to be exact.

"Are you coming to bed?" asked Alicia.

It was almost eleven, and he was seated in a rocking chair on the screened-in porch, facing their backyard. Crickets made their music in the bushes. Water gurgled from the fountain in the garden. Vince was on his third beer since the Miami Heat had fallen hopelessly behind in the third quarter of the LeBron James show.

"In a little while," he said.

His wife waited, and he sensed her concern. Finally, her footsteps trailed away to the kitchen, and Vince returned to his thoughts.

Actually, when Vince was a little boy, it wasn't just Sunday nights that he'd hated. Bedtime in general was a problem. Vince was afraid of the dark. He would lay awake for the longest time—for hours, it seemed, the covers pulled over his head, too scared to make a move. "Just close your eyes and go to sleep," his mother would say. But Vince couldn't do it. The Scooby-Doo night-light was of some comfort. But closing his eyes would have meant total darkness, and it was in that black, empty world that monsters prowled.

Ironic, he thought, that he now lived in that world—and that it was indeed a monster who had put him there.

Over the past three years Vince had tried not to think about the day he'd lost his sight, or at least not to dwell on it. Hindsight could eat you up, even on the small stuff. Going blind was definitely not small stuff. How many people could say, *If only I hadn't opened that door, I would never have lost my eyesight*? Of those, how many could actually live with the result—truly *live* with it, as in live a happy life. Vince was determined to be one of those people.

There had been major adjustments, to be sure. For a time, he'd given up active duty completely to teach hostage negotiation at the police academy. Of all the skills that made a talented negotiator, sight was not chief among them. He was still a good listener, with sharp instincts, common sense, and street smarts. He could still intuit things from a hostage taker's tone of voice over the phone, or from a mere pause in the conversation. In fact, losing his sight had seemed to strengthen those other, more important skills. Proof of that had come just a few months after his return to work, when, in his first job as a blind negotiator, he'd talked down a homeless guy from a bridge. That feat paled in comparison to the subsequent crisis that had put him in the national spotlight. A delusional and well-armed gunman took four people hostage in a motel and demanded to speak with the mayor's daughter. One of those hostages was Theo Knight—Jack Swyteck's best friend. And now Swyteck was returning the favor by defending Jamal Wakefield.

You're welcome, asshole.

Alicia came up behind him and slid her arms around his shoulders. "Why are you so quiet tonight?"

He took a long pull from his beer bottle, as if to tell her that he was in no mood to talk.

"Mind if I join you?" she asked, but he didn't answer.

"I'll get a couple more beers," she said.

"I'm good," he said.

"Then I'll get one for myself," she said as she started toward the kitchen.

It was hard for Vince to imagine life without Alicia, even if he had broken off their relationship after the accident. They'd reunited and then married only after Vince was convinced that there was no pity in those beautiful eyes he could no longer look into. At the first sign that she had stood by him out of sympathy, he would relieve her of that obligation and move on with his life. And he would be happy. That was a solid place to be, emotionally, and it had taken him many months—years—to get there.

The apprehension of Jamal Wakefield had sent him tumbling back to square one.

"I brought you a frosted mug," she said.

"I said I was good," he told her.

He heard Alicia put the mug on the coffee table and settle into the rocking chair beside him. "Knock the *Biggest Loser*–sized chip off your shoulder, Vince."

She was right, and he knew it. "Sorry."

"Apology accepted."

Somewhere in the yard, bullfrogs croaked in the night. A cool breeze through the screen felt good on his face. Alicia reached over and touched his hand, which felt even better.

"Are you going to make me drag it out of you," she said, "or are you going to tell me how your meeting went with Detective Lopez?"

Lopez was the unit supervisor of the Crime Scene Squad at Miami Beach Police Department, and he was working the suspicious death on Lincoln Road Mall. Vince's meeting with him had lasted almost an hour that morning, while Alicia was in church.

"Dead guy's name is Ethan Chang," said Vince. "A twenty-nine-year-old ex-pat who was living in Prague."

"What was he doing over there?"

"No idea. Probably chasing Czech fashion models."

"Probably the same reason he went to Miami Beach last night."

"Only if he works fast. He flew into MIA yesterday and was ticketed on a return flight to Prague tonight."

As if on cue, the rumble of a jet at thirty thousand feet cut through the night sky. Vince waited for the distant noise to fade away completely, then said, "He had pictures of Jamal Wakefield with him."

"Pictures?"

"He had a cell phone, too. Jack Swyteck's number was in the call history."

"He talked to Swyteck before he died?"

"Turns out Swyteck was at a sidewalk café about fifty feet away when the guy dropped dead on Lincoln Road Mall. Detective Lopez took his statement last night."

"Is Swyteck a suspect?"

"No. His story is that an anonymous informant called him yesterday and told him to meet at eight o'clock on the mall. The guy promised to bring Swyteck some photographs to support Jamal Wakefield's alibi."

"What alibi?"

Vince told her, and he took the long pause as a sign of her incredulity. Finally, Alicia said, "So the photographs show that Wakefield was held in some kind of a detention facility in Prague when McKenna was murdered?"

"I'm sure that's what Swyteck will argue in court."

"Exactly what did Lopez tell you is in the pictures?"

"It's definitely Jamal. He's handcuffed. He looks tired and scared. But there's no way to tell where he is or when the photos were taken."

"Does he look like Jamal Wakefield from Miami, or like Khaled al-Jawar from Somalia?"

"Clean shaven, like Jamal. But he didn't have long hair and a beard when he arrived in Guantánamo. So these photographs could have been taken when he was in Gitmo—*after* the murder."

"Could have been? Or were?"

"Were," said Vince. "Definitely were, if you ask me."

"Are they ruling his death a homicide?"

"Toxicology report will take a few weeks. But they found a suspicious mark on his ankle. So, unofficially, yeah. Lopez is going with foul play. Probably will call in Miami-Dade Homicide."

Alicia couldn't help chuckling. "What's the theory—somebody jabbed him with a poison-tipped umbrella à la James Bond?"

Vince didn't answer.

"You're joking, right?" she said.

He turned in his chair and removed his sunglasses, as if to look her in the eye. "Do I look like I'm joking?" he asked, his tone taking on an edge. "Is there anything about this that should strike me as remotely funny?"

"Vince, come on."

"No, I've kept my head about this for three years. I've been upbeat. I've been positive. I've done all the things that make people say they admire me right before they go home and tell their wife, 'Thank God I'm not Vince Paulo.'"

"They don't say that."

"Yes, they *do*, Alicia. And I'm okay with it. Most of the time. But not right now. Jamal Wakefield is back, he's got himself a couple of smart lawyers, and they've cooked up a really clever alibi. How do you expect me to act?"

"I don't expect anything. I'm just a little worried about you."

"Of course you are. Everybody is. The blind guy gets sad, and it's because all blind people are depressed. The blind guy gets angry, and it's because all blind people are bitter. Why can't I have the same emotions everybody else has? Why does everyone assume that if there's a smile on my face, it's fake, and if there's no smile on my face, it's because I hate my life? I hate Jamal Wakefield—that's what I hate. And there is nothing wrong with my wanting to nail the son of a bitch who butchered McKenna Mays and left me like this."

He felt her touch again, but he pulled his hand away.

"Vince, I don't think I like what I'm hearing."

"Then go to bed," he said as he reached for his cell phone.

"Who are you calling?"

"Jack Swyteck," he said, dialing.

"Vince, don't. You've been drinking."

He kept dialing.

"It's after eleven," said Alicia.

Vince ignored her. On the third ring, Swyteck answered his cell.

"Swyteck, it's Vince Paulo."

Jack hesitated, obviously caught off guard. "How are you, Vince?"

"Been better. I know it's late, but there are a couple things I just need to get off my chest."

"Okay," said Swyteck, some trepidation in his voice. "I'm listening."

"None of this would be an issue if we didn't know each other. But you and I have some history, so it needs to be said."

"You're right. That history, as you say, is one of the reasons I've been so reluctant to get involved. And I didn't want to rush into making ridiculous accusations against the U.S. government about black sites. I've gone back and forth on this, but there's too much tipping the other way, Vince. Even Chuck Mays seems to have his doubts, and now we have Mr. Chang suddenly silenced. I'm taking the case. I was actually going to call you."

"When? After the opening statement?"

"I don't want this to become personal."

"Funny," said Vince, "but the only time people say that is when they know it already is."

The lawyer didn't answer.

Vince said, "Chuck Mays told me about the conversation he had with you at his house yesterday morning."

"I figured he would. I know you two are friends."

"But friends don't always agree," Vince said. "You understand what I'm saying?"

"I think I do."

"Well, let me spell it out for you. You mentioned Chuck as a reason for taking the case. If, in any way, Chuck conveyed some concerns about indicting the right man, I want you to know that I don't share his doubts."

"That's your view."

"If you want to get literal about it, you might say it was my *last view.* I was the one who found McKenna in her room. I was holding McKenna in my arms when she tried to look up and told me who did it. But all that will come out at trial."

"It will, which is why I don't think this conversation is—"

"No, you need to hear what I have to say. You go ahead and represent Jamal Wakefield. I don't care. The truth is, I want him to have a good lawyer. Because I want him convicted, and I don't want him filing appeals for the next ten years claiming that his counsel was ineffective. I want the conviction to stick."

"I understand."

"No, you don't understand, Swyteck. You can't possibly *understand.* I want it to stick, and I will do what it takes to make it stick. Count on it."

Vince hung up, and it was only then that he realized how tightly he was squeezing the phone. He breathed in and out, then massaged the pain between his eyes.

"Vince, I—"

"Don't say it," he told her.

Alicia reached out and laced her fingers with his. "I love you," she said.

Vince let out another deep breath. "That's the best news I've heard all day."

Chapter Seventeen

Jack was still stinging on Monday morning. The phone call from Vince Paulo hadn't gone as badly as he thought it would; it had been even worse. Jack probably should have been the one to initiate the call; maybe he should have even told him about the polygraph. But that probably wouldn't have made a difference. Vince's anger was completely unavoidable. Maybe even justified.

You don't understand, Swyteck.

Jack closed his eyes for a moment—and held it. It could actually feel soothing, even calming in a way. Until you wanted it to end. Jack pushed himself to get to that point—eyes closed until he couldn't stand the darkness any longer—and then he forced himself to remain without sight. Sixty seconds passed. It felt like an hour. Two minutes went by, and he was in hell. After five minutes, he would have cut off his legs rather than stay this way forever. And he realized Vince was right.

You can't possibly understand.

At nine A.M., Jack had a court hearing in a foreclosure action—was there a condo anywhere in Miami-Dade County *not* in foreclosure?—and by midmorning he had returned to his office in Coconut Grove. It was an old one-story cottage on a forested stretch of Main Highway, near a three-way intersection that, depending on the chosen path, could lead to a chic shopping district, where hippies had once run head shops; waterfront mansions, where those former hippies now lived; or the Grove ghetto, where their children and grandchildren cruised in their BMWs to buy drugs. A ninety-year-old clapboard cottage wasn't what Jack had envisioned when his lease in Coral Gables had expired, but it was "loaded with charm"—real-estate-agent speak for caveat emptor.

Jack pushed through the door—it always stuck on humid mornings—and his secretary nearly tackled him as he stepped inside.

"You had eleven calls," she said, "including three from a woman who refused to leave her number and would identify herself only as"—Carmen stopped to check her notes—"oh, here it is: 'the most beautiful and intelligent woman in the world.'"

Jack rolled his eyes. "By any chance did that woman sound a little like Andie?"

The lightbulb went on. "As a matter of fact, she did!"

Jack's cell had been turned off in the courthouse, and in a free moment Andie had obviously tried to touch base with him at his office.

"Oh, one more thing," said Carmen, and then she lowered her voice, as if it were a secret. "You have an unexpected visitor. She's waiting in your office."

Jack read between the lines and tried not to groan. He loved his maternal grandmother—Abuela—but it was a busy Monday morning, and she had a way of just showing up at his office whenever it had been too long since he'd last visited her. Usually, it was to wonder aloud if she was going to live long enough to teach Spanish to the great-grandchildren who, by the way, Jack and Andie needed to hurry up and give to her.

Jack whispered his reply. "I really don't have time this morning."

"But she was practically in tears."

"Abuela?"

"No, Maryam Wakefield. Jamal's mother. She came all the way from Minnesota."

"You put her in my office? I don't even know the woman."

"Where else could I put her?"

Jack glanced at the tiny waiting area, but it was packed with dozens of exhibit boxes from a five-week trial in a bank fraud case, no place for anyone to sit. Just six months into a new lease, and he'd already outgrown the space.

"All right, hold my calls."

Jack stepped around a few boxes and entered his office. Maryam Wakefield rose from the armchair, quickly introduced herself, and immediately apologized for having arrived unannounced.

"To be honest," she said, "I hadn't planned on coming to see you. I'm in town to visit Jamal. In fact, I just came from the . . ."

Her voice cracked. For Jack, she was hardly the first mother to get emotional about a son in jail on charges of first degree murder. That first look at a loved one on the other side of the glass was rarely a comfort.

"Please, have a seat," said Jack.

She lowered herself into the chair, and her eyes begged for a tissue. Any experienced criminal defense lawyer kept plenty around.

"This is such a roller coaster," she said, taking the Kleenex. "It's like someone calling to say, 'Good news, Mrs. Wakefield: After three years, we finally found your son. The bad news is that he's in jail and, with any luck, he might not get the death penalty.' "

She dabbed away a tear, though few were left after her visit to the jailhouse.

Maryam Wakefield was not much older than Jack, probably no more than twenty years old when she'd given birth to Jamal. She was an attractive woman with a few strands of gray, but the strain of the past three years had aged her, and the tired eyes and sad expression seemed almost permanent. Jack knew from Jamal that she was of Somali descent on her mother's side, but the name

"Wakefield" had come from a father who was the descendant of slaves and not sure of his African roots.

"Anyway," she said, "the reason I came is because Jamal told me how hard you have been working for him. I'm not rich by any stretch, but it's important for Jamal to have a good lawyer," she said, her hand shaking as she pulled her checkbook from her purse. "If you can hold this check until my daughter's disability check clears next Thursday, and then hopefully I can write you another one after I sell off some of my—"

"Put that away," said Jack. "I volunteered for this case. The only person to thank is Neil Goderich at the Freedom Institute."

"Will he take a check?"

Jack couldn't help smiling. "Yes, but usually it's from rich people who didn't see him sneaking up at a cocktail party and missed their chance to turn and run."

She didn't seem to get it, but that wasn't important. She closed her purse, folded her hands in her lap, and heaved a heavy sigh of what seemed like a combined sense of relief and *Now what?*

"Jamal tells me you're working on the alibi," she said. "I might be able to help with that."

Jack paused, trying to be discreet. A mother helping her son with an alibi. *Now there's a twist.*

Maryam continued. "I know what you're thinking. But Jamal was crazy about McKenna. He called me when she broke up with him. He sounded devastated."

"On a help scale of one to ten," said Jack, "I'd have to rate that as 'not so much.' "

"I realize that it cuts both ways."

"Obsession usually cuts only one way," said Jack.

"You don't understand. Before he disappeared, the last conversation I had with my son, he told me he was coming home—back to Minnesota."

"When was that?"

"I don't remember the exact date. But it was on his cell, so I'm sure there are phone records."

Jack made a note to get it. "You're sure it was before the murder?"

"Of course I'm sure. I called him the next morning to check on his travel plans, but he didn't answer. I kept calling his cell, his apartment. No answer. I called McKenna's father at work, Jamal's friends. No one knew where he was, but his car was still in Miami—still parked outside his apartment. I was hoping he'd bought a bus ticket and just slept on the trip, but it was like he'd vanished. That was when I filed a missing person report, which of course got me nowhere."

"None of that's in dispute," said Jack. "The prosecutor will simply say that the breakup sent him into a reclusive funk. Maybe he drank himself unconscious and slept under a bridge or on the beach for a night or two. He snapped, killed McKenna, and went on the run."

"Let me ask you this, Mr. Swyteck: How does a nineteen-year-old kid with a warrant out for his arrest get all the way from Miami to Somalia, completely undetected?"

"The same way as any other kid whose father has alleged connections to a Somali terrorist organization."

She looked away, and Jack could see that the lasting stigma of that relationship cut very deep. "Sorry," he said. "I wasn't accusing you or anyone else. I'm just thinking like a prosecutor."

Her expression was still one of shame—and anger. "I hardly knew Jamal's father," she said. "We never married. Jamal did a family tree for one of his eighth-grade projects, and after that, he wanted to know more about his father. He was good with computers—a genius, really—and when Jamal was in high school they developed an online relationship. If I'd known what kind of things he was involved with, I would never have let Jamal communicate with him."

Her hand was a tight fist, the tissue balled up inside it. Jack sensed she had more to say, so he merely listened.

"My son is not a terrorist." She drew a breath, as if she resented having to say it. "If he was, the government wouldn't have failed so miserably at that court hearing you handled in Washington."

Logic supported her, but so far, logic hadn't been the test in this case. "You're right about that," said Jack.

"I didn't help my son run from the law," she said. "I spoke with Jamal only once after McKenna's death. He was calling from Prague."

"Tell me about that," said Jack.

"It was a total surprise. I could hear the fear in his voice. He didn't have any money or a credit card, so he called collect. He told me how he'd been abducted, drugged, and taken to some kind of interrogation facility. That would have sounded crazy to most parents, except for what was going on in our neighborhood."

"Meaning what?"

"American boys of Somali descent recuited to fight for al-Shabaab. It's been all over the news for several years now. There were two boys from Jamal's high school who ended up dead."

"Is that what they grilled Jamal about in Prague?"

She hesitated, as if suddenly suspicious. "Jamal must have told you what they grilled him about."

"I want to know what your son told you when he called from Prague."

"Are you testing me?"

The woman was no dummy. "No," said Jack. "I'm testing him."

Again she paused, as if she didn't see the difference. "He told me that they wanted to know about his work for McKenna's father. The encryption stuff. Isn't that what Jamal told you?"

It was, but Jack didn't answer. "What else did he tell you?"

"Nothing. That was when I told him about McKenna. The only thing that shocked him more was when I told him he was wanted for her murder."

"Did he deny killing her?"

She looked up at him, meeting his gaze. "Of course he did. I told him to come home to Minnesota. But he was too scared. I had no idea what he was going to do. Only after you got involved did I find out that he contacted his father, who managed to get him to Somalia under the name Khaled Al-Jawar. You know the rest."

Jack came around the desk, trying to soften his approach. "Let me play prosecutor again, Ms. Wakefield. How do you know that your son didn't just make up all that stuff about being abducted and interrogated in Prague?"

"Because I talked to him on the phone. I heard his voice. I know my son, and I know he wasn't lying."

"You're his mother. I want you to try to put that aside."

"What mother can put that aside?"

"What I'm trying to say is that his mother won't be a juror at the trial. How do we convince a jury that Jamal didn't kill McKenna, run off to Prague with help from his father, and then make up a story about a secret interrogation facility just to support an alibi?"

She thought for a moment, trying to put motherhood aside. "Jamal's father has no connection to Prague. But the man you were supposed to meet at Lincoln Road Mall on Saturday night did."

"What do you know about that?"

"Just the things I read in the newspaper. But it helped make some sense of the lies the police have told."

"What lies are you talking about?"

"Many of them—starting with what happened to McKenna's mother."

"You mean her suicide?"

"That was no suicide. They never found her body."

"They found her canoe upside down in the Everglades and an empty bottle of sleeping pills in her car. She drove to her favorite spot in Biscayne National Park and floated off peacefully."

"Not even the police believe that."

"How do you know?"

"A homicide investigator came to talk with me."

Jack did a double take. "When?"

"Several times. In between the time McKenna died and when her mother disappeared."

"What about?"

"There were e-mails or Internet chat communications or something of that sort that Shada Mays was having. I don't know specifics, but the detective made it clear enough to me that the police suspected Shada was onto something."

"What do you mean 'something'?"

"Chuck Mays wasn't the only person in that family who knew how to use a computer. Shada was tracking her daughter's killer on the Internet and got too close to him."

"The detective told you that?"

"Yes. Because the theory was that Jamal killed McKenna, and that McKenna's mother was talking with him online, luring him back to the States so that he could be brought to justice."

"I haven't heard anything about that."

"Of course you haven't. Because it doesn't wash anymore. The theory was that McKenna's mother talked Jamal into meeting with her in person, but when she tried to turn him in or get him to turn himself in, Jamal killed her and covered his tracks by making it look like suicide. Now the cops know that Jamal was in Guantánamo when McKenna's mother was having those online chats with her daughter's killer. I may be going out on a limb here, but I don't think enemy combatants at Gitmo had Internet."

Jack went cold. He'd smelled cover-ups before, but this one had a capital *C*. "So they can deny that Jamal was in a black site in Prague when McKenna was killed," said Jack.

"But they can't deny that he was locked up in Gitmo when McKenna's mother was talking to McKenna's killer."

"Which, of course, leaves the big question," said Jack. "Who was Shada Mays having those online communications with?"

"Answer that," she said, "and I think you'll know who killed McKenna Mays. And her mother."

Jack was beginning to wonder if this could also explain the inexplicable, the thing that had puzzled him since his meeting with Chuck Mays. It was one thing for the victim's family to question whether the police had the right man. It was another thing entirely for Chuck Mays to express those doubts *to Jack*, the lawyer for the man accused of murdering his daughter.

"Thank you," said Jack. "This has been an eye-opener."

"I didn't come for 'thanks.' I want to know what you think."

Jack walked around the desk to his phone, ready to speed-dial Neil Goderich. "If what you're saying is true, I think your son has sat in jail long enough."

Chapter Eighteen

Andie rode the Green Line into Washington for a status meeting with the supervisory agent in charge of her undercover operation. Her Metro stop was U-Street/Cardozo, near Howard University, and she took the escalator up to the Thirteenth Street exit. A cold front was pushing through that afternoon, and the temperature had dropped almost ten degrees since lunchtime. January was not her favorite time of year to visit the capital, and this latest trip north had confirmed that her Seattle roots had dissolved and that she was officially a thin-blooded Floridian.

Andie cinched up her coat and started toward the Hotel LaDroit. Her undercover role was a round-the-clock commitment, and meetings at FBI offices were out of the question. Andie wondered what Jack would have said about her meeting an ex-marine like Harley Abrams at a cheap hotel. Before she could even laugh at the thought, however, Harley stopped her on the sidewalk. He'd just walked out of Ben's Chili Bowl—A WASHINGTON LANDMARK, the sign above the window said, famous for its place in civil rights history and its "Chili Smokes" hot dogs.

"Whoa, I don't need to eat for a week," said Harley. "Let's talk while I walk this off."

Andie was almost shivering. "Aren't we meeting indoors?"

"This way," he said. "Ten minutes, tops."

"Let's make it five," said Andie. She set a brisk pace to the corner, where Harley led her up a side street.

"This wasn't on my original agenda," he said, "but I got another call this morning from Justice about your fiancé. To put it mildly, there are serious concerns about the direction his defense strategy is taking."

They stopped at a traffic light. There was a dentist's office on the corner, and it occurred to Andie that between the worsening weather and the continuing assault on Jack—this was not the first conversation with her supervisor about Jamal Wakefield—today's status meeting was turning out to be about as pleasant as a root canal.

"How do they know what Jack's defense strategy is?" she asked.

"Well, the lawyers at Justice are making certain assumptions."

"They can assume all they want," said Andie. "It's like I told you before: If Jack wants to defend Jamal Wakefield, that's his decision."

The light turned green. Andie buried her hands in her coat pockets, and Harley matched her stride across the street.

"Don't get defensive," he said. "I'm sharing this with you only because I thought you should know. That's all."

Andie paused to consider the source. Harley was one of the good guys, and it was pointless to kill the messenger. "Okay, sorry. I appreciate the heads-up."

Harley stopped midway down the block. Andie was eager to find warmth inside a comfortable lobby, but there wasn't a hotel in sight. In fact, the neighborhood had turned questionable.

"Don't tell me you got us lost," said Andie.

They were standing in front of a hardware store, but Harley's gaze had drifted toward a small shop across the street. The plate-glass windows were blacked over, but the sign on the door—CAPITAL PLEASURES, it read—featured a tall blonde in tight black leather with strategically placed nickel studs.

"Harley, this seems inappropriate."

"That's why I'm going to let one of our female agents handle this. Cherie Donner from the Washington field office is sort of an expert in this field. She'll be here any minute, take you inside, and show you around. Then the two of you will meet in private. She can explain everything."

"Explain *what*?"

"Let me put it this way," he said. "Your undercover role is entering a new phase."

Andie let it sink in. She'd played a prostitute on her first undercover assignment in Seattle, but this was her first venture into the world of leather and chains.

"Are you asking me to play some kind of dominatrix?"

"I would have volunteered myself, but does anybody really want to see *me* in a getup like that?"

Andie shook off the thought in a hurry. "Definitely not, but I—"

"Relax," he said. "I was just kidding about wearing the stuff. It's more of an education into a lifestyle and certain male fetishes that Agent Donner will introduce you to."

She took another quick look across the street, wondering what Jack would say about her visit to Capital Pleasures.

Honey, do you like the riding crop with the rhinestones, or without?

"You're okay with this, right?" he asked.

"Sure, I'm fine. There's just one thing."

"What?"

"Don't expect me to whip my husband into dropping his case," she said as she thumped him on the chest.

Chapter Nineteen

On Monday evening Jack got his first taste of Somali cuisine. It was at Cafe Nema—in Washington, D.C.

Proving that Jamal had been held at a secret detention center in Prague was step two of the alibi defense. Step one was proving that a facility had ever existed in the Czech Republic in the first place—an even bigger hurdle. The defense team needed a heavy hitter, and it was Neil who had arranged for them to meet with Stan Haber, a corporate litigator who believed that everyone deserved a lawyer. That belief wasn't incompatible with profit: Over the years, Haber and his powerful Washington firm had logged thousands of billable hours trying to convince juries that Big Tobacco didn't know cigarettes were addictive. Lately, he'd spent his time defending Gitmo detainees free of charge.

"Who ordered the sambousa with basmati rice pilaf?" the waitress asked.

Flaky fried triangles of dough filled with curried vegetables weren't exactly exotic, but Cafe Nema was more about the experience. At the basement level, a few steps below U Street, the dimly lit room was ripe for conversation, a cozy mix of foreign ex-pats and hip U-Streeters. Battered brick walls displayed a collage of brightly colored oil paintings, and a large Somali flag hung on a section painted fire-engine red. Photos of Miles Davis and Duke Ellington hung above the worn wooden bar, where counter and stools bore the nicks, scratches, and other badges of use.

Older men spoke French and Arabic, savoring plates of kibeh (a torpedo-shaped pastry filled with beef and onions). Students from nearby Howard University gathered at tables to kibitz or send text messages from their cell phones. Jazz music set the mood without interfering with the buzz of voices.

"Sambousa is mine," said Jack.

The waitress served the platters and quickly brought another round of beers. Neil steered the conversation back toward business.

"Stan has been on top of black detention sites ever since the *Washington Post* broke the story in 2005."

Jack already knew all that, but Neil's brief segue was all the encouragement Haber needed to remind them that he had been among the first volunteers to visit Guantánamo, and that he'd played a key role in securing the game-changing decision of the Supreme Court that detainees must be treated in accordance with the Geneva Conventions.

"Obviously, we'd love to have someone like you on board," said Jack. "But here's my concern. Our job is to get Jamal acquitted on charges of first degree murder. Nothing more. I don't want to turn his case into a foreign-policy battle where my client is collateral damage in a war against the CIA."

"Then you're dreaming," said Haber. "The CIA doesn't care *why* you want the information. You want to prove that secret detention sites existed in Eastern Europe—something the United States and every Eastern European country has denied for years. Even the Red Cross had to push for five years to get access to the detainees, and they still didn't get information about all the black sites."

"Are you saying you can't help us?" asked Neil.

Haber emptied his beer bottle into a tall glass. "When you represent a detainee from a black site, you're fighting every step of the way for information that the CIA does not want to be made public. My client is a good example. Mohammed was thrown into the back of a van by a group of strongmen who wore black outfits, masks that covered their faces, and dark visors over their eyes—probably commandos attached to the CIA's paramilitary Special Activities Division. He was hog-tied, stripped naked, photographed, hooded, sedated with anal suppositories, placed in diapers, and transported by plane to a secret location. It's the beginning of a process designed to strip the detainee of any dignity."

"Sounds like what Jamal described," said Jack.

"Disorientation is also a big part of it. For my client it was twenty days in a pitch-black cell with Eminem's 'Slim Shady' and Dr. Dre blaring nonstop. Then it was day after day of ghoulish Halloween sounds, always in total darkness, always in solitary confinement. They'd chain him to the ceiling hanging by his wrists so that his toes could barely touch the ground, then they'd bring him down for waterboarding. He spent hours in something called a dog box, which, as the name, implies isn't big enough for a human being. These are all tactics that were used effectively by the KGB, but you have to remember that the KGB was interested in securing false confessions to crimes against the state, not the gathering of reliable intelligence. It got to the point where my client tried to kill himself by running his head into the wall. Didn't work. He just knocked himself unconscious."

"He's probably much better at flying airplanes into buildings," said Jack—and he'd shocked himself, the words having come like a reflex.

"Whoa," said Neil.

Jack's mouth opened, but the explanation was on a slight delay, as if his brain needed extra time to process what was going on. "It's not that I make light of torture," he said, still trying to comprehend. "I just . . . I think I had an Andie moment."

"A what?"

"My fiancée," said Jack. "She's an FBI agent. You kept going on and on about the treatment at these black sites, and suddenly I could almost hear Andie whispering into my ear: 'Before you get all ACLU on me, remember what most of these guys would do if given the chance.'"

The other men exchanged glances, and Neil tried to lighten things up. "These things happen with Jack. Not many guys spend four years at the Freedom Institute before jumping ship to be a federal prosecutor."

"Ah, a wolf in sheep's clothing, are you?" said Haber.

"A sheep in wolf's clothing, if you ask my fiancée. I lasted only two years at the U.S. attorney's office."

Haber drank from his beer and nodded. "I guess none of us is easy to figure out. Look at Neil and me: a couple of Jews defending Islamic extremists."

"Funny, Grandpa Swyteck said the same thing about me."

Haber looked confused again, so Jack explained. "Since getting Alzheimer's, my grandfather thinks that he's Jewish."

"Where's he from?"

"Chicago. Both of his parents were born in Bohemia. Somewhere around Prague."

"Are there any Czech Jews named Swyteck?" asked Haber.

"I don't know," said Jack. "The name is another one of those Ellis Island disasters."

"For your grandfather to be Jewish, it really matters what his mother was."

"Her maiden name was Petrak," said Jack, "which I checked out on the Internet. It means 'Peter the Rock'—as in the Apostle Peter being the first pope, the rock upon which Christ founded his church."

"That doesn't sound too Jewish," said Haber.

"You never know," said Neil. "A lot of Eastern European Jews had good reason to assume a gentile surname, even before the Nazis. How do you think Goldsmith became Goderich?"

Jack hadn't thought of that.

Haber said, "Maybe someday you'll want to go to Prague to check it out."

"And while you're there, look for black sites," said Neil.

"Don't waste your time," said Haber, his expression turning serious. "Even former detainees can't locate them. About the only thing my client could tell me about the one in Kabul was that it was underground and close to the airport. Everything else was nondescript or utterly black. The place was known for its absolute lack of light. Detainees even called it the Dark Prison."

Jack froze.

Haber looked at him curiously. "Did I say something wrong?"

"The Dark Prison?" said Jack.

"Yeah, why?" said Haber. "Does that strike you as particularly inventive?"

"Inventive, no. But incredibly coincidental."

Jack told him about the informant he was supposed to have met at the Lincoln Mall on Saturday night, the man falling over dead, and the handwritten message Jack found on the napkin when he returned to his table.

" 'Are you afraid of The Dark?' was what he wrote," Jack said. "It was a curious message. And I thought it was interesting that the *T* and the *D* were both capitalized."

Jack looked around the table, and suddenly it was as if the wheels in their heads were all turning in the same direction.

"But why would you be afraid of a secret prison in Kabul?" asked Haber.

Jack thought for a moment. "Maybe it wasn't actually directed at me. Maybe the threat was intended for someone else—someone who's sure to read it and who has reason to be afraid."

"Afraid of what might become public about the black sites," said Neil, "like the Dark Prison."

"Or afraid of the things he had done there," said Jack.

"You mean afraid of being held accountable for what he's done," said Neil.

"That may be," said Jack. "But people who inflict torture on other human beings—especially under orders—can pay a heavy psychological price. Being afraid of the dark could be, as you say, the fear of criminal prosecution. But it could also be the nightmares that haunt them for having crossed the line—for having literally and figuratively traveled to such a dark place."

Laughter drifted over from the old men drinking large cups of kahawa at the bar, the smell of freshly ground beans in the air. Finally, Neil spoke up.

"Well, gentlemen, that's one more thing to look into."

"One more thing," said Jack, his gaze drifting across the room and coming to rest on the Somali flag hanging on the wall. "Just what we needed."

Chapter Twenty

From the backseat of a cab, the lighted monuments of the capital were a blur as Jack and Neil rode in silence to their hotel.

Stan Haber had lined up several meetings for them in the morning, including one with a representative from the International Committee of the Red Cross, who had presented the "ICRC Report on the Treatment of Fourteen 'High Value Detainees' in CIA Custody." Jack had read the report and had found it interesting that detainees were held in as many as ten different black sites before their arrival in Guantánamo. The Red Cross was careful to point out, however, that "this report will not enter into conjecture by referring to possible countries or locations of places of detention beyond the first or second countries of detention," and that "the ICRC is confident that the concerned authorities will be able to identify from their records which place of detention is being referred to and the relevant period of detention." All of that was code for the fact that sometimes the only way the Red Cross gained access to prisoners was by promising to keep certain things confidential, which was just fine for the "concerned authorities." Probably not so fine for Jamal Wakefield and his lawyers.

Jack went back to the Internet on his smart phone.

"What are you, a teenager?" asked Neil.

Jack looked up from his display, his face aglow from the Web site. Behind Neil were the illuminated stone columns of the Treasury Building, lending an oddly weighty tone to his question.

"What do you mean?"

"I can see what you're up to," said Neil. "My daughter does the same thing about every five minutes. Updating your Facebook status."

Busted. It was the international obsession for people half Jack's age: logging onto Facebook and telling the world in real time what they were doing. *"Having pizza at Casola's with my BFF." "In my room, bored out of my mind."* It was such a compulsion that two girls had made headlines around the globe by getting lost in a stormwater drain and updating their Facebook status rather than calling for help. Crazy thing was, help had arrived.

"I'm sort of into it," said Jack.

"Sort of?" said Neil. "That's the tenth time you've done it since we left Miami."

Jack couldn't argue. It was probably double that.

The taxi stopped in front of the hotel, and the cold winter air reminded Jack that they weren't in Miami. They were traveling with just their laptops and a change of clothes, which made check-in a breeze.

"I'm going to turn in," said Neil.

Jack glanced toward the lounge. It was one of those dark, cherry-paneled rooms with coffered ceilings and red velvet draperies that made Jack think of nineteenth-century robber barons feasting on caviar and smoking cigars while trying to decide which congressman to buy next.

"I'm going to hang here for a while," he said. "Get a little work done."

They said good night, Neil headed to the elevator, and Jack found a cozy leather sofa in the lounge. He ordered from the waiter, and then updated his Facebook status: *Alone in the lobby with a glass of port.*

Jack was halfway through his drink and rereading the ICRC

detainee report when the lights went out—or so it seemed. Her hands felt warm over his eyes.

"Guess who," said Andie.

He smiled, jumped up, and held her tight. It felt beyond good, and her hair still smelled the same, even if it was an unfamiliar shade of undercover blond.

"You need to be careful with those Facebook updates," she said. "You never know what kind of derelict is going to track you down."

It was their way of communicating under rules that prohibited Jack from contacting her directly. "Neil thinks I'm a teenager."

"Well, you did have the stamina of a nineteen-year-old the other night."

That triggered some nice memories. "How long can you stay?"

"Just a few minutes. Sorry. My sexually deviant boyfriend is around the corner waiting in the car."

"Not the kind of thing your fiancé wants to hear."

She sat beside him on the couch, and Jack felt that empty silence that was becoming too much a part of their relationship. It lasted only a few seconds, but it was there whenever Andie worked undercover: the hesitation as Jack checked his train of thought, knowing that he couldn't even ask how her day had gone, much less what the hell was up with the "sexually deviant boyfriend."

"Did you get my phone messages this morning?" she asked.

"Yes. Of course I knew it was you."

She took his hand, but her touch was a little stiff.

"Is something wrong?" he asked.

"Not between us," she said. "But there is something I need to tell you."

Jack braced himself for another one of those FBI-agent-to-lawyer lectures. "Please don't try to talk me out of representing Jamal. I'm more committed than ever."

"I know, and that's your business. But . . ."

"But what?"

She created some separation on the couch, positioning herself so that she could look him in the eye as she spoke. "What I'm about to say . . . you can never tell anyone that you heard it from me."

He hesitated. "Andie, I don't want to hear anything that puts you in an uncomfortable position with the bureau."

"I'm fine. This isn't classified. Some of it's even been in the newspapers. All I'm doing is helping you put two and two together so that you can make the right decision about Jamal Wakefield."

"I think I have made the right decision. Everything I'm learning about this case tells me this guy is innocent." It was the first time Jack had said it aloud, and it rang so true that it actually surprised him.

"That's what I want to talk about," said Andie. "Obviously, you know about certain black sites run by the CIA. But have you heard anything about the insurance policies?"

"No. What kind of insurance?"

"After it became public that the CIA had these black sites, some CIA officers started to get nervous about it."

"Imagine that," said Jack.

"Just listen. They were worried that they would need lawyers to represent them in civil or criminal lawsuits, or maybe even congressional hearings. So the government set up a private insurance plan that they could buy in to."

"Wait a minute. You're saying that while the administration was denying the existence of these black sites, the Pentagon was setting up an insurance plan to protect the interrogators in case they were accused of torturing the detainees?"

"Stop editorializing—but, to answer your question, yes."

The waiter came by. "Another port, sir?"

Jack was massaging the pain between his eyes, still trying to get his head around Andie's news. "Got any aspirin?" said Jack.

"I can check," he said.

Andie waited for him to leave, then continued. "The important thing here is that the insurance is private. Which means you have people outside the CIA involved—people who, theoretically, you could talk to."

"You mean people who could confirm that there was a black site in the Czech Republic?"

"I mean *theoretically.* Because here's what I'm really trying to tell you. That guy who died at the Lincoln Road Mall on Saturday night, Ethan Chang."

"The man who said he had photos of Jamal in a black site in Prague."

"I told you to stop editorializing. If you were to talk to the right person in the private insurance industry, she would tell you that Mr. Chang approached her about insurance."

"So he was CIA?"

"No. That's my point. He wanted to know if the same insurance that was available to CIA interrogators was being offered to private interrogators."

Jack knew exactly what she was saying, but he was thinking aloud: "The site was run by one of those private contractor security firms," he said, "like a Blackwater."

"Blackwater is now called Xe Services, but there are others. ArmorGroup North America, Inter-Risk, to name just a couple."

"That makes things even tougher."

"Jack, I'm not telling you this so that you'll go the extra mile and prove the existence of a black site run by a private security firm. Don't you get it? The CIA has deniability—there was no Czech facility run by the CIA. Your chances of getting the CIA to admit that it had a black site are slim to none. The chances of proving a *privately run* black site are less than zero."

"I don't care what the odds are. It's his alibi."

"Jack, sweetheart. As a former CIA director once said on his way to the White House, 'Read my lips.' There is no way in hell you are going to establish this alibi in a criminal trial in Miami-Dade County, Florida."

"What do you expect me to do?"

"Do I really have to spell it out for you?"

"No, but do it anyway. And say it so I believe it."

She leaned closer, looking him in the eye. "Find another way to win your case, Jack. Or your client is looking at the death penalty."

Chapter Twenty-one

Vince squeezed the trigger and caught his breath. He'd been at it for almost forty minutes. Since losing his sight, this was the first time he'd discharged his Glock 9-millimeter pistol without a sound beacon attached to the target.

"Nice shot," said the firearms trainer.

At first, his supervisors had scoffed at the idea of target practice for the blind, but Vince had made them believers. A series of slow rhythmic beeps from the target worked best for him. He'd learned to measure the pulses in each ear until the sound was equal in the left and right—which meant that the beacon was centered on his nose. From there, it was all about technique, focus, and instinct: Square your shoulders; draw an imaginary line from your eyebrows, heart, and shoulders to the target; raise the gun slowly to check the alignment from your heart to your palms holding the gun; and, finally, using your mind's eye, picture the gun's barrel before you and the target beyond, and when you can "see" one last imaginary line from your center of gravity, between your wrists, and along the image of the gun's sights . . . *pow*!

Brainport changed the game entirely.

Vince worked as a training advisor on "human issues" with the Academy Detail, but the new Miami Police Training Center in downtown Miami had been built after his accident. He'd never had an actual *look* at the new Firearms Unit. His role was to teach courses on "mental preparation" and "ethics and professionalism" with the Officer Survival Detail, and to conduct advanced multijurisdictional sessions on crisis negotiation skills, which covered everything from outright hostage takings to convincing an armed drug addict not to commit suicide. Stimulating work, but it was still just the classroom. He longed to get out, and a morning at the Firearms Detail with Brainport was a big step in that direction.

"I never would have believed it, but you could very well get to a passing level on stationary targets at close range," the trainer said. "Moving targets . . . well, we'll wait and see."

Vince focused the Brainport camera lens on a black-and-white target peppered with gunfire. The stated policy of the Institute for Human & Machine Cognition was never to let the device leave the Pensacola campus, but Chuck Mays had a way of making things happen. It made Vince's heart race with excitement to see—literally—the results.

Vince removed the mechanical "lollipop" from his mouth. "This is so unbelievable."

He hated to shut down the device, but he was authorized to use it only in controlled environments like the Police Training Center. If he stumbled down the stairs or tripped on the sidewalk and broke it, he'd not only be on the financial hook to replace the prototype, but they'd drop him from the pilot program.

The firearms trainer helped him put the components back inside the carry case. Vince used his walking stick to find the door. Sam was waiting for him in the hallway.

"One day I'll take you huntin', Sam," he said as he folded away the stick. Together they went to the elevator and rode down to Vince's office. Sam brought them to a stop in the open doorway, and Vince sensed that someone was waiting inside.

"Hi," said Alicia.

Alicia's police work often brought her to the department headquarters next door, but even so, unannounced visits from his wife weren't the norm. "What's up?"

Vince heard more than one person rising from the chairs in

his office. Alicia said, "I have Detective Burton with me from Miami-Dade Police. He's from the Homicide Division, working the Lincoln Road Mall case."

Miami-Dade was the countywide force, akin to a sheriff's office, and it wasn't surprising that Miami Beach Police would bring them into the investigation once a homicide was suspected. Vince shook the detective's hand, invited him and Alicia to return to their seats, and made his way to the chair behind his clunky metal desk. For the hundredth time, he nearly sliced open his thigh on the pointy metal corner of the government-issued furniture. Whoever was in charge of procurement definitely wasn't blind.

"You didn't mention that you were working with Miami-Dade on this case," Vince said.

"I'm not," said Alicia.

"I'm here on what you might call a professional courtesy," said Burton. "After I interviewed Jack Swyteck, it was clear that my investigation ties in pretty closely with the criminal case against Jamal Wakefield. It seemed appropriate for you to be informed, given your—you know, given what happened to you. I thought you might want your wife present."

Vince didn't make an issue out of it, but the detective's actions were so typical. You go blind, and the world thinks you can't do anything alone. Still, Alicia knew better. She should have told Burton that there was no need for her to tag along.

Why did she come?

"There are a couple of things you might like to know," said Burton.

"Okay, shoot."

"One, we're still waiting on the final toxicology report, but the medical examiner suspects some kind of quick-acting toxin that induced cardiac arrest."

"I'd heard that," since Vince. "Detective Lopez from Miami Beach gave me an update before handing the case over to you. Any idea how the toxin was administered?"

"That's the tricky part. The body shows no puncture wounds—no sign of a needle injection. It's possible he ingested it. But we also have some footage from an outdoor security camera that raises an interesting possibility."

Miami Beach PD hadn't mentioned anything about a videotape. "What's it show?" Vince asked.

"There are surprisingly few security cameras in the area, but they do have one at every cross street. About an hour before the paramedics arrived, we have a series of frames showing the victim in the crosswalk at Jefferson Avenue, which bisects the mall. He's headed east. Another pedestrian is headed west, and the two of them collide."

"What's wrong with that guy, is he blind?" said Vince, smiling.

"Actually, he is," said Burton, his tone serious. "That's the interesting thing. We don't have an ID yet, but whoever ran into Chang was using a walking stick, and the tip of it jabbed Chang in the ankle. The medical examiner notes a strange discoloration of the skin at the point of impact."

Vince waited for him to say more, but the ball seemed to be in his court. "Anybody get a look at the suspect?" asked Vince.

"No. It was after dark, and the quality isn't that good, even with digital enhancement. The camera has a head-on view of Ethan Chang, so we can tell that it's him, but the suspect is filmed from behind. The dark sunglasses and hat don't make it any easier."

"Might not even be blind," said Vince. "Could have just been a disguise."

"That's possible," said the detective.

"Seems more than possible, when you consider the note Swyteck found on his table. Not an easy thing for someone to do without the benefit of sight—find his way to someone's table and scribble out a note on a napkin."

"Another valid point," the detective said.

Vince listened as the detective filled in a few more details, but he was less than totally engaged, still wondering why Alicia had felt it necessary to come with him.

"Anyway," said the detective, "I won't take up any more of your time. Let me just say that before I made detective, I was in charge of the team that ran perimeter control around the motel on Biscayne when you were lead negotiator. I have tremendous respect for how you've bounced back. For what it's worth, I hope the state attorney nails the son of a bitch who did this to you."

"I appreciate that," said Vince.

Alicia and the detective exchanged good-byes, and Vince thanked him. The detective closed the door on his way out, leaving Vince alone with his wife.

"You didn't tell him about Brainport," she said.

"What?"

"You told him how hard it would be for a blind guy to write a note on Jack Swyteck's napkin, but what if the blind guy was using Brainport?"

Vince smiled and shook his head. "Alicia, that device is still in research and development. You can't just go buy it. So far, the only people who have ever used the device outside of a clinic are me and Erik Weihenmayer—and he's the only blind person ever to climb the Seven Summits. I don't think Erik is a murderer."

He and Alicia sat in silence, and he sensed that there was something she needed to say. Then she said it: "I was looking through the things from your visit to Pensacola."

Vince just listened.

She paused, then added, "There were some handwritten notes."

"Yeah, pretty primitive, wasn't it?"

"To be honest, it surprised me how good it was."

"I was doing really well with letter recognition, so we spent some time on writing. We'll work on that more on the next visit. Like everything else in life, it should improve with practice."

More silence.

"Vince," she said, "can I ask you something?"

"Sure."

She hesitated, and the question seemed a very long time coming. Finally, she spoke.

"Where were you on Saturday night?"

Chapter Twenty-two

The following afternoon, Jack returned from Washington to find a box waiting for him in his office. In it was the evidence that the state attorney had presented to the grand jury to secure an indictment for murder in the first degree. Jack was in no mood to sift through it.

Not in a box. Not with a fox.

The morning meeting at the Red Cross with Neil and Stan Haber had brought Jack no closer to proving Jamal's alibi, and his review of the box of grand jury materials convinced him of one thing: Jamal was in deep trouble. The recording from Vince's answering machine was especially powerful. Jack listened to it once, and when the chills stopped coursing down his spine, he played it again. At moments like these—when he was alone in his office and there was no need to hide his emotions from a judge or the jury—it didn't matter how many murder cases he'd taken to trial. There was nothing, absolutely *nothing*, like the sound of a teenage girl struggling to name her killer as her young life drained away.

"Tell me," he heard McKenna whisper, *"am I dying?"*

Jack envisioned her lying on her bedroom floor, her body limp and wrapped in a blood-soaked blanket, her vision fading as she looked up into Vince's eyes and heard his lie.

"*No, sweetheart. You're gonna be just fine.*"

No videotape was needed to see Vince switching into cop

mode, unable to save McKenna but finding the wherewithal to build the case against her killer.

"Who did this to you?"

A weak cough was her response, the end nearing.

"McKenna, tell me who did this to you."

It took a moment, but then came the one-word answer that was the heart of the state's case: *"Jamal,"* she whispered.

"Your boyfriend?"

"My first," she said, her voice barely audible. There was no rhythm to her breathing, the noise more like a gurgle of fluids in her throat. Then there was silence, followed by Vince's emotional outburst.

Jack hit the STOP button, knowing how it had ended, unable to listen a second time to Vince's efforts to revive her.

Two hours passed before Jack looked at the clock again, and it was well past dinnertime when he finally got through the rest of the evidence in the box. Jack had handled other murder trials in which the victim had been stabbed to death, but this case was very different. There were no photographs of the victim. The crime scene was literally a pile of ashes, and the forensic and investigative reports read more like a prosecution for arson than homicide. Investigators had isolated the propane tank that was believed to have caused the explosion. It was the fire marshal's expert opinion that it was gunfire—probably an errant shot at Vince by the attacker—that had ruptured the tank. The ensuing fire had consumed virtually all physical evidence relating to the homicide, including McKenna's body. The only knives recovered in the rubble were in the charred remains of the kitchen drawers, and there was no way to know if any of them was the murder weapon or if the killer had brought his own and escaped with it. The state's case was built on McKenna's own words and a detailed statement of Vince Paulo.

Jack kept coming back to the answering machine recording—as he expected the prosecutor would at trial. It was a dramatic contradiction of his client's claim of innocence, and a jury would demand an answer to the same question that was dogging Jack:

If Jamal didn't do it, why did McKenna say it was him?

Jack packed up the box of evidence, called it a night, and met Neil for a late bite at Cy's Place in Coconut Grove. They sat on stools at the long mahogany bar, the television on the wall tuned to ESPN. Cy's Place was better known for its late-night jazz than its food, but if Jack didn't eat there at least once a week, he risked serious bodily injury at the hands of the owner.

"Try the fish sandwich," said Theo. "The dolphin were practically jumping into the boat. I caught 'em myself this morning."

Having spent the morning in meetings trolling for evidence to support an alibi, Jack was wrestling with another why-can't-I-be-Theo moment. Fishing in the warm waters of the Gulf Stream was one of the many reasons to live in south Florida, especially in January, but Jack hadn't been out since September. If it weren't for Theo's what's-yours-is-mine philosophy, Jack's boat would have rotted on the dock.

"Make it two," said Neil. "And a couple cold drafts."

"Cool," said Theo. "Yours is on the house, Neil."

"What about mine?" said Jack.

"You I charge double."

Neil laughed, but Jack knew he wasn't kidding. "What did I do to piss you off?"

Theo went to the tap and starting pouring. "Vince Paulo basically saved my life two years ago," he said. "And now you're defending the guy who blinded him."

Jack was all too aware of that dilemma. "First of all, Neil asked me to help with the case. Second of all, he's more convinced of Jamal's innocence than I am. So why is his food free?"

Theo set up the beers in front of them. "Neil can't help himself. He thinks everyone is innocent. You know better."

"He has a point," said Neil.

"Stay out of this," said Jack. He tasted his beer, and an idea came to him. "I tell you what, Theo. You can bill me double for a month, if you can explain one thing to me about this case."

"I assume you mean the month of March, not February."

"All right. Thirty-one days."

"Hold on," said Neil. "You can't discuss the case with a bartender."

"Theo is my investigator," said Jack. "This is a privileged conversation."

"It's more like a bet involving the price of fish sandwiches," said Neil.

"Then let's do this by the book. Theo, in accordance with the rules of criminal procedure as approved by the Supreme Court of Florida, I hereby retain you as a certified expert on phony alibis and bullshit accusations. Tell me what you think of this one."

Theo came closer, resting his arms on the bar top. "Let's hear it, dude."

Jack took a minute, his smile giving way to a very serious expression. The $64,000 question that had popped from the box of evidence from the state attorney was still eating at him, and he was no longer just kidding around.

"Answer me this," said Jack. "Why would a girl like McKenna Mays tell a cop that her boyfriend stabbed her if he didn't?"

"Easy," said Theo. "The guy who did it told her he'd come back and slit her throat if she named him. She's bleeding, scared, confused, and blurts out the first name that comes into her head."

"Doesn't exactly line up," said Neil. "The girl was dying. No reason to fear her attacker coming back to hurt her."

"Maybe he threatened to come back and kill her entire family. Or maybe she didn't know she was going to die."

The last point had Jack and Neil exchanging glances. Lawyers could agonize over evidence for hours, days, even weeks.

A former gangbanger from the 'hood who'd spent four years in Florida State Prison could look at the same set of facts and make things just so simple.

"Take it one step further," said Jack. "It's not that she isn't sure if she's going to live or die. Maybe she's absolutely convinced that she is *going to live*."

"Convinced by someone she knows and trusts," says Neil.

The lawyers were silent, but Jack didn't need ESP to know where the other legal mind at the bar was headed.

"I don't want to go after Paulo directly," said Jack, shaking his head.

"I can't blame you a bit for that," said Neil. "But you know as well as I do that trying to prove up a secret detention facility in Prague is headed nowhere fast. So here's the thing."

"Tell me."

He glanced at Theo, then back at Jack. "It's like I told you before. They got the wrong man, which means that whoever stole Vince Paulo's sight and killed McKenna Mays is still out there. The way I see it, you're actually doing Paulo a favor."

Jack lowered his eyes, talking into his beer. "Yeah, a favor," he said with a mirthless chuckle. "I'll probably get a thank-you note from the whole damn department."

Chapter Twenty-three

On Friday afternoon, Jack and Neil were back in the Justice Building. Seated between them at the nicked and scratched defense table was Jamal Wakefield, who looked almost boyish in his orange prison jumpsuit. The prosecutorial team sat closer to the empty jury box. Once again, Assistant State Attorney McCue had brought along the lawyer from the National Security Division of the Department of Justice.

"Good morning," said the judge, and Jack did not take that as a good omen. It was three P.M.

"Good morning," said the lawyers, no one pointing out his error. It was an unwritten rule in Judge Flint's courtroom: Suck up or shut up.

Bail hearings were not usually closed to the public, but this hearing was unusual for many reasons, not the least of which was the fact that in Florida there was no guaranteed right to bail in a first degree murder case. The accused could be released only after an Arthur hearing, named for one of the Florida Supreme Court's most famous decisions of the early 1980s—which, for the record, had absolutely nothing to do with Dudley Moore, Christopher Cross, or getting caught between the moon and New York City. In theory, the burden was on the prosecution to establish that the proof against the accused was evident and the presumption of guilt was great. In *State v. Jamal Wakefield*—a case tinged with national security concerns—Jack was practical enough to realize that the defense would have to put on evidence to establish a right to pretrial release.

The prosecutor spoke first. "Judge, we have a defendant who was picked up in Somalia after the commission of the murder and is a clear flight risk. This is a frivolous motion and a colossal waste of this court's time. For purposes of this hearing, the state of Florida relies on the evidence that it's already presented to the grand jury."

"Thank you," the judge said, and his appreciation seemed sincere, as if he were still under the impression that it was morning and that he had an important lunch date. "Mr. Swyteck, the ball is in your court."

Jack rose. "Your Honor, in due time we'll explain how Mr. Wakefield ended up in Somalia. But first, the defense will show that the case against Mr. Wakefield is a weak one, and that he should therefore be released on bond pending trial."

The judge groaned as he rocked back in his tall leather chair. "Let me be up front about this, Counselor. I am not going to allow you to try this case twice. Your client has a right to a speedy trial, where you can present your evidence soon enough."

"We may need just one witness to call the prosecution's case in question," said Jack.

The judge seemed pleased by that announcement. "I'm going to hold you to that, Mr. Swyteck. Proceed."

"The defense calls Vincent Paulo."

Jack's voice carried across the empty seats in the public galley and almost echoed off the rear wall, a bit too loud for a courtroom with no observers. The double doors in the back of the courtroom swung open, and Sergeant Paulo entered. He wore a business suit and tie, his eyes hidden behind a pair of dark sunglasses. In his right hand was a white walking cane. His wife was standing at his left, a strong and beautiful woman, which made it seem all the more tragic that Vince could no longer see her. Vince tucked away the cane and laid his hand in the crook of her right arm. Together they came down the aisle, though it seemed to Jack that Vince could have done it without assistance. In a moment of uncontrollable defense-lawyer cynicism, Jack wondered if the prosecutor had told Vince to bring his wife, make himself look more helpless—and make the judge hate Jack even more for attacking the cop that his client was accused of blinding.

"Do you swear to tell the truth . . ." said the bailiff, administering the familiar oath.

"I do," said Vince. He climbed into the witness stand and settled into the chair.

Jack stepped forward and, to his surprise, felt at a decided disadvantage before he'd even started. The key to effective cross-examination—and this *was* cross, even though technically the defense had called Paulo to the stand—was to control the witness. In the courtroom, control was like any other form of communication: Least important was what you said, more important was how you said it, and most important of all was body language. Out of habit, Jack planted his feet firmly on the courtroom floor, squared his shoulders to the witness, and stood tall, but Vince was unflappable, impervious to the nonverbal cues.

"Good afternoon, Mr. Paulo."

Vince showed little expression. "*Sergeant* Paulo," he said.

"Sergeant," said Jack. "First, let me say that I regret having to subpoena you to appear in court today. I know—" he started to say, then stopped himself, thinking of their phone conversation. "I can only imagine how difficult this must be."

Vince did not reply, and for Jack the silence was somewhat unnerving.

Jack continued. "I've read the sworn affidavit of your testimony that the prosecutor presented to the grand jury. I've also listened to the recording of your last words with McKenna Mays on the day she died. I understand that you were a police officer at that time, but just to be clear, you were not on the scene in response to a call for help, were you?"

"No, I was not."

"I believe you stated in your affidavit that Mr. Mays was out of town, and you went to the Mays residence to check on McKenna."

"Actually, Mr. Mays told me that he was concerned about—"

"Excuse me, Sergeant. Judge, what Mr. Mays told the witness is inadmissible hearsay."

The prosecutor rose. "Is that some kind of objection?"

Even without a jury—judges were human, too—Jack couldn't let the witness testify that McKenna's father feared Jamal might come around while he was out of town. "Your Honor, what I'd like is simply an answer to my questions."

"The witness will answer the questions asked," said the judge, "without mention of what others may have told him."

"Let me restate it," said Jack. "You went there to check on McKenna, but not on official business."

Vince shifted in his chair, and it obviously pained him not to be able to take a shot at Jamal. "Basically, yes."

"You and McKenna's father were friends?"

"Yes."

"How long?"

"At that time, I'd say about seven years."

"Since McKenna was in elementary school, then?"

"That sounds right."

"Would you describe your relationship with McKenna as close?"

"She used to call me Uncle Vince, if that answers your question."

"Would you say that she regarded you as someone she could trust?"

"Of course," said Vince.

"Someone she could rely on?"

"There was nothing I wouldn't have done for McKenna."

"Someone who would tell the truth?"

"Objection," said the prosecutor, rising.

"Overruled. The witness will answer."

Vince paused, but Jack didn't read it as any kind of confusion as to courtroom procedures. It was the question that had given him pause—Vince's acute awareness that defense lawyers didn't ask questions without a hidden agenda. "She certainly had no reason to think I was a liar," said Vince.

"Exactly," said Jack. "McKenna Mays had no reason to believe that her uncle Vince would lie to her. Correct?"

Again he hesitated, but Jack had left him little wiggle room. "I would say that's true."

Jack faced the judge. "With the court's permission, I would like to play the answering machine recording of McKenna Mays. It's the key piece of evidence in the state's case against my client."

"No objection," said the prosecutor.

"All right, let's hear it," said the judge.

Neil came forward to help the judicial assistant find the CD among the grand jury materials. She marked it, inserted it into the player, and then waited for Jack's cue.

"Just to set the stage," said Jack. "Sergeant Paulo, can you tell us exactly where you were at the time of this recording."

Vince was slow to respond. "I was in her bedroom," he said, his tone forced, as if it were a struggle not to get emotional.

Jack knew that these were painful memories for him, but seeing his reaction—and knowing that he had no choice but to take him down this road—was almost equally painful for Jack. "Where was McKenna?"

"On the floor," he said softly. "I knelt at her side, and raised her head up."

Jack wished he didn't have to ask the next question. "How was McKenna doing at this point?"

"Not well," he said, and the words hit Jack sharply, as if Vince had reached inside his tormented self and told Jack, "*Up yours for asking.*"

"She'd been stabbed?"

"Several times," Vince said. His voice almost cracked, but he drew a deep breath, and he sounded like a cop again. "She had defensive wounds on her hands, and a large puncture wound to her rib cage that was spewing bloody foam from her lungs. She was also bleeding heavily from a slash across the left side of her neck. Her pulse was weak. When I called her name, her eyes opened, but her body was going cold. I pulled a blanket from the bed and covered her, tore a sheet into bandages and applied them to the wounds. It didn't do much good."

"Was that when you dialed nine-one-one?"

"Redialed. I had already called once, and the second time was to find out what was taking so long. Then I noticed that McKenna was trying to say something."

"So you hung up and dialed your answering machine?"

"At this point . . ." He paused and gathered himself. "It looked bad for McKenna. My law enforcement instincts took over. If she was going to tell me what happened, I wanted to have a record of it. I was in no position to take notes and didn't have a recording device. The idea popped into my head to get it on my answering machine. So that's what I did."

Jack gave him a moment, then signaled to the judicial assistant. "Let's listen," said Jack.

The assistant hit PLAY, and after brief static, there was noise on the line, probably the sound of Vince holding the phone to McKenna's lips. Then in a faint voice, the victim spoke:

"Tell me," she whispered. *"Am I dying?"*

"No, sweetheart," said Vince. *"You're gonna be just fine."*

Jack paused the recording.

"That's the first time you told her she was not going to die—correct, Sergeant?"

Vince seemed momentarily confused, as if he hadn't expected the question. "Yes," he said.

"Thank you," said Jack, and then he glanced back at his client.

Jamal was staring at the carpet, his forehead resting on the table's edge, as if it were all unbearable. The recording resumed.

"Really?" said McKenna.

"Who did this to you?" said Vince.

"Am I going to die?"

"No, McKenna. You're going to be fine. Who did this?"

Jack paused the recording again. "Sergeant, am I correct that this is the second time you told her she was not going to die?"

"Yes."

"Thank you," said Jack, and the recording continued with McKenna's ever-weakening voice.

"You really think I'm going to be okay?"

"Yes, it's not your time. I saw much worse than this in Iraq, and they're all fine. Tell me who did this to you."

Jack hit PAUSE once more.

"Sergeant Paulo, that makes three times that you told her she was not going to die."

"Yes."

"In less than a minute."

Vince swallowed hard, seeming to sense where this was headed. "I . . . yes."

"And after you gave her those three separate assurances, you asked her, 'Who did this to you?'"

"I believe so."

"And her answer was 'Jamal.'"

"That's correct."

Jack glanced over his shoulder at his client, and their eyes met. Jamal looked scared, terrified, really. Jack wasn't sure if he looked innocent, but he didn't look guilty, either. If he had, Jack wouldn't have found the strength to go on.

He took a step closer to the witness. "Your intention was to make McKenna believe that she was not going to die," said Jack.

"She was scared. So scared she couldn't even talk."

"Scared of dying, right?"

"Yes."

"So you told her she was not going to die."

"Right."

"Three times."

"Only so she wouldn't be scared."

"And your words removed her fear."

"Objection," said the prosecutor. "How would the witness know what was in the victim's head?"

"Your Honor, based on his own perception, Sergeant Paulo just testified that the victim was too scared to talk. I'm entitled to an answer, again based on his own perception: Did his words allay her fears?"

"I strongly object," said the prosecutor.

The judge frowned with thought. "There's no jury here. I'll allow it. The witness may answer."

Vince considered it, then said, "I'm sure it helped."

It wasn't a perfect answer, but this was unpleasant work for Jack, and he had pushed Vince as far as he cared to push.

"Your Honor, at this time . . ."

His voice halted, and Jack was suddenly at war with himself. Again, he glanced over his shoulder. *What if Jamal is guilty?*

The question gnawed at his soul, but Jack fought through it, reminding himself that he wouldn't have come this far if Jamal hadn't passed a polygraph examination. If McKenna's own father hadn't expressed doubts about Jamal's guilt. If the government hadn't pushed back so hard against Jamal's alibi. If the witness who had flown all the way from the Czech Republic to support the alibi hadn't died so mysteriously at Lincoln Road Mall.

If the message scrawled on Jack's napkin hadn't read "*Are you afraid of The Dark?*"

"At this time," Jack continued, "the defense moves to exclude the answering machine recording as hearsay."

The prosecutor was on his feet. "It's admissible as a dying declaration," he said, noting one of the oldest exceptions to the hearsay rule.

Jack said, "The premise underlying a dying declaration is that a victim of a violent crime has no reason to lie about the identity of her attacker if she knows that she is about to die. The key concept is that she must know—or at least *believe*—that death is imminent. The opposite is true here. Sergeant Paulo told her repeatedly that she was *not* going to die."

"To put her at ease," said the prosecutor.

"Precisely my point," said Jack. "Sergeant Paulo testified that the victim was so scared that she couldn't even speak. After he told her *three times* that she was not going to die, she was able to name her attacker. Clearly, she did not believe her death was imminent—or even likely."

The judge seemed troubled. The prosecutor was clearly worried.

"Judge, we—" said the prosecutor, but the judge cut him off.

"Hold it, Mr. McCue. I'm thinking."

Jack glanced at Neil, who looked almost as surprised as Jack. This was a long shot that had played out much better than either of them had anticipated.

The judge asked, "What is left of the government's case against Mr. Wakefield if this recording is excluded?"

"Virtually nothing," said Jack.

"That's not true," said the prosecutor.

The judge asked, "Is there any physical evidence linking the defendant to the commission of the crime?"

"None," said Jack.

"It burned in the fire," said the prosecutor.

"It never existed," said Jack. "My client was in a detention facility in the Czech Republic at the time of the crime."

The Justice Department lawyer was suddenly yanking at the prosecutor's sleeve, and the two of them huddled into an intense exchange of whispers. The judge leaned back in his chair until he was staring up at the ceiling tiles, retreating even deeper into thought.

"Judge, we'd like a recess," said the prosecutor.

"I'm in the middle of my examination," said Jack.

The judge ignored the exchange between the lawyers, rocking in his chair and thinking aloud. "If I rule this recording inadmissible," he said, "I would imagine the defense will be filing a motion to dismiss the indictment."

"That would be correct," said Jack.

That sent the prosecution scrambling. "Judge—"

"Quiet, Mr. McCue."

"Judge," said the prosecutor, "I have an announcement. The state of Florida withdraws its objection to the release of Mr. Wakefield on bond."

The judge seemed poised to rebuke him for the sudden change of position, but he quickly appreciated that his own butt was off the hook. Throwing out McKenna's dying declaration would have been front-page news—and letting accused murders go free was generally not a career-enhancing move for an elected state court judge.

"That certainly changes things," said the judge.

Smart move, thought Jack. The government was better off letting Jamal out of jail on pretrial release than digging in its heels and losing the entire case at a bail hearing.

"We would ask for release on the prisoner's own recognizance," said Jack.

"Bail should be set at one million dollars," said the prosecutor. "And Mr. Wakefield should be required to wear a GPS tracking bracelet."

"A tracking device seems like a reasonable request in a case of first degree murder," said the judge. "But a million dollars? Really now. Anything further from the defense?"

Jack knew when to cut and run. "No, Your Honor."

"Bail is set at seventy-five thousand dollars," said the judge. "The prisoner is to be released on the condition that he remain in Miami-Dade County and wear an ankle bracelet at all times. The witness is dismissed. We're adjourned."

With a bang of the gavel and bailiff's announcement—"All rise!"—the judge started toward his chambers.

Jack looked at Vince. He was frozen in his chair, as if he were reliving McKenna's funeral, so distraught that the bailiff's command to rise probably hadn't even registered. As Jack started back toward the defense table, Alicia caught his eye. She was on the other side of the rail in the first row of public seating behind the prosecution. Her stare was deadly. She moved to the defense side of the courtroom, came to the rail, and practically leaned over, leaving just a few feet between her and Jack.

"Shame on you," she said.

Jack could find no response. It wasn't the foulmouthed vitriol he might have gotten from other cops or their wives, but that only made it worse.

"Shame on *you*," she said, and it was even worse the second time. She walked to the center of the rail, pushed through the low swinging gate, and went to her husband on the stand.

Neil laid his hand on Jack's shoulder. "That was a great piece of lawyering, my friend. I'm proud of you."

The words were lost on Jack. His client attempted to shake his hand in gratitude, but Jack's gaze was fixed on the witness stand. Vince was still in a state of shock, his wife trying to console him.

At that moment, Jack hated his job.

Chapter Twenty-four

For the first time in three years, Jamal Wakefield was a free man.

His mother had come up with the 10 percent fee for F. Lee Bail-me Inc.—the only bail bondsman in Miami with a sense of humor—to post the $75,000 bond. It was just *pretrial* release, and he was a long way from an acquittal, but that was not going to spoil his Saturday night on South Beach. A 5.3-ounce Omnilink ankle bracelet was a small concession in the big scheme of things. Some chicks might even think it was cool. Jamal the bad boy. Computer genius. Smarter than the losers in law enforcement who monitor ankle bracelets. Smarter than the guy who invented the damn device. Smarter than the interrogators who had thought barking dogs and waterboarding would make him talk. Smarter than Vince Paulo, the prosecutors, and his defense lawyers put together. Smarter than anyone he'd ever met.

Except Chuck Mays.

"Lookin' hot," Jamal said to a couple of young women who were too busy to notice him. They were dressed to kill and pleading their case to a rock-solid bouncer who was the keeper of the gate to the hottest new dance club on South Beach. The waiting line extended down the sidewalk, around the corner, and halfway up the block again. Most of the hopefuls would never see beyond the bouncers. Fat chance for the khaki-clad conventioneer from Pittsburgh who was dressed to sell insurance. The Latin babe in the staccato heels was a shoo-in. Most of the rejects would shrug it off and launch plan B. Others would plead and beg to no avail, only embarrassing themselves. A few would curse at the bouncers, maybe even come at them, driven by a dangerous combination of drugs and testosterone, only to find out that the eighteen-inch biceps weren't just for show.

After three years of incarceration, Jamal wasn't wasting any time. He walked straight to the front of the line. "Hey, good to see you, my friend," he said as he slid a wad of cash into the bouncer's hand.

The guy was a tattooed pillar of Brazilian marble, but money always talked.

"Next time don't pretend to fucking know me," he said as he tucked away the cash and pulled the velvet rope aside.

The main doors opened, and Jamal was immediately hit with a flash of swirling lights and a blast of music.

Club Inversion was once known as Club Vertigo, a hot nightclub that Jamal and McKenna used to hit with fake driver's licenses that had made them of age. It had a new name and a new owner, but the look and feel of the place was the same, the inside of the four-story warehouse having been gutted and completely reconfigured with a tall and narrow atrium. The main bar and dancing were on the ground floor, and several large mirrors suspended directly overhead at different angles made it difficult at times to discern whether you were looking up or down. With even a slight buzz, the pounding music, swirling lights, and throngs of sweaty bodies were enough to give anyone a sense of vertigo. The sensation worked both ways, with hordes of people watchers looking down on the dance crowd from tiered balconies. Jamal wasn't sure why they'd changed the name to Club Inversion, but it seemed a bit ironic.

You want inversion? Try it with your face completely covered by a wet cloth that they keep soaking and soaking with a steady stream from a canteen until your breathing is so restricted that you're sucking nothing but water into your lungs, and it hurts so much and you're so sure you're gonna die that you'd confess to any—

Jamal shook off the thought.

A woman at the bar was checking him out, peering over the sugar-coated rim of her cocktail glass. She appeared to be alone, which was a little strange, since women in South Beach typically arrived in groups. Maybe her girlfriend had already hooked up for the night, and she was on her own. Jamal made eye contact but kept cool about it. She was a dark-haired beauty wearing a clingy white dress and a gold necklace that played off her brown skin. He could feel the pulse of the music beneath his feet, almost smell the mix of perfume and perspiration wafting up from the crowd. Albino Girl was on stage at the other end of the club, a Vegas-style act in which a dancer managed to keep time to the music while a thirteen-foot lemon-yellow albino python coiled around her sculptured body.

The woman at the bar tossed her hair, and then she glanced again in Jamal's direction. Three years of detention had made him rusty, but not oblivious. He walked toward her. She smiled and said something as he approached, but it was impossible to hear her over the music. He could have texted her, but after being off the hookup circuit for so long, he wondered if it was no longer cool to text someone who was standing right next to you. He gestured toward the dance floor, and she followed, leaving her drink at the bar.

They danced to Lady Gaga, and Jamal liked what he was seeing. It was bizarre to think that if it weren't for Jack Swyteck he'd be in prison tonight, and he wondered how many other guys in the club were wearing ankle bracelets with GPS tracking.

Probably more than anyone would guess.

"I'm thirsty," she said, shouting into his ear.

Jamal led the way through the crowd, and she had her thumb in his belt loop as they headed back to the bar. Then she gestured toward the restroom and shouted something. After a momentary delay it registered: *"Order me another drink."*

He nodded and walked back to the bar. Her half-empty cocktail was exactly where she had left it, but there was another beside it. He could only surmise that some other dude had ordered her a fresh drink, and Jamal wondered who the competition was. Then he looked closer, and he froze. The new drink was resting atop a paper cocktail napkin, and the napkin came with a handwritten note:

Are you afraid of The Dark?

His gaze swept across the bar, but it was a sea of unfamiliar faces. He turned the napkin over, and the message continued on the other side.

You should be, it read.

The music pounded, and the crowd around him was into it, but Jamal could barely breathe. The capital letters—the *T* and the *D*—were a familiar signature, even if this was the first time he'd seen it in over three years.

He glanced toward the ladies' restroom, where his best shot at a hookup for the night was making herself even sexier. He liked this girl, and he wanted her as badly as any man fresh out of prison would. But if the Dark was here, it was better to leave her out of this.

Jamal stuffed the napkin into his back pocket and headed for the exit.

Chapter Twenty-five

Jack kissed his grandfather good night at eleven.

The west wing of Sunny Gardens of Doral was entirely for Alzheimer's patients. Jack's grandfather lived on the ground floor with other "mild to moderate" residents, those with no track record of wandering off in the middle of the night. Soothing colors brightened the interior walls, sound-absorbent carpeting quieted the floors, and calming music played in the hallways. It was an instrumental version of what Jack thought he recognized as an old Cat Stevens song. His own version of another vintage 1970s hit by the same artist came to mind.

Another Saturday night, and I ain't got no Andie. . .

With Andie out of town, it had seemed like a good idea to spend time with Grandpa. Unfortunately, he'd slept the whole time, and after two hours of channel surfing through some really bad Saturday-night television, Jack decided to try another day.

His cell rang as he crossed through the lobby toward the exit. It was Andie, and it made him smile to know that he wasn't the only one feeling lonely.

"You read my mind," said Jack. "I was just thinking of you."

"Me, too."

Jack heard music in the background. It sounded like a nightclub. "Where are you?" he asked.

"*Jack*," she said, in that tone that said, *You know I can't tell you.*

"Right. Sorry," he said.

"Tell me how you're doing," said Andie.

Jack seated himself on the couch next to the birdcage in the lobby. The sleeping parakeet didn't seem to notice. "Yesterday was horrible," he said.

"Horrible?"

"The court held a hearing on bail for Jamal Wakefield. We won, but I had to cross-examine Vincent Paulo."

"*Had to*, huh? Like somebody was holding a gun to your head?"

"Andie, come on. Don't be like that."

"I told you how I feel about that case."

Jack heard laughter in the background, and then the muffled sound of Andie speaking to someone else—*"Just a couple more minutes"*—with the phone away from her mouth.

"Are you on duty?" asked Jack.

"What?" asked Andie.

"It sounds like a party going on," said Jack. "I was just wondering if you were on or off duty."

"I'm always on," she said.

Always. For an instant, Jack wondered if she was with her "sexually deviant boyfriend," but he caught himself

It's her job, Swyteck.

"Jack, I'm sorry, but I have to go. I'll call you again, next chance I get."

"Sure."

"I love you," she said.

"Love you, too," he said, and then the line was silent.

The Sunny Gardens lobby was quiet as a mausoleum, which was the very next stop on the route for just about everyone who lived there. Most were lonely widows or widowers, and probably all of them would have given up their six months or a year at Sunny Gardens for another week or even a day with the spouses who had left them. Jack had all the respect in the world for Andie and her career. But hanging around a place like Sunny Gardens did make him wonder about her readiness to volunteer for assignments that reduced their relationship to weeks or perhaps even months of catch-as-catch-can phone conversations.

You knew this was her job when you popped the question.

Jack was parked in the Sunny Gardens private lot, but without a handicapped parking pass, he had a long walk to his car. He counted thirty handicapped spots in the first row of parking alone, not a single one of them being used. It made him want to stake out South Beach and confront the twenty-five-year-old triathlete who was using his eighty-seven-year-old grandmother's pass to grab the best parking spots all over town.

Jack followed the sidewalk toward the overflow lot. The first phase of Sunny Gardens was vintage 1970s construction, which meant that there were plenty of mature olive trees along the walkway to block out the street lighting. Jack dug into his pocket for his car keys, stopped, and glanced over his shoulder. He thought he'd heard footsteps behind him, but no one was in sight. Jack continued toward the lot, but tripped over a crack in the sidewalk. The row of olive trees had given way to even larger ficus trees, whose relentless root system had caused entire sections of the sidewalk to buckle. The canopy of thick, waxy leaves made the night even darker, forcing Jack to locate his car more from memory than sight.

Again, he heard footsteps. He walked faster, and the clicking of heels behind him seemed to match his pace. He came to an S-curve in the sidewalk and, rather than follow the concrete patch, cut straight across the grass. The sound of the footsteps behind him vanished, as if someone behind him were tracing his own silent path. He returned to the sidewalk at the top of the S-curve. A moment later, he heard the clicking heels behind him do the same.

He definitely felt like he was being followed.

Jack stopped and turned. In the pitch darkness beneath the trees, he saw no one, but he sensed that someone was there.

"Andie, is that you?" It was way too hopeful to think that

she was going to surprise him again with a visit, but calling out the name of *anyone* seemed less paranoid than a nervous "Who's there?"

No one answered.

Jack reached for his cell phone. Just as he flipped it open, a crushing blow between the shoulder blades sent him, flailing, face-first to the sidewalk. The phone went flying, and the air rushed from his lungs. As he struggled to breathe and rise to one knee, an even harder blow sent him down again. This time, he was too disoriented to break the fall. His chin smashed against the concrete. The salty taste of his own blood filled his mouth.

"Why . . . are," he said, trying to speak, but it was impossible to form an entire sentence.

He was flat on his belly when the attacker grabbed him from behind, took a fistful of hair, and yanked his head back.

"One move and I slice you from ear to ear."

Jack froze. A steel blade was at his throat. The man's voice sounded foreign, but Jack couldn't place the accent. More important, the threat sounded real.

"Take it easy," said Jack.

"Shut up," the man said. "Did he give you any photographs?"

"Who? Photos of what?"

"Ethan Chang. Did he give you the photographs he told you about?"

"No. I never met him."

He yanked Jack's head back harder. "Don't lie to me."

"I'm not lying. I never met him, I swear."

"Lucky for you. But now consider yourself warned."

"Warned of what?"

"Forget everything you ever heard about Prague."

"I don't—" Jack stopped in midsentence. The blade was pressing harder against his throat.

"The lawyers have been way too subtle. Do you understand?"

"Yes."

"Good. And by the way. Remember how Ethan Chang heard you talking to your grandfather's girlfriend about Pio Nono?"

"Yes."

"I heard it, too," he said. "So believe me when I tell you this: Until you have a wife or children, there is nothing more painful than watching your grandfather suffer at a time in his life when he is too old and too confused to understand why anyone would want to hurt him."

"Leave him out of this."

"That's up to you," the man said as he pulled the blade away from Jack's throat—and then slammed the butt of the knife against the back of Jack's skull.

Jack fought to stay conscious, but he saw nothing, heard nothing, as his world slowly turned darker than the night itself.

Chapter Twenty-six

Vince woke early on Sunday morning.

He was seated on the front step outside his house, the canopy of the porch overhang shielding him from a light, cool rain.

Rain was in some ways Vince's best friend. The bond had formed on his first rainy day without sight, just moments after he'd stepped out the front door and stood on the top step. His mind was gearing up for the usual mental exercise, the memorized flower beds, shrubbery, and footpaths that defined his morning walk. But the rain changed all that. It was the sound of falling rain that brought the outdoors and all of its shapes, textures, and contours back into his world. Where there was once only blackness, suddenly there was water sloshing down a drainpipe. The patter of raindrops on the broad, thick leaves of the almond tree. The hiss of automobiles on wet streets. Even the grass emitted its own peculiar expression of gratitude as it drank up the morning shower. A sighted person would have heard nothing more than rainfall in its most generic sense, a white noise of sorts. To Vince, it was a symphony, and he reveled in his newly discovered power to appreciate the beautiful nuances of each and every instrument. Nature and his old neighborhood were working together, calling out to him, telling him that everything was still there for his enjoyment. He heard the drumlike beating on his mailbox, the gentle splashing on concrete sidewalks, and even the ping of dripping water on an iron fence that separated his yard from his neighbor's. Rain, wonderful rain. It made him smile to have such a friend. Friends were not always so loyal and dependable.

Especially the ones named Swyteck.

"Did you finally get to sleep, honey?" asked Alicia. She was standing in the foyer behind him, speaking through the screen door.

"Not really," he said.

Swyteck's cross-examination on Friday had been nothing short of torture, and it had left him tossing and turning for the past two nights. Once upon a time, Officer Vincent Paulo had been a criminal defense lawyer's worst nightmare on the witness stand. He'd anticipate their every move and thwart their clever tactics. His first experience under oath and without sight had left him doubting his ability to do real police work.

"It wasn't your fault," said Alicia.

"Tell that to the state attorney. McCue gave me an earful after the hearing."

"Tell him to go to hell."

"He had a point," said Vince. "I blew it when I called my answering machine to record McKenna's words. Calls to nine-one-one are recorded as a matter of course and are admissible as evidence in court. If I had simply stayed on the line with the nine-one-one operator and let McKenna talk into the phone, we wouldn't have to worry about this hearsay objection."

He could hear her sigh. "Vince, you loved McKenna, and she was literally bleeding to death in your arms. How on earth is anyone supposed to be thinking clearly about the legal admissibility of a recording under those circumstances?"

The rain continued to fall. Vince heard a car pass on the wet pavement. The screen door squeaked as it opened; even that sounded different in the rain. Alicia knelt behind him, and her arms slipped around his shoulders, the silk sleeve of her robe caressing his chin. Things had been a little rocky between them after she'd challenged him—albeit gently—as to his whereabouts on that Saturday night. In anger he had phoned Chuck Mays so that he could tell her directly that they were hanging out by his pool until nine o'clock, nowhere near the Lincoln Road Mall. After Friday's hearing, Alicia did a 180, seeming to appreciate how sickening it was for Vince to have to provide an alibi to his wife while Jamal Wakefield walked free.

"I've been thinking about that recording," said Alicia.

She was still kneeling behind him, her arms around him and the side of her face resting between his shoulder blades.

"What about it?" asked Vince.

"Don't you think it's kind of . . . weird? McKenna's response, I mean."

"In what way?"

She hesitated, obviously sensitive to how painful this subject was for Vince. "You said, 'McKenna, tell me who did this to you.' And she said, 'Jamal.' "

"What's weird about that?"

"Nothing. But then you asked, 'Your boyfriend?' And the natural response to that would have been a simple 'yes.' But she said, 'My first.' "

"So?"

"Why would she say that?"

Vince considered it. "I don't know. She was confused, dying. Maybe it was part of her shock and disbelief that her first love killed her."

Alicia was silent. She stayed just as she was, and the warmth of her body and the rhythm of her breathing felt good on his back.

"I suppose," she said.

The rain started to fall harder—so hard that it was no longer possible to discern the sound of water falling on leaves from the patter on pavement. It all sounded the same—like too much information, the details completely drowned out. It was no longer a friend.

"What are you thinking?" asked Alicia.

He could barely hear her over the roar of the downpour. They were protected by the overhang, but huge drops splashed up from the steps and onto his slippers.

"Nothing," he said, but that was a huge lie. Vince was thinking about the final text message that McKenna had sent to Jamal and that Vince had intercepted: *FMLTWIA*. With his help, it had remained secret. Only over his dead body would it someday land in the newspapers.

Vince would always be McKenna's friend.

"Let's go inside," he said.

He rose and took her hand. Together they retreated indoors, the screen door slapping shut on the falling rain.

Chapter Twenty-seven

Jack woke to the rumble of a motorboat behind his house. His head still hurt from last night's sucker punches, but after a minute his thoughts became less fuzzy, and he realized that it was *his* boat. Jack climbed out of bed, pulled on jogging shorts and a sweatshirt, and walked out back to the dock. Theo was already in the boat.

"Ready when you are, Ahab," he said over the idling outboards.

Jack had forgotten all about their plans to go fishing, but just the sound of the motors was making his head buzz all over again. He climbed aboard and killed the engines. The silence was sweet, as if someone had stopped hitting him in the head with a hammer.

"Got a knot on the back of my skull like a golf ball."

"What happened?" asked Theo.

Jack told him the same story he had told the police officer last night at the hospital emergency room: from the phone call he had gotten from Ethan Chang last Saturday to the Sunny Gardens employee who had found Jack lying on the sidewalk and called an ambulance.

"Scumbag," said Theo. "Theatening an old man with Alzheimer's."

"I'm not backing down. The cops kept an eye on him last night. But I'm going to have to hire a bodyguard to sit with him."

"I can help you with that," said Theo.

"Thanks."

"Oh, well," said Theo. "Looks like we'll have to wait for another perfect Sunday morning to take you to my secret spot."

Theo went to the radar and erased the GPS coordinates, which reminded Jack of the ankle bracelet his client was required to wear as a condition of pretrial release. That little intrusion was all Jack needed to stir up any number of nagging questions that had kept him awake last night. One, in particular, was gnawing at him all over again: the chain of "Pio Nono" from Grandpa to Chang to the man who threatened Jack and his grandfather.

"How do you think Mr. Chang knew about Pio Nono?" asked Jack.

Theo settled into a deck chair. "You talking about the guy who got killed on Lincoln Road Mall?"

"Right. When he called to set up a meeting with me, I didn't answer. So, to grab my attention, he texted me using the name Pio Nono."

"Pio what?"

"He was a controversial pope from the nineteenth century. My grandfather took his girlfriend to see a play about him a few years ago. I was sitting with her in the cafeteria at the nursing home talking about the play when Chang sent me a text that said, *"'It's Pio Nono. Call me. NOW!'"*

"Kind of creepy. Maybe he bugged the cafeteria."

"But how would he have known I was going to be in the cafeteria? That doesn't make sense."

"He could have planted some kind of listening device on you. Or on her."

"I patted myself down afterward and didn't find anything. And now we know that Chang had flown into Miami from Prague just a couple of hours before contacting me. How would he have had time to plant listening devices?"

Theo considered it as he glanced at the storm clouds to the west. It was definitely raining over Coconut Grove, but they were east of it on Key Biscayne.

"Have you had your phone checked for spyware?" asked Theo.

"I wasn't talking on my cell. It was a face-to-face conversation in the cafeteria with Ruth."

"Doesn't matter. They have spyware that can pick up conversations around a cell phone even if you're not talking on it. The phone doesn't even have to be turned on. It works so long as there's a battery in it."

"How would he get hold of my phone to plant spyware?"

"They don't need to touch it. They can install spyware through the Internet from anywhere on the planet. Especially people who know something about computers."

People who know something about computers. He'd met a couple of those types lately. Chuck Mays. His client.

"Every time I think I'm starting to know what I'm doing with computers, something new comes along to make me feel like an old fart."

"You've been an old fart since you were eleven."

"Thanks," said Jack. His head was hurting again, but another one of those gnawing questions was buzzing in his brain. "How do you suppose the guy who clobbered me last night overheard the same conversation?"

"He knows you were talking about Pio Nono, too?"

"That's what he said."

"Two possibilities," said Theo. "Either he's been spying on you, too. Or he was spying on Chang."

"You mean they have spyware that can pick up from Chang the information that he picked up while spying on me."

"How do you think spies get caught?"

"Good point," said Jack. He went to the cooler, grabbed a handful of ice, and placed it on his forehead. "I wish my head didn't hurt too much to think about who might be spying on Chang."

"Probably the person who stands to lose the most if word gets out about a black site in Prague."

"That question is not as easy to answer as it sounds."

"The CIA comes to mind," said Theo.

"Or a security firm that works for the CIA. Or the Czech government. Or someone who works for any of the above and has a personal interest to protect. And those are just the possibilities that come to mind with my head splitting like . . . like I don't know what."

"Like a nation split over Gitmo?"

"Dude, that was unusually deep."

"I have sex while the *Colbert Report* is on, just like the next guy."

A fifty-foot Cigarette boat roared past them in the no-wake zone. Probably a drug runner late for church. The rumble of the triple racing engines faded, and even though the black fiberglass streak knifed through the water at more than fifty yards off starboard, its long wake rocked Jack's boat.

"How is your grandfather doing, anyway?" Theo asked as the waves gently slapped the hull.

"That's the joke of it. He slept through my entire visit last night. Last time we talked, he was pretty confused. He thinks he's Jewish."

"Is he?"

"This is the first I've heard of it."

"Did you check it out?"

"I called my dad. I spoke to Grandpa's girlfriend, Ruth. Neither one of them knew anything about it."

"You need to dig deeper."

Jack was unable to hide his surprise, which Theo noticed.

"What?" asked Theo.

"I don't know," said Jack. "I guess I always gave you credit for being much more shallow than that."

Jack expected another smart-ass reply, but Theo simply gazed toward the horizon, his expression unusually pensive.

"You know what I know about my ancestry?" said Theo. "Nothin'. Don't even know who my father was. My mother's been dead since I was thirteen. Even if I had them around to help me, I'm sure I'd hit a brick wall at slavery. You've got a chance to find out who you really are, maybe. Having a couple of conversations and calling it a day is pretty lame."

Jack was speechless. To be called out by Theo on matters of family was almost beyond his comprehension. Most confusing of all, Jack realized that he was right.

"It's not that I'm not interested," said Jack. "I've just been busy. Maybe I'll spend some time on the Internet this afternoon."

Theo scoffed. "People always think the answer is online. Get serious, dude. Where was your grandfather born?"

"Czech Republic."

"Well, there you have it. An obvious opportunity to overcome the Internet and the Joe Cocker factor."

"The what?"

"You know—Joe Cocker. The rock star."

"I know who Joe Cocker is—'You are so beautiful, to me.' What does he have to do with the Internet?"

Theo sang his answer, adding the trademark affectations to another Cocker hit: " 'Lonely days are gone. My baby, she sent me an e-mail.' "

" 'Sent me the letter.' "

"That's exactly what I'm saying. The Joe Cocker factor. Sometimes the Internet is just all wrong."

"So your point is what? I should go to Prague?"

" 'Yeah she sent me an e-mail, said she couldn't—' "

"Okay, okay. I get it."

Jack's cell rang—more of the curse of technology. Andie had reset his ringtone before saying good-bye to Jack in Washington and returning to her undercover assignment. Carrie Underwood and "I took a Louisville Slugger to both headlights" on the quiet shores of Biscayne Bay on a peaceful Sunday morning.

Talk about "all wrong."

Jack checked the display. It was Neil, who wouldn't have called so early if it weren't important.

"What's up?" Jack said into the phone.

"We got a big problem with Jamal," he said.

Jack caught his breath, fearing the worst. "Don't tell me he skipped."

Neil paused, as if not sure how to put it. "He's missing."

"Damn him. He has to know he won't get far wearing an ankle bracelet."

"Actually, he borrowed his mother's rental car to hit the clubs on South Beach last night. They found the bracelet in the car."

"What? The Omnilink is supposed to be tamper proof. The alarm signals if you just stretch the band. How'd he get it off?"

"He didn't exactly remove it."

"What does that mean?"

"The bracelet is still attached to his ankle."

The image flashed in Jack's mind. "Oh boy," he said.

"You can say that again," said Neil.

"Where's the rest of him?"

"Not sure. His mother says he never came back to their hotel last night. The rental car was parked all night on Washington at about Seventeenth near Club Inversion. I'm pulling up now. Plenty of cops here. Crime scene is roped off. Maybe someone has an answer."

"I'll be there as soon as I can," said Jack, and he ended the call. He glanced at Theo, who seemed to have caught the drift of the conversation.

"No fishing again today, huh?" said Theo.

Jack shook his head. "It's getting to be a bad habit, I know."

"Pity. I got a feeling even the amateurs are catching fish this morning."

Jack glanced toward Miami Beach—toward Club Inversion. Then his gaze drifted toward the bay, which seemed to yield at least one dismembered body a year.

"I can only imagine what they're using as bait," said Jack.

Chapter Twenty-eight

Jack could smell the rain approaching. He was standing outside Club Inversion on the onlookers' side of the yellow line of police tape. A breeze kicked up and blew Neil's hat off. Jack picked it up.

"Investigators better hurry," said Neil. "Gonna rain."

The downpour in Coconut Grove was definitely headed their way. Maybe it was all the cops around, but Jack was reminded of the time Vince Paulo had shown him how the smells that warned of rain in Miami were as poignant as the sight of thunderclouds over the Everglades. Jack closed his eyes, breathing in the hint of rain—and trying to comprehend the turn of events. But when he opened his eyes, the Miami-Dade Police and Miami Beach Police perimeter control were still on the scene. Investigators were still combing over the vehicle that had given up Jamal's foot and ankle bracelet. A media van was even pulling up. It was all real.

It wasn't a dream.

Neil got the attention of a Miami-Dade officer on the other side of the tape, a woman in uniform. "Hey, can you find Detective Burton?"

Burton was the homicide detective handling the Lincoln Road Mall investigation. Obviously Miami-Dade PD had picked up on a possible connection between the two deaths and called out Burton.

"I'm sure the detective is busy," said the cop.

"I spoke to him on the phone," said Neil. "He told me that he would meet us here."

"Who are you?" she said.

Neil told her, and the words made Jack feel as if the world had been turned upside down: "We're the lawyers for the victim."

The victim.

He and Neil exchanged glances, as if they were feeling the same sense of flip-flop and disconnect.

"I'll see if he's here," the cop told them.

Jack's gaze swung back toward the rental car. It was parked at the curb on the other side of the four-lane street. Traffic was light at this hour on a Sunday, but perimeter control wouldn't let Jack close enough to see exactly what the investigators were doing. Blood samples were definitely being collected from the trunk.

"What do you think happened?" asked Neil.

"I sure as hell don't think he ran," said Jack.

"Trapped animals do it," said Neil. "They'll chew off their own feet to get free."

"He's not a mink."

Jack felt the first raindrop. He looked up to the sky, which was growing darker by the minute. The investigators moved faster, kicking into another gear to beat the weather.

"Do you think he's alive?" asked Neil.

"Not if he didn't get medical attention."

"That was one of the first things I asked Detective Burton. Unfortunately, not a single emergency room in the county treated that kind of injury last night."

"The loss of blood has to be tremendous."

"But not necessarily fatal," said Neil.

"Are you a doctor, or do you just play one on TV?"

"A few years ago I took my daughter hiking in New Mexico to a place called Sky City. It's what the Spaniards thought was the Seven Cities of Gold. Our guide told us that when they enslaved the local Indians, each adult male had a foot severed to keep him from running. I can't imagine they rushed to the emergency room in the sixteenth century."

It was an interesting story, but Jack was staying with his gut instinct. "Somebody killed him."

"Why?" asked Neil.

"Clearly, it was someone who didn't want the body to be recovered. Otherwise, they would have just put a bullet in his head and let the police find him still attached to the ankle bracelet."

"That makes no sense," said Neil. "Why leave a foot behind that allows for a positive identification, but take the body?"

Jack thought about it. "It only makes sense if they needed to keep him alive for a while. If you cut these Omnilink bracelets, an alarm goes off. Cops would have immediately come looking. Whoever did this needed to take him someplace alive and took extreme measures to make sure the police wouldn't track them down."

"Take him why?"

"So that they could get something out of him."

Neil seemed to catch his drift. "Torture and interrogate?"

"You got it," said Jack. "Maybe pick up where they left off in that secret detention facility in Prague. Get the information they couldn't get out of him three years ago."

"And then what?"

"This time they kill him," said Jack. "Just like they killed McKenna."

"Shit," said Neil. "With that kind of follow-up interrogation, it's no wonder the CIA doesn't want to talk about that secret site."

"Be careful with that," said Jack. "We're pretty sure it's not a CIA site."

"Okay, a secret site operated by a private security firm that was hired by the Department of Defense."

"I'm even having my doubts about that. A severed foot. What does that remind you of?"

It took a few moments, but Neil had a thought. "That serial

killer in Canada. Remember all those severed feet in sneakers that kept washing up on the beaches of the Georgia Straits in British Columbia?"

Jack hadn't even thought about that, but Neil had defended several serial killers over the years, so it was no wonder that his mind had gone there.

"I was thinking more along the lines of organized crime," said Jack.

"That was a severed horse head in *The Godfather*, not a foot."

"I'm talking real life. It was the discovery of a severed foot in a vacant lot that finally unraveled the mystery of how Joseph Massino got rid of three captains in one night to become the undisputed boss of the Bonanno crime family."

"How do you know that?"

"It's one of the FBI's proudest moments. You keep forgetting I'm engaged to an undercover agent."

"Mr. Goderich?" the Miami-Dade detective said.

Detective Burton surprised them, having approached from behind. Jack felt a few more raindrops as they shook hands, and it was now falling steadily enough for droplets to bead on Burton's clean-shaven head.

"Any news?" asked Neil.

"Only bad, I'm afraid," said Burton. "We found the body."

Jack knew it was coming, but the news still hit him like a punch to the gut. "Where?"

"Everglades National Park. Near a canoe launch."

It was like another body blow, but Jack kept his reaction to himself.

"I'm headed there now," said Burton. "I'll keep you posted."

Jack watched as the detective ducked under the yellow tape and walked toward his car. The rain was coming hard enough to trigger a few umbrellas. Investigators were scrambling to protect the scene with sheets of plastic.

"We should go, too," said Neil.

"Didn't you hear the location of the body?" said Jack.

"Of course. I was standing right here."

"Everglades National Park near a canoe launch. That's the same place they found Shada Mays' car after she disappeared."

"Wow, that's interesting."

"It's more than interesting," said Jack, and he was speaking his thoughts as quickly as they came to him. "Police suspected that Shada was tracking her daughter's killer when she vanished. Supposedly, Shada had some e-mail or other communications with him over the Internet. The cops' theory was that the killer was Jamal, and when Shada pushed too hard to get him to turn himself in, Jamal killed her, dumped her body in the Everglades, and tried to made it look like a suicide."

Neil had a pained expression, as if he wanted to follow Jack's reasoning, but wasn't quite with him. "So somebody cuts off Jamal's foot and dumps his body where McKenna's mother disappeared. Why?"

"Not just somebody," said Jack. "I think we're talking about McKenna's killer. The same guy who killed Shada when she started closing in on him. The same guy who killed Jamal as soon as he got out of jail and—maybe—picked up on the trail Shada was following."

"Could be," said Neil. "Unfortunately, we don't have a client anymore. So I'm not sure what we can do about it."

"I know what I want to do," said Jack.

"What?"

"I'm going to have another talk with Chuck Mays."

Chapter Twenty-nine

It was Monday evening when Jack returned to the Mays estate on Tahiti Beach in CocoPlum.

For nearly two days, his phone calls to Chuck Mays had gone unanswered, and an unannounced visit seemed too confrontational. Finally, a secretary called from MLFC headquarters late Monday afternoon to say that Mr. May's would be jet-lagged but expecting Jack at his house around nine P.M.

Jack rang the doorbell and waited.

"In the backyard," said Mays, his voice crackling over the intercom speaker at the entrance. "I'm making s'mores."

S'mores? Jack didn't verbalize his thoughts, but his expression was caught on a security camera, and Mays' voice crackled again on the speaker.

"Don't act like you don't fucking like them, Swyteck."

An Eagle Scout couldn't have said it better.

The door unlocked with an automated *click*, which Jack took as his invitation to enter unescorted. The rear of the house was a wall of windows, and from the foyer Jack could see all the way through to the backyard. Beyond the patio, on a finger of land that protruded into the moonlit waterway, a campfire glowed in the darkness. The sliding-glass door was unlocked, and Jack followed the path of stepping-stones around the pool and through the garden to find Chuck Mays seated on a log before a crackling fire. It was a cool night for Miami, but it was still south Florida, which meant that Mays was wearing hiking shorts, flip-flops, and a T-shirt that said, *1f u c4n r34d th1s, u r34lly n33d 2 g3t l41d.*

If you can read this, you really need to get laid. The speed with which he'd decoded it troubled Jack. *Damn, I miss Andie.*

Mays handed him a skewered marshmallow, seeming to sense that Jack had solved the riddle. "S'mores are the next best thing," he said.

A light breeze was blowing in from the water, but it was still too warm for a jacket. As Jack removed his, the wind shifted and the smoke overcame him, sending Jack scrambling to the other side of the campfire, where he could breathe.

"S'mores were McKenna's favorite when she was a little girl," said Mays. He stuffed the toasted marshmallow between two graham crackers and waited for the chocolate to melt. Jack found a hot spot above some glowing embers and held his marshmallow over it. Mays stuffed the gooey treat into his mouth, chewing roundly.

"So tell me what's on your mind, Jack."

It seemed absurd to discuss Jamal under these circumstances. More precisely, it *would have* seemed absurd, if it hadn't felt so choreographed. This was all staged, of course—Mays taking the steam out of a potential confrontation by holding a fireside chat with his mouth full of McKenna's favorite childhood snack.

"Jamal is on my mind," said Jack. "I'm trying to figure out who cut off his foot, tortured him to death, and then dumped his body less than two hundred yards from where your wife disappeared in the Everglades."

"You're on fire," said Mays.

"What?"

"Your marshmallow is burning."

Jack yanked it out of the fire, and the flaming mess dropped like red-hot lava onto his foot, just above the shoe leather. Jack jumped up and let out a yelp, then smothered the flame with his jacket. It had burned through his sock, and he was sure the skin would blister. Mays roared with laughter, and Jack decided not to say what he was thinking.

Mays looked at him and said, "No, I'm not."

"You're not what?" said Jack.

"You think I'm enjoying this."

Jack felt chills. He was dead-on. *The guy really is a genius.*

"Truth is," said Mays, "I haven't enjoyed a damn thing in three years."

Jack couldn't imagine ever being friends with Mays, but it was impossible not to feel sorry for a man who'd lost so much. Even though Jack knew he was risking a punch in the nose, he could think of only one response.

"Jamal didn't kill your daughter."

Mays narrowed his eyes, and Jack braced himself for that punch.

"I guess we'll never know," said Mays.

"I think his killer is the same person who killed your wife. And I think whoever killed your wife also killed your daughter."

The fire hissed, and the last remnants of Jack's marshmallow burst into flames on a charred log.

Jack continued. "Technically, the attorney-client privilege survives the death of a client, but there are things about his detention in Prague that would have come out at trial, and that Jamal wanted you to know. For one, Jamal's interrogators threatened to kill McKenna if he didn't talk."

That drew a slight reaction—enough for Jack to discern that it was the first time Mays had heard it.

"What did they want to know?" asked Mays.

"The questions were all about the work he was doing for you. Project Round Up, to be specific."

"I don't talk about that."

"Neither did Jamal—which got him killed. So tell me: Why would someone in Prague interrogate him about Project Round Up?"

No response. A burning log shifted, sending sparks fluttering upward like a swarm of fireflies.

"Does it have to do with national security?" Jack asked. "Rounding up terrorists?"

Mays stared into the fire, apparently unwilling even to consider the question.

"I know much more than you think I do," said Jack, though he was careful not to use Andie's name. "I know that the FBI seized Jamal's computers after McKenna was murdered, and that they found encrypted messages that related to terrorist organizations."

Mays leaned forward, poking at the ashes with his stick. "I don't know anything about that."

"Did you know his father was a recruiter for al-Shabaab?"

"I wouldn't know al-Shabaab from shish kebab."

"You didn't answer my question."

"Nobody told me anything about his old man until after Jamal was indicted for murder."

Jack hesitated, but this was getting frustrating. "We're tap dancing here," said Jack, "so let me just say it straight: I don't believe you."

"I don't care."

"You will. Because I've got a theory, and I think it's a good one. Like everyone else in your business, you want to be the go-to guy for technology and homeland security."

"Is that a crime?"

"No. But it's not merely patriotic. It's profitable. I think you and Jamal were working on a supercomputer that could find and tap into encrypted messages between suspected terrorists. I think Jamal was using his father to get access to those messages so that you could test your decoding algorithms. Maybe Jamal even pretended to be sympathetic to his father's cause. That's what got him on somebody's terrorist watch list. That's what got him abducted and taken to a black site in Prague for interrogation. And that's why his father was willing to help him when he ran to Somalia."

Mays mocked him with a round of slow, hollow applause. "You've given this a lot of thought, haven't you?"

"Am I right?"

"Not even close. But let me know when you sell the movie rights. I'll pop the popcorn for you."

"I can handle that on my own," said Jack. "But there's something else you can help me with."

"Yeah, there's something you can help me with, too," Mays said, his hand moving up and down in a vulgar gesture.

Jack ignored it. "After your wife disappeared, a Miami-Dade homicide detective questioned Jamal's mother. He told her that Shada was following her own leads, trying to find McKenna's killer. She had some online communications—possibly with the killer himself. Do you know anything about that?"

"Nope."

"The cops thought it was Jamal she was in contact with, but I don't believe it was. Like I said, I think there are three victims here—McKenna, Shada, and Jamal—but only one killer. I'd love to get my hands on those online communications."

"I can't help you there."

Jack could have recited the man's résumé to dispute it. "Here's the thing," said Jack. "If your supercomputers can search eight billion files in an instant—which is what you told me yours can do—then you most certainly *can* help me. What you're telling me is that you *won't*."

"Same bottom line," said Mays.

Jack rose. He knew that Mays was the key to any computer-related evidence involving his wife, but it was clear that tonight was not going to be the breakthrough. He just needed to plant the right seed.

"You're right: McKenna's killer remains unpunished, free to kill again. Same bottom line."

Jack grabbed his jacket and headed back toward the house,

feeling a surprising chill in the night air as he distanced himself from the fire.

"Swyteck," said Mays.

Jack stopped and turned. He was halfway through the garden.

"You got a few more minutes?" asked Mays.

Jack shrugged. He had all night, if that was what it was going to take. "Sure. What's up?"

Mays pushed himself up from his seat on the log and started toward him on the footpath. "There's something I want to show you."

Chapter Thirty

Jack was awake half the night thinking about Shada Mays' text message.

Last week's tip from Jamal's mother had been slightly off the mark. The police didn't have any e-mails. It was a text-message exchange—just one—between Shada and someone using a pirated cell phone (owner unknown). Shada's cell phone had disappeared along with her, so it had taken a subpoena from law enforcement to turn up the day-old text message on the carrier's server. There were also records of phone calls to and from the same pirated cell, but there was no way of knowing what was said in those conversations. The single text was chilling enough, starting with a question from the man suspected of being McKenna's killer:

"Are you afraid?"

"Not at all."

"Maybe you should be."

"No way. Never. I will see you tomorrow."

Jack probably would have guessed it, but the date on the message confirmed as much: "Tomorrow" was the day Shada had gone missing.

Still, Jack wasn't sure how to read it. Was she being defiant? *No way, you killed my daughter, but you will never intimidate me, you son of a bitch.* Was she playing the role of the "good cop"? *Don't worry, accidents happen, I'll see you tomorrow and you can tell me your side of the story.* They were merely printed words—no voice inflection, no context, no way to know for sure. The first line—*Are you afraid?*—was intriguing, and the addition of just three more words—*of The Dark*—would have all but confirmed in Jack's mind that McKenna, Shada, Jamal, and Ethan Chang were all killed by the same man. As it was, that was still a distinct possibility.

Or someone was trying very hard to make it look that way.

The telephone rang on his nightstand, and Jack shot bolt upright in bed. His room was dark, but he hadn't really been sleeping. A call at 3:40 A.M. was never a good thing, and his first thought was of his grandfather in the nursing home.

"Hello?" he said.

There was no answer, but Jack sensed that someone was on the line.

"Who is this?" said Jack.

"Is this Mr. Swyteck?" The voice was beyond tentative. It sounded like a teenage girl—a frightened teenage girl.

"Yes," said Jack. "Who's calling?"

"You don't know me, but . . . you were the lawyer for Jamal, right?"

"Yes. Who is this?"

"I—I can't tell you that."

Her English was good, but she spoke with an accent. German, maybe. "Where are you calling from?"

"I can't really tell you that, either."

Jack heard the sounds of a city over the line—the echo of a car horn, the grumble of a bus or a diesel truck. She was obviously calling from outdoors, perhaps on a busy street corner, either a cell or a pay phone. Wherever she was, the business day had already begun; it definitely wasn't 3:40 A.M.

"Did you know Jamal?" asked Jack.

"Uhm, not really. I spoke to him. Once."

"When?"

"A couple of days ago," she said, her voice quaking. "He gave me your number and begged me to call you. I told him he'd never hear from me again if he told you or anybody else we talked but . . . is it true that he's dead?"

"Yes."

"Oh my God," she said.

Jack jumped out of bed and started pacing. He wasn't sure where to go with this, but it sounded important. "What did you and Jamal talk about?"

"Was he . . . killed?" she asked.

"It looks that way," said Jack.

"Oh my God," she said, and this time Jack thought she might hyperventilate.

"Calm down, okay?" said Jack. "If you know something about this, I can help. You just have to tell me what you know."

A siren blasted in the background. She was definitely in a city.

"It's like I told Jamal," she said. "I think . . . I know who killed his girlfriend."

Jack stopped pacing, frozen in the darkness of his bedroom. "McKenna Mays? You know who killed McKenna?"

"I think so."

"Who was it?"

She didn't answer.

"I need you tell me who did it," said Jack.

"I'm afraid!"

Jack didn't want to push too hard and lose her. "It's okay. Have you gone to the police?"

"Yeah, right," she said, and Jack could hear the struggle in her voice. "I can't do that. No way."

"Why not?"

Jack heard more of the sounds of the city, but she was silent.

"Why can't you go to the police?" Jack asked.

"Because he would—"

She stopped herself. There were more urban sounds in the

background, and Jack thought he heard her breathing. No, she was crying.

"Are you all right?" Jack asked.

The crying continued, stronger but more distant, as if she had taken the phone away from her face.

"Don't hang up," said Jack. "I need to know: Are you all right?"

The crying stopped, and Jack heard her take a deep breath.

"No," she said, sobbing, "I'm not."

Before Jack could respond, the caller was gone.

Chapter Thirty-one

Her heart was pounding as she hung up the pay phone at the street corner. One thought consumed her, but she could barely get her mind around it. The gruesome photographs she'd seen weren't staged. Jamal was dead, his foot cut off.

OMG!

She was shivering, partly from the cold but mostly with fright. This time of year, sunrise didn't come to London until almost eight o'clock. Thirty minutes past dawn, the chill of night was still in the air, and the morning fog was so thick that she could barely see the top of the three-story redbrick buildings that defined the beaten-down neighborhood. She was in a place she knew well, near the Tayo Restaurant, the Hilaac Superstore, and the all-important Internet café. Neighborhood shops were opening for another business day, buses were running, and streets were lined with morning commuters. None of it put her at ease. There was no doubt in her mind that gangs like the Money Squad and African Nations Crew were still on the prowl, searching for young girls like her who were stupid enough to venture out alone. Gang violence terrified her. It had taken all the courage she could muster to head out before daybreak, and the brief telephone conversation with Jamal's lawyer had only heightened her fears. Creepy blokes were everywhere. Like that man sitting on the curb and talking to himself.

Why is he looking at me?

The other runaways at the train station had called her paranoid. "Chill out," they told her. "Bethnal Green has a reputation, but it's not that bad these days. Lots of kids and parents with babies. Certainly not the worst area in London."

Chill out? People who said that were the same morons who would tell someone in a coma to "cheer up." She knew better. You didn't stop for a cigarette, didn't load your iPod, didn't even answer your mobile on these streets. She'd read about the girl who'd disappeared outside King's Cross railway station—blond and sixteen, just like her. Scotland Yard found her on the other side of Euston Road, her throat slit and panties stuffed in her mouth. Things were no safer in Bethnal Green, even if the tube stations weren't nearly as big. There were still creeps begging for money, bumming cigarettes, asking if you're selling, tagging along, talking nonstop to you, refusing to go away, looking for runaways and teenage girls who bit their fingernails and tugged at their hair in ways that made them ripe for appropriation to whoring exercises. "Those are just the flavors of London's northern lines," people told her.

Flavors? Ha!

Sure, once you knew an area, you could spot trouble and steer away from the dodgy bloke. She knew the difference between a normal person and those who broke the conventional rules of social engagement—the skanks who stood too close, rubbed up against you, grabbed a feel. But, realistically, what could a girl do? A man might think nothing of standing alone at a bus stop two blocks away from the scene of the latest stabbing. A girl doing the same thing would quickly be asked how much she charged for a blow job. Having a dally with a creepy bloke, being half nice in case he demands money, but also trying to get rid of the unwanted visitor without offending—diffusing a potentially aggressive situation—required a bit of sharp thinking. Even a bit of paranoia.

Just a bit. I'm not PARANOID!

It was a safe bet that the jerks who'd teased her and called her chickenshit had never been dragged along by the hair on London's sidewalks. Who the hell were they to go slagging her off as paranoid? If those losers started up again, then she was going to treat them back to the playground crap they dished out.

You want war, then this is war, you shits!

She drew a deep breath, then glanced across the street. She had to focus. Jamal was dead.

Double OMG!

Her mobile rang. She was afraid to answer, but the incoming number was enough to make her shudder. It was him. He knew her every move. Sixteen years old, and her life felt like prison.

I am a prisoner.

Her mobile continued to ring, but she let it go. There would be hell to pay for not answering, but she wasn't prepared to explain what she'd been doing. And she would need a damn good explanation. He kept track of every penny he gave her, and five pounds for an international calling card from the Internet café was not an allowable expense. She ducked into the convenience store, grabbed a banana from the bin, and asked the clerk for a receipt.

"Can you make it out for five pounds?" she asked.

"What?"

"The receipt," she said. "Can you make it for five pounds?"

"You bought a banana."

"I know. But I need a receipt that says I paid five pounds."

"Then buy ten bananas."

"I just need the receipt. Can you do that?"

"Sure."

"Really?"

"Yeah," he said, and then he grabbed his crotch. "Have this banana."

Her mobile rang, and she didn't even have to check the incoming number. She was suddenly all too aware of the bracelet on her ankle. It was always there, twenty-four hours a day. It was probably a lot like Jamal's—except that hers hadn't been put there by the police. She wanted to rip it off, but that would be a very foolish move. There was a reason he had shown her those photographs of Jamal.

"He'll cut my foot off, too!"

"You want the banana or not?" asked the clerk.

She was almost too flustered to answer. "Forget it."

She hurried out of the store, her mobile still ringing, not sure what she was going to say when she got back to the flat and he grabbed her by the hair and said, *"What the hell have you been up to, you little slut?"*

Chapter Thirty-two

I'm sorry for the loss of your son," said Jack.

Neil echoed Jack's sentiment, and Maryam Wakefield expressed her appreciation quietly. She looked physically and emotionally drained, and with good reason.

Wednesday morning marked three days since Jamal's death—the end of the traditional Islamic mourning period for any relative of the deceased other than the widow of a married man. On Sunday Jamal's uncle flew down from Minneapolis to be with Maryam, but the medical examiner didn't complete his autopsy and release the body until early Tuesday. Islamic law called for a quick burial and disfavored transportation of the body. Jamal's uncle washed and wrapped the body in a shroud, a brief funeral service was held on Tuesday afternoon, and Jamal was taken directly to the cemetery and laid to rest (on his right side, facing Mecca) in Miami, the community in which he had last lived.

Jack could see in Maryam's eyes that she had slept not a wink last night.

"Come in, please," she said.

Jack was respectful of her loss, and he wouldn't have come if Maryam had not extended an invitation. Her suite had a kitchenette and spacious seating area, but it was the kind of low-budget hotel that any last-minute traveler could pick up on the Internet for the price of dinner for four at McDonald's: well within earshot of both the airport and the expressway, and last updated when fluorescent tube lighting and shag carpeting was all the rage.

Maryam introduced Jamal's uncle as Hassan. His dress was not as Western as Maryam's, and he had the full beard of a traditional Muslim male. It was Jack's quick impression that he was more religious than Maryam, and that he'd been a tremendous help with the necessary arrangements.

"Your brother?" asked Jack.

"No," said Maryam.

"I am the brother of Abukar," said Hassan. "Abukar is Jamal's father."

The terrorist recruiter, thought Jack—and then he immediately chided himself about the whole guilt-by-association thing.

"Pleased to meet you," said Neil, seeming to recognize that Jack was momentarily tongue-tied.

Maryam led them into the seating area and took the armchair. Jack and Neil sat on the couch facing her. Jamal's uncle sat away from them on a barstool at the kitchen counter. He read in silence from the Koran, seeming to ignore the company.

"It wasn't my plan to call you," said Maryam. "But Detective Burton from MDPD came to see me this afternoon. He told me about a lead they were pursuing. A message of some sort that was written on a cocktail napkin from that club he went to."

Jamal's uncle looked up from his Koran. The mere mention of a cocktail napkin from a club on South Beach did not sit well with him.

"What kind of message?" asked Jack.

She opened her purse and handed Jack a paper. "Here, I wrote it down exactly as the detective described it."

Jack inspected it, and immediately felt chills. "Are you afraid of The Dark?" Jack said for Neil's benefit. "It's identical to the one I got on the night Ethan Chang was murdered. Right down to the capital *T* and capital *D*. Also written on a napkin."

"I know," said Maryam. "Detective Burton seems unwilling to share his theories as to who wrote them. I wanted to hear yours."

Jack again caught a glimpse of Uncle Hassan. He was clearly listening from across the room, and it bothered Jack that he was pretending not to.

"I honestly don't have any ideas," said Jack.

"Detective Burton also told me about the phone call you received."

Jack had, of course, reported it to the police. "What did he tell you?"

"Everything," she said. "Except where it came from."

"Did you ask?"

"Yes. He said he was not at liberty to say."

Jack had heard of detectives keeping certain facts secret in an ongoing investigation, but he had another theory here.

"Were you alone when you met with Detective Burton?

"No. Hassan was with me."

Jack wondered if Hassan's presence had caused the detective to hold back—if Burton had given in to the same guilt-by-association prejudice that Jack was fighting now.

Maryam slid to the edge of her chair, her dark eyes like lasers aimed right at Jack. "I need to know where that call came from."

Jack looked back at her, then shifted his gaze toward Hassan. It was purely instinct, but Jack sensed that Hassan wanted to know as much as she did.

"At the time, I didn't know where it was coming from," said Jack.

"But surely you've checked the number," said Maryam.

"Yes."

"And?"

Again Jack glanced across the room at Hassan. Jack could have lied and said he didn't know, but in the end, the balance tipped in favor of a mother's right to know.

"It was from a pay phone," said Jack. "In London."

Maryam froze. Hassan rose and crossed the room, no longer pretending to be an outsider. "Where in London?" he asked.

"Bethnal Green."

Maryam closed her eyes for several seconds, as if to absorb the news. Finally, she opened them.

"Is something wrong?" asked Jack.

Hassan spoke up. "That's where my brother and I parted company. Sixteen years ago."

Only then did Jack pick up the hint of a British accent. "What do you mean?"

"You know what I mean," said Hassan. "My brother is the only sympathizer of al-Shabaab in our family, though I suppose that, to you, I look like a terrorist, too."

Jack suddenly felt small. "No, uh—not at all."

Maryam said, "That area along the Mile End Road between Whitechapel and Bethnal Green underground stations is called Somaal Town. Lots of Somali ex-pats, and also some cool clubs and pubs. I met Hassan's brother when I was visiting London one summer. He and Hassan were sharing an apartment, but they were never anything alike."

"Still aren't," said Hassan.

"Are you saying that Jamal's father is behind this phone call?"

"Who knows?" said Maryam.

"We do know this much," said Hassan. "That area has changed over the years. It's what some people would call eclectic, but you still have gangs, more crime. To be blunt about it, there are a lot of dead-end Somali teenage boys, which makes it a fruitful recruiting area for al-Shabaab. And there is one thing we all know about my brother."

"He's a recruiter for al-Shabaab," said Jack.

"Exactly."

"I still don't see the connection to a panicked young girl who calls me in the middle of the night to tell me that she knows who killed McKenna Mays."

"You haven't looked," said Hassan.

Maryam was suddenly emotional. She'd held herself together

well, but it was all too much. Hassan went to her and gave comfort. Tears were in her eyes as she looked at Jack.

"Someone has to find out what happened to my son."

"I'm sure the police . . ." Jack stopped himself. With the resistance he'd faced at every turn—the Department of Justice, the state attorney's office, the CIA, the private security firms, even his own fiancée—he couldn't peddle false hope that the police would get to the truth.

Hassan took her hand, and then looked at Jack. "Our faith teaches that when one dies, everything in this earthly life is left behind. There are no more opportunities to perform acts of righteousness and faith. But the Prophet Muhammad once said that there are three things that may continue to benefit a person after death. Charity given during life, which continues to help others. Knowledge, which grants enduring benefits. And third, a righteous child who prays for him or her."

Maryam wiped away a tear. "I've lost my righteous child," she said. "My only son."

"I'm so sorry," said Jack.

"For whatever reason, Jamal trusted you. So I trust you. And that is why I'm asking you this favor: Help me find the man who took my child away from me."

"I honestly don't know what I can do."

"Please," she said. "Help me."

"It's not that I don't want to. But I'm a lawyer, and the sad fact of the matter is that my client is dead. I'm not a private investigator."

"You missed the operative words," said Hassan. "Jamal trusted you, so we trust you."

"Right now," said Maryam, "we don't trust a lot of people."

Jack wasn't sure where this was headed, but it would have taken a heart of stone not to at least listen.

"All right," he said. "What is it that you want me to do?"

Chapter Thirty-three

Jack took a seat at the bar in Cy's Place, where Theo was mixing cocktails for a jazz-loving crowd. Neil had agreed to meet him after work, and Jack wanted to bounce Maryam's request off him. For once, Jack was the one to arrive early, and he had a little time to kill.

He ordered a beer and updated his Facebook status again—his fourth update in the two hours that had passed since he'd said good-bye to Maryam Wakefield. He hoped that Andie—wherever she was—would see it and call him. He didn't want her to worry about his safety, but he felt she should know about the threat against his grandfather.

"Until you have a wife and children . . ."

Jack had driven from the hotel with plenty on his mind, but Maryam's tears had triggered some very serious thoughts . . . about children. Specifically, about the teachings of Muhammad and the short list of things that may be of benefit after death—charity, knowledge, and a child who prays for you. A child. Maybe even more than one. Jack was an only child. Andie was adopted. Funny how little they'd talked about how those experiences might shape their own family after marriage. The last time—the only time, really—that they had seriously discussed children was right before Andie left for her latest undercover assignment. In fact, it had happened at this very spot in Theo's bar.

Now, with the buzz of Cy's Place in the background, Jack was thinking about how awkward it had been.

"Do you want kids?"

The question left Andie coughing on her vodka tonic. "What brought that on?"

"I sort of sprang the engagement ring on you at my surprise birthday party. You said yes on the spot. But looking back on it, we've never had a serious talk about kids."

"We've been engaged for only three weeks."

"Most people discuss it before they even get engaged. Probably we would have, too, if the leap from dating to a marriage proposal hadn't been so spontaneous. Maybe it's the reason we still haven't gotten around to picking a wedding date."

Jack hadn't intended to put a chill on the night, but the awkward silence that gripped their conversation was unlike any Jack had felt with Andie.

"Do I want kids?" she said, teeing up the question once more. "Do you?"

"Yes."

"Really? How many?"

"At least one. Maybe two."

"Really?"

Really. What a word. What a response. I like my coffee black. *Really?* The Sox are going to the World Series this year. *Really?* I'd like to saw off your right hand and superglue it to your chin. *Really?*

"Yes. Really."

Andie's cell rang. Their conversation ended right there. The call was from the assistant special agent in charge of the Miami Field Office, telling her to pack her bags and report for her assignment. Two minutes later she was out the door, seemingly relieved to leave Jack alone with the seven-pound, eight-ounce elephant in the room.

• • •

"Sorry to keep you waiting," said Neil as he pulled up the stool beside Jack.

He was actually right on time and had dropped everything at the office to meet Jack on a moment's notice. Now he was apologizing for having kept Jack waiting. *Classic Neil Goderich.*

"No problem," said Jack.

Theo came over and wiped down the countertop. "What are you drinking, Mr. Goodwrench?"

It was just Theo's way; "Goderich" had been "Goodwrench" as long as Jack could remember.

"Do you have milk shakes?"

"Do you have testicles?" said Theo.

"So . . . yes?" said Neil.

Jack translated. "Actually, he means 'no.' "

"Bummer," said Neil, letting it roll right off his back. "How about hot tea?"

It was happy hour, but apparently hot tea was something Theo could tolerate at his bar. He headed for the kitchen, and Jack picked up where his voice-mail message to Neil had left off.

"Maryam Wakefield wants to sue Chuck Mays."

"That much I gathered from your message," said Neil. "What for?"

"Money. A wrongful-death theory, I presume. She thinks Jamal was set up."

"How?"

Jack emptied the rest of his bottle into his beer glass. "Mays has been working for a few years now on something called Project Round Up."

"Yeah, Jamal mentioned that. But he didn't seem to know much about it."

"No one does, except for Chuck. Jamal's mother thinks it was something illegal, or at the very least not totally on the up-and-up."

"All these guys in the data-mining business push the envelope," said Neil.

"True. But what makes this situation a little different is that after McKenna was killed and Jamal disappeared, the FBI actually came in and found encrypted messages on Jamal's computer. Even Andie confirmed that those messages exist, but I can't get anything more than the fact that they relate in some way to terrorist organizations."

"And Mom refuses to believe that her son was in any way connected to terrorists."

"Beyond that. She thinks Chuck Mays needed a pawn to venture into a forbidden area of cyberspace as part of the research and development for Project Round Up. That way, if the shit hit the fan and the FBI swooped in with a search warrant, Chuck Mays had his own in-house Muslim to point the terrorist finger at."

"Chuck used him as the fall guy."

"That's the theory."

Theo was back. "One hot tea," he said as he placed the cup in front of Neil.

Jack's cell rang. The display read PRIVATE. "This could be Andie," he said.

"Go ahead and take it," said Neil.

Jack answered with anticipation, but it wasn't Andie. It was Dr. Spigelman.

"I'm sorry, who?"

"The doctor who gave CPR to Ethan Chang at Lincoln Road Mall. Do you have a minute?"

Jack glanced at Neil, who was multitasking between the list of tapas on the bar menu and the e-mails on his BlackBerry.

"Sure, go ahead," Jack told the doctor.

"I've been following your case for Jamal Wakefield in the newspaper, and I know that the police have been looking into a possible connection to Mr. Chang's death. Anyway, you may or may not know this, but the medical examiner's office just released the toxicology report a few hours ago."

"I did not know that," said Jack. "What did it show?"

"That's the reason for my call. It's extremely vague."

"Why am I not surprised?"

"I also wanted to let you know that I've been following this toxicology issue very closely. For reasons of my own safety."

Jack was reaching for his beer, but that halted him. "What kind of danger are you in?"

"I don't know. That's the problem. I've been thinking a great deal about that night on Lincoln Road Mall. Something wasn't quite right—from a medical standpoint, I mean. There's no doubt that Mr. Chang went into cardiac arrest, but the medical examiner states that it was induced by asphyxiation. Suffocation, in layman's terms."

"Someone strangled him?"

"No. Suffocation induced by a toxin."

"What kind of toxin?"

"The toxicology report says it cannot be identified."

"That sounds weird."

"To say the least. And I have a theory for that. Have you seen the mall's security tape where Chang has that brief encounter with someone who's probably just pretending to be blind?"

"I haven't seen it, but I heard about it."

"Action News loaded the key frames on their Web site about an hour ago. I'm sure all the networks have it up by now. Check it out. Chang clearly gets stuck in the leg with the white mobility cane. An hour a later he was in convulsions and dropped dead. I believe that something was administered at that point of contact."

"But the initial autopsy showed no sign of injection."

"That's what has me so worried. It must have been a toxin that's lethal even if just a small amount comes in contact with the skin. Possibly a synthetic, like VX, or—"

"Nerve gas?"

"In liquid form, yes. A ten-milligram drop of VX can kill you. A raindrop is eighty milligrams."

"But it doesn't just fall from the sky like rain."

"Look, I know I must sound paranoid, but I researched this. Terrorists in Japan used sarin to kill commuters on the Tokyo subway back in the 1990s. VX is even more deadly, but there are ways to get it. You steal it. You buy it from some Russian mobster who smuggled it out of the former Soviet Union. Whatever."

Jack paused, as the conversation was getting a little flaky. "Did you say you researched this?"

"Yes, don't you see what's going on? Surely the medical examiner knows what kind of toxin was involved. This report is a cover-up. Maybe the government doesn't want to send the public into a panic over fears of chemical and biological warfare."

A retiree with time enough to dream up conspiracy theories. *Great.*

"Doctor, I'm not saying you're paranoid, but—"

"Please, I need help. I don't know why the medical examiner won't say what killed Ethan Chang. The point is that if I came in contact with the same toxin when I was helping that man—or even if I just breathed in the fumes—I need to start on an antidote."

His voice was becoming increasingly urgent, and Jack needed to reel him in. "Okay, I hear your concern. But let's think about this for a second. If you were exposed, wouldn't you be dead already, or at least showing some kind of symptoms?"

"Not necessarily. Chang got a direct application and died in an hour. Depending on how much I got and how it got into my system, it could take weeks to see the effects."

"All right," said Jack, trying to keep him calm. "Let's look at this another way. What would be the downside of starting yourself on a nerve-gas antidote as a precaution?"

"For some of these synthetics the antidote is itself a toxin. I can't just be self-prescribing willy-nilly. I need to know exactly what kind of toxin was involved."

"What have you done so far?"

"I've plied every professional contact I've made over the past forty years, and I can't get anywhere. I'll be honest, I'm no fan of lawyers, but I know when I need one. You seemed like the logical choice. You're plugged into this already with the work you've done for Jamal Wakefield."

It still sounded flaky to Jack. "So you want a lawyer to go into court and get a judge to force the medical examiner to reveal the toxin that killed Ethan Chang. Is that what you're asking?"

"Bingo. If the son of a former governor can't cut through red tape, who can?"

Jack glanced at Neil, who was finishing his tea and trying to get Theo's attention.

"Mr. Swyteck?"

Jack heard the doctor's voice, but he was thinking. It had all started with a Gitmo detainee who spoke no English. Several bodies later, Jack was now discussing nerve gas with the second potential client of the day who was—in someone's eyes—nothing more than collateral damage in one hell of a cover-up.

That, or the crazy conspiracy theorists are coming out of the woodwork.

"Refill, Mr. Goodwrench?"

Neil handed Theo his empty cup, and Theo poured more hot water. It was a simple thing but a pivotal moment for Jack: the man who'd mentored him at the Freedom Institute served hot tea by a former badass from the 'hood who had been the only innocent man Jack and Neil had ever represented.

Had been. *Until Jamal came along.*

"Mr. Swyteck, are you still there?"

Jack was still taking in his Neil-and-Theo moment, and though it wasn't technically accurate, another word came to mind to describe his mentor. "Doctor, can I call you right back?" Jack said into the phone. "I need to consult with my partner."

Chapter Thirty-four

The Internet café on Bethnal Green was open twenty-four hours. At half past midnight in the middle of week, he expected to have his choice of terminals, especially on such a cold and nasty night. The rain was turning to sleet, and the sidewalks were deserted, but he was unlike most of his fellow Africans in Somaal Town. January's bite didn't bother him, and he actually preferred the shorter days of winter. The late sunrise and early sunset were his friends, and if that meant living in a colder climate, so be it. His given name was Habib.

To his victims, he was known as the Dark.

He shook out his umbrella and entered the café. The fluorescent lighting assaulted his eyes and, for some reason, triggered a yawn. His quick trip to Miami and back had left him drained. As a rule, he didn't sleep well on airplanes, no matter how exhausted he was. This time his work had been especially taxing. Everything had come off without a hitch, thanks to his 24/7 approach to preparation, coordination, and execution. After landing at Heathrow, all he could do was climb into bed and sleep for eighteen hours. He still didn't feel rested.

The clerk behind the desk was reading a graphic novel online. She looked up and directed him to a terminal. He pulled up a chair in front of the monitor, logged on, and created a new Internet account. Using the same account twice was out of the question; it was important that his messages never be traced back to him. This account would be in the name of Doris Lader, a fifty-two-year old woman from Las Vegas who had provided her credit card number and other personal information in response to a phishing e-mail that she had thought was from Citibank.

Americans had to be the stupidest people on earth.

He quickly entered the necessary information to create the account, then typed in his screen name. It was the same one he used for all his phony accounts, the same mix of lowercase letters and capitalized initials:

ruaoTD.

Are you afraid of The Dark.

He was up and almost ready to go. The only remaining step was to choose the preferred language. Sometimes he used English, sometimes he used Somali modified Latin script. It didn't really matter this time. The message was short, and he banged it out in just a few quick keystrokes. He always created the message and proofread it before typing in the address. It was good practice to prevent a half-baked message from sailing off accidentally. He read it one last time.

"I killed your son. I wanted you to know that."

Satisfied, he typed in the address and hit SEND. It was gone in an instant, headed to Mogadishu.

He logged off, and the clerk didn't even look up from her LCD as he exited the café. A cold blast of wind hit him as soon as the door opened. His flat was just a block away, but even so, he was tempted to go back inside and wait for the weather to improve.

Which could be June.

He popped open his umbrella and headed out into the night, walking with purpose. There was one more thing to accomplish tonight. He rounded the corner, passed the street entrance to his flat, and walked down the alley to the cellar door.

The international call from the pay phone had pissed him off in a big way. It was her first offense, and a very foolish one at that. Did she think she could buy a calling card without his finding out about it? Did she think she could do *anything* without his knowledge? He turned the key and shook his head with amusement as he unlocked the door. There was no doubt in his mind that she would tell him who she had called, why she had called him, and what she had said. If she lied, he would not be fooled—because he already knew everything there was to know about that call. He just wanted to hear her say that she was sorry for what she had done.

Oh, so sorry.

He entered, closed the door behind him, and climbed down the steep stairs. The cellar had just one small window at street level, which had been made translucent with a streaky coat of paint on the outside. The streetlight glowed behind it, and the shadow of iron bars cast a zebra pattern across the floor.

He watched her sleeping on a mattress in the corner. Finally, she seemed to sense his presence.

"Who's there?" she said, only half awake.

He didn't answer. She reached for the lamp switch.

"Leave the light off," he said, and his command halted her.

"You're back," she said.

It was that frightened and timid voice that had lured him into complacency. The one that had led him to believe that, after almost six trouble-free months, she could be trusted with a modicum of supervised free time. The one that had made it almost inconceivable that she would find the courage to venture out to a pay phone.

He grabbed the covers at the foot of the bed and peeled them back. She jerked away, but he grabbed her by the ankle. The monitor was still in place.

"I never really left," he said.

Chapter Thirty-five

"Douglas Road," the driver said as the Metro-Dade bus squeaked to a stop.

Vince rose and offered a sincere "Thank you" on his way out; bus drivers were supposed to call out stops for the blind, but not all of them did. The smell of diesel fumes engulfed him as the bus pulled away, and Vince could hear the *click-clack* of Sam's nails on the sidewalk as his four-legged friend led him to the crosswalk.

"Time for a doggy pedicure, buddy."

Vince stopped at the crosswalk, checked his GPS navigator, and waited for the familiar female robotic voice: *"Go one hundred yards, and your destination is on the right."* The traffic light changed with an audible *click*, and Sam led the way across the street.

Vince had visited MLFC headquarters before, but his mental image of it was sketchy. Although he had received a full tour, Chuck Mays' idea of being descriptive for the benefit of his blind friend was simply to add his all-purpose adverb to everything. The offices weren't big; they were f-ing big. The computers weren't superfast; they were super f-ing fast.

"You have arrived," announced the navigation system. Sam stopped, and by Vince's calculation, they were directly in front of Chuck's building.

"Over here, Paulo," said Chuck. "What are you, fucking blind?"

The guy had a way with words.

"Too nice of a day to sit in the office," said Chuck. "Thought we'd walk down to the pond and feed the ducks."

Vince hesitated. No matter where they were, whenever Chuck said something about a walk down to the pond to feed the ducks, Vince detected the distinct odor of marijuana in the air. Some guys just seemed to get a rush flouting the law under a cop's nose, even if the cop was blind.

"There's no pond here," said Vince, "and probably no ducks, either."

"Busted. Guess I'll settle for a cigarette."

They found a bench in the shade on the other side of the building, away from traffic noises. A light breeze felt good on Vince's face. He opened his backpack and emptied a water bottle into a travel-size bowl for Sam. Chuck was wired on caffeine overload and dominated the small talk—everything from his new receptionist's great set of tits to the latest stupid bureaucrat at the Division of Motor Vehicles to hand over twenty thousand driver's license numbers to hackers in the Ukraine by clicking on a bogus link for free porn. Finally, Chuck took a breath, and Vince got straight to the point of his visit.

"This isn't easy for me to talk about," said Vince, "but sometimes I can't remember what McKenna looked like."

It was a rare occurrence, but Chuck was actually silenced. Vince heard only the breeze stirring the palm fronds overhead.

"Don't worry about it," said Chuck, clearly not knowing how to respond.

Vince sensed his uneasiness—"a guy thing"—but there was something he needed to say. "It's strange. My grandmother, who has been dead for over two decades, I can picture perfectly in my mind. But with my brother, who I see every week, it's now almost impossible for me to attach a face to his voice."

Chuck lit up another cigarette. "What about me? How can you forget my ugly mug?"

Vince stayed on a serious track. "The way I described this to Alicia is to imagine that there is a big photo album in my mind. If people are part of my past, they stay there forever, just as they were. But if I make them a part of my new life, their image fades. The more contact I have with them, the more they are defined by things that don't depend on sight."

"Well, if that's the case, shouldn't you remember McKenna?"

"She's the exception. When I think of that night, I don't see McKenna the young woman anymore. I see McKenna the five-year-old girl who used to jump into my arms when I came to visit. It's getting so that my memory of that day—that horrible day—is one of a five-year-old girl."

"There's nothing wrong with that."

"On the surface, you're right. But she wasn't five when she was murdered. And no matter how much evidence we concealed, we weren't going to make her five."

"Nobody hid any evidence, Vince."

"I'm talking about the text message from her cell phone. *FMLTWIA.*"

"I know what you're talking about. Hacking into her provider's network and zapping it from her cellular records was my version of child's play."

"And I never told anyone a thing about it."

"There was no reason for anyone to know."

Vince shifted uneasily. He hated moments like these, when people could see the angst on his face and he could see nothing on theirs.

"Look, at the time, we were of one mind," said Vince. "The last thing we wanted was a rag-sheet reporter dragging McKenna's reputation through the mud. But without that text message, the only evidence we had was the recording of her dying declaration—which *I* screwed up. The text would have put Jamal Wakefield at the scene of the crime. What nineteen-year-old guy wouldn't have come running in response to a message like that?"

"It's hard to run from a secret detention facility."

"You don't really believe that line Swyteck has been selling, do you?"

Chuck took a long drag from his cigarette. "Jamal didn't kill McKenna."

"Don't patronize me. If I had stayed on the line with the nine-one-one operator and let McKenna talk to her, the case against Jamal would have been a lock. There was only a hearsay problem because I recorded it to something as unreliable as my home answering machine."

"You need to stop beating yourself up over that. The text message doesn't convict Jamal. It actually proves his innocence."

"How can you say that?"

"For one thing, McKenna would never have sent a text like that. Not that I knew everything about my daughter, but that much I did know. The man who killed her picked up her cell phone and texted Jamal. It was all part of setting up her ex-boyfriend."

Vince paused, confused. "When did you decide this?"

"After I heard Jamal's alibi, I did the math."

"Math?"

"The time of death was a time certain. So was the time of the text message. We also know the severity of McKenna's wounds. With a little input from medical and forensic experts, I was able to make a fairly reliable calculation of how long a healthy teenage girl of McKenna's height and weight could survive those injuries. That gave me an approximate time of the attack. The bottom line is that McKenna was probably stabbed *before* the text was sent."

Vince considered it. Some things weren't measurable with mathematical certainty, but if anyone could do it, Chuck could. "So Jamal was framed?"

"That's my calculation."

Sam rested his head on Vince's leg. Vince patted his huge head, then scratched him in his favorite spot: on the forehead, right between the eyes. Sam's eyes. *Vince's* eyes. "Which means that the son of a bitch who did this is definitely still out there."

"Three years and running," said Chuck.

"Which means Swyteck was right."

"Yeah," said Chuck. "So right that Jamal's mother intends to sue me under some bullshit theory."

"How do you know that?"

"Jamal's uncle called me. He said he was hiring Jack Swyteck, and that it was going to be the courtroom equivalent of jihad."

"Well, if it's war they want . . ."

A puff of smoke hit Vince in the face.

"I got a better idea," said Chuck.

"Tell me."

There was another cloud of smoke, then Chuck turned into Marlon Brando. "I'll make him an offer he can't refuse."

Chapter Thirty-six

Jack entered the MLFC Computer Center through a fireproof door and in the company of Chuck Mays, Vince Paulo, and a security guard who made the other men look like Lilliputians.

"Watch your step," said Mays.

Boxes of records and supplies cluttered the ramp, and it impressed Jack the way Paulo negotiated his way with just a walking stick. The guard left them at another glass door, which Mays opened with a passkey. It led to a large open space that was so well air-conditioned that Jack felt an immediate chill. Inside, rows of supercomputers hummed beneath an expansive drop ceiling with cool fluorescent lighting.

"This single computer center is bigger than my entire first company was," said Mays.

Jack didn't fancy himself a computer whiz, so rather than interrupt with a stupid question, he simply let Mays keep talking.

Mays continued. "If you pulled up these floors, you'd see miles and miles of cables. That's our information pipeline. Every minute of every day we're sucking in new names, ages, addresses, phone numbers, IP addresses. We get records on your marital status, employment, home values, estimated income. Your children's ages, your ethnicity, your religion, the books you read, the products you order by phone or online, and where you go on vacation. And that's just the purchase behavior and lifestyle data."

"There's more?" asked Jack.

Mays smiled. "Follow me."

He led them around a pod of work cubicles to another row of smaller computers.

"Don't let the size fool you," said Mays. "These are my fastest ever, and they hold more information than you can fathom. Ever heard of a petabyte, Swyteck?"

"No, but I'm sure a shot of penicillin will clear you right up."

"Funny. The computer memory here is measured in petabytes."

"I have no idea what that means."

"Imagine a stack of King James Bibles that's fifty thousand miles high. That's one petabyte."

"That's a lot of 'thees' and 'thous,' verily I say unto you."

"We call it grid computing, which is basically a network of supercomputers. All day long we're analyzing and matching the information we gather to create a detailed portrait of hundreds of millions of adults. And it all happens in seconds, because each portrait has its own sixteen-digit code unique to each person."

Jack's gaze swept the room. Each computer looked identical to the one beside it, except for a somewhat goofy motif that was unique to each machine. Some were marked with the characters from *The Simpsons* or *SpongeBob SquarePants*. Others were identified by muscle cars, like Maserati or Ferrari.

"What kind of information is collected here?" Jack asked.

"I can't tell you," said Mays. "But you might have guessed that the shark fins are for legal actions—divorces, foreclosures, and bankruptcy filings, mostly."

Jack wondered what nuggets from his own divorce were in there.

"So that's the end of our tour, ladies and gentlemen," said Mays. "Now let's talk settlement."

"Settlement?" said Jack.

"Jamal's mother wants to know who killed her son," said

Mays. "I want to know who killed my wife and daughter. My friend Vince wants to know who turned him into the only guy in the room who can't see what's going on. So let's cut through this bullshit about Jamal's mother suing my ass because it's somehow my fault that her son is dead."

"What are you proposing?" asked Jack.

"After you left my house the other night, something stuck in my mind. Basically, we shared information. I gave you a copy of a text-message exchange between my wife and the man who the police think was her killer. You told me something that Jamal said to you in private."

"That his interrogators in Prague threatened to kill McKenna if he didn't talk."

"Exactly," said Mays. "You said that it was technically still covered by the attorney-client privilege even though Jamal was dead."

"Fortunately, it was something that Jamal had already authorized me to make public, so I was free to share it."

"Yeah, brilliant," said Mays. "Jamal's dead. Now we want to nail the son of a bitch who killed him and the two most important people in my life. So fuck the attorney-client privilege. You have information straight from Jamal that I can't get from any other source, am I right?"

"That's a fair statement," said Jack.

"Here's the deal: We pool our knowledge. Everything Vince and I know about McKenna and Shada goes into the pot. Everything you and Jamal's mother know goes right in with it. And I mean everything. Anything you learned from anyone about Mr. Chang who died at the Lincoln Road Mall. Everything you know about the girl who called you from London. And most important, everything Jamal ever told you."

"It's the broadest net possible," said Vince. "We realize this might include some things that Jamal's family might not want to tell the police. That's why we're doing this privately, through Chuck. Not through the police."

"We plug all of it into my supercomputers," Chuck said with a wave of his hand. "We run the same kind of searches I run for Homeland Security when they ask for help finding terrorists. And we find this fucker."

Mays' emphasis was on finding the killer, but Jack was hung up on the first point. "Wait a second," said Jack. "You run searches for the government?"

Mays chuckled. "No offense to my friend Vince here, but do you think the government has this kind of capability? The fires were still burning in the World Trade Center when the FBI came calling on the major players in information technology for clues about the nineteen hijackers and their accomplices. For a stretch, half my company was on it, all on my own dime."

"Are you still doing national security work?"

"That's none of your business."

"Is that what Project Round Up is about?"

"I said it's none of your business."

Jack glanced at Paulo. With a cop for a best friend, Mays was already connected to law enforcement. Jack probably shouldn't have been surprised that the ties ran deeper than the Miami Police.

"I believe there's a proposal on the table," said Vince.

"Let me say a couple of things," said Jack. "First, I have tremendous respect for you, Vince, even though it may not have seemed that way in the courtroom."

"I'm over that," said Vince. "You did what you had to do. I understand."

"It's important to me that things are cool between us."

"We're cool," said Vince.

"Good," said Jack, and then his gaze swept across the computer center. "But I have to be honest. This business gives me the creeps. Not just your company. I'm talking about the whole information revolution. Call it a Big Brother complex. There's a bias in me, and that bias makes it hard for me to trust guys like Chuck Mays."

Mays was completely unfazed, as if he'd heard that speech before. "You probably weren't whistling that tune on September twelfth. But that's another debate. Does your client want to find out who killed her son or doesn't she?"

"I understand what you're saying. And I will speak to Maryam about your offer."

"You do that. And here's something to sweeten the pot. Tell her that if she agrees to my proposal, I'll pay her five hundred thousand dollars."

Paulo looked surprised, which Jack noted.

"You're actually going to write a check to Maryam Wakefield?" said Jack.

"Not exactly," said Mays. "I would sign over my rights as beneficiary under Jamal's life insurance policy."

Jack did another double take—but it was mild compared to Paulo's visceral expression of disbelief. Like a smart cop, Paulo had the good sense to hold his tongue until he and his friend were alone. Jack felt no such constraint.

"Are you saying that you took out a half-million-dollar life insurance policy on Jamal Wakefield?" said Jack.

"Actually, it was a million. But I'll give his mother half, and I'll keep half. That's fair."

"Chuck, let's talk about this later," said Paulo.

"What?" said Mays. "I have life insurance on everyone who works for me."

Jack said, "A million dollars on a nineteen-year-old employee who also happens to be dating your daughter? That strikes me as a little . . . awkward, shall we say?"

"A lot of companies have life insurance on their employees. It's cheap, especially on the young guys, and it pays a nice benefit. What's the big damn deal?"

"No big deal at all," said Jack, his stare tightening. "So long as you had absolutely nothing to do with the disappearance and murder of the man who was accused of killing your wife and daughter."

Mays narrowed his eyes with anger, and Jack got the distinct impression that, had Paulo not been in the room, Mays would have grabbed him by the throat.

"My offer is good for twenty-four hours. Get me an answer from your client—before I change my mind."

Chapter Thirty-seven

Neil Goderich spent all of Thursday in court and ate a microwaved frozen dinner at his desk in the office. Long days were the rule for him. Friends often asked him what his tiny salary came out to on an hourly basis, but he would just smile and shake his head. People didn't get it. There was no minimum-wage law for lawyers at the Freedom Institute.

"Can you please turn on the air-conditioning?" asked the doctor.

The day had been unusually warm even by Miami standards, and Neil was in a windowless room with a new client: the doctor who had come to Ethan Chang's aid on the Lincoln Road Mall, and who feared he had been exposed to the same deadly toxin.

"Sorry," said Neil, "there's no budget for AC after five P.M."

The doctor dabbed his sweaty brow with a handkerchief. "I'd sure hate to be in here in the summertime."

"You get used to it," said Neil, and he meant it. In twenty-eight years, the run-down house on the Miami River that was the Freedom Institute had changed little. Four lawyers shared two small bedrooms that had been converted into offices. The foyer doubled as a storage room for old case files, one box stacked on top of the other. The bottom ones sagged beneath the weight of denied motions for stay of execution, the box tops warped into sad smiles. Harsh fluorescent lighting showed every stain on the indoor/outdoor carpeting. The furniture screamed "flea market"—chairs that didn't match, tables made stable with a deck of cards under one leg. The vintage 1960s kitchen was not only where lawyers and staff ate their bagged lunches, but it also served as the main (and only) conference room. Hanging on the wall over the coffeemaker was the same framed photograph of Bobby Kennedy that had once hung in Neil's dorm room at Harvard.

The other lawyers had gone home, and Neil was with Dr. Spigelman at the kitchen table. The old refrigerator made a strange buzzing noise, which Neil silenced with a quick kick to the side of the appliance. It didn't exactly convey the image of powerhouse legal representation, and Neil could hear the concern in his client's voice.

"Are you sure you're equipped to handle this case?" the doctor asked.

"Absolutely," said Neil. "Granted, our typical client is not a retired physician."

"Unless that retired physician is also a murderer, I presume."

"Accused murderer," said Neil. "But let's get beyond that. Jack Swyteck steered this case in my direction because he thought it was a cause I would want to fight for. And he was right. You were a doctor for forty years. You witnessed a man die with your own eyes. You've clawed for information as to the cause of death, and in your professional opinion, the medical examiner may be covering up evidence that a synthetic toxin was released in one of the most famous outdoor malls in the country."

"In a nutshell, that's it. But hearing you repeat it back to me gives me some pause. Do I sound paranoid?"

"A little. But you came to the right place."

"What do you mean by that?"

"We know things about Ethan Chang that lend credence to your concerns."

"Like what?"

"The night he was killed, Chang was on his way to see Jack Swyteck. He was going to hand over photographs about a government secret that would help us defend a man who was held overseas as an accused terrorist. When you're talking about government secrets and accused terrorists, there are any number of entities, foreign and domestic, that could have access to nerve gas or a similar toxin."

"Holy cow," said the doctor. "I really could be at risk."

"I don't mean to diminish your personal right and need to know if you should start taking an antidote. But if someone used a weapon of mass destruction—and that's what these synthetic toxins are—then the *public* has a right to know."

"So how do you get the medical examiner to give us the information we need?"

"Obviously, time is of the essence. I'll draft the complaint and emergency motion tonight, file the papers in the morning, and request an immediate hearing. The case will go before the emergency duty judge, and—"

Neil halted at a loud crash in the other room.

"What the hell was that?"

Neil started toward the hallway, but the café door flew open before he got to it. A man dressed in black burst into the room. A ski mask covered his face, and in one quick motion, he raised his right arm and took aim with his pistol.

"No!" the doctor shouted.

Neil braced for the crack of a gunshot, but it was the muffled sound of a silenced projectile. The doctor's head snapped back, and as he tumbled backward in his chair, the crimson spray of blood reached all the way to the framed photograph of Bobby Kennedy.

Neil shrieked and ran for the other door. It led to the alley, but the second half of the attack team was right outside, dressed in the same black fatigues and playing lookout. The triggerman grabbed Neil by the ponytail and took him down hard. Neil's spectacles flew from his face and slid across the linoleum. The wind rushed from his lungs as the attacker drilled his knee into Neil's back.

The man yanked harder at the ponytail, forcing Neil's chin up from the floor. A cold, serrated blade was pressed so firmly to his throat that he could feel the blood starting to trickle down his neck, moistening his shirt collar.

"This is not going to end well for you, Mr. ACLU. So you might as well talk."

Neil's body was shaking, and his mind flashed with the memory of what Jamal had told him about his abduction three years ago.

"What . . . do you want to know?"

The masked man leaned closer, burrowing his knee deeper into Neil's spine.

"I want to know everything about Jamal Wakefield," he said, hissing into Neil's ear. "You can start with what he told you about Prague."

Chapter Thirty-eight

Midnight was fast approaching in central London—lunchtime in a day in the life of the Dark.

The tube ride from Bethnal Green to King's Cross was about twenty-five minutes, most of which the Dark spent reviewing his plan. The man seated behind him was snoring like a drunk, and the grind and hum of the underground railcar had lulled a handful of other riders to sleep, or near sleep. The Dark, however, was wide awake. His regular six hours of rest were from nine A.M. to three P.M., which meant that London's winter suited his needs perfectly. Some days he never saw the sun. Still, he wore his sunglasses everywhere, including the underground. He was no vampire; even artificial light bothered him. Not that vampires were a bad thing. Hell, the number of schoolgirls reading *Twilight* on the tube was enough to make him bloodthirsty.

"Farringdon Station," came the announcement over the loudspeaker. One more stop until his destination.

The train squeaked to a halt, and the doors opened. The smell of urine and feces entered the car, and the Dark spotted the mess someone had left on the platform. He ignored it, but not entirely. He'd read somewhere that memory was most closely linked to the sense of smell, and this unmistakable odor was indeed taking the Dark around a strange bend of memory lane. It smelled like the central market in Mogadishu, and the fact that his mind was making that connection was far from random. He'd been thinking about the Bakara Market on and off, ever since he'd sent that e-mail to Jamal's father.

The e-mail hadn't been part of the original plan. It was definitely beyond the scope of what he'd been hired to do. But getting paid for this job was just the icing on the cake. The Dark wanted that Somali son of a bitch to know that his son was dead, and he wanted to be the one to break the news. There was history between the two men, and the root of his animosity was burned into the Dark's memory. As much as he wanted to stay focused on the present journey to central London, his mind was taking him back to that hot summer day in the Bakara Market, when the East African sun made the stench unbearable, when the sounds of war were never far away, and when the smell of newly spilled blood was in the air. To a time when he was known only as Habib, a foot soldier for al-Shabaab, and he worked under a cell leader named Abukar—Jamal's father.

It was midmorning, and Habib was looking east across the Bakara Market from the charred second story of yet another building that had been destroyed by mortar fire. Years of armed conflict had reduced the Italian architecture of Somalia's colonial period to rubble. Despite the recent shelling, Somalia's biggest trading center was alive with the dangerous blend of war and commerce. It was just Habib and his cell leader on patrol, each of them well armed with an AK-47 rifle.

"There," said Abukar, pointing.

The market was mostly shanty shacks made of old wood, rusty corrugated steel, and any piece of cloth that was large enough to provide shade. With temperatures exceeding 110 degrees, the stench of raw sewage and garbage rose up from the streets. At the whim of the breeze, Habib caught whiffs of the business being conducted at the various kiosks. He could smell live animals—camels, chickens, and goats—and the putrid piles of guts and puddles of blood that baked in the sun after the animals were slaughtered on-site. He detected sour goat and camel's milk in unrefrigerated steel drums, which stank like a rotting corpse. There were rancid meats, many of them unidentifiable. Habib did not smell it today, but he'd been told of kiosks where human corpses—villagers dead from disease or starvation—were butchered and sold as animal feed for the dogs and hyenas that the poorest of the poor kept as pets, watchdogs, or a future meal.

And there were the arms traders. An RPG-2 grenade launcher would set the buyer back about five hundred American dollars. Ammunition for your AK-47: just seventy-five cents. Around these booths, it didn't take a trained nose to breathe in the smell of gunpowder.

"The man by the orange tent?" asked Habib, his gaze trained on the kiosk to which Abukar had pointed.

"Yes. That one. He sold to the alliance."

Abukar meant the Alliance for the Restoration of Peace and Counter-Terrorism (ARPCT), a group of secular warlords that was funded in part by the CIA. Militia loyal to the Islamic Court Union had driven the alliance out of the capital in what had come to be known as the *Second* Battle of Mogadishu, though to most Somalis it was all just one continuous battle with no beginning or end. In a single month Habib had been all the way down the coast to Marka, yanking out teeth because gold and silver fillings were sinful. Next it was Awdheegle, to punish women who did not wear the veil, with a stop along the way to carry out the sentence—public whipping—for two boys caught playing soccer. Then it was on to Afgoye, to destroy American textbooks in schools; to Baidoa, to defile the graves of infidels and loot the UN offices; and to Balcad, where Islamist clerics belonging to the Ahlu Sunna Wal-Jama faction were beheaded. More blood was spilled in northern Mogidishu's Maslah Market: firing squads for spies and public amputation of hands for anyone caught stealing—common punishment for common thieves. Next week his team would take over six UN vehicles for use in suicide bombings against the African Union's main base.

Important work, to be sure. But Habib's calling was the high-tech stuff. He got started by simply monitoring reports about al-Shabaab on the Web—"100 Britons a year coming to Somalia Training Camps," or "American from Seattle Kills 21 Peacekeepers in Suicide Bombing"—and reporting back to his superiors. His goal was to work with the production team on the latest propaganda video in progress, *At your Service, Osama,* in which al-Shabaab would formally and publicly pledge its allegiance to Osama bin Laden.

Habib checked his watch, then glanced at Abukar.

"One minute," said Habib.

Timing was critical. They were implementing one of two separate but simultaneous suicide attacks in the city. It was Habib who had delivered the stock of explosives for use in the Bakara Market bombing: forty kilograms of fertilizer, the same amount of ammonium nitrate that last week had delivered up a thirty-year-old husband and father of four to martyrdom. Habib was dependable in all he did for al-Shabaab, and his reward was to witness firsthand the fruits of his labor.

"Ah," said Abukar as he peered through his binoculars into the busy market. "She is right on time."

"She?" asked Habib. He didn't know the bomber's identity; very few did.

"They will not suspect a woman."

"She must be very brave."

"You should be proud. It's Samira."

Habib did a double take. "My sister?"

"Our *shaheeda.*"

Habib glanced at the bustling marketplace, then at Abukar, then back at the crowd. He spotted several women dressed in traditional black burkas, any one of whom could have been a human bomb. Before Habib could speak—before his anger could even begin to find words—a huge blast ripped through the usual daily commerce. Screaming bystanders scattered as bloodied body parts flew through the air.

"Samira!" he cried out, invoking his youngest sister's name.

"Allahu Akbar!" his cell leader shouted.

"King's Cross St. Pancras."

The crackle over the loudspeaker stirred the Dark out of his memories. The blur of the platform whizzed past in the train's window, slowing steadily to a stop. He was the first one off when the doors parted, and he walked straight to the escalator.

The largest tube station in central London was so named because it served two rail stations: King's Cross and St. Pancras. Forty million riders coursed through the complex each year. The Dark was interested in a select few of them. The tube had delivered the goods in the past, but tonight he would try the Suburban Building. Platforms 9 and 10 to be exact.

In the Harry Potter series, King's Cross is the starting point of the Hogwarts Express. Riders enter secret platform 9¾ by passing through the brick-wall barrier between platforms 9 and 10. The books and movies are set in the main part of the station, but platforms 9 and 10 are actually in a separate building. Nonetheless, authorities did their best to capitalize on the phenomenon, erecting a cast-iron PLATFORM 9¾ sign on a wall in the right building. Part of a luggage trolley has also been installed below the sign, half of it seeming to have disappeared into the wall. Fans of the series were always flocking there for photographs, one after another taking a turn at pretending to push the cart through the wall.

That was where girls of the right age would be. Silly girls who hung out in train stations late at night and who wanted to disappear like Harry.

The Dark passed a row of shops in the concourse, checked his reflection in a storefront window, and smiled to himself.

Disappear, they will.

Chapter Thirty-nine

Jack's voice cracked for the third time. Lengthy eulogies were inappropriate at a Jewish funeral on a Friday afternoon, but delivery of even a short one was painful.

"Neil Goderich was my mentor and my friend," Jack said, fighting back tears. "And he was the kindest soul I've ever met."

The entire memorial service was kept short, as it was the wish of the Goderich family to bury Neil before sundown on Friday, rather than hold the body over until after the Sabbath. Jack was the only gentile among the pallbearers, so the family provided him a yarmulke. The casket was a simple wooden box adorned only with the Star of David. The procession stopped seven times, in accordance with Jewish custom, each stop symbolizing the liberation from the vanity of this world and transfer to the world without vanity.

An easy transition for Neil, a man of remarkable humility.

By the time they reached the burial plot, the sun was low in a cloudless blue sky. A slight chill in the air forced Neil's widow to drape a sweater over her shoulders, another layer of black atop her traditional black dress. About twenty other mourners gathered at graveside. Among them was Theo Knight, who was forever indebted to "Mr. Goodwrench " for mentoring Jack through a case that could have ended with Theo in the electric chair. A rabbi, the only speaker at the cemetery, led prayers in Hebrew and in English. As the casket was lowered slowly into the grave, one verse from Psalm 91, in particular, caught Jack's attention:

"Thou shalt not be afraid of the terror by night, nor of the arrow that flieth by day; Of the pestilence that walketh in darkness . . ."

Terror by night . . . darkness . . . The Dark.

Jack shook off thoughts of how Neil might have died—and who could have murdered him.

One by one, the mourners stepped forward for *k'vurah.* Jack followed Neil's brother. He took the shovel from the pile of dirt. Using the back of the shovel—a showing of how hard it is to bury a loved one—Jack pitched a scoop of earth onto the wooden casket below. It landed somewhere in the darkness with a hollow *clump.* Jack hadn't expected it, couldn't even really explain it, but that sound triggered a flood of memories, and it sounded like so many things—all at once. It was like Jack's eager knock on the door when he showed up at Neil's office for his first interview out of law school. Like the bang of a gavel when Jack tried his first case with Neil at his side. Like the clop of Neil's vintage Earth Shoes, which he'd resoled a half-dozen times since the 1970s.

"Good-bye, my friend," Jack whispered through the lump in his throat.

It was after dark when Jack reached the Sunny Gardens Nursing Home.

Grandpa Swyteck was in bed, staring at the television on the credenza, as Jack entered the room. The other bed was empty, and a nurse was emptying drawers and bagging up the roommate's belongings. Jack didn't have to ask what that meant, not in a place where most residents were eighty-five or older. Just twenty-four hours earlier, Jack would have bet his car that the next funeral in his life was going to be his grandfather's.

Life's weird.

The Goderich family returned to the house after the internment. Shivah—the period of mourning when visitors would stop by to express their condolences—would not begin until after the Sabbath. Although Neil's widow had invited Jack to join them for Shabbat eve dinner, he sensed that it was best to leave the family to itself. As much as Jack didn't want to be alone, he didn't feel like stopping by Cy's Place to watch Theo work. He wished Andie were back, but he hadn't heard from her, which surely meant that, wherever she was, news of Neil's death had not yet reached her.

"You can take a break," Jack told the hired bodyguard. Theo had kept his promise and found serious muscle to sit with Grandpa after the threat. This guy had to be six feet eight, Jack estimated as he watched him leave the room.

"Hi, Grandpa," said Jack.

The older man gazed in Jack's direction, showing little reaction at first. Truthfully, Jack barely recognized *him* anymore. He'd shed twenty-five pounds in the nursing home, and it showed in his face. Jack had always known his grandfather as having long wisps of silver hair, but now a buzz cut was necessary to keep him from yanking it out in fits of confusion. Breathing through his nose was too much effort anymore, so his mouth was constantly agape. Finally, the recognition flashed on Grandpa's face.

"Jack, how are you?"

Jack smiled. It was hit-and-miss with Grandpa, some good days and some bad days. Nighttime was generally tougher than daylight. Sunset was worst of all—sundowner syndrome, they called it.

The nurse kept busy packing, but she glanced over and said, "We didn't have a good sunset at all today. Lots of confusion. But he seems to be coming back a little. You can give it a try. He may have a few good minutes left for you tonight."

Jack held his tongue. He knew she was trying to be helpful, and he was fully aware that his grandfather's condition was irreversible. But it still bothered him the way so many people felt free to talk about his grandfather's condition right in front of the man, as if he were already gone.

Jack reached through the bedside restraining bars and took his grandfather's hand. Grandpa's gaze slowly rolled in Jack's direction. A little smile creased his lips, and he raised a crooked finger, pointing at Jack's head.

"You see?" said Grandpa. "I told you."

Jack was confused, but then it hit him. He'd been in such a daze that he was still wearing the yarmulke from Neil's funeral, completely unaware of it.

"I wore it out of respect for a friend," said Jack as he removed it. "We buried Neil today."

"Neil who?"

It saddened Jack that his grandfather didn't remember. "Neil Goderich."

"Goderich? That sounds about as Jewish as Petrak."

"The original family name was Goldsmith. They changed it to hide from the Nazis."

Grandpa nodded—as if he truly understood—and it had Jack's mind working overtime. For more than a week, Jack had been thinking about his conversation with Grandpa's lady friend—specifically, Ruth's mention of how the stage play about Pio Nono and Edgardo Mortara had deeply affected Jack's grandfather. Then, in Washington, Neil had explained his own family name change, which prompted Jack to do some research on Jews who had fought to survive by hiding their Jewishness from the Nazis. Sometimes a name change was just the start. Some Jewish children were sent to live with gentile families. In the saddest cases, young children whose parents were taken away to die in concentration camps grew up in non-Jewish homes without knowing that they were Jewish. As the Greatest Generation passed, deathbeds and nursing homes had a way of letting those secrets loose.

Jack presumed that his grandfather still had relatives named Petrak in the Czech Republic. He was starting to wonder if he had lost other relatives on his great-grandmother's side—perhaps those who hadn't changed their name to Petrak to survive the war.

"Grandpa?" asked Jack.

His eyes were closed. Jack was about to nudge him, but his cell rang. Not even the Carrie Underwood ringtone that Andie had programmed into Jack's phone was enough to get a reaction from Grandpa. The caller ID said PRIVATE, and Jack had a feeling that it was Andie. He was right.

"I'm so sorry," said Andie. "I just heard about Neil."

Jack rose and went to the other side of the room, away from Grandpa, to bring Andie up to speed. He hit the highlights quickly, ending with the double murder of Neil and his new client—and how it was no coincidence that they were on a mission to unravel one of the threads that seemed to lead all the way back to a secret detention facility in Prague.

"I'm coming home," said Andie.

"How long can you stay?"

"I'm putting in a request for at least a week. Longer, if I can swing it."

That was good news on one level, but it gave Jack pause. "Honey, I want to see you, and I'm definitely down in the dumps. But I don't want your career to take a hit over this."

"Don't you understand how dangerous this has become? Your client and your partner are dead: first Jamal Wakefield, now Neil. Has it occurred to you that someone out there might think that the third one's the charm?"

It had, especially after the threat against his grandfather, but Jack didn't want to go there.

"Harry!" Grandpa shouted, calling for Jack's father. "Harry, where are you?"

Jack asked Andie to hold on, went to the bedside, and spoke in a soothing tone. "Harry is not here, Grandpa."

"Harry!" he shouted.

The nurse muttered under her breath about his "combativeness," and she grabbed him hard by the wrists. Jack reached over and grabbed hers. She didn't seem to like it, either.

"Grandpa, it's okay," Jack said as he stroked his head. Grandpa settled down, but he continued to mumble about Pio Nono and his curious obsession with Pope Pius IX.

Andie's voice was on the phone. "Jack, is everything okay?"

"Yes. Just a little confusion, that's all."

Jack glanced at the nurse, and she seemed to take his cue that gentle was better, even if it did take a little more time than grabbing an octogenarian like a steer and strapping him to the bed. Jack stepped aside but stayed in the room to keep an eye on things.

"Listen to me," said Andie. "I'm coming home as soon as I can. Hopefully this weekend. But promise me that you are not going to take this into your own hands. You have to let the police do their work."

"Sure."

"Don't say 'sure.' I want you to promise that you *won't*."

Jack struggled for a response. As the future Mrs. Swyteck, Andie was perfectly within her rights to reel him in, and her concern wasn't at all out of line. There was just one problem. Neil was gone. And he was never coming back.

It was personal now.

"I promise you," said Jack, "that I will never make you a promise that I can't keep."

Chapter Forty

Chuck Mays woke early on Sunday, skipped breakfast, and drove to the cemetery. Vince and Sam rode along, the dog in the backseat with his snout out the window. The Maserati handled the curves along the tree-lined highway with ease, and the way Sam was breathing in another perfect south Florida morning almost made Chuck jealous. It was Chuck's intention to express his condolences to Neil Goderich's widow at some point. But not today. In fact, he was nowhere near Miami Beach, where Neil had been buried two days earlier. Charlotte Jane Memorial Park was in Coconut Grove. It was McKenna's final resting place.

Sunday would have been her nineteenth birthday.

Chuck parked on Franklin Avenue and followed the sidewalk around the corner to the main entrance. Older than the city of Miami itself, and situated on a few silent acres in West Coconut Grove, Charlotte Jane Memorial Park was in some ways the departed soul of a neighborhood that was rich in history and plagued by crime. Multimillion-dollar estates lay between the bay to the east and, to the west, the old Grove ghetto, where gunfights in run-down bars and package stores were all too common, and the "have-nots" tried not to get caught in the crossfire. After dark, street corners on Grand Avenue could service just about anyone's bad habit, from gangs with their random hits to doctors and lawyers who ventured out into the night in deference to their addictions. But within Charlotte Jane's iron gates rested the early settlers who sailed across the Florida Straits from the Bahamas. Shada's family was from the islands, and she had chosen this historic cemetery for McKenna. Chuck was ashamed to admit it, but he had been too distraught to make such decisions. The fact that it was within a stone's throw of south Florida's oldest African-American Baptist church hadn't fazed his wife. Shada's father was Muslim, but religion had never been important in her life.

Chuck stood beneath the arching ironwork at the entrance gate and drew a breath. Even by Coconut Grove standards, Charlotte Jane was a unique burial ground. As was the old Bahamian way, bodies rested aboveground in tombs that looked like stone caskets. Tombs were so close together that visitors barely had enough room to step between them. Some were their original stone color, but others were painted white or silver and looked brilliant in the Florida sun. Many were in disrepair, however, either deteriorating with age or the target of vandals. Spanish moss hung from sprawling oak limbs like dusty old spiderwebs from a chandelier, and the overall impression was more one of haunted than hallowed ground. Chuck was fine with it. McKenna probably would have found it cool that Michael Jackson had filmed part of his famous *Thriller* video here—or at least that was the Miami lore.

"You okay?" asked Vince.

"I guess so."

A large sign at the entrance warned him to lock his car and take his valuables with him. He hadn't bothered. Visiting his daughter's grave made it impossible to give a hoot about petty theft.

"Damn it," said Vince.

Chuck turned and saw his friend sitting on a tomb and rubbing his shin. Vince's guide dog had a sorry look on his face.

"What happened?" asked Chuck.

"Either I tripped over a tomb or a dead guy jumped out and kicked me in the shin. What do you think happened?"

Chuck gave him a minute, but he didn't dare help him up. He knew how much Vince hated that.

"Sorry," Vince said, rising. "I didn't mean to snap at you like a royal smart-ass. Especially here. Today of all days."

"Forget it," said Chuck. He turned and continued toward the north end of the cemetery. Sam followed, and Vince was right behind his guide dog.

McKenna was buried beneath two large oak trees in one of the oldest sections of the cemetery. Hers was among relatively few tombs from the twenty-first century. The cemetery had been essentially full for years. Space came available only as the oldest tombs, holding bodies unknown, disintegrated. But it wasn't just the new tombs that were decorated with flowers. Even Mrs. Blackshear, "Asleep in Jesus" since 1927, had a vase filled with plastic carnations. It was a touching gesture, even if by a stranger, but it saddened Chuck to wonder who might visit McKenna in eighty, ninety, or a hundred years.

And then he froze: A hundred yards ahead, between two oak trees, someone was at McKenna's grave.

"What's wrong?" asked Vince, sensing his vibe.

"Wait here," said Chuck.

He started toward the grave, moving quickly between the tombs—much faster than he could have with Vince following behind him. The going was getting tougher, however, as he moved into the oldest part of the cemetery. Tombs were so crowded together that he had to put one foot directly in front of the other to walk between them. He was about fifty yards away when he noticed that it was a woman at McKenna's grave. She was on her knees, clearing away weeds around the marker. But she wasn't dressed like a maintenance worker. Her head was covered by a large scarf, hijab style.

Chuck picked up the pace until he was almost at a jog, but with his eyes riveted on the woman who was wearing the hijab scarf, he tripped and knocked over a porcelain vase. It crashed into pieces against the concrete base of a tomb.

The woman at McKenna's grave looked up. Just thirty yards

separated them, and Chuck's gaze cut like a laser over the ragged rows of tombs. The scarf covered her hair, but she wore no veil or sunglasses. She stared back at him for a moment—and then she sprang to her feet and ran.

"Stop!" Chuck shouted. He started after her, but the tight spaces between tombs made it impossible to gather speed. The north end of the cemetery had no fence, and the woman was getting away.

"Wait!" Chuck shouted, but the gap between them was widening. Meaning no disrespect to the dead, Chuck hopped up on a tomb and ran at full speed, leaping from one to the next the way superheroes leaped from building to building. The woman was doing the same, but she was much lighter on her feet. Chuck was losing ground.

Come on, Mays, faster!

He picked up the pace, but the older crypts were spaced so irregularly that it was hard to hit his stride. He hopped from a white tomb to a silver one, and then to a crumbling marker for a pioneer unknown. He was keeping one eye on the woman, who was pulling away, when he caught sight of trouble. Vandals had destroyed the next tomb in his path. The lid was a pile of rocks, and the empty tomb lay open. Chuck reached for another gear and soared right over the battered tomb. He landed hard—all 240 pounds of him—on the next tomb over. It was a century old, however, and it couldn't support his weight. Chuck crashed through the lid like a human cannonball. He was almost up to his knees in a smashed tomb, but the pain made the horror of it almost irrelevant.

"My leg!"

Chuck pulled himself out, rolled onto the adjacent tomb, and lay on his back. Surely the woman in the hijab scarf was long gone, and even if she weren't, giving chase was out of the question. His only hope was that he hadn't destroyed his ankle. He was staring up at the sky, trying to bring the pain under control, when he heard Vince approaching with his guide dog.

"I heard you yelling at someone," said Vince, "and then a crash. What happened?"

Chuck groaned, then fed Vince his own line: "Either I tripped over a tomb or a dead guy jumped out and kicked me in the shin."

"I'm serious," said Vince. "Were you chasing after someone?"

Chuck was winded from the chase and needed to catch his breath. He listened for a car engine or other sound of the woman's getaway, but the streets around the cemetery were quiet, and he was still trying to understand what had just happened.

"You're going to think I'm crazy," said Chuck.

"I already think you're crazy."

Chuck would have laughed under any other circumstances. Instead, he sat up, scratched his head in disbelief, and said, "I think I just saw Shada."

Chapter Forty-one

Andie spent Sunday morning coloring her hair. Luckily, raven black looked best all one shade, no highlights, so it was easy enough to do it herself, given the time constraints. Losing the blond was for Jack, but she also hoped her boss would like it. Or more precisely, Lisa Horne's boss. Danilo Bahena was the principal reason that the FBI had arranged for Andie's crash course in male fetishes at Capital Pleasures. Andie caught up with Bahena at a private heliport in northern Virginia. Bahena took her inside the executive waiting room, away from the noise of the company's Agusta AW-139, where they could talk in private.

"Black is more . . . authoritative," Andie said. "A good thing, don't you agree?"

Bahena stepped closer for a better look. As usual, his expression was about as easy to read as tea leaves in a windstorm.

Bahena's official title was vice president of training and recruitment for Vortex Inc., and Andie—Lisa—was a trainee on the cusp of what Vortex referred to as "activation." Vortex was a privately held company, a subsidiary of a foreign corporation of obscure ownership, which made it impossible to know what the real business of Vortex was and who was actually running it. Bahena was equally enigmatic. He claimed to be from Los Angeles, California, but Andie and the FBI knew better. His closer ties were to Angeles, Pampanga, in the Philippines—a hotspot for human trafficking and sex trade. The skinny on Bahena was that, before he'd moved to Pentagon City and become such a friend to the U.S. government, the Japanese Yakuza and Chinese Triad had paid him a small fortune to feed their insatiable appetite for young prostitutes. He was built more like a wrestler than a businessman, and Andie could easily have envisioned him standing up to any element of organized crime. He was also a man of few words, which made him a tough study.

"I like it," he said finally.

"I thought you would," said Andie.

Bahena went to the coffee machine and poured himself a cup. He didn't offer Andie anything.

"Now for the bad news," said Andie. "I need a week off. Family emergency."

"No," he said.

"Sorry, maybe you didn't hear. It's an emergency."

"I heard you fine. I said no."

Andie disliked Bahena more than anyone she'd ever worked for—which was saying something, since in actuality she didn't even work for him. "Look, I wouldn't ask, but it's my mother. She needs—"

"I don't give a shit about your mother. We've got too much invested in you, and we're on a strict timetable."

"I'm only asking for a week."

"I said *strict*. If your mother's sick, hire a home health-care nurse."

"It's not a medical emergency."

"Then call your sister."

"My sister—"

Andie stopped herself. She'd never spoken of a sister to Bahena, and in her FBI undercover profile, she was an only child.

Did Bahena just bait me?

"My *step*sister, I mean," said Andie, her heart pounding and her mind racing as she backpedaled her way out of blowing her own cover. "I have a stepsister who is useless. So unless you're planning to put me in handcuffs and drag me to the airport, I'll see you in a week."

Bahena unleashed his patented stare of intimidation, but Andie gave it right back to him. She had him pegged for the kind of man who didn't respect any woman who wasn't prepared to spit in his eye, and it was time to turn on the attitude.

"Have a nice flight," she said as she started for the door.

"Lisa," said Bahena.

She stopped and turned quickly—quickly enough to disabuse him of the notion that her real name was anything but Lisa.

"I'll give you till Friday," he said.

Andie didn't nod her agreement, and she sure as hell didn't thank him. She opened the door and left the heliport without another word, kicking herself for the lapse about a sister. And wondering if she could ever come back.

Chapter Forty-two

"It's nowhere near as bad as twenty years ago," said Theo, "but it's straight out of the bad old days."

Jack parked his car down the street from the cemetery, directly across from Tucker Elementary—where Theo had gone to school in the sense that, on occasion, he had physically occupied space there. Charlotte Jane Memorial Park was part of Theo's old neighborhood, just two blocks away from where someone had slit his drug-addicted mother's throat and left her to die on the street. Theo had been just thirteen when he'd found her body outside Homeboy's Tavern.

"I know you hate coming around here," said Jack. "But I didn't know what to think when Mays called and said he had to meet me at McKenna's grave. Every time I start to see Mays as a potential ally, he says something that makes me think he's nothing but trouble."

"You want me to kick his ass?"

"No," said Jack, groaning. "Chuck Mays thinks he's the smartest person in the world, which means I don't want it to come down to my word against his if there's ever a dispute about what was said between us."

"So you want me to *threaten* to kick his ass."

"*No.* Just keep your mouth shut and listen. Believe it or not, life doesn't always come down to kicking somebody's ass."

Theo glanced at the school's graffiti-covered entrance, shook his head, and chuckled. "Dude, you wouldn't have lasted five minutes at Tucker Elementary."

It was late Sunday afternoon, but the cemetery was open to the public until sundown. They climbed out of the car and walked to the west entrance on Charles Street. The sidewalk was dimpled and rutted with symbols that gangs had etched into eternity when the cement had been poured twenty years ago. Jack even found one from the Grove Lords—Theo's old partners in street crime. The rusted iron gate creaked as it opened, and Jack spotted Chuck Mays and Vince Paulo standing beneath the two large oak trees that Mays had described to Jack in his directions. Jack led, and Theo followed. The sun was low enough in the sky to cast long shadows, and they'd passed just two rows of old tombs when Theo broke into his singing voice, quietly but predictably invoking the memory of Michael Jackson:

"*It's close to midnight, something something, something dark . . .*"

Theo's recollection of the lyrics expired quickly, but he was still humming the tune as they reached McKenna's grave. Jack silenced him with a glare and introduced Theo to Mays and Paulo as his "investigator." It wasn't exactly a lie. Theo had worn many hats throughout their friendship—all of them size XXL.

"Sorry about your friend Neil," said Vince.

"Ditto," said Mays.

It was already feeling awkward, standing around McKenna's tomb in an old Bahamian cemetery, talking about Neil in the past tense.

"I appreciate that," said Jack.

"It changes things, doesn't it," said Mays, "having skin in the game?"

"That's one way of looking at it," said Jack.

Mays glanced at Theo, gestured toward the bench beneath the oak tree, and said, "Have a seat, big guy." He wasn't being polite. Theo was the tallest man in the group, and Mays clearly wasn't used to looking up at anyone.

"I'm good," said Theo.

Jack said, "What is it that you wanted to show me, Chuck?"

"You see where you're standing?" asked Mays.

Jack looked around, orienting himself. Family plots marked GUILFORD and SANDS were directly behind him. His left foot was practically touching McKenna's tomb. "What about it?" said Jack.

Mays' expression turned very serious. "This morning when I came here, I saw Shada kneeling in that exact spot."

Jack glanced at the plaque beside McKenna's grave: IN MEMORY OF SHADA MAYS, it read. "You're one strange guy, Chuck. Let's go, Theo."

Mays grabbed Jack by the arm and said, "I saw her."

"Yeah, and I once had a client who looked down at his grilled cheese sandwich and swore he saw the Virgin Mary. Now let go of my arm."

"This is not a joke."

Theo grabbed Mays, his huge hand making Mays' considerable forearms seem slight. "Let go," said Theo.

Mays released, and so did Theo, but the tension hung in the air between them. It was palpable, no gift of sight required.

"Chuck is telling the truth," said Vince.

Jack still had doubts, but if Vince was vouching for his friend, Jack owed them the courtesy of an ear. "Did you talk to her?" asked Jack.

"No," said Mays. "She ran as soon as I spotted her."

"How close did you get?"

"Twenty yards."

"Show me an eyewitness who was standing twenty yards away, and I'll show you a dozen first-year law students who could rip him to shreds."

"I know it was her," said Mays.

"How can you be sure?"

"She left me a message."

Jack did a double take. The story had suddenly taken on an entirely different quality. "What kind of message?"

Mays went to McKenna's grave and knelt beside it. "Have you ever heard of a memory medallion?"

"No," said Jack.

"It's nothing super-high-tech, but it's about as computer savvy as graves get." He brushed away a little dust from a metal plate on the stone marker. It was about the size of a quarter.

"It's an added feature you can order through just about any funeral company," said Mays. "The marker comes with a weatherproof portal. If you know the password, you can hook up a USB cable and view photographs or read stories that others have left. Or you can leave something for others to see: pictures, poems, stories. Or you can do what Shada did this morning: leave a message for your husband."

"That makes no sense," said Jack. "Let's put aside all the other questions raised by her resurrection from the Everglades. If she wanted to get in touch with you after all this time, why wouldn't she just call or e-mail you?"

"Calls and e-mails can be traced. This can't. We're the only two people on the planet who even knew it existed."

"She could have just knocked on your door," said Theo.

"Not if she didn't intend to stay. Obviously, she didn't. She ran as soon as we made eye contact."

A million questions came to mind, but Jack was speechless, not sure what to ask. "Why did she run in the first place?"

"I don't know," said Mays.

"Because she thinks she can," said Vince.

Vince had a troubled expression on his face, and Jack worried that it wasn't his place to probe. But he needed to understand. "What does that mean, Vince?"

Vince patted his guide dog, and Sam sat up straight, as if his master had something important to say.

"It doesn't matter where I go, what I do, or who I'm with,"

said Vince. "I could change jobs, change my name, change my life—change my gender, if I want to get crazy about it. No matter what, I'm still blind. The man who butchered McKenna left me that way. It hasn't been easy, but I've accepted it. Shada—and this is just my take—is another story. She hasn't accepted anything. She thinks that if she runs far enough and long enough, she can get away from what happened."

No one spoke, but after a minute or two, Mays was shaking his head. "You've known a long time, haven't you, Vince?"

"Suspected. It was all so amateurish. The sleeping pills in the car. The canoe in the Everglades. Today cinched it for me. You tried to sound surprised, but—"

"I actually was surprised to see her," said Chuck. "But not because I thought she was dead. I just never thought I'd see her again, after she left."

"She just left you?" asked Jack.

"It was her idea. But I let her go."

"What do you mean you let her go?"

"Shada was a mess. She lived in fear of McKenna's killer coming back for her. She blamed me for leaving the country and not doing something about Jamal before it cost McKenna her life. She wanted out of her life, out of everything she'd ever known. I let her go."

"Why did she come back? Why now?"

"She didn't say in her message."

"Exactly what *did* she tell you, Chuck?"

"She told me that she was sorry it had to be this way. And she told me not to worry."

"Worry about what?"

"Being charged with murder."

"Whose murder?"

"Hers, of course."

Jack blinked hard, not comprehending. "Why would you be charged with Shada's murder?"

"As much as Shada tried to make it look like she committed suicide, the investigation was homicide all the way. Like Vince said, it was pretty amateurish. Is anyone here *really* that surprised that it turned out to be bullshit? Jamal was the chief suspect for almost three years, but now we know he was in Gitmo when Shada disappeared. The cops are back to square one. Any time a wife disappears, square one is the husband."

"So when Shada told you not to worry, she meant what? She's officially coming out of hiding?"

"She's coming out of hiding if—and only if—the same assholes who can't catch McKenna's killer try to pin something on me that I didn't do. Like killing her. Killing Jamal Wakefield. Or killing your friend Neil."

"Are you saying that she knows who killed Neil?" asked Jack.

Mays didn't answer. Jack pressed: "Did she tell you that in her message?"

"She told me more than she realizes," said Mays.

"Stop being so damn coy," said Jack. "What does that mean?"

"It means that Shada's message reveals enough for me and my computers to figure out where she's been for the past three years. And that's key for everyone here. Because I believe she's spent all that time—every minute of every day for the past three years—looking for the monster who killed McKenna and blinded Vince. And I think that same son of a bitch is the guy who murdered your friend."

Jack had the same suspicion, but he had no proof. And until now, he had no conceivable way of getting it. "What are you proposing?" asked Jack.

"I'm proposing that you get off the dime. We're right back where we left off before you buried your friend. Except now the pot is sweeter."

"How much sweeter?"

"My supercomputers are only as good as the data I input, and now all the pieces are within reach. I know I can find Shada. If

I can add what Shada knows to what I know, what you know, what Jamal told you, what Jamal's mother knows . . . bingo. This fucker is mine."

"You mean mine," said Vince.

"He's not anyone's," said Mays, "unless the rest of us are all on board. So what's it gonna be, Swyteck?"

A cool breeze whispered through the oak limbs overhead. Day was turning into night, and the shadows across the cemetery were now so dark that the marker on McKenna's tomb was no longer readable. A strange feeling hit Jack, but it was nothing supernatural. It was the survivor's paradox that follows every funeral—that moment when you're faced with a decision because a friend or loved one is dead, and you catch yourself wishing he were there to help you decide.

Jack glanced at Theo, but it wasn't up to him. Then he looked at Mays, and he went with his gut.

"I'd say he's *ours*," said Jack.

Chapter Forty-three

Brent and Bradley Hellendoorn, please come to the check-in counter," said the gate attendant.

Shada Mays grabbed her purse and carry-on bag, hoping for her name to be called next. The gate at the Miami International Airport's Terminal A was jammed with three-hundred-plus passengers, several of whom seemed more than capable of felony assault, if that was what it took to snag an upgrade to business class. Shada had the last available seat in the waiting area. It was right next to a family of seven, and three toddlers were tumbling on the floor in front of her. The 747 was right on the other side of a large plate-glass window, however, so at least she could keep an eye on it and make sure the flight didn't leave without her. She didn't normally worry about such silly things, but flying out of her hometown after a day like today was beyond stressful. She'd taken extra precautions to make sure no one would recognize her. Her traditional hijab dress included a half niqab, a veil tied on at the bridge of the nose that falls to cover the lower face. Only Homeland Security officers would see her full face. In hindsight, she should have worn a full niqab to the cemetery.

I can't believe Chuck came before nine o'clock in the morning.

Shada had disappeared a month before her daughter would have turned seventeen. For three birthday anniversaries running, Shada had returned to Miami to visit McKenna's grave. Any hour before noon should have been a safe time to make the pilgrimage.

Never had Chuck been a morning person—especially a *Sunday* morning person. Apparently he wasn't the late-Saturday-night party animal he used to be.

Admit it: You wanted him to see you.

Shada shook off the thought. If she'd wanted it, she wouldn't have dressed like a Muslim. Shada had never worn the hijab—never practiced any Muslim traditions—as long as she'd known Chuck. The clothing was purely an expedient form of concealment that she'd adopted since her disappearance. It fooled most people. It was funny, however, the way a man could recognize his wife with so little to go on—maybe just the way she cocked her head, the way she lifted her chin, or the tilt of her shoulders. Chuck had recognized her, all right. Even at a distance, she'd felt it register.

"Maysoon Khan, please come to the counter."

Shada immediately rose from her seat. "Maysoon" had been her name for more than two years now, and it had become as familiar to her as Shada. No longer was there even the slightest hesitation in her response to her assumed name.

There was a short line ahead of her at check-in, and she had to wait as the two brothers ahead of her insisted that they *not* sit together. It was starting to fray her nerves, all these little delays and bumps in the road. She needed to be on a plane and flying out of this city *now*, away from the most terrible of memories, beyond the reach of her old fears. Fears that kept her up at night. Fears that she had struggled to conquer since that text-message exchange on the day before she had driven her car to Everglades, staged her own suicide, and disappeared.

Are you afraid?

Not at all.

Maybe you should be.

No way. Never. I will see you tomorrow.

Beneath the veil, Shada bit her lip, trying to stop it from quivering. This time, she hadn't returned to Miami simply to visit McKenna's grave and mark another birthday never reached. For nearly three years, Shada had believed that Jamal was McKenna's killer. For nearly as long, she had lived in fear that he would find and kill her, too. She'd come to Miami to see him brought to justice. Now Jamal was dead, leaving questions unanswered as to his whereabouts not only at the time of McKenna's death, but also at the time of Shada's disappearance. It was the latter that had prompted Shada to leave the message for Chuck at their daughter's grave.

Dear Chuck,

I can never come back, not even if you wanted me to. It won't erase the past, but I promise I won't let anyone blame you for what happened to me. Or for what I made them believe happened. I'm sorry it had to be this way.

"Can I help you?" asked the attendant.

The line in front of her had disappeared, and it was Shada's turn to upgrade from coach. She placed her documents on the counter. "I'm Maysoon Khan," she said.

"Lucky you. I have one seat left in business class."

Shada watched in silence as the attendant checked her passport. With the push of a button, he reprinted her boarding pass to London/Heathrow.

"Have a nice trip home," the man said.

Home, thought Shada. It didn't feel anything like home.

"Thank you," she said as she retrieved her documents. "I will."

Chapter Forty-four

There was only one woman Jack wanted to see when he reached the airport. He found her at baggage claim.

"I missed you," said Andie as they locked in a tight embrace.

Sunday evening at MIA at the height of tourist season was like the running of the bulls in Pamplona, complete with the trampling of stragglers and the goring of innocent bystanders. Parking was out of the question, so Jack met up with Andie on the lower level as Theo burned through a half tank of gas circling the terminal. Andie was carrying a heavy winter coat and wearing a black sweater, which was way too warm for a balmy night in Florida. Jack liked her in cashmere, however, and he was feeling her warmth and breathing in the familiar smell of her hair when he realized that she was no longer a phony blond.

"Your hair—it's like it used to be," he said, smiling.

"I like things the way they used to be."

"Me, too," said Jack, his smile turning a little sad.

Two days had passed since Neil's burial, since Andie had promised to get out from undercover and return to Jack and Miami as quickly as possible. She already had her bag, but out of curiosity Jack checked the flight information on the nearest luggage carousel. She'd flown in from JFK, but Andie was on to his detective work, and she shot down immediately any notion that he had uncovered the location of an FBI operation.

"You don't really think I fly home direct from an assignment, do you?"

He supposed not. "Speaking of," said Jack, touching her newly restored hair. "I hope this doesn't mean you did something drastic . . . like quitting?"

She shook her head. "I got a week. I just thought you might like to spend it with the real me."

"You're the best."

Jack took her bag. They exited through the pneumatic doors, continued on the sidewalk past the long line at the taxi stand, and stopped at the curb. A cabdriver laid on his horn, which set off the audio version of the domino effect. Traffic was endless, eight lanes of cars and shuttle buses streaming by at something less than cruising speed at Grandpa Swyteck's nursing home. Somewhere in that mess was Theo, unless he'd gotten fed up and ditched them.

The horn blasting subsided, and Andie took his hand. "Have you thought about what I asked on Friday?"

"About what?"

"Buying us a snowblower," she said, shooting him a look. "About letting law enforcement do its job."

"Yes. I've thought about it."

Jack wanted to drop it, but Andie seemed determined to secure his agreement that trying to find out what had happened to Neil could be hazardous to his health.

"Have you been talking to Vince Paulo and Chuck Mays?" Andie asked.

Theo pulled up to the curb and popped the trunk—*Perfect timing.* Jack wedged the bag between the golf clubs and spare tire, then climbed into the rear seat with Andie. Theo steered back into the incredibly slow flow of traffic. They might as well have been moving backward.

"Welcome to the Bob Marley Taxi Company, mon," said

Theo, putting on a Jamaican accent, "where da whole world move like a stroll on the beach."

Andie rolled her eyes. "Hello, Theo."

"I like the new hair," he said, glancing in the rearview mirror. "Old hair."

"Thanks. Jack was just telling me about his talks with Chuck Mays."

"You already told her about—"

Jack groaned, and Theo caught himself, but it was too late.

Andie's expression demanded an explanation.

"Come on, Andie," said Jack. "Mays has resources that even the cops don't have. You know as well as I do that even the FBI turns to guys like him when they really need to find someone."

"Then let the FBI turn to him. You don't need to get involved."

"With all due respect to your fidelity, bravery, and integrity," he said, invoking the slogan on the FBI shield, "I'm not convinced that the FBI is entirely committed to solving this crime."

"We think it's a cover-up," said Theo.

"Thank you for translating," said Andie.

"So does Chuck Mays," said Theo.

"I'm not surprised," said Andie.

"So does Shada Mays," said Theo.

"Shada?" she said, looking at Jack.

"She's alive," said Jack.

Andie massaged between her eyes, as if staving off a migraine. "Did Chuck tell you that?"

"Yes."

"And you believe him?"

"I think so."

"She just vanished, is that it?" said Andie. "No reason."

"We don't know the reason," said Jack.

Theo wedged his way into the next lane, but traffic was still barely moving. "But we do know that Shada was cheating on her husband when she ran."

"What?" said Jack.

"It's obvious," said Theo. "Didn't you read the memorial plaque at the cemetery? 'In memory of Shada Mays.' That's it. No 'loving mother and wife.' Nothing."

"That doesn't mean anything."

"Maybe not by itself. For me, the clincher was when Paulo came to Shada's defense and said the only reason she ran was to escape from the daily reminders of her daughter's murder. Makes sense, I guess. It's also the only explanation that makes you feel sorry for a woman who basically abandoned her husband. And what does Mays do? He turns it all around and paints himself as the saint who *let* her go. A guy with an ego like Chuck Mays doesn't let go of anything, least of all his beautiful wife. She cheated, and he kicked her ass out the door. Maybe the only reason she cheated was so that he *would* kick her ass out the door. But the bottom line is the same."

"That's a big leap of logic," said Jack.

"Dude, you're talking to a bartender. You know how many guys I've talked to who got that same chip up their ass?"

Jack blinked, confused. "I think you're mixing up chips with bugs or shoulders with—"

"You know what I'm saying," said Theo.

"So she wasn't the perfect wife," said Jack. "It doesn't really matter."

"It *does* matter."

"He's right," said Andie. "It matters."

Jack did a double take. Andie had been curiously silent since the conversation had turned to adultery.

"It matters how?" asked Jack.

"You said it yourself: You think someone is trying to cover up the fact that Jamal Wakefield was in a secret detention facility when McKenna was murdered. That gives you one motive for two murders: first Jamal, and then Neil."

"Don't forget about Chang," said Theo.

"Okay," said Andie. "Throw him in there, too. It all breaks down if Shada was cheating on her husband."

Jack made a face, not comprehending. "What am I missing here?"

"Good grief," said Andie. "Don't you get it? Chuck Mays had reason to kill Jamal—or to have him killed—even after he found out that Jamal didn't kill his daughter."

"Why?"

"Dude!" shouted Theo. "Jamal was banging his wife!"

They fell silent, and Jack suddenly felt stupid. It wasn't the kind of thing he normally missed. Andie took his hand.

"Jack, this is why you need to stop playing detective. You're a smart man, but you're grieving. You were too close to Neil to see all the possibilities."

Jack glanced out the window. "How long has the FBI known?"

"Known what?"

His gaze turned back to Andie. "That Shada Mays was cheating on her husband. And that she's still alive."

"You know I can't answer that question."

"This isn't idle curiosity," said Jack. "We're talking about Neil."

"It doesn't matter who we're talking about. I can't tell you what the FBI knows."

"Then I'll make you a deal," said Jack. "Let me know when you *can* tell me. That's when I'll stop playing detective."

Chapter Forty-five

British Airways Flight 208 from Miami landed at Heathrow as scheduled. By ten thirty A.M. London time, Shada emerged from the sausage grinder that was the immigration chute and ducked into a public restroom. Ten minutes later, she was dressed like a Westerner.

Returning to her neighborhood wearing a hijab and carrying a suitcase wouldn't have been smart. There were religious laws against Muslim women traveling alone, and there were men in Somaal Town who took it upon themselves to enforce them. The hijab had been a charade anyway, simply a disguise to make Shada unrecognizable while in Miami. Maysoon Khan had never dressed that way in London.

The tube ride from the airport was over an hour, and Shada was so sleepy that she nearly forgot to change lines at the Holborn Station. The final leg of the trip home took her to Bethnal Green, and she could walk to her apartment from there.

Northeast London had been overcast and chilly when she'd left six days ago, and it was even colder this morning. Or maybe it just felt that way after the warmth of Miami. She walked briskly, her suitcase on wheels clicking at each crack in the sidewalk behind her. Every half block or so she glanced over her shoulder, back toward Somaal Town, where gangs had been known to crack skulls just to protect their turf. Even in daylight Shada checked for trouble sneaking up from behind. Her own neighborhood, up around Wadeson Street, was only slightly better, though a steady increase in trendy clubs and restaurants like Bistroteque and Bethnal Green Working Men's Club drew crowds from all over the city.

Shada climbed the front stairs to her building, dug the key from her purse, and entered the apartment. It wasn't much warmer on the inside. She left her bag at the door and walked straight to the thermostat to crank up the heat. Hunger pangs growled in her belly, but instead of going to the kitchen she went to her small study and switched on the computer. It was something she and Chuck had in common, this obsession with information. The PC took a moment to boot up, but finally the screen blinked on and brightened the room, bathing her in the blue light of her digital desktop. She jumped onto the Internet and went to the home page for the *Miami Herald*.

Shada wasn't technically a news junkie, but she had followed the local news in Miami daily since McKenna's death. The Internet made that a snap even from London. Most days were the same: nothing about McKenna. Until recently. Out of the blue, she'd read about the return and arrest of Jamal Wakefield. Each day since had brought new developments—often several breaking stories in a span of hours. The latest headline jarred her:

> Data-Mining Pioneer Is Prime Suspect
> in Wife's Disappearance

Shada knew immediately what the story meant, and the feelings of guilt and regret almost made her dizzy. But she read on:

> Three years after his wife's disappearance, Miami businessman Charles "Chuck" Mays, a pioneer in the personal information industry, is the focus of a criminal investigation. According to sources at the Miami-Dade Police Department, Mays could face charges of first degree murder.

A sick feeling welled up in Shada's throat. She forged ahead, skimming over the part about how Chuck became a millionaire, her hand shaking on the mouse as she read about McKenna's death and then about her own disappearance:

> Six months after her daughter's death, Mrs. Mays' kayak was found floating upside down in the Florida Everglades, less than a mile from her parked car. An empty bottle of sleeping pills was in the front seat. "Clearly someone was trying to make it look like suicide," said Miami-Dade homicide detective Jim Burton, but her body was never recovered.
>
> For nearly three years, police theorized that Mrs. Mays and her daughter were killed by the same man. Jamal Wakefield, a U.S. citizen and alleged "enemy combatant" of Somali descent, lived under an assumed identity at the Gitmo detention facility until January of this year, when he was transferred to Miami and charged with McKenna's murder. Just one day after his release on bail, Wakefield was brutally murdered, his body found less than a mile from where Mrs. Mays had disappeared in the Everglades.
>
> "We still believe Wakefield killed McKenna Mays," said Detective Burton. However, new evidence has led police to suspect that Mrs. Mays was killed by her husband.

Shada scrolled down, but the story offered no clue as to the nature of the "new evidence," concluding with a quote she would have expected from Chuck: " 'The charge is total bull—.' " Clicking on links to "related stories" pulled up nothing but earlier postings that she had read before.

Shada sat perfectly still, her face aglow in the warm light of the computer screen. The words she had written to Chuck at her daughter's grave replayed in her mind: "I promise I won't let anyone blame you for what happened to me. Or for what I made them believe happened."

Now what?

There was no clear answer. She owed Chuck, but was now the time to honor her promise? Or later, if and when he was formally charged? Her head hurt too much to think about it.

Shada closed out the Web page. She thought about going to bed, but her information addiction kicked into another gear. Unopened e-mails beckoned. It took her ten minutes to get through the ones under her main identity. Then she switched to another screen name—one that allowed her to be the person she wasn't. Seven messages, one for each day Shada had been gone. The first had hit just a few hours after Shada had left for Miami. The most recent was from last night. All were from the same woman. A lonely woman whom Shada had met only in cyberspace. They had been exchanging instant messages for almost a month, but of course Shada had told her nothing about her trip out of the country. Shada knew her only as kitty8.

kitty8: Hi cutie.

kitty8: Miss u.

kitty8: Where r u?

kitty8: r u playing hard to get?

kitty8: Been thinking about u soooo much.

kitty8: Do u have any clue what u r passing up?

The string of messages ended with a playful threat: *Last chance. kitty8 n88ds a FB.*

Shada smiled. She'd sent enough text messages and IMs to know that "8" was code for oral sex, and that "FB" in this context was a kind of buddy, not "Facebook." A photograph was attached, and upon opening it, Shada had to catch her breath. She'd worked hookups online before, but this was one of those rare instances where the photograph actually lived up to the "as advertised" hype. And it left no doubt as to the kind of buddy that kitty8 needed.

Shada typed a short reply—*Let's meet!*—and hit SEND. The message was on its way.

And kitty8 was in the bag.

Chapter Forty-six

The lunch crowd was thinning as Jack settled into a booth at Grunberg's Deli in downtown Miami.

"I'll have the Reuben," Jack told the waitress.

"Same," said Vince.

Vince had called that morning to suggest they talk. Jack hadn't visited Grunberg's in years, but it had been one of Neil's favorites, which made it the first place to come to mind when Vince had asked, "Where do you want to eat?" Real Jewish delis were becoming somewhat of a dinosaur in Miami. Jack could remember bygone places like Wolfie's, Pumpernik's, and Rascal House—sticky and shopworn institutions that were last refurbished when *The Honeymooners* was live on television, where the food was plentiful but never really outstanding. The experience was the draw. As Neil used to say, the hamantaschen were passable and the macaroons were okay, but there was strange comfort in knowing that perhaps it was a long-dead relative who'd left that stuffed cabbage leaf wedged beneath your booth.

"Nothing for me, thank you," said Alicia.

Jack hadn't expected Vince to bring his wife to their meeting, but it made sense. Jack had the advantage of being able to read Vince's expressions. Alicia leveled the nonverbal playing field.

"Eat *something*," said the waitress. "You're too thin."

It was standard banter between strangers in a deli like Grunberg's, but Alicia didn't quite know how to respond.

Vince said, "You do seem to have lost a couple pounds, honey."

"I'm the same weight I've always been."

"I'm not so sure about that," said Vince.

It occurred to Jack that the only way for Vince to have gained that impression was through the sense of touch. There was something to envy in a married man who knew his wife's body so thoroughly. Jack wondered if he could have done the same with Andie.

Alicia caved and ordered a bowl of matzoh ball soup, barely enough to make the waitress tuck the lunch ticket into her apron and leave them alone.

"Again, I wanted to say I'm very sorry about Neil Goderich," said Vince. "This is not an official police visit, but I did want to give you my thoughts on the man who killed your friend."

Jack helped himself to a pickle from the platter on their table. "I'm all ears."

"First, from what I've learned, it seems obvious that the killer was not blind."

Jack did a double take, then glanced at Alicia. She leaner closer to Vince and took her husband's hand.

"I didn't know anyone had suggested the killer was blind," said Jack.

Vince laced his fingers with his wife's. "The same goes for the man who killed Jamal Wakefield. Definitely not the work of a man without sight."

Again Jack glanced at Alicia, but she cast her eyes downward as she gently stroked the back of her husband's hand.

"No one would dispute that," said Jack.

"Which is what makes the case of Ethan Chang so interesting," said Vince. "The medical examiner won't say what killed him, but it was a toxin that entered his body through the top of his foot. The mall security tape captures a highly suspicious moment of contact."

"Yes, I've seen it."

"Then you know," said Vince. "Someone pretending to be blind jabbed Ethan Chang with his walking stick."

"How do you know he was posing, as opposed to really blind?"

"Generally speaking, blind guys don't have that good of an aim."

Brilliant question, Swyteck. "I guess you got me there," said Jack.

"It's not just that," said Alicia. "Tell him."

Vince drew a breath, then let it out. "If you think about it, someone went to a lot of trouble to orchestrate the death of Ethan Chang. If Chang had information about a secret detention site that someone would kill to keep secret, the easiest thing would have been to put a bullet in the back of his head. Instead, the killer pretended to be blind and jabbed him with his stick. You have to ask yourself: Why?"

Jack considered it. "No good reason comes to mind."

"He's jabbing *me*," said Vince, his voice tightening. "There is no doubt in my mind that this is the work of McKenna's killer. Which makes him the same guy who took away my sight. He's jabbing me with the stick he gave me."

Jack didn't know how to respond, but the reasoning was far from flawed. "So this is personal," said Jack.

"Isn't it for you?"

Jack didn't have to answer.

Alicia touched her husband's shoulder, and Jack noted their silent communication, the connection between them. It wasn't overdone, but it was constant in one form or another—the hand-holding; the gentle touches; the way they sat so close to each other, with shoulders, elbows, and forearms brushing together. It didn't bother Jack, except for the way it served as such a vivid reminder that he and his fiancée—sighted couples all over the world, for that matter—were moving into the digital world of texting and tweeting, the complete loss of communication through physical contact. Vince and Alicia had what Jack and Andie had lost, in spades.

The gift of blindness. The curse of sight.

"Excuse me for a minute," said Alicia. She squeezed Vince's hand as she rose, as if the unsaid words were passing from her hand to his. They had an understanding. This was the predetermined point in the conversation where Alicia was supposed to leave, and she was keeping her end of the agreement. This would be between Jack and Vince, and no one else. She gave him a kiss and left the table. When the click of her heels on the tile floor faded, Vince spoke.

"Chuck Mays knows where Shada lives. She's in London."

"I just read in today's paper that he's about to be arrested for killing her."

"That's a plant," said Vince. "I fed that story to my contacts in the media."

"Why?"

"Shada promised to come out of hiding if Chuck needed her. The media coverage about his impending arrest on murder charges will hopefully make her think it's time."

"How did he find her?"

"His supercomputers. I can't tell you the methodology."

"Have you told the FBI?"

"No. And I'm not going to."

"Why not?"

"I believe there's a cover-up surrounding Jamal Wakefield that reaches all the way back to McKenna's murder. I believe it relates to black sites, and I believe the U.S. government is involved on some level."

"Neil would have agreed with you," said Jack.

"Do you?"

Jack suddenly heard Andie's voice in his head, chiding him for even entertaining such wild conspiracy theories. "I don't know," said Jack. "But let me run wild with that thought for a second. Has anyone considered the possibility that Shada works for the government?"

"I'm betting that Shada knows something about the cover-up

and who's involved in it. Chuck wants to know what Shada knows, and he doesn't trust any government to get that information out of her without also getting her killed."

"You mean killed by a government agent?"

"More likely, killed by law enforcement incompetence. Someone in some agency failing to keep her whereabouts secret, which means that Shada could end up like Ethan Chang or Neil Goderich."

"Obviously, you have a plan," said Jack.

"I do," said Vince. "But let me be clear. I couldn't care less about terrorists who were held in black sites. My only goal is to find the man who killed McKenna. And who did this to me."

"How are you going to do that?

"It's just like Chuck told you: We pool information—including what Shada knows. Which means the next step is London."

"What makes you think Shada will even talk to you?"

"I lost my sight trying to save her daughter. Shada will talk to me."

"But she ran from her life before, and she ran from Chuck when he saw her at the cemetery. She obviously didn't want to talk to anybody. Especially her husband and his best friend."

"First of all, Shada and I were always good with each other. I warned Chuck for years that he was going to lose her if he didn't stop being such a jerk of a husband, and Shada knows that. Chuck and I agree that if there's anybody she'll talk to, it's me. Second of all, Chuck's not going with me to London."

"Not going?"

"No," said Vince. "With all this talk about a possible arrest, he doesn't want it to look like he's fleeing the country."

"You just told me that the story was a plant. And even if it wasn't, Chuck Mays doesn't strike me as the kind of guy who worries about appearances."

Vince smiled. "True enough. Which leads me to the real problem: There's this little thing about an arrest warrant out of the Old Bailey. Ten years ago, Chuck was pretty careless about what he smoked and where he smoked it. If he sets foot in the U.K., he's going straight to the slammer."

"So your wife is going with you?"

"Do you see Alicia sitting at this table?"

"No, but—"

"Look," said Vince, "what I do with my own badge is my business, but my wife is also a cop. She understands that I have a score to settle. She also understands that I can't let her throw her badge away watching me settle it."

Jack measured his words, not wanting to insult Vince. "You're going . . . alone?"

"No. Even with Sam, that would be an ambitious trip."

It was clear where this was headed, and Jack wasn't sure how to react. "You want me?"

"It was Alicia's idea. She thinks that having a criminal defense lawyer around will keep me from stepping too far out of bounds."

"What do you think?" asked Jack.

"I agree with Chuck: After what happened to Neil Goderich, I think this criminal defense lawyer has almost as much skin in the game as I do."

Jack paused. *Vigilante* was the last word Jack would have used to describe Neil. But that didn't lessen Jack's need to find his friend's killer.

"When do you leave?" asked Jack.

"This evening. Chuck is covering all expenses—airfare, hotels, meals. It won't cost you a dime."

Jack thought about Andie. Something told him that he should talk it over with her. Something told him that he shouldn't.

What would Neil do if the tables were turned?

"Guess I'd better make my sandwich to go," said Jack, flagging their waitress. "I need to pack."

Chapter Forty-seven

"Are you sure you don't want me to go with you?" asked Andie.

Jack checked on his grandfather before heading to the airport, and it was the third time Andie had asked the same question since entering the nursing home. At least she'd stopped trying to unpack his bags.

"I'm sure," said Jack.

"Go where?" Grandpa Swyteck asked.

Jack did a double take. Andie was seated in the armchair, and Jack was standing at Grandpa's bedside, but Jack thought he had fallen asleep after *Wheel of Fortune*.

"Jack is going to London," said Andie.

"Of course he is," said Grandpa. "That's where they all ran off to."

Jack had no idea what he was talking about. Too often that was the case anymore. "And then I'm going to Prague," said Jack. "I want to look up your mother's family. The Petraks."

The older man's brow furrowed into little steps of confusion, as if he were struggling to make a connection between Prague and family. Jack's gaze shifted back to Andie.

"I'm glad you're staying," Jack said quietly. "Even with Theo's friend as bodyguard, it's important that one of us be close by."

"I suppose," said Andie.

"He's still there, you know," said Grandpa, following up on his original thought. "Still in Britain."

Jack almost asked *who*, but he caught himself, recalling the neurologist's advice: Just roll with it. "Still there? Wow."

"No, I'm wrong about that," said Grandpa. "He left for the South of France in 1940. A town called Agde, I think."

"South of France," said Jack. "Sounds nice."

"Nice, yeah," Grandpa said, scoffing. "If you're a Nazi." Then he fell silent. He wasn't making much sense today, but Jack wished he would keep talking, as Andie picked up her thread of the conversation.

"I don't have a good feeling," she said, shaking her head. "I respect Vince and all he's accomplished as a cop. But the fact remains: He is blind. And you're . . . well, you're Jack."

"What does that mean?"

"I'm just saying. This could be dangerous."

"Way too dangerous!" Grandpa shouted. "That's what everyone told him. And even if he pulled it off, any fool would know there would be payback in the long run. The Germans don't just take things lying down."

Jack didn't know how to "just roll" with this one. He stayed on track with Andie. "Would you feel better if I was going with Theo?"

"No," she said. "Definitely not."

"Now I remember," said Grandpa. His finger was in the air, as if the lightbulb had come on. "He went back to Liverpool. Is that far from where you're going?"

"Not too far."

"Good. Go see him."

"I'm sorry. See who, Grandpa?"

"The general, of course. And when you see him, kick his ass. You hear me? You kick General Swyteck's ass for me!"

General Swyteck? Alzheimer's or not, Grandpa suddenly had Jack's complete attention. Even the neurologists had told him that people with Alzheimer's could have solid memories of the distant past.

"Is there really a General Swyteck?" asked Jack.

"No!"

"Then why—"

"Nono!

"Grandpa, why did you say—"

"Pio Nono! Pio Nono!"

Jack's heart sank. More ranting about the pope was not a good turn of events.

"Harry!" Grandpa shouted, calling for Jack's father. "Harry!"

The nurse entered the room, her tone soothing. "Harry is not here, Joseph."

"Harry!" he shouted, swinging his fists at the nurse. She tried to get out of the way, but Grandpa landed a punch squarely to her chest, then another to her shoulder. Jack grasped his hands, and the nurse pushed the red panic button on the wall.

"No, no! Pio Nono!"

"Grandpa, it's okay," said Jack.

The old man shouted even louder. It pained Jack to watch, pained him even more to think that his question about General Swyteck had brought about the outburst.

The nurse's aides raced into the room. Two large men went to the bed, one coming between Jack and his grandfather, the other positioning himself at the opposite rail. Jack backed away.

"It's best if you wait in the hallway," the nurse told him.

"I'm not going anywhere," said Jack.

She persisted, but Jack wasn't listening. Even with the Alzheimer's, Jack wondered if there was some thread of truth running through Grandpa's confusion over the Petraks, Czech Jews, and now this mention of a General Swyteck.

"Please, sir," the nurse said, "wait in the hall."

"I'm staying," said Jack.

"But—"

"No buts," said Jack, and then he reached for the little bit of Yiddish he'd learned from his friend Neil. "I'm here for my zeyde."

Chapter Forty-eight

Chuck Mays spent Monday evening alone at his computer, surfing the Internet. The dark side of the Internet.

Peer-to-peer (P2P) file trading was nothing new in the digital world. For years, software has allowed complete strangers to connect online to search for shared files on the computers of others. Any content that can be distributed digitally can be downloaded directly from "peers" on the same network. Most people shared music or video, which grabbed the attention of the music industry in a big way. Lawsuits over illegal trading of copyright-protected material shut down Napster in 2001, but the battle continued. Of greater interest to guys like Chuck Mays was the fact that, on the most popular peer-to-peer networks, roughly two-thirds of downloadable responses with archival and executable file extensions (especially responses to movie requests) contain malware—viruses, worms, Trojan horses—that turn personal information on a home computer into the cyberspace equivalent of an unlocked and unattended vehicle with the keys in the ignition and the motor running. P2P was a virtual smorgasbord for identity thieves.

And for all kinds of criminals.

Mays tried another P2P program and entered his password. The usual self-serving disclaimer popped up:

> This program enables access to the Gnutella file-sharing network, which is comprised of the computers of its many users. There is no central server for the files that populate Gnutella. We cannot and do not review material, and we cannot control what content may exist in the Gnutella.

Mays scrolled through the legal mumbo jumbo, then stopped at the italicized words at the bottom of the page: "*Be advised that we have a zero-tolerance policy for content that exploits children.*"

It almost made him laugh. *Yeah, and Big Tobacco has zero tolerance for sales of cigarettes to minors.*

His sardonic smile faded. It was time to get down to business. Mays was no stranger to the darkest doors in P2P, and with just a few choice keystrokes—abbreviations for words that should never be linked together in the English language—he was knocking on an old standby. With a click of the mouse, a menu popped up on his screen. A list of files followed, digital content that network peers were offering for trade. *Bloody Hairbrush Spanking* caught his eye, but he'd seen that one before, and it was tame compared to what he was trying to find. He typed in a query—*AV/IF/IB*—and waited.

A P2P chat room was a lively marketplace, and for the next several minutes, Mays stared at his screen and watched this trader link up with that trader right before his eyes. It took a little imagination, but for him, the bartering harkened back to the Roman forum. Much of it was legal. An unknown quantity was patently illegal, but no one seemed to worry about getting caught. The typical trader who flouted copyright laws was basically of the mind-set that there was no reason to pay for something that could be downloaded for free. Traders in this chat room came from a different place entirely. No matter how much money was in your bank account, you couldn't go on Amazon and buy this kind of content. You couldn't even buy it at pornstars.com. These weren't girls gone wild. These were girls gone missing.

Mays' computer chimed. His query of *AV/IF/IB*—Asian virgin in the front or in the back—had drawn a quick response. It was from someone who called himself Mustang.

What are you trading?

That was always the question. Mays took his time to formulate the right response. In a world where mere possession of illegal files meant prison time, only undercover cops posing as traders answered quickly. Sixty seconds passed. Long enough.

FMLTWIA, he typed, waiting another sixty seconds before adding the all-important number, the girl's age: *16*.

Then he drew a long drag on his cigarette, and he waited for Mustang's reply.

Chapter Forty-nine

Jack did all the right things to avoid jet lag. His wristwatch was set to London time before boarding. Plenty of water, no alcohol on the flight. He even managed to sleep a few winks before landing. Still, as they settled into their hotel room, he was having a hard time accepting that it was lunchtime Tuesday.

"You have to force yourself to stay awake until bedtime," said Vince. "Napping is the worst thing you can do on day one."

Jack was curious: *When it came to international travel, was it an advantage to be blind—no disorienting change from night and day?* But he didn't know Vince well enough to ask the kind of questions that sighted people were always embarrassed to ask.

Chuck Mays had put them up at the Tower, a business hotel and convention center north of the Thames and a couple miles south of Somaal Town. They had a junior suite on the eleventh floor with two double beds. The feather pillows looked tempting, but Jack resisted. He went to the window and opened the blinds.

"Wow, check out the view."

It was his first gaffe, but Andie's words of worry popped into his head: *Vince is blind, and you're . . . well, you're Jack.* "Sorry," he said.

Vince just smiled. "No need to apologize. Tell me what you see."

Their room faced the Tower of London, and Jack tried not to sound like a tour guide as he described the historic buildings and concentric stone walls on the bank of the river, the oldest of which dated back almost a millennium. But he was suddenly philosophical.

"It's kind of ironic," said Jack. "This whole nightmare started when Neil asked me to represent a Gitmo detainee. Now I'm on the other side of the ocean trying to find his killer, just a few blocks away from one of the most notorious torture chambers on earth."

"I seriously hope you're not comparing Gitmo to the Tower of London. Because if you are, that makes you the blind guy in the room."

Jack thought about it. "You're right. No comparison. The weather is much better in Cuba."

"That was a joke, right?"

Vince was still learning Jack's intonations, and Jack was still adjusting to a roommate who couldn't see his smirks and half smiles. "Yes," said Jack. "That was a joke."

Jack unpacked in silence—not because of any tension in the air, but because Vince was orienting himself to the floor plan, silently pacing off steps from the bed to the dresser, from the closet to the bathroom, from the desk to the minibar. Jack pretended not to notice when he banged his leg into the bedpost.

"I bet you're wondering how I'm supposed to find a killer," Vince said as he rubbed the pain out of his shin.

It was meant as a joke, but Jack picked up a hint of frustration in his voice. He imagined that if Vince were to roll up his pant leg, there would be plenty of black-and-blue badges of persistence.

"We'll figure it out," said Jack. "But on the subject of finding people, I am still curious to know how Chuck was able to track Shada back to London."

"I guess I can tell you now that you're on board. It was simple, really, once Chuck knew that she was disguising herself as a Muslim woman."

"What do you mean?"

"You won't find many women dressed in hijab who travel by themselves. It's not allowed under Muslim law. Chuck checked the flight manifests to and from Miami, looking for women with Muslim-sounding names who were traveling alone. His supercomputers narrowed things down pretty quickly."

Vince's cell phone chimed, and a mechanical voice told him who it was:

"Call from: Chuck . . . Mays."

"That's weird," said Vince.

Jack wondered how much of a coincidence it was, never underestimating Chuck's technological ability to know that they were talking about him. He continued to unpack as Vince took the call.

At first, Vince did nothing to prevent Jack from overhearing his end of the conversation, but about three minutes into the call he noticeably lowered his voice. Another minute later he went into the bathroom, taking extra care to maneuver around that dreaded bedpost.

What's the big secret?

Jack was tucking socks and underwear into the dresser drawer when he heard the toilet flush. If Vince was trying to make him think that he had really needed to use the bathroom, Jack wasn't buying it. Vince's cell was clipped to his belt, the phone conversation over, when he returned to the room.

"Chuck wants me to meet someone," Vince said.

"Who?"

"He wouldn't tell me."

"Cut the bullshit."

"I know, it's annoying. But Chuck was up all night in some kind of paranoid mood. I had to flush the toilet to convince him that I was in the bathroom, away from where you could overhear. Even then, he wouldn't tell me who he wants me to meet."

Jack was skeptical, but he wanted to believe that Vince was being straight with him. "Who do you think it is?"

"Probably a local private detective."

"When is the meeting?"

"One o'clock."

"Where?"

"A pub called the Carpenter's Arms, up on Cheshire Street. Chuck says it's about a ten-minute cab ride from here."

Jack checked his watch. "We'd better leave now."

"Well, like I said: He wants *me* to meet someone."

"You're saying I can't go?"

"For whatever reason, Chuck doesn't want you there. Don't take it personally."

Jack blew out a mirthless chuckle. "What did I come all the way from Florida for, the beaches?"

"There will be plenty for you to do. Just let me get this first meeting out of the way, and then I'll straighten things out with Chuck."

"Call him back and straighten him out now."

"Jack, come on. You of all people should understand the kind of hoops you have to jump through when your best friend is also a royal pain in the ass."

Jack wasn't totally cool with it, but Vince did have a point. Jack already had a half-dozen text messages from Theo listing all the crap he wanted Jack to buy for him in the duty-free shops.

"All right, you go," said Jack. "But are you able to get there on your own?"

"My cell has GPS navigation. If you can get me down to the taxi stand, I'm good."

Jack grabbed his coat and followed Vince out of the room. His walking cane and his memory seemed to be all the assistance Vince needed to find the elevator at the end of the hall. The lobby was bustling with conventioneers at check-in, however, which required some assisted maneuvering. With Vince at his side, Jack gained a whole new take on revolving doors. It was almost like something out of the Tower of London, and Vince seemed to be on the same wavelength.

"Is that the wheel of death I hear at the end of the gauntlet?" asked Vince.

A bellboy steered them toward a handicapped exit. Outside in the covered motor court was more chaos, and Jack led the way through a logjam of cars and buses to the taxi stand. Even with space heaters glowing overhead, the damp air was chilly enough for Jack to see his breath as they waited. Finally, a couple of tourists in front of them stopped arguing about whether or not they could walk to the Tower, and it was Vince's turn. Jack held the door open as Vince climbed in the backseat and told the driver the destination.

"Do you need me to meet you here on the way back?" asked Jack.

"No, I should be able to find my way upstairs."

Jack wished him luck, closed the door, and watched the black taxi pull away. Immediately, a feeling of complete and utter uselessness fell over him. The next cab pulled up, and the porter opened the rear door. Jack stood there. The driver called to him.

"You want a cab or not?"

Jack was about to step aside, but then he caught a glimpse of Vince's taxi at the stoplight, less than a half block away. He hadn't flown across an ocean to hang out in the hotel room. The whole exchange upstairs was gnawing at him, particularly the part that Vince had told him not to take personally: "*For whatever reason, Chuck doesn't want you there.*"

To hell with Chuck. Jack hopped into the cab and pulled the door shut.

"Where to?" asked the driver.

It suddenly amused Jack that this was his chance to say something Bond-like to a London cabbie—except that it sounded too goofy to actually say it.

"Do you see the taxi that just pulled out ahead of us?" Jack asked. "The one waiting at the red light?"

"Yeah, what about it?"

"Well . . . just do whatever he does."

The driver glanced over his shoulder and shot him a curious look. "You want me to follow that cab?"

Jack sighed, resigning himself to it. "Fine, if you must: Follow that cab."

Chapter Fifty

Vince was halfway to the Carpenter's Arms pub when his phone chimed. Again it was Chuck Mays.

"Swtyeck is following you."

"How do you know?" asked Vince.

"I'm watching it right here on my computer screen."

"You have a GPS tracking chip on Jack?"

"It's a remote installation through his cell phone. I put one on you, too."

Vince bit his lip to stem the eruption. "Chuck, you need to stop doing things like that without telling people. It's a violation of privacy."

"People need to stop telling themselves that there is such a thing as privacy."

Spoken like a true data miner, but that was another debate. "Do you want me to go back to the hotel?"

"I don't know," said Chuck. "Let me think this through. You didn't tell Swyeck who you're meeting with, did you?"

"I lied and said it was probably a detective."

"Good, then just lose him."

"What do you expect me to do, roll down the window and throw a box of roofing tacks on the road?"

"Just give the driver an extra twenty pounds to ditch him."

"That won't work," said Vince. "I told Jack the meeting was at Carpenter's Arms at one o'clock."

"Damn it! Why'd you do that?"

"Probably because I'm not at all comfortable lying to him. The three of us made a deal. This was supposed to be a team approach."

"Fuck the team! Just call Swyteck and tell him that the meeting was canceled."

The cab stopped, and Vince heard the meter register. "Seven pounds," said the driver."

Vince checked his wallet for a ten—tens were folded in half, twenties in thirds—and he told him to keep the change.

"Would you mind directing me to the pub's entrance?" he asked the driver.

Chuck overheard. "Vince, don't get out of the cab."

"Sorry, I'm going in."

"It took a lot of coaxing to arrange this. I promised it would be just you. You can't go in with Swyteck on your tail. Let me reschedule."

"I've waited long enough for answers."

"You know how skittish she is. All I did was look at her and she ran from me."

Vince climbed out of the cab. A cool mist greeted his skin, and he heard the Cockney accents of passing pedestrians—the nuances of northeast London in his perpetual world of darkness.

"I can't look at her," he said as he stepped onto the sidewalk, "which is why Shada won't run from me."

Chapter Fifty-one

Stop here," Jack told the driver. They were in Bethnal Green, a half block away from the Carpenter's Arms.

Like it or not, Jack had received a crash course in East End pub history from a driver who was apparently determined to become his new best friend. Plenty of pubs in the area claimed a connection to Ronald and Reginald Kray, the East End's kings of organized crime in the 1950s and 1960s. Carpenter's claim was more real than most. Once upon a time, it was actually owned by the Kray twins and run by their dear old mum. Somehow over the years the tiny old pub had avoided conversion to flats, and it stood in refurbished splendor at the corner of Cheshire and St. Matthew's Row.

"Try the Greene King IPA or Staropramen ale on draft," the driver said as Jack climbed out of the cab.

"Will do," said Jack.

The cab pulled away, leaving Jack alone on the sidewalk. He was standing in front of a vacant shop that had apparently sold shoes of some sort; a tattered old sign in the window read THE DEVIL WEARS PRADA, BUT THE PEOPLE WEAR PLIMSOLLS—£5. The narrow and crooked one-way street was made even narrower by a block-long construction site across from the Carpenter's Arms. Jack peered through the cold mist and saw Vince at the pub's entrance.

Jack felt a pang of guilt for tailing a blind man, but Vince's claim that he didn't know who he was going to meet was a crock, and but for the jet lag, Jack would have called him on it immediately. Factor in the pain he was still feeling over Neil's death, and maybe Andie had been right about the wisdom of deferring to the police. Chuck Mays was not to be trusted, and even if Vince was reliable under normal circumstances, these were not normal circumstances. Jack was starting to feel used, and it wouldn't be the first time that someone like Chuck had tried to hire the name Swyteck—the son of a former governor—to legitimize some scheme.

Jack was about two hundred feet away, his anger rising, when he saw Vince reach for the door at the pub entrance. Then Vince stopped. Jack's cell rang, and he answered.

"Stop following me," said Vince.

The words hit him like a brick. Jack didn't know how Vince knew, but it didn't matter. "If I go back to the hotel, I'm going back to Miami," said Jack. "Either I'm part of this, or I'm not."

"Don't be a jackass. It's not my decision. Chuck set up the meeting."

"Chuck is about to be indicted for murder."

"For the third time: That news story was a plant. Chuck didn't kill his wife."

"I'm talking about the murder of the guy who was sleeping with her. Who killed Jamal Wakefield?"

"Jamal was butchered. They cut off his foot."

"I've seen more grisly murders for hire."

"Now you're talking crazy."

"Am I?"

"Yes. But let's have this conversation later. You have no idea what you're screwing up."

"Who is your meeting with?"

"I'm not meeting with anyone if you don't get out of here."

Jack picked up the pace, now almost close enough to read the chalkboard in the window. "Are you meeting with Shada Mays?"

"I told you: Chuck set it up."

"That's the point. I'm not going to lend my name and reputation to secret meetings that I'm not a part of."

"What are you talking about?"

Jack was acting on a gut feeling that wasn't his own, but he trusted Andie and Theo, and the fact that they were of the same mind about Shada's infidelity was enough for him.

"Don't be a fool, Vince. Don't let Chuck use you."

"Use me to do what?"

"To strong-arm Shada Mays into helping Chuck get away with the murder of Jamal Wakefield."

"What?"

"You heard me," said Jack. "Are you or are you not meeting with—"

Jack stopped cold, nearly flattening a woman who had rounded the corner from the opposite direction. She, too, was frozen in her tracks—and their eyes locked.

"Jack, please," Vince said over the phone, but Jack wasn't listening. Images flashed in his mind—photographs he'd seen of Shada Mays before her disappearance. And he knew.

"Shada?" he said.

She didn't answer, and before Jack could say another word—before he could even react—she turned and ran.

"Shada, wait!"

Jack sprinted after her, trying his best to keep up. Two minutes into the chase, Jack was digging for a gear he didn't have. She was pulling away, a blur of buildings flying by as the distance expanded between them.

"Shada!" he called out.

She never looked back, never broke stride. Jack hadn't logged a five-minute mile since high school, and Shada was bettering that pace on a wet sidewalk. He pulled up at a zebra crossing, exhausted and fighting to catch his breath. The mist was turning to rain. Hunched over, hands on his knees, Jack looked up and watched Shada disappear into the old neighborhood. He wasn't surprised in the least that a woman on the run could run like the wind.

Jack was still catching his breath when a taxi pulled up at the curb. The rear window rolled down, and he spotted Vince in the backseat.

"Get in," Vince said.

Jack turned and walked the other way. The cab came up slowly beside him, matching Jack's walking pace. Vince spoke through the open window.

"I made a mistake," said Vince.

Jack didn't answer. The cab pulled ahead with a quick burst of speed, and then it stopped at the corner. Vince got out, and the cab pulled away. He waited for Jack, who had no intention of stopping. In fact, Jack already had his smart phone in hand, searching the Web for return flights to Miami.

"I'm sorry," said Vince.

Jack stopped. It wasn't every day that a criminal defense lawyer got a heartfelt apology from a cop, and Jack found himself unable to ignore it. He put his phone away.

"You should have told me you were meeting with Shada Mays."

"You're right, I should have," said Vince.

"It was beyond a mistake. Meeting with Shada Mays was the most important thing that could have possibly come out of this trip. You not only excluded me, but you flat-out lied to my face. There is absolutely no way for me to trust you anymore."

"Let me try to explain."

"Forget it," said Jack. "I never trusted Chuck, and you may not be a murderer, but now I don't trust you, either."

"Chuck didn't kill anyone."

"Obviously, he didn't kill Shada. But like I said: I have serious questions about what happened to Jamal. I should have listened to my fiancée and never come on this trip."

"Does your fiancée seriously think that Shada was sleeping with Jamal?"

Jack was silent.

Vince shook his head, scoffing at the thought. "Look, Chuck and Shada didn't have a perfect marriage. But Shada loved McKenna. She was not the kind of mother who would bed her teenage daughter's first love."

Vince was making sense, and it surprised Jack that Andie hadn't thought of that. Or maybe the whole theory that Chuck killed Jamal in a love-triangle homicide was more posturing on her part to keep Jack from going to London.

"You did the right thing by coming," said Vince. "Let me talk to Chuck and see what he can do to make this right."

Jack stopped. He'd come this far, and now he had leverage. The next nonstop to Miami was not until Wednesday morning anyway. "All right, here's one way to make amends. Chuck can tell me all about Project Round Up."

"Exactly what do you think you can learn from Project Round Up?"

Jack remembered that Jamal had been working with Chuck on Project Round Up before he'd gone missing. "My bet is that it will tell me how Jamal ended up in a detention center, and why Chuck never really believed that Jamal killed his daughter."

Jack studied his expression. Those were two huge pieces of the puzzle, but it was hard to read a man who lived behind dark sunglasses.

"It might even tell me what Shada has been doing in London for the past two and a half years," said Jack.

He was fishing, and for Jack, the trust had indeed worn thin. But it spoke volumes that Vince didn't deny any of the importance that Jack attached to Project Round Up.

"All right," said Vince. "Let's see if Chuck thinks you've earned your way into Project Round Up."

Chapter Fifty-two

Shada ran all the way to her front step. Even then, she didn't really stop. She pushed open the door, raced through the flat, and headed out the back.

Trusting Chuck had been a huge mistake. She wasn't sure how he had found her online, but he *was* in the personal information business, and it had never been Shada's intention to let her husband face charges for murdering a woman who wasn't dead. A promise was a promise, and she had tried to keep hers by agreeing to meet with Vince Paulo at the Carpenter's Arms. Instead, Chuck had sent a lawyer. Jamal's lawyer. The lawyer for the monster who had murdered their daughter.

How could you, Chuck?

It was just over a mile to her flat from Cheshire Street, but she had taken the long route around Weavers Fields to lose Swyteck. Shada had set a school record for the 10K back in the Bahamas, and with her adrenaline pumping, she was barely winded. It was unlikely that a forty-year-old lawyer had kept up with her, but she wasn't going to hang around her place to wait and find out. She ran down the alley, down the old brick streets of Vyner, past the picnic tables outside the Victory pub, past the whitewashed buildings spray-painted with gang graffiti. *Smash the Reds.* She remembered that one. She was getting close. She was running so fast that she slipped at the corner, but she caught her balance, ran inside the apartment building, and gobbled up two steps at a time to the second floor.

Her hand was shaking as she aimed her key at the lock. Even though it was crazy to think that Swyteck was closing in on her, Shada felt the need to hide, and no one would ever find her here. At least, no one had found her in the last two years.

The door squeaked as she opened it, which made her cringe. It was the middle of the afternoon—he always slept in the afternoons—and he would be furious if she woke him. She closed the door with extra care and set the deadbolt as quietly as she could, but the apartment was quiet as a tomb, and merely turning the lock sounded like a shotgun shucking.

"Maysoon, is that you?" he said, grumbling.

Funny, but the only time her new name gave her pause was when she heard the angry voice of the man who had given it to her.

"Yes, it's me," she said.

"Come here," he said.

She hesitated. The shades were pulled, and with the door closed, the apartment was black as midnight. She needed time for her eyes to adjust.

"Maysoon!"

He was definitely angry. She took a deep breath and started down the hall. The bedroom was on the left, and she stopped in the open doorway.

"What are you doing here?" he said.

Her throat tightened. Even if she had known what she was going to say, she couldn't have spoken.

"Maysoon, I asked you a question," he said, his voice taking on an even harsher edge. "What are you doing here?"

She knew that tone, and it frightened her. Telling him about Chuck and the would-be meeting at the Carpenter's Arms was not an option. She needed to deliver good news—and then it came to her.

"I have something for you," she said.

"I'm not in the mood."

She removed her coat and laid it on the chair. "You will be," she said as she stepped toward the bed.

"Let me sleep."

She pulled her smart phone from her pocket and sat on the edge of the mattress. The glowing screen assaulted his eyes.

"I said let me sleep, damn it."

She adjusted the brightness. "Check this out," she said.

His eyes narrowed as he tried to focus, and slowly the scowl on his face became a smile. The photograph obviously pleased him.

"Who is that?" he asked.

"Kitty eight," she said. "Pretty, no?"

"When did that come in?"

"Last night. She desperately wants to meet you. LMIRL," she said, invoking the texting shorthand: *Let's meet in real life.*

"When?"

She reached beneath the covers and grabbed him where it counted. "Whenever he wants."

Habib pulled her closer. "You are so good, Shada," he said, reverting to her real name.

Shada felt him getting bigger already. She pulled away slowly, laid her phone on the nightstand, and turned on a little five-watt night-light. Then she started to undress for him. Slowly. With the lights low.

The way kitty8 would.

Chapter Fifty-three

The hotel suite was quiet, but Jack and Vince were not alone. Jack's computer was on the desk, the LCD aglow with a live video feed from across the ocean. Chuck Mays was connected by webcam. Jack positioned himself in front of the built-in camera on his laptop so that Chuck could see him back in Miami. Vince sat off to the side in the armchair, close enough to hear Chuck's voice on the speaker.

"Project Round Up is by far the most important work I've ever done," said Chuck, his mouth moving a second or two behind the words, "even though I'll never make a dime from it."

"You're doing this for free?" said Jack.

"This isn't about money," said Chuck.

Jack glanced at Vince, then back at the screen. "Exactly what is it about?"

Chuck paused. He wasn't happy about it, but Vince had convinced him that the only way to make up for the way he'd treated Jack was to share the details of his prized project.

"It's about catching criminals on the Internet," said Chuck.

"Terrorists?"

"Worse."

It took only a moment for Jack to conjure up images of those newsmagazine shows on television where fifty-year-old men meet teenage girls on the Internet and show up naked at their door only to find a camera crew waiting in the kitchen. "Pedophiles?"

"Even worse," said Chuck.

"Worse than a pedophile" was a short list in anyone's universe, but Jack had met and even defended them on death row. Chuck spelled it out:

"We're talking about the sick bastards who not only savage the endangered runaways you see on the back of milk cartons, but who share their homemade videos over the Internet."

Jack bristled at the thought. "That's not at all what I expected Project Round Up to be."

"You were thinking terrorism, I presume."

"How else can you explain how Jamal ended up in Gitmo?"

"Let me rephrase your question," said Chuck, "and you can probably answer it: What do terrorists and pedophiles have in common?"

Vince chimed in. "You mean other than the fact that they should both have their balls dipped in honey and fed to fire ants? Skip the guessing game, Chuck. A little history on Project Round Up might be helpful to Jack."

"All right, here's the quick version," said Chuck. "Two months after the 9/11 attacks, Italian police raided a mosque in Milan and, to their surprise, found computers filled with images of sexually abused children. Five years later, British antiterrorism police focused on a preacher at the East London Mosque who also happened to be a former Mujahideen. They couldn't get enough to convict him on terrorism charges, but again, police were shocked to find computerized images of hard-core child pornography. Fast-forward another couple of years, again in the U.K. A Nazi sympathizer was convicted on terrorism charges, and police found thirty-nine thousand indecent images of children at his flat in Yorkshire. I could go on, but the question is obvious: Were all these terrorists into the exploitation of children for personal gratification? Or was something else involved?"

"My guess is that the 'something else' would be encryption," said Jack.

"You got it," said Chuck. "The first reports out of the *London Times* were about terrorists encoding secret messages in the digital images of child pornography."

"That seems really stupid," said Jack, "considering all of the scrutiny it gets from law enforcement. Seems like it would be a much better idea to hide messages in pictures of cookware or something else random and off the radar."

"Exactly," said Chuck. "My take was that it wasn't steganography—terrorists embedding messages in child porn. It was terrorists learning about encryption by studying the way online pedophiles traded files in peer-to-peer networks. That was when it hit me: If terrorists could go to school on these guys, so could I. Project Round Up was born."

Jack knew about P2P, but something was missing. "I'm still not clear on what your project is," said Jack.

"Show him," said Vince.

Chuck nodded readily, as if the initial reluctance to share his work had faded. In fact, he seemed proud of what he was doing, almost eager to be able to demonstrate it. "Keep your eyes on the screen," he said.

Jack braced himself, fearful that the horrific image of a pedophile's work might appear. Instead, the image of Chuck's face blinked off the screen, and it was replaced by a map of south Florida. A red dot appeared over a street on Key Biscayne.

"The dot on the screen marks the address of a convicted sexual predator who traded on the P2P network," said Chuck.

"That's less than a mile from my house," said Jack.

"That's why I chose it. Kind of brings it home, doesn't it?"

"He was trading child pornography?" said Jack.

"Not just trading. He created it. What I'm going to show you is the digital version of time-lapsed photography. You're looking at zero-hour for the launch of one of his video files. The first trade."

There was a blip on the screen, and the map enlarged from south Florida to the eastern United States. A second dot appeared over Richmond, Virginia.

"Is it that easy to track P2P trades?"

"If you know what you're looking for. Watch what happens twenty minutes later."

The map grew again, now showing the entire United States. Jack counted six dots, one as far away as Oregon.

"Two hours later," said Chuck, and suddenly there were several dozen dots spread across North America. "Four hours," said Chuck, and the map stretched to the entire Western Hemisphere. Hundreds, maybe thousands of dots from Brazil to Vancouver to Budapest and everywhere in between.

"That's Project Round Up?"

"No. Project Round Up is the ability to work backward."

"What do you mean?"

"Look at that map," said Chuck. He continued to advance the timeline—one day, three days, a week—until there were so many dots that virtually every major city on the map was covered in red. "If you didn't know that the file started in Key Biscayne, could you tell me who created it?"

"No way."

"Unfortunately, that's the point where law enforcement—usually undercover agents trading online—gets involved. After the file has been traded around the world. You nail these creeps for possession and trading, but not creation. This is what I want to do. Watch."

There was another blip on the screen, and the timeline was in reverse—the map shrinking, red dots disappearing. Finally, they were back to the first frame: one red dot over a house on Key Biscayne.

"You can do that?

"I'm almost there. My goal is to be able to work back to the camera that made the video. Like ballistics for a bullet."

"How does that work?"

The map vanished from the screen, replaced by the image of Chuck's face. "That's for me to know and the sick bastards to find out."

"Is that what Jamal was working on when he disappeared?"

"We were in the very early stages of creating algorithms to unravel trades of encrypted files. Basically he was cataloging the most popular encryption methods used by sexual predators. As I mentioned, some terrorist organizations have essentially borrowed those encryption methods from the pedophiles."

Jack worked through the implications. "So Jamal was all over the Internet downloading files that were encrypted the same way al-Qaeda files are encrypted."

"Not necessarily al-Qaeda," said Chuck, "but yes, known terrorist organizations."

"Couple that with the fact that he was of Somali descent, his father is a known recruiter for al-Shabaab, and two of his high-school classmates left Minnesota to fight in Somalia, and I can see where he would end up on an antiterrorism watch list."

"A watch list is one thing," said Vince. "A secret detention facility in Eastern Europe is another."

Jack considered it, but he didn't want to put words in anyone's mouth. "What are you saying, Vince?"

"I'm saying that we still don't know for sure that there ever was a secret detention facility in Prague. Even if there was, we don't know if it was government run."

"Actually, I'm convinced that it was not government run," said Jack, though he still did not divulge Andie as his source.

"Hell, if that's the case, maybe it didn't even have anything to do with the war on terrorism."

Jack glanced at Chuck's image on the screen, and with the slight transmission delay, the import of Vince's words hit Jack first and then carried across the ocean like a tidal wave.

"I feel stupid for saying this," said Jack, "but I've never actually considered that possibility."

"Maybe it's time we did," said Vince.

There was a flicker on the computer screen. The map reappeared, but this time it was focused on London, and the city was covered with red dots.

"Maybe Shada already has," said Chuck.

Chapter Fifty-four

Shada lay sleeping at his side. Habib was staring at the ceiling, deep in thought.

The sex had been good. Not as good as their first time, of course, but it was hard to top the illicit thrill of throttling another man's wife in his own castle. To say that he had come between Shada and Chuck Mays would have been overstatement. Never had a married woman been so ripe for the picking. It had started with the exchange of e-mails, a little flirtatious online banter, and the eventual trading of photos. Things quickly heated up with the webcam, where it was her idea to undress for him, his idea that she touch herself, their idea to meet. From then on it was good-bye to the virtual world and hello to the real pink. Habib had the perfect arrangement. Until Vince Paulo came along. And now Paulo was pounding the sidewalks of London with Jamal's lawyer. Or so Shada had told him.

Habib glanced at Shada, who was still sound asleep. The room was awash with shadows, brightened only by the dim night-light. He quietly rolled out of bed, walked to the bathroom, and washed up at the sink. Then he went down the hall to the study, unrolled his prayer mat on the floor, and faced toward Mecca. It was almost *Isha*, the last of the daily prayer times for Muslims around the world.

Salat—the formal prayer of Islam—is one of the Five Pillars of the religion, an obligatory rite for practicing Muslims that must be performed five times each day at the specified time. Habib tried not to miss *Fajr* (sunrise), *Magrhib* (sunset), and *Isha* (nightfall). *Zuhr* and *Asr* were another matter. Praying at noon and midafternoon would have required him to set an alarm clock. Sometimes he would wake himself and combine the two into one, a permissible practice known as *Jam' bayn as-Salaatayn.* More often, he slept through and substituted a late-night prayer, twisting the words of `Amr ibn `Absah, who claimed to have heard Muhammad say, "The closest that a slave comes to his Lord is during the middle of the latter portion of the night, so if you can be among those who remember Allah the Exalted One at that time, then do so." Never mind that the Prophet was talking about non-mandatory nighttime prayer *in addition to* Salat. It was one of the small ways in which Habib had distorted the teachings of Islam to suit his personal needs. He was guilty of bigger distortions. Much bigger.

Habib went to the dresser for his crocheted kufi, then stopped. Even after washing his face and hands, the smell of sex lingered, which made *Ghusl*—the cleaning of the whole body—mandatory before prayer. The removal of such impurities involved a certain step-by-step ritual, but he asked for Allah's forgiveness and simply jumped in the shower.

The drafty apartment had a perpetual chill in winter, and the hot water felt so good that Habib could have stood there for another thirty minutes. But he had missed *Magrhib* as well as *Zuhr* and *Asr,* so he was determined to be timely about *Isha.* The starting time changed each day; it began when complete darkness arrived. Some Muslims were quite scientific about it, setting the time at precisely when the sun had descended at least twelve degrees below the horizon. But no one could pinpoint the commencement of *Isha* better than a man who thought of dusk as dawn—a man who, for the past three years, had called himself the Dark.

Habib peered through the shower glass and looked out the

bathroom window. The city lights had a certain glow when it was truly nightfall, and by his estimation, he had at least another fifteen minutes. He squeezed a glob of shampoo from the bottle, his mind awhirl as he worked the lather through his hair.

The news from Shada had surprised him. It had come while they were lying naked on the bed, his heart still thumping from an intense climax. Out of the blue, she'd told him about Paulo. Habib had pressed her for details, but she'd denied that it was a prearranged meeting, and she'd offered up nothing in response to his questions:

"What is Swyteck doing with him?"

"No idea."

"How did they track you down?"

"I swear, I don't have a clue."

Habib still wasn't sure if he believed her. His initial reaction had been to blame her for being careless and somehow blowing their cover. On reflection, however, perhaps it was his own damn fault.

Could they know about the e-mail?

He was thinking about the e-mail to Jamal's father. *"I killed your son. I wanted you to know that."* Sending it had been risky. But he couldn't help himself. Memories of his sister—of how Jamal's father had gotten her to "volunteer" for martyrdom in Mogadishu—still burned like a firestorm.

I'm glad I sent it.

The bathroom light switched on, and the blast of brightness was more than he could stand.

"My eyes!" he shouted.

"Oops, I'm sorry," said Shada, and the light cut off.

He closed his eyes, soothing them with darkness, and then he opened them slowly. It was all he could do since the explosion. Sleeping by day. Working by night. Living in shadows. Running from the sun. Showering in the dim glow of a tiny night-light. Photophobia was what the doctors called it, a diagnosis that spoke more to the symptoms than the cause. For three years he'd suffered, and even though it was his own bullet that had punctured the propane tank and unleashed the destructive flash of heat and light, there was only one person to blame.

This is all your fault, Paulo. Even if you did get the worst of it.

He turned off the water, stepped out of the shower, and toweled himself dry. The bathroom window had darkened. It was past *Isha*, but he didn't feel like praying. His friends at the mosque would have told him he wasn't a good Muslim, and they would have been right.

I am The Dark.

He pulled on a bathrobe and went to his computer. Shada was only pretending to be asleep, but he didn't care, so long as she left him alone. A three-year-old anger burned inside of him. Vince Paulo had already lost his sight in the same explosion, and the Dark had shown him the mercy of leaving it at that. But if Paulo had come here like a blind fool thinking he could settle an old score, it was the Dark's intention to make him pay an even steeper price. And just as he'd done with Jamal's father, the Dark wanted the pleasure of telling him so.

He entered a stolen user ID and password to log on to an e-mail account. It wasn't the same account he'd used to contact Jamal's father, and he used a new screen name as well. One that would definitely mean something to Vince Paulo. He banged out a quick message, then stopped.

FMLTWIA. The simple act of typing in the screen name—seven letters that summed up his work for the past three years—triggered a brainstorm. The work had begun with McKenna, but it was ongoing, as enduring as the memory of what had happened to his sister in Mogadishu. He was suddenly thinking of the other little whore in the cellar, of her breach of security during his trip to Miami—her phone call to Swyteck.

That's why Swyteck is here.

Maybe she had reached out to Shada, too. The thought chilled him, but he quickly calmed himself. There was no way. It would have taken a major breakdown in his spyware for any communication to Shada to have gone undetected. And Shada would never have set up a LMIRL hookup with kitty8 if she knew about a sixteen-year-old runaway in the cellar.

Assuming there really was a kitty8.

He retrieved Paulo's e-mail address from the Miami Police Department home page before putting the finishing touches on the draft message. It didn't matter if Swyteck had brought Paulo to London, or if Paulo had brought Swyteck. They were here together, and that made for a single threat. The draft e-mail seemed fine, but he didn't want to fire off anything in knee-jerk fashion. He took a couple minutes to get dressed, then returned to the computer to read it again.

Perfect. He hit SEND, then started across the bedroom.

"Where are you going?" Shada asked from the bed.

He put on his coat—the one with the key to the cellar in the pocket—and turned to face her in the darkness.

"Taking care of business," he said.

"What does that mean?"

He stepped closer to the bed, his expression deadly serious. "It means *none* of your business," he said, letting her feel the weight of his stare for a minute. Finally, he turned and left the room, closing the bedroom door behind him.

Chapter Fifty-five

Jack was glad to hear Andie's voice on the line. It was lunchtime in Miami, and she had only a few minutes. Vince had gone down to dinner by himself to give Jack time alone to talk in the room. Jack wanted to tell her how much he missed her, but Andie wasn't one to get all sloppy on the phone in the middle of her workday.

"Theo wants to know if you're planning to hit the Tanqueray distillery," she said.

Theo was like those relatives up north who expect you to bring them back a bag of grapefruit every time you visit Florida. Jack would rather fork over twenty bucks with directions to their local grocery store. He changed the subject.

"How's Grandpa?"

"He's doing surprisingly well. We've had some good talks since you left."

"You have?"

"It's weird. Your trip to London seems to have energized him. Or at least triggered some long-term memory."

"Are you telling me there really was a General Swyteck?"

"No, but Grandpa was convincing enough that I did some research on your family."

Jack caught his breath. An FBI agent doing research on your family could be dangerous, even if she was your fiancée. "What did you find out?"

"No General Swyteck, but it turns out there was actually a Czech general who went into exile in the U.K. right around the time period your grandfather was talking about—early 1940s. And his last name was Petrak."

"Is it the same Petrak as my grandmother?"

"I haven't gotten that far yet."

The landline rang. Jack's first thought—that Vince had gotten lost in the lobby and was calling for help—was a stupid one, as he quickly realized that somehow Vince had managed to survive pretty well without him for the past three years. He put Andie on hold and picked up. It was Chuck Mays.

"Did you look at the file I sent you?"

Chuck had e-mailed Jack a key file that he had obtained through Project Round Up. It wasn't that Jack didn't appreciate how important the work was. It just took some emotional preparation to dive into this particular type of P2P trading.

"Not yet."

"What are you waiting for? Another dead friend?"

Chuck had quite the way of reminding him that he was here for Neil. But he had a point. "I'll do it tonight," said Jack.

"Let's do it now."

"I said I'd get to it."

"I'll walk you through it. It will be better that way."

Again, he had a point. Jack took a minute to say good-bye to Andie on his cell. Then he returned to Chuck on the landline and booted up his laptop. Chuck gave him click-by-click instructions to bring up the file. It was a video, as Jack had expected, and a thumbnail bearing the name Project Round Up appeared on Jack's LCD.

"That's obviously not the original thumbnail," said Chuck. "But everything else about the file is intact, exactly the material I traded for on the P2P network. Left click once, and that will bring up the original thumbnail; click again, and that will enlarge it to screen size."

Jack clicked once, and even though the icon was the size of a postage stamp, it was enough to give him pause. He clicked again and looked away.

"Do you see it?" asked Chuck.

Jack's gaze returned to the screen. The girl staring back at him was wide-eyed with fright. Jack guessed that she was sixteen, at most, and her long brown hair was tied in pigtails to make her look even younger than she was. She was wearing only the skirt from a cheerleading outfit, and across her smallish breasts someone had written a message in bold red lipstick: *FMLTWIA*.

Chuck said, "If you click again—"

"Is it really necessary that I watch this?" said Jack.

"Hey, if you want to understand the artist, you have to look at the art."

Jack had heard that analogy before, even from elite FBI profilers, and he'd never liked it. It was running way too far with Warhol's concept that "art is what you can get away with," as if there were art in savagery.

Jack took a breath and clicked again. The image shocked him, as he wasn't prepared for instant hard-core sex.

Chuck said, "The guys who crave this stuff aren't into foreplay."

The man was unidentifiable, his face completely off screen, his body filmed from the big hairy stomach down, the phallic version of the proverbial Everyman. Nothing about the girl suggested a willing participant. Jack looked away, but the audio was equally disturbing—the man inside her shouting at his underage victim, berating her on his way toward climax.

"Who did this to you, huh?

"You did."

"No! Who did this to you? Who made you into such a little slut?"

"Me."

"Say it again!"

"I did."

Jack closed the file, ending it. "That's enough. I get it."

"No, you don't," said Chuck. "I've been studying these sick sons of bitches for three years, and I still don't get it."

Jack felt a sudden urge to shut down his computer—to grab it and throw it out the window, he was so repulsed. He collected himself and said, "What I'm saying is that I 'get' the FMLTWIA. That was the text message that McKenna sent to Jamal before she was murdered."

"Let's be more precise," said Chuck. "The man who killed McKenna used McKenna's phone to send that message to Jamal. That made it look like Jamal was the killer. That's why I was so encouraged when I found these FMLTWIA videos being traded in the P2P networks."

"There are more?"

"Many more. Some sick pervert took the text acronym that high-school girls send to their boyfriends and turned it into his pornographic video signature."

Jack was almost afraid to ask, but he had to know. "Is there a McKenna video?"

"Not that I've been able to find. But my theory is that her killer made one before . . . you know."

Jack noted the break in Chuck's voice, and it was a painful reminder that this was a father talking about his child. Chuck was a tough guy, but no one could be a John Walsh all of the time.

Chuck continued, his composure restored. "That's what drives me with Project Round Up. If I can find McKenna's video, and if I can use Project Round Up to unwind the trades all the way back to the camera that created it . . . bingo."

"You found her killer."

"In fact, it may be the only way to catch this guy," said Chuck. "There are no witnesses. All physical evidence was destroyed in the fire."

"Which would give McKenna's killer good reason to go to great lengths to stop Project Round Up."

There was silence on the line, as if they were both ticking off the lives that had been lost so far. Finally, Chuck said, "I realize there are missing pieces to this puzzle."

"A few," said Jack.

"I think they'll fall into place once we get an answer to the one part of the equation that doesn't seem to add up."

Jack thought about it, and intuitively he knew it was the one thing that had troubled him all along. "Why did McKenna say Jamal did it?"

"Remind me to ask that question," said Chuck, "just as soon as I get my hands around this monster's throat."

Chapter Fifty-six

It was cold in the backseat of the taxi, but Vince didn't ask the driver to turn up the heat. A little chill in the air would keep him alert.

It was important to be alert around guns.

Vince had lied to Jack about going down to dinner. Food was the furthest thing from his mind. He was singularly focused on the e-mail message that had landed in his work mailbox, and which his screen reader had converted from text to mechanical audio. "*Are you afraid of the Dark? Admit it. You are. You shouldn't have come to London. May the best blind man win.*"

The city streets were wet, and the *whump-whump* of the windshield wipers gave rhythm to his ruminations. *The Dark.* He imagined the words were capitalized in the e-mail, and the significance wasn't lost on him. He'd heard about the signature before—scrawled on the cocktail napkin in a message to Jack at the Lincoln Road café; on the napkin from Club Inversion that police had found in Jamal's back pocket after he was killed. In is own mind, Vince had already made the connection between McKenna's killer and this man who called himself the Dark. But the reference in this e-mail to "the best blind man" was confusing. Was he blind, too? Was he talking about blindness in some other sense? Was it just more taunting? Vince wasn't sure. Nor had he determined how the Dark knew he was in London. But he recognized fighting words when he heard them. If it was a showdown he wanted, then yes, by all means: Let the better man win.

"Right turn at White Chapel High Street in twenty-five meters."

It was the computerized voice of his GPS navigator. He didn't trust taxi drivers, who had been known to rob blind people . . . well, blind.

The driver turned right, and Vince was glad to have kept him honest. They were headed for Brick Lane, an East End area once prowled by Jack the Ripper, now famous for curry houses and everything Bangladeshi. Streets were narrow and the one-way traffic was slow, so Vince used the travel time to phone his wife. The call went straight to voice mail. At the tone, he left a simple message.

"I love you."

The taxi stopped. "I love you, too," said the driver. "Four pounds fifty."

The GPS navigator announced, *"You have arrived at your destination."* It was nice to have the reassurance of technology that he wasn't being dropped off just anywhere, even if the satellite was a few seconds late.

"Which way is the Kushiara ATM?" asked Vince.

"Get out and you'll be standing right in front of it."

That was exactly where Vince wanted to be—the corner of Brick Lane and Fashion Street, south of the old Truman Brewery. He paid the fare, stepped out to the sidewalk, and closed the door. The taxi pulled away, and even though he was alone, his old friend was with him. Rain. It was abundant in London, creating a world that didn't depend on sight. Vince popped his umbrella and listened. He could hear footsteps around him, easily differentiating between the heavy plod of a passing jogger and the lighter step of a woman walking in high heels. He could feel the breeze on his face and smell the curry from the restaurant down the street. He heard a flag flapping in the breeze overhead, the clang of a bicycle bell. With a little extra concentration he could distinguish buses from trucks, trucks from cars, little cars from motor scooters. Nearby, a pigeon cooed, then another, and it sounded as though they were scrapping over a piece of bread or perhaps a muffin that someone had dropped on the sidewalk. A car door slammed. Men were talking in the distance. In some ways, he was more aware of his surroundings, or at least of certain details of his surroundings, than many sighted persons.

Are you afraid of The Dark?

The question had been poignant. Yes, sometimes he was—when he used his mind's eye to step outside of himself, and he remembered a world that was so much more than sound, smell, taste, and touch. The fearful Vince was all too aware that he lived his life largely in a reactive posture—that things still existed even if they concealed themselves and did not call out to him for recognition. He wondered what lay hidden on these old streets, how close he really was to danger—to the Dark.

"Are you Vince?"

He turned at the sound of the man's voice. "Who's asking?"

"Prince Charles."

The guy was every bit the smart-ass in person that he had been on the phone, and the Bangladeshi accent was just as prominent. Vince took the envelope from his pocket and handed it over. He could hear the man open it, presumably counting out the two hundred pounds in cash.

"You sure you don't want the submachine gun?" the man said. "It's only another hundred pounds."

The U.K. had some of the toughest gun laws in the world, but the guy was only half joking. Even semiautomatic weapons could be had for as little as three hundred pounds, and bootleg DVDs and black-market tobacco weren't the only illegal trade in Banglatown. It was all a matter of knowing the right person, and Chuck Mays had assured Vince that if he needed anything—*anything*—in the East End, an ex-pat from Dhaka named Sanu Reza was the go-to guy.

"The Glock will do," said Vince.

"We have to walk about two blocks," Reza said.

Vince unfolded his walking stick, asked the man for his arm, and placed his hand in the crook of the man's elbow. "You lead," said Vince.

"I've never brokered a sale to a blind guy before," he said as they started down the sidewalk.

Vince smiled to himself, mildly amused that both Reza and the Dark were under the same misapprehension.

"No worries," he said, thinking of the precious time he'd logged at the shooting range with Brainport back in Miami—and of the prototype of the device that his friend Chuck had shipped to the hotel. "This blind man isn't as blind as some people think he is."

Chapter Fifty-seven

It was well beyond nightfall, and the Dark walked down the alley with purpose.

Part of him had wanted to go straight from his computer to the cellar, but he kept his urge under control. The self-storage unit for his equipment was eight blocks from his flat, and it had taken almost forty minutes to walk there. It was a discipline he'd learned with al-Shabaab: Never go directly from point A to point B. Take the long route, then go around the block again, until you're absolutely sure that no one is following. Everything he needed from storage fit into his backpack, and in minutes he was on his way. The diversion had fueled his intensity, however, and he took a less circuitous route to the cellar.

He checked over his shoulder once, then put down his backpack and aimed the key at the door lock. The tumblers clicked as the lock received the key, and the feel of a perfect fit was a sensual rush—a sign of what was to come.

The Dark had waited a very long time for this, having resisted the temptation to take her so many times in the past, before the moment was exactly right. It had been six months since she had fallen into his trap. The first four had been the usual conditioning: sixteen weeks of confinement and total isolation in the cellar. She ate, slept, and bathed only when he allowed it. She wore the clothes he gave her. The lights went on or off when he said so. She had no television, no radio, no iPod, no CDs, no computer.

Then, at week seventeen, he started leaving magazines for her. Soft-core things at first, partially clothed young girls in provocative poses. At first she ignored them, but eventually boredom or curiosity got the best of her. She bit. He'd changed the material daily, each magazine a little more explicit than the one before it. The conditioning had gone much better than with her underage predecessors. She'd soaked it up, thumbing through even the images of old men having the time of their life with the oral-sex-is-not-sex generation. It had gone so well, in fact, that at week twenty he'd started letting her venture out for an hour each day with an ankle bracelet. The plan was to turn her into a recruiter, his link to more teenage girls—the way he'd trained Shada to be his link to other women.

You're next, kitty8.

The deadbolt turned. The Dark pushed the door open, locked it behind him, and started down the concrete staircase. He was just ten steps away from the secure metal door that he had installed at the lower entrance to the cellar apartment. His pack of tools was starting to feel heavy. He'd taken only the bare essentials from the warehouse, but filming without a crew wasn't easy. He needed two cameras with tripods and remote-controlled zooms for wide shots, and a handheld for close-ups. He would cut and mix later. One shotgun microphone would catch the audio. A Paglight would eliminate the grainy amateur look, even if his hypersensitive eyes did force him to wear dark glasses suitable for the snow-blind. No glasses for her. Just gold stiletto heels, a black lace thong, rope, and handcuffs.

A rush of adrenaline coursed through him as he fumbled for the second key. He was already thinking of camera angles and positioning. First-class footage was not required, but material on the P2P networks did need to be trade-worthy. The quality of some downloads he'd watched was abysmal, and once upon a time, quality hadn't mattered. His earliest ventures into P2P weren't about titillation. He was studying the ways of encryption and secret communications among pedophiles, seeing how those methods could be applied to al-Shabaab's communications. Sometimes it angered him the way this dark world had sucked him in. Sometimes.

He turned the knob and pushed open the door.

"Is that you?" she asked.

She always asked that same question, but he knew what she was really asking: *What do you want from me?* That fear in her voice was a good thing; he wished the camera were already running. He adjusted the dimmer switch on the wall to bring a little light to the room, then started toward her. She lay on the mattress in the corner, which was a good place for them to start. She'd end up on the floor. There was no written script, but as he drew closer, he could hear the first take in his head.

"Who did this to you, huh?"

"You did."

"No! Tell me who it was."

"Me."

"Who made you into such a little slut?"

"I did."

"No!" he shouted, emerging from his thoughts. "That's the wrong answer!"

The outburst made him stop, and he worried that his voice might have been heard outside the cellar. The girl looked up from the bed, her eyes wide with fear.

"I didn't say anything," she said.

He knew she hadn't, but the anger inside him was uncontrollable. Girls blaming themselves used to work for him, but not anymore. Not after what had happened in Mogadishu.

A scream—not the girl's—cut through the silence as the closet door flew open. It was as if the Dark had been hit by a charging rhinoceros. He was suddenly on the floor, flat on his back. The weight of his attacker was on his chest, and a pair of very strong hands was at his throat. He gasped for air, but his windpipe was closed.

There was another scream—it was the girl this time—and the Dark had just enough oxygen flowing to his brain to process what was happening to him. His eyes were bulging, his head was on the verge of exploding, and the man with his hands around his throat was obviously not taking prisoners. The Dark hadn't come this far to die on the cellar floor. His backpack was within reach, right where it had fallen. Even though it had seemed heavy a minute earlier, he found the strength to grab it by one strap and launch it from the floor with the force of a catapult.

Something cracked inside the backpack—or maybe it was the attacker's skull. The grip on his throat eased for an instant, as if the blow had dazed his attacker, and the Dark seized the moment. He pushed with all his strength and sent the man flying across the room. But he came right back at the Dark, and the momentum sent them both crashing into the wall. A hot wet spray slapped the Dark across the face.

Am I bleeding?

The man grabbed the Dark by the hair and slammed his head against the floor—once, twice, a third time. Each time, the Dark felt that hot spray on his face, but each blow was weaker than the last. With the fourth, his attacker fell backward, a battered heap.

It's not my blood!

The Dark tried to push himself up from the floor, but the cellar was awhirl, and he couldn't move. He couldn't even turn his head. He thought he saw the girl standing over him, but he was barely able to focus. She stepped past him. The Dark heard her voice, but she wasn't speaking to him. The words didn't register, but her tone was one of concern. She wasn't talking to a stranger.

She knows the guy.

It was his last conscious thought before the dimly lit room turned completely dark.

Chapter Fifty-eight

Jack went out looking—for what, he wasn't sure. For Vince. For Shada. For answers. He was finding none of them.

His coat was barely warm enough for a Miami winter, and his new leather gloves were touring around London in the backseat of the cab that he and Vince had grabbed at the airport. But he braved the chill, needing to get out of the hotel room and clear his head. Walking certain areas of the East End after dark was not a good idea, so Jack stuck to the route suggested by the concierge. London's streets were laid out long before surveyors with precision instruments platted the emerging cities of the New World into grid systems. Jack soon learned that it was not unusual for London streets to change names three times in the space of three blocks.

How the heck is Vince getting around here?

He stopped at the corner to check his map, but the one he'd picked up from the hotel was essentially a walking tour of World War II memorials. The East End was especially hard hit by Hitler's air raids, partly because of its proximity to the docks, partly because the attack on its heavily Jewish population fit nicely with the Nazi agenda. The dates on the memorial plaques along the route—the bombing of the Great Synagogue, Duke's Place, May 1942; the Bethnal Green Tube Station disaster, March 1943—were right around the time period that Jack's grandfather had been talking about. It got Jack to thinking about Grandpa and General Swyteck. Petrak. Whoever. Maybe he could stop by the

Czech Centre in the morning and straighten it out: *Excuse me, my eighty-seven-year-old grandfather, who talks to a dead pope and who suddenly thinks our family is Jewish, says we're related to an ex-pat Czech general from World War II. Can you help me? Oh, and did I mention he has Alzheimer's?*

"Come with me!"

Jack resisted the strange woman pulling on his arm, and when she tugged harder, he swung in self-defense, forcing her to duck out of the way.

"It's me, Shada Mays!"

Jack froze, but her grip tightened around his forearm as she led him into the pub at the corner. They settled into the darkest booth available, where Jack stared at her from across the table, too stunned to talk. She seemed out of breath, and for a moment Jack wondered if Shada had been running one continuous marathon since they'd bumped into each other outside the Carpenter's Arms.

"Where's Vince?" she asked.

"I don't know. Tell me what's going on."

She glanced nervously over her shoulder, and in the dim glow of a neon sign in the window, Jack noticed the abrasions and swelling on the side of her face.

"What happened to you?" he asked.

"I thought he was going to kill me."

"Vince?"

"No. This guy who . . . it's a long story."

"Do you need a doctor?"

"No, I'm fine. Just a little sore."

"Tell me who did this to you."

"His name's Habib. He fooled me for a long time, but I'm starting to think he killed my daughter."

Jack was speechless for a second. "Okay, I've got a lot of catching up to do."

Even the short version took several minutes. She covered everything from her infidelity before McKenna's death to the recent blows that marked her face. Jack leaned close as he listened, arms resting atop the table, trying to absorb the enormity of what she was saying.

"When I ran from you today," she continued, "I went over to his flat. After we were together, Habib went out, but he wouldn't tell me where he was going. I had a bad vibe, like something was about to snap. Sure enough, he came back a couple hours later looking like he'd been fighting. He started shouting, accusing me of double-crossing him and setting him up. Crazy stuff about how I'd blown six months of work."

"What kind of work?"

"I have no idea."

Jack retrieved his cell phone from his coat.

"Who are you calling?" she asked.

"I agreed to keep the police out of this until Vince and I were able to talk to you. Now I'm hearing that the man who beat you up may also have killed your daughter, but clearly you're not telling me everything. So I'm calling the police."

She grabbed his phone. "I'm not ready to go to the police."

"You mean Chuck's not ready to go to the police."

Her mouth fell open, and the reaction confirmed Jack's suspicion: Coordination of some sort was stretching across the ocean. "What kind of weird thing do you and Chuck have going on?"

Again, she had no answer. Jack snatched his phone back from her. Lawyer's instinct told him to make the phone call and turn this over to the police—to let Scotland Yard find McKenna's killer, perhaps Neil's killer, too. But tonight might be his only chance to find out what Shada knew. Neil would have run with an opportunity like this—and that was a good enough barometer for Jack.

"He's tracking me, isn't he? Chuck has GPS spyware tied to my cell phone, and that's how you found me on the street."

"Well . . . that may be."

"I'm giving you five minutes to make sense of this," said Jack.

"I hardly know where to start."

"Start by telling me why you think this man may be your daughter's killer."

"Habib told me he was there—in the house—when she was killed."

"He told you that today?"

"No. We talked the day after McKenna died. That was when he told me."

Jack paused, not comprehending, not sure what to ask next. One question loomed largest. "How in the world could you run off to London with the man who murdered your daughter?"

"I didn't," she said. "In fact, a big part of the reason I left Chuck—left the country—was to get away from the reminders of what had happened to McKenna. I didn't think I was running off with her killer. I was sure Jamal did it."

"Because McKenna named him?"

"Not just that. Habib told me what happened."

"His version of what happened, you mean. What was his story?"

She winced with pain, not from his question but from the bruises. Jack slid out of the booth, quickly got some ice from the bartender, and wrapped it in a napkin for her. She pressed it to her face as she spoke.

"That day McKenna died, Chuck was out of the country. Habib came over to see me. I wasn't there, but as he was walking back to his car, he heard a scream from inside the house. He knew where we hid the house key—under the pot on the porch—and when he opened the door he saw Jamal running down the stairs. Habib chased him through the kitchen and into the garage, and Jamal hit him over the head with a rake or something. Habib came to after a few minutes and heard another noise. He tried to get up but was so shaky he knocked over the garbage can. Next thing he knew, the door flew open and Vince Paulo shot at him. The bullet hit the propane tank on our barbecue. You know the rest."

It was barely plausible, and Jack called it what it was. "Everything he told you is a crock. Jamal wasn't even in the country when McKenna was killed."

"I didn't know that at the time. I kept getting threatening e-mails from Jamal all the way up until Habib and I came up with our plan—until I became Maysoon and went to live with him here in London."

"Jamal was in Gitmo when you were getting those messages."

"How was I supposed to know that? I wanted to believe what Habib was telling me. It wasn't Chuck's fault—the way he took McKenna's death so hard and blamed himself for being out of the country. But honestly, if I had stayed around Chuck another day, I probably would have ended up committing suicide for real. I thought I could start over with Habib. I thought I knew him." She moved the ice to the darkening bruise on her cheekbone. "Until today."

"You need to tell me how it got to this point."

"I told you: This is the first I've seen this side of him."

"Really?"

"Do you think I would have given up my life in Miami and moved to London for this?"

"Do you think I came all the way from Miami to get half the story? Talk to me, Shada. *Now.*"

She looked away, ashamed, then spoke in a soft voice of resignation. "My relationship with Habib had its kinky side, I guess you'd say. Never anything illegal, but he was after me to find women and set up a threesome for him. But is that so bad? Isn't that every man's fantasy?"

Jack let that one go. The walls had ears, and Andie's middle name was Walls.

"Anyway," she said, "Something set him off today."

"*What* set him off? That's the thing I'm trying to understand."

"I really don't know. He's been edgy lately, and when he came back from wherever he went tonight, it was like a bomb exploding. I had to fight my way out of the apartment. Thankfully, I can outrun just about anyone."

Jack could attest to that.

"Anyway," said Shada, "I started this conversation by asking you where Vince is."

"Chuck doesn't know?" asked Jack. "Why doesn't he just track him down with his cell phone spyware the same way you found me?"

"We tried," said Shada. "But the spyware doesn't work if you remove the battery from the cell. Vince knows that, and that's what has Chuck a little worried."

"Maybe I should check in with his wife."

"Chuck did already. If you call, she'll just worry even more."

The only other option was to call the police, but he knew the cops wouldn't help find someone who'd been missing for just two hours.

"Let's go to the hotel and wait for him," said Shada. "I need your computer."

"To find Vince?"

"No." Shada put down the ice. "I've been getting more and more suspicious since I heard Jamal was dead. Once I get a bad feeling about someone, I don't just sit around and play victim."

"Meaning what?" said Jack.

Shada dug into her pocket and pulled out a handful of USB flash drives. "While Habib was out today, I copied some files from his laptop."

"Does Chuck know about this?"

"Why do you think we tracked you down so fast when we couldn't find Vince?"

Jack was suddenly feeling better about the trust issue. "Can I see those files?"

"Not without Chuck."

"Naturally," said Jack, wondering how the world had turned before Web conferences. "Let's patch him in."

Chapter Fifty-nine

It was a ten-minute walk to the hotel. Not surprisingly, Shada was facile with the computer, and Jack zoned out as she set up communication with Chuck. Funny how the mind works, but Jack spent half that time trying to remember the name of the pub they had just left. Too many authentic pubs had converted into gastro bars—not much profit in Scotch eggs, but tuna tartare was a whole new world—and Jack thought he might want to return someday with Andie, when this insanity was over.

Hamilton Hall. That's it.

"We're good to go," said Shada. "Chuck, can you hear me?"

Jack expected to see Chuck's face on his computer screen, but it was his usual desktop even when Chuck's voice came over the speaker.

"Yeah, I'm here."

Shada explained. "Chuck has control over your computer now. We can watch what he clicks on, what files he accesses. It's as if he's in the room with us and we're looking over his shoulder."

Jack wondered how many times Chuck had done one of these remote-access jobs without people knowing it.

"Go ahead and insert the flash drive," said Chuck. He was talking about the files Shada had copied from Habib's computer.

"Which one?" she asked.

"How the fuck would I know, Shada?"

"You don't have to be nasty about it," she said.

Jack detected the tone of a man none too keen on his wife's sleeping habits. *So much for any likelihood of long-term coordination between these two.*

"I really don't know which one to choose," she said.

"Just pick one that has video content. I'm most interested in seeing what this fucker has been downloading."

His tone wasn't getting any sweeter. Jack just hoped Chuck could control his anger long enough to get the information they needed from Shada.

Shada sorted through the flash drives. She'd numbered them, presumably based on the order in which she'd copied the files. Jack filled the lull with what was on his mind. "Chuck, do you know where Vince is?"

Chuck didn't answer right away, and it was more than just a Web transmission delay. Finally, the response came over the speaker: "I haven't heard from him."

"That's not what I asked," said Jack.

More silence. Jack pressed. "Chuck, do you know something?"

"Vince is a big boy. I'm sure he's fine. Shada, the flash drive, please."

Shada selected one and inserted it in the USB port.

"I don't like being kept in the dark," Jack said.

"You're seeing the files the same time I'm seeing them," Chuck said. "How is that being kept in the dark?"

"I'm talking about Vince. You don't sound very happy with Shada, and I have this feeling that you've pressured her into creating this complete diversion to keep me from finding out what Vince is really up to."

"The files are encrypted," said Chuck.

Jack was being ignored.

"Can't you break the code?" asked Shada.

Ignored by both of them.

Jack's cell rang. He checked the number but didn't recognize it. He answered on the third ring, and the urgent voice on the line was strangely familiar.

"Mr. Swyteck? Is this Jack Swyteck?"

"Yes, who is—"

Jack stopped himself, suddenly recognizing the voice. It was the teenage girl who'd called him from Bethnal Green, who'd talked to Jamal right before he was killed, who'd claimed to know McKenna's killer—and who was too frightened to call the police. Jack drew a breath and tried not to spook her this time.

"I was hoping you'd call again," said Jack in a calm voice. "Are you doing okay?"

"No—I don't know," she said, straining with confusion.

Jack wasn't sure if it was the right thing to say, but he said it anyway: "You may not know this, but I'm in London right now. Probably not too far from where you are."

"How do you know where I am?" She sounded more than a little paranoid.

"Don't worry, I'm not following you. But I would like to meet with you, if—"

"No! I'm not meeting with anybody!"

Jack glanced at Shada, who was suddenly more interested in Jack's phone call than in Chuck's work on the computer screen.

"That's okay," Jack said into the phone. "You don't have to do anything you don't want to do."

"Is he dead?" she asked.

"Is who dead?" asked Jack.

"The man who killed McKenna Mays."

"We don't know who killed McKenna. Do you?"

"Yes! I told you before, and I told Jamal, too. He's creepy and scary and showed me pictures on his computer, and he said if I ever tried to escape I'd end up just like McKenna Mays."

Jack glanced at his computer, wondering if those pictures were among the files that Shada had copied onto the flash drive.

"What's his name?"

"I don't know."

"When did you see him last?" asked Jack.

"A couple of hours ago," she said, her voice cracking. "He came to the cellar and . . ."

"And what?" asked Jack.

She didn't answer, and the crack in her voice had mushroomed into outright sobbing. Jack wasn't sure how much longer he could keep her on the line.

"Listen to me, please," said Jack. "It's okay if you don't want to tell me where you are, but can you tell me where that cellar is?"

"No! Not if he's not dead. I saw the pictures. He showed me what he'd do to me if I ever told anyone!"

"He doesn't have to find out you told me anything."

"He knows everything! This sucks so bad. Why couldn't he die? He looked dead. "

Jack did a double take. "He looked dead when?"

"When we left."

"We?" said Jack. "Someone was with you in the cellar?"

"There was a big fight, and he just laid there as I cut off the ankle bracelet. Then we ran."

"Ankle—" he started to say, but the bracelet was secondary. "Who was with you?"

She didn't answer.

Jack tried again. "Please, I need to know who was with you."

He heard her talking away from the phone. A few seconds later, she was back on the line. "I don't know his name. And he's not answering me."

"What do you mean he doesn't answer?"

Her voice was suddenly racing. "It was really a bad fight. They both got hurt, and he seemed okay when we ran. But I'm not so sure now. I'm taking care of him, and if he has to go to the hospital I'll call an ambulance. But right now I don't want to go anywhere until you tell me that I'm not going to end up like McKenna."

"I promise that is not going to happen."

"You don't *know* that."

"I know that I can help you."

"No one can. Not until the Dark is dead!"

The Dark? "Did you just call him the Dark?"

"That's what he told me to call him—what he told me to be afraid of."

"Please, you have to tell me where you—"

Jack stopped. The line had gone silent, and he could tell she was gone. Jack immediately dialed back, but she didn't answer. It went straight to voice mail.

"Hello, this is Hassan, I can't come to the phone right now . . ."

Jack knew the voice, and it gave him chills. It was Maryam Wakefield's brother-in-law.

Jamal's uncle.

Chapter Sixty

It was almost six P.M. in Arlington, and Sid Littleton was working through dinner. The offices of Black Ice Security were on the Virginia side of the Potomac, and at sunset the shadows on the partially frozen river looked like black ice. It was on a winter day like this one, six years earlier, that Littleton had named his private military firm.

Littleton was meeting with his Washington lawyers when his cell phone rang. He checked the number. It was from London. He excused himself from the conference room so that he could return the call in private on a more secure line.

Congressional hearings into the possible existence of black sites in Eastern Europe had started on Monday. The highly politicized inquiry was making little headway, but at least one member of the House Committee on Oversight and Government Reform was chomping at the bit to grill the arrogant CEO of Black Ice Security. Littleton's testimony would begin at nine A.M., and his lawyers' job was to make him the most prepared witness from the handful of private military firms summoned to the Hill. Littleton wasn't worried. He assured his counsel that it would be over his dead body that the committee would get to the bottom of any privately run black sites. He didn't mention the other dead bodies—most recently, Neil Goderich.

Littleton stepped into his corner office, where floor-to-ceiling windows offered power views of the Pentagon and the upscale area known as Pentagon City. Seated behind the two-hundred-year-old walnut desk that his father had used as director of the CIA, Littleton picked up the phone and dialed the number. He never took a call from his chief special operations man directly. They needed to account for the possibility that Habib might be calling with a gun to his head. The protocol was for Littleton to return the call using Diffie-Hellman top-military-level cell-encryption methods. If Habib answered with the correct greeting, Littleton knew that he was talking under his own free will.

"F-M-L-T-W-I-A," said Habib.

It was the correct greeting. The men could talk freely.

"Go ahead," said Littleton.

"Major problem. I have reason to believe that some files from my computer may have been copied."

"Which files?"

"The ones Chang had."

Littleton sank in his chair. The elimination of Ethan Chang had been an easy decision. Chang had transported several detainees to the Black Ice site in the Czech Republic, and he'd even created videos of what went on there—including a few videos of Jamal Wakefield. It was brazen enough that Chang demanded serious money from Littleton to keep quiet about it. When he threatened to give the images to Jack Swyteck if Black Ice didn't pay up, he'd left Littleton no choice. The CEO did, however, have issues with the Bond-like assassination technique that Habib had chosen.

"You were supposed to destroy those files," Littleton said.

"Obviously, I didn't."

"Why not?"

"Look, if you want to second-guess, go back to three years ago, when you should never have let Jamal Wakefield leave the Czech Republic alive."

"A nineteen-year-old kid doesn't deserve to die just because he's a stupid punk in over his head."

"I beg to differ."

"I ordered his release because you were learning more about Project Round Up from Chuck Mays' wife than our interrogators could ever squeeze out of one of his employees. So don't put this problem on me, Habib. You should have destroyed the videos of what went on at that facility. Period."

"Fine, I should have. But I didn't. Right now, it doesn't matter why. We've got a problem that we have to deal with."

Littleton tried to control his anger. For purposes of handling the immediate problem, Habib was right: It mattered not why he had failed to destroy the files. But Habib would have some explaining to do once this fire was out.

"How big is the problem?"

"The only safe assumption is that the files are going straight to Chuck Mays."

"Son of a bitch! Do you understand what that means?"

"Yes."

"I don't think you do," said Littleton. "The same technology that Mays is applying to kiddy porn can be used to reverse engineer the technological DNA of *any* video he gets his hands on. He can trace those black site videos back to Black Ice, and the things we did to those detainees make Abu Ghraib and Gitmo look like a spa."

"Fortunately, you're not in the videos."

"It doesn't matter! If Mays can link that kind of abuse to my company, I'm dead. You hear me? I'm not just talking about the cancellation of DOD security contracts in Iraq and Afghanistan. I mean this literally: *I'm dead*."

"Sounds like you're hitting the panic button."

"I want to know what you are going to do about it?"

"I have the upper hand on Chuck Mays. All I need from you is a green light."

"A green light to do what?"

"To play my ace in the hole."

"Do I want to know what your ace in the hole is?"

"That's a good question. Do you?"

Littleton considered it. There was always a danger of asking one question too many in this line of work.

"You have the green light," said Littleton. "Do what you gotta do."

Chapter Sixty-one

"Your boyfriend is the Dark," said Jack.

Jack's use of "the Dark" meant nothing to Shada, but he put the pieces together and brought her up to speed on the string of notes with the same creepy messages: *Are you afraid of The Dark?*

"He killed your daughter," Jack said. "He killed Jamal. He killed a guy named Ethan Chang. He probably killed my friend Neil and Dr. Spigelman along with him. And now it sounds like he almost killed Jamal's uncle."

Chuck's reply rattled over the computer's little speaker. "How did Jamal's uncle get involved with this?"

"I've got a better question," said Jack, looking at Shada. "Who is the girl in the cellar?"

"I don't know," said Shada. "This is the first I've heard anything about that."

"It's obvious that's where Habib—the Dark—went today after he left you. And you're telling me you had no idea—"

"I had absolutely no idea," she said firmly.

"This wasn't one of your threesomes you arranged for him?"

"No way. I told you it wasn't anything illegal. And it definitely wasn't about sex with underage girls."

"Threesomes?" said Chuck.

"Oh, Chuck, like you didn't enjoy them."

"Oh, sure, here it comes. You're sleeping with the sick son of a bitch who killed McKenna, and it's all *my* fault because I turned you on to threesomes."

"I didn't say it was your—"

"Can we focus here, people?" said Jack, reaching for his cell. "Or I'm calling the police."

The sparring stopped.

"Good," said Jack. "I'm not asking you to settle all the issues between you here and now. Just behave yourselves. Now, whether you like it or, I'm calling Jamal's mother. She deserves to know."

No one argued.

It was midafternoon in Minnesota. Maryam Wakefield answered on her home phone, and Jack could hear her concern as soon as he said he was calling from London. He delivered the news as gently as he could. She caught her breath, but she didn't sound totally shocked.

"Is Hassan dead or alive?" she asked.

"We don't know," said Jack.

"I told him not to go," said Maryam, her voice quaking. "Islam has no place for vigilantism. But Hassan was convinced that there would be no justice for Jamal in a court system that treated an innocent boy like a terrorist."

"I understand," said Jack.

"When I asked you to help us sue Chuck Mays, and, instead, you teamed up with him and Vincent Paulo, that pushed Hassan over the edge."

Jack understood that, too. "How did Hassan track down the Dark?"

"His brother."

Jack started pacing as he spoke, as if energized by his own confusion. "I thought Hassan hated his brother for going over to al-Shabaab."

"He did, but Hassan would do anything for Jamal. His brother forwarded me an e-mail that he received: 'I killed your son,' it said. I showed it to Hassan, and he took it from there. I told you that the three of us used to live together in London before Jamal was born. Both brothers still have contacts in London—Hassan, especially, at the East End Mosque. As much as he hates his brother, he swallowed their differences and found Jamal's killer."

"Who is he?"

"I don't have a name. But it's someone who used to be part of al-Shabaab with Jamal's father."

Jack could hear the strain in her voice. She couldn't afford to lose Hassan on top of Jamal. "Maryam, everything is going to be okay. I want you to take a minute to collect yourself, and then you and I are going to get on a conference call with Scotland Yard. You need to tell them everything you just told me."

"No," said Chuck. "We can't call the police."

"Watch me," said Jack.

"Stop," said Chuck. "Listen to this for one minute."

"Listen to what?"

"I was treating it as my business. Now we all have to deal with it."

"Look," said Jack, "I agreed to keep the police out of this at first, but that doesn't make any sense now."

"Just listen," said Chuck. "It's the tail end of a phone call I got about twenty minutes ago."

The computer screen flickered. The transmission was audio only, and the band on the audio tracker spiked up and down with each voice inflection on the recording.

"Listen up, Mays."

Even though Jack didn't recognize the voice, he somehow knew it was the Dark. The recording continued: *"I have someone you'll want to hear from."*

Jack waited, the audio line on the LCD went flat, and suddenly it wobbled again with the beaten-down voice he instantly recognized.

"The Dark is in charge," said Vince, obviously saying what he had been told to say. "Do not come looking for me, and do not call the police. If you do, he will kill me. I'm afraid of the Dark. You should be, too."

The recording ended, and the audio line went flat again.

Chapter Sixty-two

"Good news, Paulo. The boss says I can take off your blindfold."

The Dark grabbed him by the hair, then slapped his hostage upside the head, as if Vince were the absentminded one. "Oh, I forgot. You're *not wearing* a blindfold."

He laughed way too hard at his own stupid joke, but Vince said nothing. He was seated in a desk chair, hands tied behind his back, unable to move. The Dark walked to the window and double-checked that the plywood over it was secure. They were in a spacious suite on the third floor of an abandoned hotel that was scheduled to be gutted and converted to flats. The nicest furnishings had been hauled away for auction, and only a wobbly table, a few old chairs, and a beat-up leather couch remained. There was no water or electricity, but the battery-powered lamp on the table was adequate, and when nature called, the toilet in the suite across the hall would suffice, even if it didn't flush.

"Who's your boss?" asked Vince.

The Dark pulled up a chair and straddled it backward, his chin resting on his forearms as he stared at Vince. He was close enough for Vince to feel his presence—a technique he'd perfected on blindfolded women.

"Let me explain something to you, Paulo. Your life is in my hands, which means that you will live only as long as you are of use to me. You're not the hostage negotiator here. You don't get to ask questions."

"Why did you kill McKenna?"

"Cute," he said, scoffing. "Uncle Vince wants to know *why*. After I tell you, then what are you gonna do? Fly back in your time machine and make it all better?"

The Dark glanced across the room. The device that he'd ripped from Vince's head in the scuffle outside his flat was on the floor. "This Brainport thing comes with a time-machine function, right?" he said, mocking Vince.

Vince said nothing, but the Dark could read his expression. The sunglasses had been smashed in their struggle, and Vince looked so much weaker without them.

"Very foolish of you to try to ambush me," the Dark said. "Desperate, really, even with this cool technology."

The Dark gave the device a closer look. He put on the headgear with the mounted camera, but he wasn't sure what to do with the tongue sensor. "What's this little lollipop thing for?" he asked.

"You stick it up your ass," said Vince.

The Dark pulled off the headgear, threw the Brainport onto the chair in the corner of the room, and punched Vince in the stomach so hard that it hurt his own hand. Vince gasped for air, hunching over.

The Dark shook the sting out of his fist. "How do you like that, smart mouth?"

"Did you rape McKenna?"

The Dark hit him again, and Vince let out a loud groan. "Yell, scream all you want," said the Dark. "I can fire off my gun if I want to. No one is going to hear you, except maybe a crack addict or two on the first floor."

Vince caught his breath. "Did you . . . rape her?"

"Kind of a one-track mind you've got there, partner."

"Did you?" asked Vince.

"What do you think?"

"I think you're a sick bastard."

The Dark gave him another blow to the solar plexus, the hardest one yet.

"Typical hostage negotiator's seat-of-the-pants psychology. It always boils down to sexual sadism. I hate to disappoint you, genius, but I killed McKenna because she was in the wrong place at the wrong time. It's as simple as that."

"You're a liar."

The Dark grabbed him by the jaw and held his head up, as if daring Vince to stare at him through his blindness.

"My job was to find out as much as I could about Project Round Up. If that meant sleeping with Chuck Mays' wife, so be it. If that meant hacking into Chuck Mays' home computer while he was out of the country, no problem. Unfortunately, I had no idea McKenna was home at the time. She caught me red-handed."

"There was no reason to make her suffer."

"If you gotta do it, you might as well make the most of it."

Vince lunged forward from the chair, but his hands were tied behind his back. The Dark dodged the head butt and pushed him hard to the floor. Vince was facedown, and the Dark bore his knee into Vince's spine as he pressed the cold muzzle of the pistol to the base of his skull.

"That's your second silly move of the day, Paulo."

"You're lucky I'm blind."

"No, *you're* lucky you're blind. You weren't the only one injured in that explosion. If you had walked away unscathed, I would have killed you three years ago. Probably after making you watch your wife have a go with me."

Vince jerked his shoulders back, but his resistance was futile.

"Oh, did I hit a sore spot?" said the Dark. "I thought you knew your wife sleeps around on you."

"Shut your mouth."

"A beautiful woman like that. Of course she feels sorry for

you and wants to be the good wife. But how long did you really expect her to hang with a blind guy?"

"You don't know Alicia."

"Oh, I know her all right. I'm sure she's thrilled about this Brainport contraption you've been testing. The less dependent you are on her, the less guilty she'll feel about leaving. She *is* going to leave you, Paulo. Don't mistake pity for love."

Every muscle in Vince's back tightened, and the Dark sensed the hot rush of anger, but then he could almost feel the air escaping from Vince's lungs. It was satisfying to have touched a raw nerve—to have literally deflated him.

The Dark leaned closer, whispering into Vince's ear: "Yes, I raped McKenna. I stabbed her with a kitchen knife. And I enjoyed it."

Vince lay motionless.

"Now you know everything, Paulo. Except for the one thing that I will let torment you all the way to the grave." He waited for Vince to say something, but he had gone silent. The Dark said it for him:

"Why did she tell you Jamal did it?"

Chapter Sixty-three

Jack was feeling the jet lag. It was technically still day one in London, but his body was telling him that he'd gone too long without rest. His chin snapped up off his chest as the sound of Chuck's voice roused him from a state of semisleep.

"I cracked the code," said Chuck, speaking over the computer.

"What took you so long?" asked Jack.

He was being facetious. Anything less than intelligence-grade encryption was no match for Chuck's supercomputers.

"Does that mean we can view the files now?" asked Shada.

"No need," said Chuck. "I ran them through my database. Part of Project Round Up is the cataloging of every single video file traded over the worst of the P2P networks. Trust me on this: The files that you copied from that creep's computer are not the kind of things that any normal human being would want to watch."

Jack was almost afraid to ask. "What kind of content are we talking about?"

"Some people would call it sexually explicit. I call it graphic violence."

"Not against children, I hope."

"No children in these videos. Interestingly, the violence is against grown men. By women."

That took Jack aback. "Dominatrix stuff?"

"It goes beyond that. From a trading-frequency standpoint,

the most popular video shows a woman ripping out a man's pubic hair with her teeth."

Jack squirmed at the thought, then refocused. "So are you saying that every single file that Shada copied has already been traded on the P2P networks?"

"All of them—except one."

"Which one?"

"Jamal's."

Jack went cold. "What does that one show?"

"I haven't watched it yet, and since it's never been traded on the P2P networks, I don't have the content cataloged. I thought I would pull it up now for the three of us to see."

Jack and Shada exchanged uneasy glances.

"I don't need to see it," said Shada. "This may not matter to you, Chuck, but I feel bad enough for the mistakes I've made without watching these videos."

Chuck didn't bite, unwilling to acknowledge her contrition just yet.

"What about you, Swyteck?" he asked. "Jamal was your client."

Jack wasn't eager to say yes, but if Jamal's mother was going to hear about this from anyone, he wanted it to be from him, not Chuck. "I should," Jack said, bracing himself, "so I will."

Chapter Sixty-four

Andie put her head down, pulled her wool scarf up over her nose, and walked into the wind. It was snowing in the Washington area. Tiny flakes fell from the night sky, flickered beneath the glow of streetlamps, and gathered on the wet sidewalk in front of her. No doubt some tourist was giddy with excitement over postcard-quality photographs of the illuminated Capitol or Jefferson Memorial. Andie wished she were in Miami. The Ritz-Carlton Hotel was right across the street, which made her think of Jack. He'd probably booked the romantic-weekend package a half-dozen times at the Ritz on South Beach, but something had always come up and forced them to cancel. "Something" was code for the FBI.

Sorry, Jack.

Andie still wasn't convinced that it was safe to return to Vortex. She'd left the company heliport on Sunday with the definite impression that Bahena was having doubts about his trainee. But it wasn't Bahena who had called to insist that she return tonight to discuss her "immediate activation." The call had come from the top. From the CEO of Vortex's parent company. From Sid Littleton himself.

"You're close," Harley had told her. "You have to go back."

Andie knew her supervisor was right.

An inch of new snow blanketed the sidewalk, and it squeaked beneath each step. Commuters had been heading home since lunchtime in anticipation of the coming storm. Even so, a long line of glowing orange taillights streamed up the street toward the on-ramp to the expressway. There were few pedestrians—just Andie and a lone lunatic jogger. A woman, Andie noted as she trudged by her. A pregnant woman. Now *that* was dedication: In her sixth month, easily, and superwoman was out jogging in a snowstorm. She probably worked sixty hours a week at a major law firm, too. Dropped off her three older children at three different private schools on her way to work. Hit the gym every morning at five A.M., even if it meant getting up at four to put the cookies in the oven for the Cub Scout bake sale. Teleconferenced with teachers over lunch, organized charity events on weekends, sang the barking puppy to sleep at two A.M., always had her highlights done before her hair hit "scare alert," and made love to her husband four times a week whether they wanted it or not.

Is that who Jack thought he was engaged to marry?

Andie hurried up the granite steps to the building's after-hours entrance. The adrenaline was kicking in. From the very beginning, Black Ice had been an exhilarating mission: uncover the truth about the interrogation tactics used at black sites operated by Black Ice through its highly secretive subsidiary, Vortex Inc. The plan was to place an FBI agent in the role of an interrogator in training. And now the reason was clear why it had to be a female agent: Black Ice used female interrogators to berate and humiliate Muslim men in the name of "enhanced interrogation."

Still, there was the question: Why her? Of all the female FBI agents who worked undercover, why did the bureau choose Miami agent Andie Henning? True, she was an experienced undercover agent who, over the years, had fooled everyone from cult leaders to Wall Street investment bankers. But she was no expert in counterterrorism. And that was beginning to bother her. *Really* bother her.

She stopped at the top of the steps before entering the building and dialed her supervisory agent.

"Harley, it's me."

"Everything okay?" he asked.

"Fine. Before I go back in, there's just something I need to get off my chest."

"What is it?"

Andie stepped closer to the building, away from the falling snow. "I'm in this role, and it's my duty to see it through. But I'm not naïve about why I was chosen."

"What are you talking about?"

"This is a broad investigation into private security firms. I don't see it as coincidence that I'm investigating Black Ice."

"Of course it's no coincidence. There is a key role for a woman."

The cold air made her sniffle. "Or is it a key role for Jack Swyteck's fiancée?"

"What do you mean?"

"I don't know for sure yet. But my instinct tells me that I'm about to find out that I'm investigating the same black site in Prague that was at the heart of Jack's alibi defense in the murder case against Jamal Wakefield."

There was silence on the line. Andie took it the only way she could.

"I knew all along that Jack and I were playing on the same field," she said. "But I can't believe the bureau would put me in a position where my job would intersect with Jack's like this."

She heard his sigh on the line. "I'm sorry," said Harley.

"It's sleazy, at best," she said.

"I agree," said Harley. "I want you to know that I was just as surprised as you are."

Andie paused. Something about the way he said it—something about Harley—made her believe him. "I'm still going to raise hell about it when this is all over."

"Okay. But there's something else I want you to know," he said.

"What?"

"I'll help you."

"Thank you," she said.

Andie ended the call and tucked her phone away. She brushed the snow off her shoulders, then slid her passkey through the electronic reader at the main entrance.

The door to Vortex Inc. opened. The security guard greeted her in the lobby.

"Welcome back, Ms. Horne."

"What do you think, Leon?" she said as she shook the snow from her scarf. "Do we get extra points for working the night shift in a blizzard?"

"No, ma'am. But at least we're not alone. Mr. Littleton still hasn't gone home yet."

"That's good to know," she said—and she meant it.

Chapter Sixty-five

Jamal's video was short. Jack's recovery time would be much longer. It was amazing how high a naked man could be made to jump from the table with a well-placed cattle prod. More than the image, however, it was the sound of Jamal's screams that would stay with Jack.

"Okay," said Jack, collecting himself. "If being Jamal Wakefield from Miami gets you this kind of treatment, I now have a better understanding of why he went to Gitmo pretending to be a Somali peasant who didn't speak English."

"Not to mention the fact that being Jamal Wakefield could land you on death row for a murder you didn't commit," said Chuck, who was still on speaker.

Shada shook her head. She hadn't watched, but Jack's summary gave her the flavor. "I don't understand why they would record this kind of conduct on video."

"This came up at Gitmo," said Jack. "It's a matter of interrogation expedience. If I'm questioning you, it may be that all I have to do is show you the video of what I did to Jamal. You'll probably start talking before I do the same thing to you."

"Let me make sure I understand," said Shada. "All those videos that I copied from Habib's computer—those are all men who were tortured at the same black site Jamal was at?"

"It looks that way," said Chuck. "The interesting thing is that we would never have made that connection if you had not brought us the Jamal video."

"Explain that to me," said Jack.

"I mentioned to you before that one of the functions of Project Round Up is to trace video files all the way back to the camera that created them. My computers confirm that all these files—Jamal's included—were created with the same camera. Without Jamal's file, you might think that all the other files were just more sick pornography traded on the P2P network. Jamal's was the only one not traded on P2P. His video is the missing piece in the puzzle that links all of this activity to torture at a black site."

"There's something that still doesn't add up for me," said Shada.

"Tell me," said Chuck.

"I understand what Jack said about interrogation expedience as a reason to create these videos. But creating them is one thing. Somebody took these files and put them on the P2P network. Why?"

"That's a good question," said Jack.

"I can answer that in two words," said Chuck. "Trade value."

"What does that mean?" asked Shada.

Jack was with him. "It means that the way to get content on a P2P network is to trade something in return."

"You got it," said Chuck. "In plain English, if I'm a sick son of a bitch who wants to watch movies of a preteen girl having sex with her mommy's boyfriend, the easiest way for me to get it is to trade something for it."

"Hard to imagine someone wanting to watch a woman rip out a man's pubic hair," said Shada.

"Are you kidding me?" said Chuck. "Do you remember the photos of that female soldier sitting on a pile of naked men at Abu Ghraib? That left a lot of men clamoring for more explicit abuse. For some guys, this stuff is very sexual, very much a turn-on."

"Obviously someone saw this black site as a P2P trading gold mine," said Jack.

"And that someone was Habib," said Chuck. "He had a steady

supply of videos that showed leather-clad women torturing men. Not simulated stuff. Real blood, real violence. He could trade that for whatever turned him on. Torture of women. Child pornography. Snuff. You name it."

Shada closed her eyes, absorbing the blow, as if the pain of her terrible miscalculation kept digging deeper.

Jack heard a phone ringing over the speaker. Someone was calling Chuck.

"It's from London," said Chuck. "Let me plug you guys in so you can hear. Don't say a word."

Jack moved closer to the computer, and Chuck answered. The voice on the line matched the one in the recording Chuck had shared earlier—but this was live.

"I want two hundred fifty thousand pounds, cash," the Dark said. "Small bills. Or I kill Paulo."

"When?" asked Chuck.

"Tomorrow morning. Early."

"That's very short notice."

"You're a rich man. Make it happen."

Jack wanted to speak, but he held his tongue and, instead, fired off an e-mail to Chuck.

"How do we make the exchange?" asked Chuck.

"I'll call you tomorrow at half past five with instructions."

"Five thirty A.M. *London time*?"

"Yes."

"You must be joking."

"I'm joking only if your idea of a punch line is a bullet in your friend Paulo's head."

Chuck paused, and Jack hoped he was reading his e-mail. "One thing," said Chuck. "I want to talk to Vince. I need to know he's alive."

Jack could breathe again; his e-mail had gone through.

"Blow me," said the Dark. "Get the money and you get to talk to Paulo. And by the way: Shada, if you're listening, I know you copied some files from my computer."

Shada stiffened, and Jack squeezed her hand for reassurance—and to make sure she said nothing.

"That makes me very angry," the Dark said, "but I'm a reasonable man. I want you, personally, to deliver the money tomorrow. If you do, we'll call it even. If you don't . . ."

The line went silent. The Dark was gone.

Jack tried to get Shada to look at him, but she was staring at the floor, numb. "Listen to me," said Jack. "If that's the game he wants to play—insisting that Shada deliver the ransom—we need to revisit the idea of just calling the police."

"No," said Shada. "He'll kill Vince."

"It's not an option," said Chuck. "I could run this guy through every conceivable database, and I guarantee you he'd show up on every terrorist watch list in the world. You know what that means for hostage negotiation."

Shada looked even more worried. "What does it mean?"

Until now, Jack hadn't thought it all the way through, but he quickly caught Chuck's drift.

"The United States has repeatedly stated that as a matter of official government policy it does not negotiate with terrorists," said Jack. "Even though we're not on U.S. soil, Vince is an American law enforcement officer. Scotland Yard will likely respect U.S. policy."

Shada's eyes widened. "If we don't negotiate, Vince is a dead man."

Chuck said, "Do you disagree with that analysis, Jack?"

Jack processed it. "I can't disagree."

"So what's it going to be, Shada? Can you deliver?"

She was staring at the computer screen even though it was blank.

"Shada," Chuck repeated, "what's it gonna be?"

Chapter Sixty-six

Vince was alone in the hotel room. His ribs ached. The side of his face felt swollen. The Dark certainly knew how to deliver a punch. But Vince was proud of himself.

If the Dark knew Jack Swyteck was in London, he hadn't heard it from Vince.

Vince had spent his time alone counting steps, trying to diagram the floor plan in his head. More precisely, he was counting the sound of the Dark's footsteps each time he crossed the room. Eight steps, twelve o'clock, from the door to the chair Vince was tied to. Six steps, one o'clock, from Vince to a table or a counter where the Dark had popped open a beer or a soda after beating the daylights out of him.

Three steps, nine o'clock, from Vince to the chair on which the Dark had tossed the Brainport after Vince had told him to stick it up his ass.

You weren't the only one injured in that explosion.

Those words kept swirling around in his head, and he wondered what the Dark had meant by that. Vince's memory of the explosion in the Mays garage was fuzzy—pushing through the door, the gunshot, the deafening percussion, the flash of light . . . and then nothing until he awoke in the hospital. Rescuers were already in the driveway and acted fast enough to save his life, but not his sight. Firefighters arrived too late to keep the house from burning to the ground. He was lucky to be alive, was the way he tried to look at it—which meant that the Dark, too, was lucky.

You weren't the only one. . .

Vince could only speculate, and his thoughts ran the gamut on the possible injury to the Dark. Third-degree burns to his skin? Ringing in his ears? Vince wanted the satisfaction of knowing that the Dark had gotten the worst of it, that the man who had murdered McKenna had paid a price. Short of death, what could be worse than blindness? *Millions of things*, Vince told himself.

But at that moment, he couldn't think of one.

The door opened, and Vince heard someone enter. It closed quickly, and the chain lock rattled. Then Vince heard footsteps . . . *one, two, three* . . . and the sound of a heavy sack or backpack dropping onto the luggage rack. A zipper opening—too long for a backpack, maybe a suitcase. Finally, there was the unmistakable sound of a magazine loading into a firearm. The Dark had been out gathering supplies.

"Amazing how much crap you can accumulate in self-storage," the Dark said smugly.

It was a safe bet that there was more than one handgun in that suitcase. It had sounded like an arsenal, the thud with which it had landed on the luggage rack.

"I have to use the bathroom," said Vince.

"Go in your pants."

"You won't like the smell in the room."

The argument was a convincing one, even if Vince didn't really have to go.

"Fine," said the Dark, starting toward him.

Vince was immediately counting footsteps again. *One, two, three . . .*

The Dark put a gun to Vince's head before untying him. "Don't try anything stupid."

Six steps, at eleven o'clock, from Vince to the suitcase filled with weapons.

"No problem," said Vince, the floor plan etched in his brain. "Nothing stupid."

• • •

Andie was still in the main lobby and waiting for an elevator, surrounded by polished granite, glass, and chrome. Her cell chimed. The number was familiar, but it was a dummy—merely a trigger for her to call in to her supervisory agent. Less than five minutes had passed since her last conversation with Harley. The quick callback was cause for concern.

She glanced across the lobby, and on the other side of the plate-glass window the snow was falling even harder. She would never have called her contact from the Black Ice offices on the twelfth floor, but the building lobby was essentially public space. She dialed, gave her contact name, and listened.

"Bad news from Scotland Yard," said Harley. "They lost track of Hassan."

"We've been tailing him for two months, and they lost him in *two days*?"

"He attended a prayer session at the East End Mosque. They watched him go in, but they didn't see him come out."

"How can that be?"

"In the Yard's defense, twenty thousand people come and go from that mosque every week. They lost him for about eight hours."

"So they've reconnected?"

"Only because he's in the Royal London Hospital. Someone found him unconscious in a public park or athletic field in the East End and called for an ambulance. Paramedics picked him up and brought him to emergency."

"How did he get hurt?"

"Hassan isn't talking. I don't know if he's in a coma, but he still has not regained consciousness. The only report I have is that he took a bad blow to the head."

"Any idea who did it?"

"No confirmation yet. But it's possible that an order issued out of Black Ice."

She knew what he was saying: Hassan had gotten too close to the truth about his nephew's detention, and one of Littleton's special-ops guys was on the job. But that didn't mean the FBI's read of the situation was correct. "What do you want me to do?" she asked.

"I just want you to be aware and know that I have a team on alert if you need to be extricated."

"Is Jack in any danger?"

Harley paused, as if reluctant to say what he had to say. "Andie, I understand your concern about the way your assignment intersects with Jack. I told you I would be on your side when the time comes to make an issue out of it. *Now* is not the time."

"I'm not saying I'm going to make an issue out of it."

"You can't call him. Not at this juncture."

A janitor rolled a trash can past her. She waited for him to pass, which gave her a moment to think about her response. But she still didn't know what to tell her supervisor.

"Andie, you can't jump in and out of role as you please. I promised you that this operation was on the verge of wrapping up, and you agreed to come back and finish what you'd started—no more leaves of absence. That's the assignment, and that means you can't call Jack."

She considered it further.

"Andie, did you hear what I said?"

"Yes, I heard you," she said, acknowledging only that.

Jack and Shada rode down the elevator in silence. Step one was to get their hands on the cash, and Jack had to defer to Chuck on that part of the plan. For the next couple of hours, at least, Jack had no choice but to follow Chuck's instructions.

The elevator doors opened to an empty lobby. A black taxi was waiting in the motor court on the other side of the revolving door. Before heading out, Jack took the opportunity to pull Shada aside and make one last plea.

"You don't have to do this," he told her.

"We can't call the police. You and Chuck are in agreement on that. I'm the one Habib wants."

"The delivery is always negotiable, especially when all we're talking about is the person who makes the drop. Chuck can manufacture an excuse for you."

"Then who is going to do it?"

Jack paused, not quite believing what he was about to say. "I will."

"You? Why should you do it?"

"Why shouldn't I?"

"Because you don't owe Vince anything."

That wasn't exactly true, but the fact that Vince had once stood up to a crazed hostage taker and negotiated for Theo's release wasn't the driving force here. "This isn't about who owes what to whom," said Jack.

Her eyes welled. "You couldn't be more wrong."

"What do you mean?"

"Don't you understand? I owe everybody. I betrayed my husband. The lover I took turned out to be the man who murdered our daughter. Vince lost his sight trying to save McKenna from him. It's time for me to step up and do something about it."

Jack couldn't argue with her feelings.

"I'll make the delivery," she said. "That's final."

Jack followed her through the revolving door, and they climbed into the back of the cab. Shada announced the address.

"Bengali Town?" the driver said. "Nothing much open up that way at two A.M."

"You'd be surprised," said Shada. "Hurry, please."

Chapter Sixty-seven

The cell rang just as the Dark finished untying the ropes. He pressed the gun to Paulo's forehead and checked the incoming number. It was Littleton calling from his encrypted line at Black Ice. The Dark took it, but only briefly.

"I'm not alone," he said. "Call me back in ten minutes."

He tucked his cell away and started retying the knots.

"What are you doing?" asked Paulo. "I have to use the bathroom."

"You're just going to have to wait."

He pulled the rope snug and placed duct tape over Paulo's mouth. "Just a precaution," said the Dark. "Like I told you: Yell, scream, kick, and stomp all you want. We're the only ones in this building."

He tucked his pistol into his belt and locked the door on his way out. There was an emergency stairwell at the end of the hall, and the LED on his key chain provided sufficient light to find it. The lock on the fire door at street level was busted—probably the work of vagrants—making it easy to come and go. He stepped into the cold night and checked things out. Traffic was nonexistent, and the wet pavement glistened in the fuzzy glow of streetlights. Hanging out in front of the abandoned hotel could draw the attention of the police, so he walked to the corner and waited for Littleton's call.

The neighborhood was in late-night lockdown, storefronts

hidden behind roll-down security shutters or accordion-style metal doors. A stray cat scurried past him on the sidewalk and disappeared into a burned-out shell of a condemned building. Windows in the flats above the shops were dark, save for one. Standing on the corner, he could see right inside. A television threw more than enough light to reveal all to the outside world, and it was surprising how many residents lacked the sense to pull the bedroom shade. Not long ago that the White Chapel rapist had walked these streets. People had short memories. Most people. Not the Dark, especially not when it came to rape—the rape of his youngest sister.

Stop it, the Dark told himself, angry for having allowed his thoughts to turn to his own ugly past. He checked his watch. Four more minutes until Littleton would call back—an eternity when there was nothing to do but dodge his own memories. In his mind's eye, he could see the tears on her face, the terror in Samira's eyes.

Her clothes were torn, and when she finally stopped sobbing, he could hear the fear in her voice. She didn't want to talk, but as he dragged the truth out of her, Habib could almost smell the other men—men she did not know by name, but from her description, the Dark knew it was al-Shabaab. Probably even men he had worked beside in Mogadishu. Habib took his sister to Abukar—Jamal Wakefield's father—for justice.

"Do you have four male witnesses?" asked Abukar.

"Samira was raped," said Habib. "The only witnesses are the men who did this to her."

"Have these men confessed?"

"The punishment is death," Habib said. "Why on earth would they confess?"

Abukar waved his hand, dismissing them. "Then there is no rape to be punished."

"What?"

"The law is clear," said Abukar. "The rapist must confess, or there must be four male witnesses."

Samira spoke up. "The Koran requires four witnesses to prove that a woman has committed adultery, not to prove that she was raped. You are twisting things for your own purposes."

"Quiet!"

"You're twisting it the way Westerners do when they want to defile Islam!" she shouted, her voice shaking.

"Stop, woman!"

"I was raped!"

"Enough with your false accusations!" said Abukar. "You have brought shame on your family."

"Shame?" said Habib. "Look at her!"

"I've seen how she looks at men," said Abukar, "the way she tempts them. Her thoughts are impure. The shame is on Samira and her family!"

The Dark's cell rang, jarring him from his memories. It took a moment to shake off the anger—the stinging memory of how, brainwashed by a cunning and convincing older woman chosen by Abukar, Samira had walked into a crowded market in Mogadishu and "cleansed herself" of her shame.

"Go ahead," the Dark said into his cell phone.

"I've been thinking about our conversation," said Littleton. "We need a plan to recover those files that were taken."

"That's impossible. Even if I get the originals back, there is no way to account for every possible copy that could exist. It's the technological version of trying to put the genie back in the bottle."

"Damn you, Habib! How could you have been so stupid? You should have destroyed those files!"

Littleton was shouting a string of obscenities, as if that would change the fact that the videos were out there. It only made the

Dark angrier. He was a young man who had believed in a cause when, years ago, he'd spent countless hours online for al-Shabaab, studying the state-of-the art encryption methods of pedophiles, trying to duplicate their methods for terrorism. It wasn't Habib's fault that, after viewing thousands of explicit videos, sex with underage girls didn't just seem normal. It became a turn-on. It remained his obsession.

"I don't understand it, Habib! What in the hell were you thinking?"

What could the Dark tell him? That the cloud had a silver lining? That if Project Round Up hadn't led Chuck Mays to the black site torture videos that the Dark was trading on the P2P networks, the Dark might never have discovered that Jamal Wakefield was actually Abukar's son? That this bit of good fortune was the only reason the Dark even bothered to prostrate himself in daily prayers anymore? That it had been worth all the pain and aggravation to show Abukar that he couldn't even protect his son by harboring him on the run and turning him into Khaled al-Jawar?

It would have been perfect, in fact, had it not been for Vince Paulo and the explosion.

"No more!" he shouted into the phone.

"No more what?" asked Littleton.

"I made myself clear in the last call," the Dark said. "I warned you that the files were out there. I didn't need your permission to play my ace in the hole, but I asked for it anyway, which put you on notice that dead cops might be involved. Now it's every man for himself."

"So your ace in the hole is what—your exit strategy?"

"Yes. And I suggest you get one. Because in less than eight hours I'm playing my hand, and my ace in the hole will be a dead man."

He ended the call, tucked away his phone, and started back to the old hotel.

Chapter Sixty-eight

Their taxi stopped in front of a tiny East End establishment with a big sign that read BANGLATOWN CURRY SHOP. Jack counted at least twenty restaurants up and down the narrow street that looked almost exactly like it. Not one was open for business.

"I told you everything would be closed," the driver said. "If you're hungry, I know a little place not far from here."

"This will be fine," Shada said.

Jack paid the fare, and when the cab left, they were the lone signs of life on the block. It wasn't hard to imagine the street clogged with cars and delivery trucks, the sidewalks jammed with people from all walks of life from around the world. In a matter of hours, tourists and regulars alike would stop to decipher exotic menus posted in the windows, and by the end of the day, the guy at the pushcart on Brick Lane would hear customers order the jellied eels in at least twenty different languages. From two A.M. to four A.M., however, was a dead zone, when the eerie pall of urban quiet fell.

"I guess this is why they call New York the city that never sleeps," he said.

"Don't kid yourself," said Shada as they passed a wall covered with BLM gang graffiti. "This is Brick Lane Massive territory."

Jack followed her around the corner to the back of the curry shop. Many of the windows along the alley had been bricked over, and burglar bars and metal shutters covered those that remained. Jack recognized more BLM graffiti tags on the walls, but most of them had been spray-painted over by "White Flatz" and "Bow E3," suggesting a turf war. It made Jack want to walk faster. Chuck had called ahead to say they were coming, and the light burning over the rear entrance indicated that someone was indeed expecting them. Rather than knock, Shada made a quick call on her cell. Someone on the inside started working the locks, and from the sound of it, Jack had visited jails with less security. Finally, the door opened.

"Come in, please," the man said.

Jack followed Shada inside, and the man introduced himself as he closed the door and refastened the locks. His name was Sanu Reza from Dhaka. Chuck had already told them about Reza's earlier meeting with Vince.

"I'm so sorry to hear about Mr. Paulo," he said.

"I'm sorry you sold him a gun," said Jack.

"I do as Mr. Mays requests. That makes tonight your lucky night."

Jack could only wonder.

Reza led them down a dark hall past the kitchen, and the lingering smell of curry made Jack hungry. They stopped at the solid metal door at the end of the hall. A separate alarm system protected whatever was beyond that door, and Reza entered the pass code. There was another set of locks to unfasten, too. Finally, he pushed open the door and switched on the light. Bags of rice were stacked from floor to ceiling. Boxes of spices lined another wall. Reza directed them inside and locked the door.

"An awful lot of precautions to protect rice and spices," said Jack.

Reza smiled. "Old family recipe."

A PC hummed on the desk in the corner. Reza took the chair in front of the glowing LCD and logged on. "You there?" he asked.

The computer screen flickered and Chuck's image appeared.

"Welcome to Banglatown," he said. "First things first: Reza, show them the money."

Reza popped a switchblade and cut open one of the bags. Rice spilled to the floor, but not much. Reza reached inside and, by the handful, pulled out twenty-five bundles of fifty-pound-sterling notes. Jack didn't ask where it had come from, but with the East End's history of organized crime and gang graffiti all over the neighborhood, he didn't really want to know. Reza stacked the bundles of cash into four neat piles on the table.

"Two hundred fifty thousand pounds," he said.

It wasn't nearly as bulky as Jack had expected; he could have stuffed it in his coat pockets and walked out.

"What will I carry it in?" asked Shada.

"How about a big bowl of yogurt and cold cucumbers?" said Jack. It was how patrons of Bengali restaurants put out the fire in their mouths.

"Good one, Yank." Reza pulled a backpack from a shelf and handed it to Shada. "In my neighborhood, this will draw much less attention than a briefcase."

Jack picked up one of the stacks and examined it. "Is this real or counterfeit?"

"Absolutely real," said Reza. "The only qualification is that in one of the stacks I will insert a bogus bill that contains a miniature GPS tracking system. Chuck will be able to follow the money after Shada delivers it."

"Doesn't GPS require a battery?" asked Jack.

"It's all in the same bill. I'm talking *miniature.* The battery will only last twenty-four hours and is set to beep out the coordinates every fifteen seconds. It sleeps between signals."

"Which bill gets the GPS system?" asked Shada.

"That's not important," said Chuck.

"I'd like to know," said Shada.

"I'm not telling you," said Chuck, his tone taking on an edge.

"What do you mean you're not going to tell me?"

"It's better that you don't know," said Chuck.

"Better for *whom*?"

"It's for your own safety."

"That's bullshit, Chuck, and you know it. Tell me which one has the damn chip in it."

"Shada, back off," said Chuck.

Jack could see the anger in her eyes, and even though Shada had expressed remorse for what she had done, it was also clear that she was approaching her limit with Chuck. Jack jumped in before they could tell each other to shove it.

"Folks, can we all take a deep breath and remember why we're here?"

Slowly, the tension drained from the room, and before anyone could stoke the fire, Jack changed the subject.

"I understand that there is no talking Shada out of making this delivery," Jack said. "I can also understand why she feels the way she does. But I'm here for a reason, too." He paused as thoughts of his friend caught up with him. "If Shada is going to put herself at risk, I want to provide backup."

"No," said Shada.

"Why not?" asked Jack.

"It's better that you don't," she said, glancing at Chuck's image on the screen while parroting his words. "It's for your own safety."

"Now we're getting petty," said Jack. "I'm sure everyone is overtired."

"I agree with Shada," said Chuck.

"What?" said Jack.

"There's no reason for you to tail her," Chuck said. "We've got the GPS tracking embedded in the bills. If something goes wrong, we'll call the police."

It didn't sound like Chuck—taking the safe route and suggesting that they call the police in a pinch—but Jack was getting too tired to argue. "We have a little more than two hours until the call," said Jack. "Let's all try to get some rest."

Reza said, "There's a two-bedroom flat upstairs that you can use."

"Works for me," said Shada.

"Me, too," said Jack.

"Shada, no hard feelings?" said Chuck. It was the first bone he had tossed since finding out about the Dark, and it seemed to take Shada by surprise.

"Whatever," she said.

"Good night, everyone," said Chuck.

Reza logged off the computer and led them from the storage room, locked the door behind them, and reset the alarm. A back stairwell led them up to the second-floor flat. Reza directed Shada to the bigger of the two bedrooms, and Jack took the small one with the twin bed. He needed sleep, and he hoped his mind would shut off and let him rest.

"I'll wake you at five," said Reza.

"Thanks," said Jack. He sat on the edge of the mattress, and even though it was lumpy, all worry about falling asleep vanished. One shoe was off when his phone chimed with a text message. It was from Chuck: *Just between u and me*, it read, and the last two words were in all caps: *FOLLOW HER*.

Jack pulled off his other shoe, typed a response, and hit SEND: *Do you trust her?*

He settled back onto the mattress, exhausted and staring at the ceiling, his phone resting on his chest. Chuck's response came sooner than he'd expected: *Would you trust your wife after she cheated?*

The question hit Jack hard. Shada had been so contrite that he'd actually let himself believe that Chuck should be more like those I-love-you-no-matter-what guys who forgive and forget. But when the question was turned around on him—would *you* trust *your* wife?—he realized that this was the real world, not Lifetime TV or the Oxygen Channel. Jack typed out his response, then rolled over and turned out the light as he hit SEND once more:

OK. I'll follow.

Chapter Sixty-nine

Sid Littleton watched from his office window as the snow fell on the illuminated buildings and monuments of the capital.

The phone call from London had been unsettling, but Littleton always had a backup plan. The plan's name was Lisa Horne—or whatever her real name was—and he just hoped the weather wasn't going to screw things up and keep her from coming to the office on short notice.

"She's in the building," said Bahena.

Littleton turned away from the window and saw his right-hand man standing in the doorway. Danilo Bahena had been with Littleton since the formation of Black Ice. Most of the company's four hundred employees didn't know him. Very few knew he was the mastermind of the black sites that the company ran for the CIA. Only Littleton knew him as the specialist who would do *anything* to see a mission succeed.

"Good," said Littleton. "Go down, take her to the limo. I'll meet you there."

"You sure? I could just take her for a ride. Very treacherous roads tonight. Accidents could happen."

"No," said Littleton. "We need to know who she is first."

"Her name is not Lisa Horne, that much is for sure."

"If she's an investigative journalist chasing rabbit holes, that's one thing. If she has some other agenda, I want to get to the bottom of it."

"Whoever she is, she knows too much."

"That may be," said Littleton. He turned back to the window, thinking. The gist of the warning from London replayed in his head: *I have my exit strategy. You need yours.*

"Get the limo," he said, watching his own reflection in the window. "And let's be quick about this."

Chapter Seventy

Jack lay awake in the glow of his smart phone.

The text message from Chuck had made it impossible to sleep, and Jack made the mistake of surfing the Internet to numb his brain. For the heck of it, he followed up on Andie's conversation with Grandpa Swyteck and searched "General Petrak." He could have spent all night reading about the daring plot of the Czech resistance to assassinate Reinhard Heydrich, Hitler's planned successor, and how the general in exile coordinated it from the U.K. It didn't make them Jewish, but Jack hoped that there was *something* to his grandfather's ramblings, that perhaps they were somehow related to this Petrak—but that was for another day.

He put the phone away and closed his eyes. He wasn't dreaming—sleep that deep didn't come so soon—but in his mind's eye he saw himself at Brookfield Zoo with his grandfather. He was five years old and enthralled by the polar bear exhibit. Suddenly, Grandpa was gone. Jack was alone and surrounded by strangers.

He shot up in bed and grabbed his smart phone. Jack had been getting lost in strange places since childhood. Tailing Shada would require a working knowledge of the area, and Jack spent the next hour studying maps of the East End. In Miami, the rule was CRAP: Courts, roads, avenues, and places flowed north and south—top to bottom—like the stuff we get from our bosses. As best Jack could tell, the only way to make sense of London was to ask, "Which way to the nearest tube?"

"It's five o'clock," said Reza. He was outside the door.

Jack couldn't believe it. "Be right down," he said.

Jack went into the bathroom and splashed cold water on his face. He'd had no sleep in the last twenty-four hours and about five hours total—thankfully, he'd slept on the flight from Miami—in the last thirty-six. He'd tried murder cases on less rest. Another two hours tonight would have been just enough to revive the jet lag. A quick shower brought him to life, and he was downstairs in fifteen minutes.

The kitchen was already bustling. The Banglatown Curry Shop was a traditional Bengali restaurant where spices were ground by hand and mountains of vegetables were chopped with pride and precision. One team filleted the morning's delivery of fresh fish, while another cut whole chickens into parts. Two men by the wood-burning oven were arguing in their native tongue, and Jack guessed it had something to do with the cooking temperature.

"Hungry?" asked Reza as he handed Jack a plate. It was fruit, a multigrain bread, and yogurt. Jack thanked him as they headed down the hall, but before they reached the locked door to the storage room, Reza pulled him into a tiny office and closed the door. "Shada is already inside," said Reza, "so let me be quick. Chuck is going to extend an olive branch and tell her which bill has the GPS in it."

That didn't jibe with last night's text message from Chuck, but Jack kept quiet, not sure if Reza knew about the exchange.

"Of course, there will be a second bill that we don't tell her about." He handed Jack a cell phone. "As for the backup, use this when you follow Shada."

"My cell works fine here."

"This one is linked to Shada's cell. Chuck and I installed spyware last night while she was asleep. It allows you to hear what she says so long as she has her cell with her, even if she's not talking on the phone."

"How close do I have to be?"

"Technically, it's supposed to work up to six or seven kilometers. But wireless can be dicey in urban areas, especially if she goes indoors. To be safe, Chuck wants you to stay within two hundred meters."

"What if she sees me?"

"That's more than likely, but it doesn't matter. Chuck played it perfectly last night, and telling her where the GPS chip is this morning will reinforce the trust. The important thing is that she thinks it's *your* idea to follow her, not Chuck's. People get nervous when Chuck has one of his men on their tail. No offense, but you're an amateur. She might get her knickers in a knot if she sees you, but she won't abort the mission."

Jack tried not to feel insulted.

"I've also programmed a panic button," said Reza. "Just hit the star key if you want to call the police. For all other calls, use your own cell."

Jack tucked the spy phone into his pocket. Reza unlocked the desk drawer and removed a pistol. "Chuck also thinks you should be armed. I have a Glock nine millimeter. Do you know how to use it?"

"No gun."

"Chuck thought you might know how to use it, being engaged to an FBI agent."

"Andie has actually turned me into a pretty good shot. But this is the U.K., not Texas. Not the place to risk arrest for carrying a concealed weapon."

"Suit yourself." He put the pistol away and locked the drawer. "Any questions about the cell phone?"

"Just one," said Jack. "How long has Chuck had that same spyware on *my* cell?"

"Good one, Yank," he said, smiling and shaking his head as he led Jack out of his office. "That's a real good one."

Chapter Seventy-one

The Dark slept not at all, which was a normal night for him. He would sleep on the plane to Hong Kong after the money was in hand and Paulo was dead.

Last-minute changes to the plan had necessitated another trip to the storage shed. That little unit would have been the envy of al-Shabaab, had he still been loyal to them. Somewhere down the road, when the bodies were recovered and the Dark was on the other side of the globe, Scotland Yard would uncover the cache, and the Western media would report that another Muslim was preparing for jihad. As if every jihad involved war and violence. As if this struggle had anything to do with Allah.

The Dark stopped at the corner. Sunrise was still hours away, and it was cold enough to see his breath. Morning rush hour was just barely beginning, a few cars streaming by. A man and a woman huddled beneath the shelter at the bus stop. The nearest tube station didn't open until five thirty A.M., but an hour from now waves of commuters would flood into the underground like water into a storm sewer. The Dark was eight blocks from the abandoned hotel, just in case anyone was triangulating his wireless call and trying to pinpoint his location. Chuck Mays' cell was on his speed dial. He punched "8" and waited.

"I'm here," said Chuck.

"Is Shada in or out?"

"She's in."

The Dark smiled thinly. "I knew she would be. Now listen

closely, because I'm not going to repeat this. Shada must come alone. Tell her to take the money to Billingsgate Fish Market."

"The fish market?"

"Just *listen*. I know Shada a hell of a lot better than you ever did, and I'm being very reasonable about setting up the exchange in a public place. The fish market is probably the busiest place in London this early. Hundreds of people around, so there's no reason for her to get scared of her own shadow and freak out. The ground floor has two cafés. Shada is to find the one nearer to the shellfish boiler room, take a seat, and wait."

"When do we get Vince back?"

"When I get the money. Understood?"

"Yes, but—"

"No 'buts.'"

"But you—"

"Quiet! Do you want your friend dead or alive?"

"You said I could talk to Vince in the morning."

The Dark gripped the phone, angered by the audacity. "There's plenty of morning left," he said, seething as he ended the call.

For some of us.

He tucked the phone away and started back to the hotel.

Jack's cell rang as he stepped out of the Curry House's storage room.

The Web conference following the Dark's ransom demand had gone exactly as Chuck and Reza had choreographed it. Shada was ready to make the delivery. Jack would tail her—after he took this phone call.

He ducked into Reza's office and answered it.

"It's me," said Andie. "First thing I want to say is that I'm sorry."

"For what?"

"For pressuring you to drop the Jamal Wakefield case."

There was a knock, and then Jack heard Reza's voice on the

other side of the closed door. "We have to go, my friend."

"Andie, don't worry about it," said Jack. "We can talk when I get home."

"No, you don't understand. When I found out that you were trying to prove the existence of a black site, I had no idea that I was investigating the same black site that was at the end of your trail."

Jack's jaw dropped. "What?"

"It's complicated, and I'm so angry with the bureau right now that I can hardly stand it. But you were representing Jamal ever since he was Khaled al-Jawar, Prisoner No. 977 at Gitmo. Obviously, the FBI knew he was really Jamal Wakefield, which means they knew his lawyers would eventually get into the issue of black sites in Prague. It was no coincidence that I was given this assignment. Someone high up thought they could play the national security card and pressure me into compromising your case. Or at least throw you off the trail of the black site in Prague, if need be."

Jack lowered himself into the desk chair. He was having trouble getting his head around this one. "Wow. Andie, it's five thirty in the morning here, I've hardly slept, and . . . just, wow."

There was another knock at the door. "Jack," said Reza, "we *really* have to go."

"Andie, this is all good to know," said Jack. "But I—"

"*Good to know?*" said Andie, incredulous. "Jack, I could be fired for telling you this. But here's the point. I don't know what exactly you're doing over there in London, but you need to know that the people who ran this black site are beyond evil. Don't kid yourself into thinking otherwise. Please, *please*, don't take unnecessary chances."

The door opened, and Reza stuck his head into the room. "Hang up the phone. We're leaving."

Andie asked, "Who was that?"

Jack hesitated too long, but Andie's tone changed abruptly. "I gotta go," she said. "Be careful, Jack. I love you."

"I love you, too," he said, and the call ended.

Chapter Seventy-two

The Black Ice limo cruised through the night at forty miles per hour, top speed in a snowstorm like the one that was slamming the Mid-Atlantic region. Andie glanced out the dark-tinted windows. She'd seen few cars on the road tonight, virtually none since they'd exited the expressway. Bahena had told her that they were headed for the airport, but she had her doubts.

"Doesn't look like a good night to fly," she said.

Littleton didn't answer. He was seated across from her, facing forward. Andie was in the other bench seat with her back to the cockpit. The chauffer's partition behind her head was closed, leaving her and Littleton in privacy. They were forty minutes into the drive, and he had yet to speak a word to her.

Not a good sign.

Andie had ended the phone call with Jack in the nick of time, before Bahena had come around with the company limo. She'd made riskier calls while working undercover, and this one should have gone undetected. But she was beginning to have doubts.

The limo slowed, then pulled off the road to a stop. Andie glanced out the window. They were outside the glow of city lights, nowhere near an airport—nowhere near anything she recognized.

"Why are we stopping?" she asked.

Littleton stared at her, his face illuminated only by the dim, blue glow of the liquor cabinet to Andie's right.

"Who are you?" asked Littleton. His tone was not cordial.

"What do you mean?" she asked.

He folded his arms across his chest. "Who do you work for?"

"Vortex," she said.

"I mean who do you really work for? Amnesty International? Some other NGO with a left-wing agenda?"

"I work for your company," she said.

Littleton tightened his stare, saying nothing, or rather letting his silence do the talking. Andie didn't flinch, but she noticed the file folder on the seat next to him. Littleton picked it up, opened it, and said, "Bad weather or not, there's a plane waiting for you."

"Yes, I understand I'm being activated."

He smiled sardonically, then shook his head. "You're not being activated."

"What's the problem?"

Littleton pulled a photograph from the file, switched on the interior spotlight in the ceiling, and held the before her eyes. "This is Olga," he said.

Olga looked to be at least six feet tall and about 180 pounds of solid muscle and steroids. The tight black hot pants, studded leather jacket, and black lipstick were straight out of Capital Pleasures. Her head was shaved, except for a single wisp of red hair that hung in her eyes. Her nose, lips, and ears were pierced with multiple metal rings, and she had her mouth wide open to reveal the tongue piercing. Tattoos covered her neck and right arm, mostly Chinese characters and random figures that vaguely resembled them. Andie took special notice, but she didn't recognize any gang symbols.

"Olga is one of our most successful level-five activations," said Littleton.

He returned the photograph to the file and removed another. "This is the last person we sent to meet Olga."

Andie tried to show no reaction, but the difference between her level-one activation and level five was more dramatic than she'd thought. Olga appeared to be removing the man's pubic hair with her teeth.

Littleton closed the file and put it aside, but he laid the last photograph faceup on the seat, where Andie could still see it.

"We can go one of two ways here," he said. "You can tell me who you are and what you're doing here. Or we can put you on that airplane, you can meet Olga, and you can tell *her*."

Andie glanced at the photo, then back at Littleton. "I told you the truth. Would you like me to tell you again?"

Littleton's smile was even more condescending than the last one. "Yes, tell me again," he said as he switched off the light.

The partition behind her head slid open and Bahena grabbed her by the hair, jerking her head back. Andie was staring up at the base of his chin. Even in the darkness, she could tell that he was enjoying himself.

"But this time," said Littleton, "Danilo will make sure you don't lie to me."

"You're making a mistake," said Andie, her heart pounding.

"No," said Littleton. "*You* made the mistake."

Chapter Seventy-three

Poplar is the nearest tube station to the Billingsgate Fish Market, but with a quarter million pounds in her backpack, Shada sprang for a cab. The market complex covers thirteen acres, and the driver dropped her as close as he could to the trading hall. Doors opened at four A.M., and as Shada approached the entrance, buyers were already walking out with fish. The surrounding neighborhood wasn't the Cockney crime scene of Hawthorne's day—"a dirty, evil-smelling, crowded precinct, thronged with people carrying fish on their heads." But it was still the East End before dawn, and the shadows were plenty dark. Shada tried not to look paranoid by checking over her shoulder too often as she hurried into the building.

Habib had called it the busiest place in London before sunrise, and once inside, Shada found that was no exaggeration. Billingsgate merchants sell over twenty-five thousand tons of fish and fish products annually, much of it straight out of ice-packed coolers at one of ninety-eight booths in the trading hall. The floors were wet, the noise was constant, and with open warehouse doors inviting January inside, Shada kept her coat on. Porters wore traditional white sailcloth smocks, and salesmen didn't just sit on their coolers and wait for the fish to go bad. Like the fishmongers of old, they made sales by pulling people in and outshouting one another's claims of freshness—most with civility, a few with the age-old flair that put the second definition of "Billingsgate" in the dictionary: coarse, vulgar language.

"Best halibut in the world right here, ma'am."

The porter's Scottish accent brought Shada to a stop. "I'm looking for the café," she said.

"Straightaway," he said, pointing.

She looked ahead, then checked over her shoulder. It felt like she was being watched, and she didn't think she was paranoid.

"Thank you," she said, moving on toward the café.

Jack was trying to keep a safe distance, watching from behind a merchant's signage for FRESH PRAWNS. A borrowed winter coat and knit cap from Reza made him less recognizable. Shada was wearing a yellow scarf that made her easy to spot in a crowd. She was in his sights, and he could see her conversing with a porter, but Jack wasn't hearing any of it over the borrowed cell phone. Too much background noise in the hall, perhaps. Jack continued to follow her down a long and crowded row, passing booth after booth, cooler after cooler. Halibut from Scotland. Trout and salmon from Norway. Lobster and eel from New Zealand.

I wonder where they keep the psychopaths from Somalia.

From just beyond a booth offering smoked fish, he watched as Shada entered the café, bought a cup of coffee, and took a seat at an open table. She looked around, and Jack tried to remain inconspicuous by moving to another booth and feigning interest in a cooler of tuna steaks. A man entered the café and approached Shada, which caught Jack's attention. Jack put Reza's phone to his ear, trying again to eavesdrop, but he heard nothing, even though the man was clearly asking a question. Shada answered him—something along the lines of "this seat is taken," Jack surmised. The man left her alone. A false alarm—but there was still reason for concern. Jack made a quick call to Chuck.

"She's at the café, but I can't overhear anything with this phone Reza gave me."

"He should have known better," said Chuck. "The spyware won't pick up conversations if she has her cell phone tucked away in her purse or her pocket."

Great, thought Jack, and then an idea came to him. "Can you make her phone ring without displaying an incoming number?"

"I can make her phone sing 'God Save the Queen,' if I want to."

"Then make it ring."

"What for?"

"Just make it ring, but hang up and don't let her know where the call came from."

Jack ended the call and watched. Thirty seconds later, Shada dug her cell phone out of her coat pocket and answered it. From her reaction, Jack knew it was Chuck's prank ring. She looked around, a little nervous. Jack crossed his fingers.

Don't put it away.

She laid the phone on the table in front of her, as if waiting for it to ring again.

That's it, Shada. Leave it right there.

The crank call left Shada a little jittery. It was odd that no incoming number had flashed on the display. She kept one eye on the phone and one on the active trading hall as she waited for the cell to ring again.

Her feet hurt and she needed sleep, but she wasn't sure how long she could sit and wait. She was too on edge to stay in one place. The knots in the back of her neck were like golf balls, and if she came through this ordeal without a stomach ulcer, it would be a miracle. No one would ever understand. She had no one to talk to about it anyway. She certainly couldn't tell Chuck or Jack everything there was to tell about Habib and her.

"Is this seat taken?"

Shada looked up, ready to shoo away another unwanted visitor, but she recognized the pretty face. They'd met once before. It was a hookup that Shada had arranged for Habib over the Internet, but Shada had cut it off because she was too young—just a girl, not a woman.

"What are you doing here?" asked Shada.

The girl stood there, silent, the expression on her face a whirl of angst and confusion. Perhaps there was some fear, too, but Shada didn't have enough time to read every emotion. Without invitation, the girl took a seat, leaned on the tabletop, and broke her silence.

"What do you *think* I'm doing here, Maysoon?"

For no apparent reason, the girl dug her cell phone out of her coat pocket and laid it on the table between them. Shada had learned enough about computers from her husband to understand what that meant: Someone was listening to their conversation. The girl had activated the spyware with typical teenage awkwardness, which made Shada wonder about the crank ring right before the girl's arrival. It hardly seemed like a coincidence that it had prompted Shada to lay her own cell on the table in front of her, where the right spyware could pick up her conversations.

Shada removed her cell phone's battery and tucked the separated components into her pocket. Then she leaned into the table, choosing her words carefully, speaking not to the girl but to the girl's phone—and trusting her instinct as to the eavesdropper's identity.

"Habib," Shada said, "let's talk."

Chapter Seventy-four

Shada is sitting with the girl!" said Jack.

Jack was speaking into his cell phone, pacing back and forth in front of a crowded merchant booth. He had Chuck on the line.

"What girl?" asked Chuck.

"The one who called me yesterday after Jamal's uncle rescued her."

"Are you sure?"

A couple of restaurant owners were haggling with a South African lobster salesman, and it was getting loud. Jack stepped away.

"I'm sure it's her," Jack said. "I recognized the voice right away. Then I lost audio. I'm still in the trading hall about two hundred feet away, but I think I saw Shada take the battery out of her phone."

"That's the one way to deactivate the spyware," said Chuck. "What can you see now?"

Jack's gaze shifted back to the café. "They're still sitting at the table talking to each other. No, wait. The girl just answered her cell phone. She's handing it to Shada. Shada's talking to someone. This is getting really weird."

"Agreed, but the possibilities are limited."

A forklift with bags of ice rolled down the aisle. Jack dodged out of the way. "Limited in what way?"

"Only two ways for that girl to have known how to find Shada.

Either Shada made contact and told her where she was going. Or she's here on behalf of the same lunatic who kept her in a cellar."

Jack thought about it. "Like I said: This is getting weird."

"Don't call the police just yet," said Chuck. "Let's see where this leads. As long as they're in the building and in your sights, the situation is under control."

"Will do," said Jack.

"I'm sorry," Shada said into the phone, pleading. "From the bottom of my heart, I want you to know that."

"You had no right to copy files from my computer," the Dark said.

"I should never have listened to Chuck."

"You screwed up everything, Shada."

"No, listen to me. I never gave the flash drives to anyone. Definitely not to Chuck. I haven't even looked at all the video."

"Do you expect me to believe that?"

"It's the truth."

There was silence on the line. The girl sat all the way back in her chair, arms folded tightly, as if trying to figure Shada out. Shada avoided making eye contact.

"Habib, are you still there?" There was just enough noise around to keep Shada from distinguishing dead air from the sound of Habib mulling things over. Finally, he answered.

"Tell me why I should believe you, Shada. Why should I believe *anything* you say?"

Shada tried to stay cool, especially in front of the girl. But it wasn't easy, knowing that the wrong words could be fatal. She cupped her hand and covered her mouth—an extra precaution against being overheard.

"Because I have a quarter million pounds in my backpack for you," she said.

"That's a good start," he said. "Give the backpack to the girl."

"It's not that simple," she said.

"*Give it to her.*"

"Wait," she said, a bit unnerved by his tone. "You need to know that there's a tracking chip embedded in one of the bills. Chuck can follow the money wherever it goes."

"Do you have any idea which bill?"

"Yes. Chuck told me this morning. But knowing Chuck, I'm sure there's more than one."

"Is there someplace you can go to check the other bills?"

Shada lowered her voice further, increasingly nervous about holding so much cash. "Even if I had the time to do that—there are five hundred notes here—it's a *microchip* I'd be looking for. It isn't easy to see, unless you know it's there."

"That's a problem."

"If your personal assistant here brings the money to you, the police are sure to follow."

"That's an even bigger problem."

"I can fix it," said Shada. "Let me come with her. I'll bring the money to you personally."

"That doesn't fix anything."

"Yes, it does," said Shada.

"What difference does it make if you come or not?"

Had the girl not been watching her, the cell phone would have been shaking in Shada's hand. She kept her nerves in check.

"All the difference in the world," said Shada. "I have a plan."

Chapter Seventy-five

They're leaving the café," said Jack. He still had Chuck on the line.

"Together?"

"Yes," Jack said. "They're heading for the main exit."

"Perfect. As soon as they leave the building, I'll be able to pick up the tracking chip in the money. Stay with them, but keep your distance. If I lose the GPS signal for some reason, my backup is you."

"Police officers are much better at this than I am."

"We can call the police as soon as these two lead us to Vince. Just stick with the plan a few more minutes."

It was after six A.M., a full ninety minutes before sunrise, peak hour for the fish market. The crowd around the exit was almost double what Jack had seen on the way in. The men walking out with coolers on their heads were especially hard to see around, so he closed the gap to under a hundred feet in order to keep a bead on Shada's yellow scarf. He phoned Chuck with an update.

"They just left the building."

"I have them on my computer now," said Chuck. "You can drop back a little farther out of sight. Stay on the line and I'll tell you where to go."

Jack pushed through the north exit doors, and a gust of cold air welcomed him to the parking lot. Security lights cast a yellowish glow around the loading docks, but most of the lot was dark, which was to Jack's advantage. Still, he walked on the other side of a long line of refrigeration trucks to make sure he remained out of Shada's sight. Chuck fed him almost step-by-step instructions past the loading docks to the fenced walkway along Aspen Way, a busy divided highway. It was the early phase of the morning rush hour. Six lanes of commuters, three in each direction, whizzed by at speeds that would have made hopping the iron fence and crossing the road suicidal.

"They're on a pedestrian bridge across the highway," said Chuck.

Jack looked up at the suspension-style bridge and saw them. It led directly to Poplar Station. "I think they're getting on the underground," said Jack. "That will kill your GPS."

"My computer says it's DLR—Docklands Light Railway. I'm pretty sure that's aboveground. But they might switch over to the underground. Stay with them."

A train was pulling into Poplar Station. Shada and the girl made a run for it, and their lead on Jack was at least a hundred yards.

"I'll do my best," he said as he tucked away the phone and sprinted toward the station.

The Dark was playing mind games. Vince was sure of it.

Vince was seated on the floor, his hands tied to an old steam radiator. The Dark had just gotten off the phone, and Vince had been able to hear only one side of the conversation—the Dark's side. The Dark was filling in the other half—the half that Vince refused to believe.

"Amazing, isn't it, Paulo? McKenna's mother begging *me* for forgiveness." The Dark stepped closer and grabbed Vince by the jaw. "So where's *your* apology? Can I hear you say you're sorry for what you did to me?"

Vince still had no idea what injuries the Dark had suffered in the same explosion that had taken his own sight. It took all his strength not to ask, but expressing any desire to know would only have given the Dark more power over him.

"Nothing to say for yourself, huh?" The Dark was squeezing hard enough to break Vince's jaw, but Vince took the pain in silence.

"Fine," he said, pushing Vince's head away. "I'll let your wife apologize—when she spreads her legs for me."

Mind games, Vince told himself, but he wasn't sure how much more he could take. Every word out of the Dark's mouth, every punch to the jaw or the solar plexus, every crack about Vince's wife, only served to remind him that the last thing he remembered seeing—*really remembered* seeing—was McKenna Mays dying in his arms. Vince knew it would all come down to the next few minutes. He needed a plan, and he was glad he had one: six steps at eleven o'clock to the suitcase filled with weapons; three steps, nine o'clock to the Brainport.

Now, all he needed was a break.

Jack pulled his black knit cap down to his eyebrows, but he wasn't sure how much good the lame disguise was doing.

He'd been the last person to board at the Poplar Station before the doors closed and the train pulled away. His car was nearly full, and he found an open seat about halfway down. Shada and the girl were in the lead car—there were only two—and Shada's was standing-room only. Ten minutes into the ride, his heart was still pounding, but not from the chase.

He was almost certain that Shada had spotted him.

Jack glanced out the window of the speeding train. Chuck had been right: The tracks were aboveground—so far, at least—which meant that Chuck's GPS was working. Jack's cell phone worked, too. The stations all along the line were elevated, and with each stop Jack got a postcard view of London in the morning twilight. He was westbound, and based on how the passengers were dressed and what they were reading, Jack's quick take was that the train was headed toward London's financial district.

"Tower Gateway," the mechanized voice announced.

Jack leaned into the aisle and peered ahead through the windows in the emergency doors between cars. Shada was moving toward the exit doors. Jack gave Chuck another update.

"She's getting off."

"Did you see *The French Connection*?"

Of course Jack had, and he didn't want to be the idiot left standing on the platform as Shada jumped back on the train and waved good-bye to him. "Got it covered," said Jack.

"The train goes into a tunnel after Tower Gateway," said Chuck. "All Shada has to do is ride through to the next station, and she's in the underground. You're the only set of eyes we have if that happens. Keep me on the cell as long as you have service. I want to hear from you in real time while the situation's fluid."

"Understood."

The train stopped, the doors opened, and Jack moved with about six other people toward the exit. He let them get off first, and by the time he stepped onto the platform, Shada was heading for the stairs.

"She's definitely getting off," Jack said into his phone.

"That doesn't make any sense."

"I'm following her down the platform now."

"It's almost like she's trying to do us a favor by getting off before the tracking chip becomes ineffective."

"Maybe she is," said Jack. "This station is less than a five-minute walk from my hotel. She couldn't have picked an area of London that I'm more familiar with."

"Then why did she remove the battery to kill the spyware on her cell phone?"

Jack didn't have an answer. He just kept walking with the morning-rush-hour crowd.

Tower Gateway is an elevated station, and Jack waited for her to ride the escalator all the way down to street level before he started down the adjacent stairway. She walked quickly, leading the girl with one hand and clutching the backpack with the other. They were out on the street faster than Jack had expected, and he had to leap down the stairway two and three steps at a time to keep from losing them. A group of lost Americans surrounded him on the sidewalk.

"Dude, which way is the Tower of England?"

Jack blew right past them—presumably they meant *London*, and if they were any closer, the old walls might have fallen on their heads—and he spotted Shada across the street. He followed her for another block beyond an old railway overpass.

"She just ducked into a breakfast shop," said Jack. He was in a zebra crossing at one of those typical London intersections where pedestrians could be killed from no fewer than seven different directions.

"One heck of a time to stop for a muffin," Chuck said.

Jack continued up Minories, weaving his way through pedestrians as he struggled to see beyond the big green lettering on the restaurant window. The charcoal sky was ebbing toward a lighter shade of gray. The end of eighteen hours without sunlight was near, and any additional light was helpful.

"It doesn't look like she's ordering food. She's definitely buying something, though."

A bus stopped in front of him, blocking Jack's view.

"Buying what?" asked Chuck.

Jack hurried beyond the bus, and the few steps forward gave him a clear line of sight into the restaurant. "She's buying aluminum foil, I think. A whole roll of it."

"And paying whatever price the clerk names, no doubt—and it's still a bargain, when you consider that the payoff is a quarter million pounds."

"What are you talking about?"

"Wrapping her backpack in all that foil will shut down the GPS. That bitch is stealing the ransom!"

"What do you want me to do?"

"Tower Hill Tube Station is about a hundred yards from you. If she gets underground, she can go just about anywhere, and if the money is wrapped in foil, I'll have no way of knowing where she pops up."

Jack's grip on the phone tightened. "I'm asking you a question: What do you want me to do?"

"Grab her!"

Chapter Seventy-six

Shada tucked the roll of foil in her backpack, careful not to let the salesclerk see all that cash inside.

"We have cellophane wrap as well," the clerk said as he stuffed the fifty-pound note into his pocket.

"Next time," Shada said. The chances were exactly one in five hundred that she'd just solved her microchip problem, but the foil would shore up those odds. She'd wrap the remaining 499 notes once they were underground. "Let's go," she said, and the girl followed her to the door.

"By the way," asked Shada, "what should I call you?"

"Call me what he calls me: McKenna."

Shada stopped cold. Had it not been for Jack Swyteck, Shada might never have found out about the teenage girl in the cellar. It had been a sickening realization this morning that the girl in the cellar was the same girl she'd met on the Internet and unwittingly brought into Habib's web. Hearing now that he called her "McKenna" was more than sickening. It was Shada's worst fear realized.

She stepped away from the door, found a spot at the counter facing the window, and hit REDIAL on the girl's cell. Habib answered, and Shada talked fast.

"I have the foil," she said. "We're a stone's throw from the Tower Hill Station. Tell me where to get off the train."

"First stop on the District Line. Aldgate East. About three minutes."

Shada was about to answer, then stopped. Through the plate-glass window, she could see all the way across the street. A street-light enhanced the light of dawn, and the man standing at the bus stop looked just like the guy on the train wearing the black cap. Shada tightened her stare, and even from this distance, it made him look away nervously. There was no doubt in her mind.

That's Swyteck.

"It might take me a little longer than three minutes."

She tucked away the phone and grabbed the girl by the elbow. "Let's go," she said as they moved quickly toward the other exit.

Chapter Seventy-seven

She saw me," Jack said into his phone.

"Then go now!" Chuck shouted.

Jack put away the cell as he darted across the street, making the American mistake of checking left instead of right. Two cars slammed on their brakes, and Jack narrowly missed mention in tomorrow's paper under the headline "Death by Mini Cooper." Shada and the girl flew out of the restaurant and ran in the opposite direction, headed down a side street. Shada covered the city block in no time, but the girl seemed to be struggling to keep up.

Damn, that woman can run.

"Shada, stop!" he shouted. It felt like the fiasco at Carpenter's Arms all over again, only this time he knew the area—he was glad he'd studied his map—and he knew that she was headed for the Tower Hill Tube Station.

Shada was in full stride, and as they made a hard left down another street, Jack could hear her yelling at the girl to keep up. Then the girl went down in the shadows beneath the overpass. Shada kept going. The girl had fallen, and Shada just left her.

Or did Shada push her down?

The girl was still on the sidewalk, holding her ankle, when Jack caught up with her.

"Are you okay?"

"Leave me alone!" she shouted. She got up slowly, then nearly fell over again when she put weight on that ankle.

Jack glanced ahead, beyond the darkness of the overpass. Shada was out of sight, long gone—with the cash. Jack hated to think what might happen to Vince without the ransom, but he couldn't let a teenage girl go back to the Dark.

"Let me help you."

"No!"

She was panic-stricken, and Jack tried his most soothing voice. "You're safe now. Stay with me."

"Leave me alone!"

Jack looked around for help and saw that they were right in front of a place called Pitcher & Piano, which, to a jet-lagged attorney from Miami, sounded like a law firm. "I'm going to take you inside here and call the police."

"No!"

"You've been brainwashed by—"

Her punch to his chest took Jack's breath away. "I'm not brainwashed," she shouted, "and I can't call the police!"

"Yes, you can."

"If I'm not back with the money in ten minutes, he'll kill me!"

"He has to find you to kill you!"

"No, he doesn't!" she shouted.

"Just let me—"

Her scream was deafening—long and shrill, like the cry of a mortally wounded animal, and the fact that they were beneath an overpass made it even louder. A man came running out of Pitcher & Piano—it was a bar, not a law firm—and grabbed Jack.

"Let go of her!" the man shouted.

"I'm trying to help her."

"I said, *Let go!*"

He took a swing at Jack, but Jack deflected it. Jack managed to keep a tight grip on the girl's coat, but she only encouraged her Good Samaritan.

"Help! Get him away from me!"

The man was smaller than Jack, but the girl's plea gave him

added strength. He pulled Jack to the ground, and the girl broke free. The two men rolled on the sidewalk, and the speed with which the girl ran away—right through the pain in her ankle—left no doubt that her life was on the line. Hers and Vince's. Jack pushed the man aside, jumped up from the sidewalk, and chased after the girl.

"Stop!"

She flagged a taxi to the curb. Jack was still a hundred feet away, but the thought of the girl getting away in a taxi made him kick into a higher gear. He had his cell phone in hand and was trying to dial the police, but that was impossible while running at full speed. He closed the gap quickly—that ankle was really bothering her—and she was almost within reach when the man from Pitcher & Piano tackled him from behind. Momentum carried them all the way to the taxi, and Jack reached for the girl's ankle as she yanked the car door open. The man knocked Jack's arm aside, and the girl jumped into the taxi.

"No!" Jack shouted, but the door was swinging shut, and the girl would soon be on her way to God only knew where. Jack was still on the ground, the man was on top of him, and he couldn't stop the door from closing. In a split-second decision, Jack tossed his cell phone onto the floor in the back of the cab.

The door slammed shut, and the cab pulled away.

"Sorry, pal," Jack said as he swung at the man's jaw. The blow stunned the poor fellow, and it was enough to discourage him from giving chase as Jack hurried down the street in pursuit of the girl's taxi. He dug the cell phone from Reza out of his coat pocket as he ran, stopped for a second to dial Chuck, and took off running again.

"You have spyware on my cell, right?" said Jack.

"Well . . ."

"It's okay, Reza told me as much this morning!"

The black taxi was well ahead of him, but in the light of dawn it was still in sight. Jack talked fast as he raced down the sidewalk. "I tossed my phone into the back of the cab."

"What cab?"

"I lost Shada, but the girl's in a taxi with my cell phone. Follow that GPS signal and she'll lead you right to the Dark."

"Where are you?"

Jack stopped to catch his breath. He could smell the River Thames. "Tower of England," he said, parroting that numbskull at the DLR Station. The lack of sleep was catching up with him, and he knew that chasing a moving vehicle on foot just wasn't going to work.

"I'll grab a cab," he said. "I want you to call the police and tell them exactly where that GPS signal is headed."

"Will do," said Chuck.

Jack spotted a taxi approaching from the opposite direction. He jumped out into the street, and the cab screeched to a halt to avoid hitting him. The driver rolled down the window, primed to give Jack a good tongue-lashing, but Jack's mouth was already running as he opened the rear door on the driver's side.

"I need to follow that cab about fifty meters ahead of—"

Jack stopped himself, having gotten a better look at the driver. It was the same cabbie from the Tower Hotel who just yesterday—it seemed much longer—had helped Jack tail Vince's cab to the Carpenter's Arms.

"You gotta be kidding me," said Jack, still holding the door open.

"Again? This is getting a bit strange, mate," the driver said, and the rear door slammed shut with the force of the taxi pulling away.

"Damn it!"

Up ahead, the traffic light changed, and Jack saw the girl's taxi pull away. Hopefully Chuck was tracking it, but GPS wasn't exactly golden in one of the most tunneled cities in the world.

Jack had to keep up. Several cars flew by, ignoring Jack's attempts to flag one down. Jack dug a handful of bills from his wallet and waved them at a boy on a bicycle.

"I'll give you two hundred pounds for your bike!"

The kid stopped. "Are you joking?"

"No joke. Here, take it."

The boy got off his bike, smiling as he grabbed the money. "Ta very much."

Jack pedaled off in pursuit of the taxi, hoping like hell for a major traffic jam ahead.

Chapter Seventy-eight

Behind the gray blanket of winter clouds, the sun was starting to rise over London. The Dark removed his nighttime sunglasses and put on a darker pair. Then he reached for his cell phone. It was the middle of the night in Washington, but he dialed the number anyway, knowing that Littleton would be awake and take his call.

"This is your final update," said the Dark.

"Tell me," said Littleton.

He was standing across the street from the exit to the Aldgate East Tube Station. Morning rush hour was at full throttle, and he had to move around to keep from being jostled by commuters.

"For what it's worth, I spoke with Shada. She admitted that she copied files from my computer. But she swears she didn't give them to anyone."

"Do you believe her?"

"In two hours, I'm out of the country with just enough money to make sure no one ever finds me. Which means there's only one question that matters: Do *you* believe her?"

"Damn it, Habib! Don't play games with me! More than just my company is on the line here. The shit that went on at that black site is nothing short of blasphemy to some Muslims. I'll be al-Qaeda's poster child for 'Death to Infidels.' Do you hear what I'm saying? Some extremist group out there will be pissed off enough to make its own video and cut my head off—literally! So tell me straight: Do you believe her, or don't you?"

The Dark kept an eye on the tube station exit. Just then, he spotted Shada in the crowd. She was carrying the backpack like a baby in her arms. A smile creased his lips.

"I wish you luck, Mr. Littleton."

The Dark put the phone away and started across the street.

Chapter Seventy-nine

Jack pedaled furiously, crouched like an Olympic cyclist, his elbows on the handlebars and the cell phone pressed to his ear.

"I can't see her!" he shouted into the phone. "Which way, Chuck?"

It was an old bicycle, but the boy had maintained it with speed in mind, having stripped away the fenders, chain guard, kick-stand, and all other unnecessary weight. A light rain was falling, and the spinning tires gave Jack his morning shower.

"Go left at the fork in the road," said Chuck. "She's headed up Mansell."

Traffic was heavy at the fork, four lanes splitting into two diverging roads, but Jack was in the bicycle lane and moving faster than the morning rush hour. He pedaled hard around the corner, concerned not in the least that the bicycle lane up Mansell was shared with buses. The last cyclist from Miami who couldn't outrun a bus had been killed decades ago.

"I see her," said Jack, and he continued to trade information with Chuck all the way up the busy street. He'd covered less than a mile so far, but his thighs were starting to burn, and he didn't know how much longer he could keep up the Lance Armstrong pace. Another quick turn put him on Whitechapel High Street, and within the span of thirty seconds, the mirrored windows of the Royal Bank of Scotland gave way to the Aldgate Warehouse and other buildings in serious need of a paint job and repair.

"She's heading up Osborn," said Chuck.

Jack oriented himself with a mental image of the East End map he'd studied last night, and he realized that the taxi was leading them back toward Brick Lane, near the south end of Bengaltown and Somaal Town. More and more of the old buildings Jack saw along the street were covered with gang graffiti. The rain started to fall harder, and it was darker now than when the chase had started.

"The taxi stopped," said Chuck.

The phone was getting wet, and Jack made the mistake of weaving through a narrow gauntlet of standing cars, illegally parked cars, and slow-moving cars while jostling the phone to protect it from the rain. It slipped from his hands and smashed on the wet pavement.

Shit!

Jack kept going. A delivery truck was blocking the one-way street and most of the sidewalk. Jack dropped his bicycle and ran around the truck. The taxi was in front of a three-story brick building that appeared to be slated for demolition. Graffiti-covered plywood sealed off the main entrance, and the windows facing the street were boarded shut. The worst of the building bordered a vacant lot to the south, where a couple of crackheads huddled amid the burned-out shell of crumbling brick walls, twisted sections of chain-link fence, and weeds.

The steady rain was suddenly a downpour, and Jack was soaking wet. He could only imagine how he must have looked to a frightened sixteen-year-old girl as he caught up with her. She shrieked as if hit by lightning upon seeing him.

"Please!" Jack said, catching his breath.

Before he could tell her that the police were on the way, she turned and ran toward the vacant lot. Jack followed her to a side entrance to the building. He'd given up trying to persuade her with words. He grabbed her by the wrist and said, "You're coming with me!"

"No!"

"Where is Vincent Paulo?"

Jack probably should have seen it coming, but the driving rain made everything a blur, and he was suddenly blinded by pepper spray. He fell to his knees, the girl broke away, and the metal door knocked him over as she yanked it open. Even with rain falling hard around him, he could hear her running up a flight of stairs, her footfalls echoing inside the stairwell. Blinded and on his hands and knees, he looked up to the sky and let the rainfall soothe his eyes. Slowly, the stinging subsided, and as his vision returned, a man's voice boomed behind him.

"What the hell is going on here?"

Jack focused as best he could, hoping Chuck had sent the police. "The girl went upstairs!"

"That little thief owes me eight pounds for the fare!"

A scream from inside the building cut through the driving rain. Jack's immediate thought was the girl, but the second scream was more like a woman's.

Shada?

"Call the police!" Jack shouted to the cabdriver, and then he ran inside.

Chapter Eighty

Shada was on the floor. A blow from Habib had put her there, but she was okay. Vince was a different story.

"You didn't have to stab him!"

"Shut up!" the Dark shouted back at her.

Vince lay on the floor next to her, bleeding badly, and Shada went to him. The knife had entered somewhere beneath his rib cage. Possibly a punctured lung. Blood from his left side had soaked through the shirt, and a dark crimson pool was gathering beside him. Shada removed her coat and used it to apply pressure to the wound.

"He needs an ambulance," said Shada.

"Why do you pretend to care?"

"You can't let him die. I warned you about the tracking chip. I brought you the money myself. I did everything you wanted."

Shada heard a whimper from across the room. The girl—the one Habib called McKenna—was in the corner, her knees drawn up to her chest. She seemed to know better than Vince or Shada that the Dark had never intended to simply take the money and run.

The Dark stepped closer to Shada. "Tell him, Shada. Tell Paulo the truth."

Vince lifted his head at the sound of his name. Shada took it as a good sign that he was not only conscious but listening.

"This man needs a doctor," said Shada.

The Dark tightened his stare, his exclusive focus on Shada. "You've known it was me for a long time. Haven't you?"

Shada didn't answer. She suddenly wished Vince weren't able to listen.

"You definitely knew yesterday," he said, "when we were having sex. When you looked in the mirror and saw what I had written on your back with red lipstick. The letters were backward in the mirror, but I saw it register on your face. Tell Paulo what it said, Shada."

She kept pressing on Vince's wound, but her hands were shaking. The Dark aimed his pistol straight at her head. He was just five feet away from her.

"Tell him!"

Shada swallowed hard, then said it slowly, each letter filled with hatred: "F-M-L-T-W-I-A."

Vince let out a noisy breath, one that was wet with blood. The sound gave Shada chills, and her feelings of shame and disgust for the things she'd done with the Dark forced an image into her head—that of Vince kneeling on the floor beside McKenna three years ago as the life drained from the stab wounds in her body. A thousand times over, she would have taken McKenna's place. Now she wished it were her own life on the line, not Vince's.

"Please don't die, Vince."

"Tell him why," said the Dark. "Tell him why McKenna said Jamal did it."

"I don't know why!"

"You *do* know! Tell him what you told me."

She knew exactly what he meant, but she tried to keep the focus on saving Vince. The Dark would have none of it. He stepped closer and pressed the gun right against her head.

"Tell him!"

Chapter Eighty-one

The outburst from beyond the closed door—*"Tell him!"*—stopped Jack in his tracks.

Rushing inside the old hotel had been an instinctive reaction to the scream, and he'd raced up three flights of stairs hoping that the Dark had already fled with the money and left his hostages behind. Clearly, that was not the case, and as Jack stood frozen in the dark hallway, not sure what to do, he wished he was packing that gun Reza had offered him. He didn't even have a cell phone, but hopefully the police were on the way. Surely Chuck had called them. Or the cabdriver. He inched closer to the door, stepping carefully on floorboards stripped of carpeting, and listened.

"Shada, do it *now*!"

He stopped and put his ear to the wall, trying to hear other voices inside the room. What he really wanted to hear were police sirens wailing on Brick Lane. If they didn't come soon, Jack would be forced to make a move—either bust down the door or run for help. A wrong decision could be disastrous, and he was deep in an anxious state of disbelief over the fact that he was in London tracking down a psychopath when his week from hell—everything from Jamal's murder and the loss of his friend Neil to the lack of sleep and Jamal's uncle in the hospital—suddenly caught up with him, propelling him to do *something.*

"Do not harm the hostages," he shouted. "I have a gun!"

The crack of gunfire was the response—a bullet exploding through the wall just inches from Jack's nose. Jack dove to the floor.

Brilliant bluff, Swyteck.

The door swung open, but no one came out. The dim lighting from inside the room spilled a faint glow into the hallway, and Jack crouched low in the shadows. The rain continued to beat down on the roof of the hotel, and his only hope was that nature's hiss would drown out the sound of his own panicked breathing.

"Toss your gun into the room," the Dark said, calling out into the hallway. "Then step into the doorway where I can see you."

Jack bit his lip, not quite believing that his bluff was going this badly. It was almost comical—until Shada screamed in pain.

"Do as I said, or the next scream is her last."

Where the hell are the cops?

"He's serious," said Shada. "He already stabbed Vince!"

The fear in her voice was palpable, and the thought of Vince down and perhaps dying raised the stakes yet again—if that was possible. But he stayed put.

"One," said the Dark, counting down.

"Jack, please!"

"Two."

It was a split-second decision, but all Jack could do was buy time. "I'm stepping toward the doorway," he shouted from the hallway, "and I don't have a weapon."

The Dark stopped counting, and for the next few seconds, there was only the sound of falling rain on the roof.

"Hands up where I can see them!" the Dark shouted.

Jack took a deep breath. This was definitely *not* the plan. Jack moved into the doorway with hands up over his head. The sole source of light in the room was a battery-powered lantern on the table, but it was sufficient, and the sight took Jack's breath away—especially the blood on the floor beside Vince. Shada was on her knees at his side. The Dark stood behind her with his gun pressed against the back of her head.

"I swear I don't have a gun," Jack said.

"It wouldn't help you anyway," the Dark said. "Come out, McKenna."

Jack did a double take at the name "McKenna," but when the girl from the fish market stepped out from the shadows in the corner of the room, he knew it was just more of the Dark's sickness.

"Everyone is going to do exactly as I say," the Dark said. "Show them, McKenna."

The girl opened her coat to reveal what she was wearing underneath. Even in the dim lighting of a boarded-up hotel room, it didn't take an expert to see that she was wired for explosives. Her earlier exchange with Jack—when she told Jack that the Dark *didn't* have to find her in order to kill her—hadn't been paranoia. Now it made sense.

The Dark showed Jack the cell phone in his free hand. "Remote detonator," he said. "Something I learned from Jamal's father. Life's funny, isn't it?"

"Nobody else has to die," said Jack. "Just take the money and go."

"I'll go," he said, shoving Shada's head forward with his pistol, "but I'm taking this slut with me."

"You don't need Shada," said Jack.

"Don't tell me what I need," he said, his anger rising. "We're talking real Internet porn-star potential—right, Shada? Let's give your friends a little sneak preview. Tell them who made you into such a slut."

She didn't answer. The Dark only berated her further. His voice turned into that same abusive rant that Jack had heard on those unwatchable P2P videos.

"Who did it, huh?" he said, getting into role. The pistol forced Shada's head forward, and again he shouted: "Who did it to you?"

She answered in a weak voice. "Not Chuck," she said. "He was number six."

"Then who? Tell me!"

"Not the men in college. Not number five. Or four. Or three."

She looked up just enough to catch Jack's eye—and Jack had a double epiphany. The Dark's interrogation of Shada was like a replay of his final moments with McKenna before stabbing her to death. He was forcing her to go back to that first lover, the one who had taken her virginity and—in his twisted mind—turned her into a slut. For McKenna there had been only Jamal, and it suddenly came clear to Jack. When Vince found her on the bedroom floor, dying and delirious, and asked her that same question—*Who did this to you?*—McKenna had been conditioned to give him the answer that she'd given the Dark: *Jamal.*

"Not that boy on the beach," Shada said. "Number two."

She paused, again catching Jack's eye, and the second half of the two-part epiphany was confirmed. Shada wasn't just counting down her lovers.

"Definitely not two," she said, making sure that Jack was with her as she counted down like mission control toward a synchronized launch time for a simultaneous attack.

"One!" she said, and they sprang into action.

Shada jerked away from the gun. Jack dove at the Dark and knocked the phone—the detonator—to the floor. His momentum carried them both all the way to an old chair against the wall. Their combined weight smashed the chair to pieces, their bodies hit the floor, and the gun discharged. The girl screamed as the errant bullet splintered the door casing behind her.

"Run!" Jack shouted.

He heard someone racing toward the door as he and the Dark fought for control of the gun. They rolled hard to Jack's left and slammed into the radiator. Jack got hold of the Dark's wrist and smashed his hand against the pipe until the gun dropped to the floor. The two men were still locked in a wrestling match as Jack swung his leg around and kicked the gun across the room. Jack saw it disappear somewhere in the shadows—but he didn't see the broken chair leg coming at his head. The blow stunned Jack, and as much as he tried to fight through the pain, he could feel the Dark slipping out of his grasp. Only then did Jack see the cell phone resting in the center of room. He knew that if the Dark got to it first, they would all be blown to bits. He tried to pull the Dark back to him, but his strength was gone.

The Dark reached for it.

"Freeze!" Shada shouted, and the crack of a pistol stopped everyone. It was her warning shot. The gun that Jack had wrestled free in the struggle was now in her hands, and the Dark was in her sights. The Dark didn't move, but his open hand hovered ominously over the cell phone on the floor.

"Put the gun down, Shada," the Dark said.

"Don't tell me what to do!"

With tentative steps, and with her gun aimed at the Dark, Shada slowly crossed the room to check on Vince. Her warning shot seemed to have roused him. Shada knelt at his side, but he didn't speak.

"Shada, I'm talking to you," said the Dark.

Jack struggled to focus, fighting off the blow to his head. "Don't listen to him, Shada."

"Quiet, everyone!" she said.

Jack backed off, but the Dark continued in a chilling tone. It was the strong, almost hypnotic voice of control.

"Shada, this isn't what you came back to do."

"Yes, it is. I want you dead."

"Only I can help you now."

"You deserve to die!"

"You need me, Shada. That's why you brought me the money."

"You killed my daughter, you monster. I brought the money so I could get close enough to kill *you*."

Jack could see the anger on his face, but the Dark continued in the same even tone that almost seemed to cast a spell over Shada. "And then you were going to make a run for it, weren't you?" he said.

She didn't answer.

"You don't have to run alone, Shada. We can run together."

"Shut up!"

"Tell Jack why you have to run, Shada."

"Quiet!"

"If you kill me and let Jack live, it's only a matter of time before he figures out that you were in Miami when Ethan Chang was killed."

"Stop it!"

"And that you were also in Miami when his friend was killed."

She didn't deny it. She wouldn't even look at Jack, and her connection to Neil hit Jack like a sledgehammer.

"You tricked me," said Shada. Her gun was trained on the Dark, but Jack could hear in her voice that she was beginning to crumble.

"Nobody tricked you, Shada. You knew the truth."

"You made me think Jamal was out to kill me, and you said Chang could lead him to me."

"That was true."

"*Not* true!" said Vince, groaning. It startled everyone. It was the sound of a dying man, and Jack wished he would save his strength.

"Don't listen to Paulo," said the Dark. "You did the right thing, Shada. Chang was a blackmailer."

Her aim was turning unsteady, even as her voice quaked. "You said it would only make him sick, not kill him."

Jack felt chills at the thought of Shada disguising herself and jabbing Chang with the toxin. He suddenly grasped the degree of control the Dark exercised over her.

"Shada, I want you to do exactly as I say," the Dark said. "Take it slow now. I want you to turn the gun away from me."

"I . . . can't."

"Turn it away from me and aim it at Jack."

She shook her head, but without much conviction. The Dark continued to work on her. "Shada, the police already know that *two* people went to Neil Goderich's office the night he was shot."

That was news to Jack, and he wasn't sure if the police knew it, either. But Shada's silence confirmed that it was true.

"Run with me," said the Dark. "That's all we can do, Shada."

Tears were streaming down her face. Shada's voice was barely audible, and even though she was staring at the Dark, Jack sensed that she was speaking to him.

"I was just the lookout," she said. "Neil wasn't supposed to get shot."

"Aim the gun toward Jack," said the Dark.

Her hand was shaking. Slowly, almost imperceptibly at first, the barrel of the gun began to move.

"I'm sorry," she said.

Shada's betrayal—and the pain of Neil's death—caught in Jack's throat. He could barely speak.

"Shada, don't do this."

The gun continued to move in Jack's direction.

"Shada, please," said Jack.

Slowly and steadily, the gun kept moving—and then it jerked toward Shada's face.

"No!" shouted Jack, and his cry seemed to jar Vince into action. He catapulted up from the floor and knocked the barrel away from Shada's mouth. Out of the corner of his eye, Jack saw Vince and Shada going down as the explosion of another gunshot rattled the room.

The next few seconds passed like minutes, as events suddenly seemed to unfold in slow motion. As the Dark's fingers wrapped around the phone, a boot came down on his wrist, clamping it to the floor. Jack looked up to see the business end of a pistol that looked exactly like the one Reza had offered him. It was aimed straight at the Dark's head. In a flash, Jack realized that Chuck had not called for help, and that he had never intended to involve the police under any circumstances. He realized that there was no outstanding arrest warrant for Chuck Mays that prevented him from traveling to the U.K., and that Chuck had been in London at least as long as Jack had.

And Jack totally understood that it was time for a father's justice.

"This is for *my* McKenna," he said, and the crack of his pistol shook the old hotel.

Chapter Eighty-two

Andie gasped for breath.

She was bent at the waist, essentially upside down in the back of the limo. Her head was hanging off the forward edge of the leather seat, and her hair splayed across the carpeted floor. Her knees were pointed at the ceiling, flexed over the headrest so that her feet dangled through the open partition and into the cockpit. Bahena held her legs still. Her arms were outstretched, each wrist tied to a door handle.

"I'll ask you one more time," said Littleton. "Who are you?"

Her lungs burned, and she could barely force out the words. "I told you," she said. "My name is Lisa Horne."

Again, Littleton covered her face with the wet cloth. Andie couldn't see, but she heard the jangle of the crystal carafe as he pulled it from the slot in the liquor cabinet. The fact that it wasn't liquor was of little consolation. A steady stream of water began to flow again, soaking the cloth. Andie tried to hold her breath, knowing how painful it would feel. The cloth became thicker and heavier on her face, absorbing more and more water. She needed air and finally drew a breath, but it was like trying to breathe through a wet sponge. The burning sensation was in her nose first, and then it shot down her throat and tore at her lungs. Her body lurched and twisted until she coughed up the water into the wet cloth. She wanted to scream—*Stop!*—but the flow of water from the carafe was seemingly without end, choking off all ability to speak. Again she struggled to hold her breath, but the lack of oxygen was making her dizzy and borderline delirious. She knew if she blacked out they would revive her, and then she would face the tough questions about her true identity. Her head seemed on the verge of explosion, but she tried to focus on who she was, who she was supposed to be. Her name was Willow, and she was part of a cult in the Cascade Mountains. No, she was Andrea, and her best friend Mallory was married to a high roller on Wall Street. Her past undercover rolls were bleeding into the present, and it was impossible to think straight.

Air! I need air!

She breathed in, but she only sucked water into her lungs. The pain this time was like a knife to her chest, a rope around her neck, and a hammer to her head—all at the same time. It was impossible to focus, and her thoughts ran wild—until everything stopped.

She was suddenly coughing and gasping for air again. She was sure she had blacked out, but she had no idea how long she'd been unconscious. The wet cloth was gone—*Thank God!*—but her pulse rate was off the charts, and she was breathing with the desperation of someone plucked from the ocean moments before drowning.

"This is the last chance," she heard a man say. "Who are you?"

The question barely made sense to her. No answer came to mind, but she wasn't physically capable of speaking yet anyway. Desperate for air, she drew in a series of short, noisy breaths.

"Who *are* you?" he said, shouting at her now.

Andie had no idea where she was. No clue *who* she was. But the man shouting from somewhere above was demanding an answer, and in a brief instant of lucidity, she heard another voice in her head. She heard her supervisor, Harley Abrams, telling her that he had a team on alert in case things went badly, and she knew that to stay alive, she would have to buy time.

"We know you are not Lisa Horne," the man said.

Buy time, buy time.

“Tell me who you are!” he shouted.

The name “Andie Henning” came to mind, but she flushed it.

Littleton draped the wet cloth back on her face, and the mere sensation sent her into a panic. She was sure that her supervisory agent was on the way, and her only chance of survival was to stall until help arrived. She had to tell this interrogator something—anything but “Andie Henning, FBI.” She searched her mind for an alias, but none of the FBI covers rang true enough for her to beat another round of waterboarding.

The carafe rattled, and she knew that in seconds the water would again begin to flow.

“Tell me!” Littleton shouted.

For reasons she couldn’t comprehend, her mind was suddenly in another time period, decades before she was even born, and she could see herself walking in the shoes of a woman she’d never met. A woman she’d heard about only a day or two ago, but whose horrible story made her seem so much more real than any FBI cover.

“My name is Katrina Petrak,” she said.

He pulled away the cloth. “Petrak? You work for the Czech government?”

“No,” she said, barely aware of her own voice, her mind awhirl as she fought to remain conscious. “The resistance.”

“What are you talking about?”

“The assassination,” she said. “Not everyone was to blame.”

“What assass—”

The explosion of a single gunshot cut his question short, and pellets of glass from the shattered window rained down on Andie. It came with another blast of wetness, but it was unlike the water-boarding, this time hot and thick as blood. She had nowhere near enough time to fear if the blood was her own. Almost instantly the dead weight was upon her, telling her it was Littleton’s.

From then on, the amount of time that passed was impossible for her to gauge. Perhaps she’d even blacked out again. The next thing Andie knew, the rear door of the black limo was open, and she was sitting up in a normal position on the door sill. Blue lights from surrounding squad cars swirled in the snowy night sky. A few yards away, a pair of FBI agents in full tactical gear led Danilo Bahena to a SWAT van. Andie was looking into the warm eyes of her supervisory agent.

"Are you okay?" asked Harley.

Andie glanced over her shoulder. Littleton's body was behind her, slumped over in the back of the limo. A shot to the side of the head had taken him out.

"Better than he is, I guess."

"I just heard from London," said Harley. "Jack's fine. You can call him now."

He handed her a phone, and the sense of relief almost made her smile.

"Thank you," she said. "I'd like that."

Epilogue
February
The Czech Republic

Snow was falling as Jack drove out of Prague. Andie was in the passenger seat. It was their first trip abroad together. It wasn't exactly a vacation.

"Funny," said Jack, "an entire branch of my family tree is from this area. And every road I turn down, I see Jamal Wakefield in the trunk of a car heading off to a black site."

Andie glanced out the window. "That location will never be public information." She was right, Jack realized. The only living person who knew the exact location was Danilo Bahena, and he was sitting in jail for the murder of Neil Goderich. The likelihood of his talking was almost nil.

"To be honest," said Jack, "it doesn't really seem that important anymore."

Andie reached across the console and held his hand. Her touch had a way of reaffirming something that he was now more sure of than ever: Andie was on his side. She'd taken a huge risk by calling him in London to explain how his case and her investigation overlapped, and to warn him about what he was up against. It was not yet clear how that would play out for her professionally, but she wasn't fired, and she had the support of her supervisor. But Jack had a feeling there was more to come.

"Are you okay?" she asked.

Jack nodded, and they rode on in silence, his thoughts drifting back to the mission at hand.

Grandpa Swyteck had died in his sleep. As best Jack could piece events together, it was right around the time doctors at the Royal Hospital of London were assuring Vince that his stab wound wasn't fatal. Jack flew home from London for the funeral. Ten days later, he was back in Europe with Andie—and with a handful of his grandfather's ashes.

"Turn left in one hundred meters."

It was the mechanical voice of the GPS. Hearing it made Jack think of fifty-pound notes wrapped in aluminum foil.

The fatal shooting of Habib Warsame Dhamac was ruled self-defense, even though it was clear to Jack that Chuck had his plan to avenge McKenna's death, and Shada had hers. The fact that neither had known what the other was doing could have gotten everyone killed—which seemed like a metaphor for their marriage. Chuck was being held in the U.K. on weapons charges. Shada had much bigger problems with the law. Her attorney would surely build a classic "Patty Hearst" defense and argue that her involvement in the murders of Ethan Chang and Neil Goderich was carefully choreographed by the Dark to cement his control over her—more specifically, that she'd had no idea she was administering a lethal dose of anything to Chang, and that she'd played lookout for Bahena outside Neil's office only because the Dark had brainwashed her into thinking that it was her last chance to learn the truth about Jamal Wakefield.

As for Chuck, he seemed more concerned that Shada get psychological counseling than legal help. A divorce was in the works, and his commitment remained Project Round Up. Nothing could have driven home the importance of that work more than seeing a teenage girl reunited with her family after months of the Dark's psychological abuse. The bomb strapped to her body had been real, and she was still looking at long-term therapy, but one life had already been saved. Jamal's uncle had played a big role in that rescue, even if her fears and brainwashing did drive her back to the Dark after Hassan had been hospitalized. Jack felt like he still owed him an apology for harboring those initial suspicions about him.

"You have arrived at your destination."

The tiny village of Lidice dates back to the fourteenth century, and by the late nineteenth century it was a busy mining village in the rolling hills of the Bohemia region. The old village was destroyed during World War II, and the new village sits near the original town site, about ten miles west of Prague. Much of the thirty-minute drive is on divided expressways, two lanes in each direction, a far cry from the roads traveled by the Nazis on their way to Prague.

Jack's grandfather had few possessions at the time of his death, and the most important provisions of his will dealt with the disposition of his remains. The instructions—worded more like a request—were to find a woman named Eliška Sokol in Lidice, who would know exactly where to spread the ashes. She wasn't hard to find. Lidice has fewer than five hundred residents, and Eliška had lived in the same house since the complete rebuilding of the village after the war.

Jack knocked on the door. He had phoned ahead so that Eliška would expect him, and she answered the door herself. She was as he had imagined her on the telephone, frail and walking with a cane, but she had a bright and determined look in her eyes. She had to be in her late eighties, perhaps ninety. Her English was passable.

"You look just like Joseph," she said.

"I've heard that from others," Jack said, and he appreciated hearing it again.

Eliška apologized for being out of coffee, but Jack wanted to get to the spot anyway. He helped her on with her coat, and Andie gave her the front seat of their little rental car. It was a short ride to the site of the original village—now a memorial.

Mention of Lidice in Grandpa's will had naturally prompted Jack to research it. It was the same piece of history that Grandpa Swyteck had shared with Andie in one of the last lucid moments in his life, while Jack was in London. Andie hadn't told him until after the funeral, and Jack was moved to hear that his grandfather's words had come back to her in the depths of her own torture, maybe even helped her survive at a time when every second mattered. It made the trip as important to her as it was to Jack.

They both knew the horrific story, but Jack let Eliška tell it in the voice of someone who had been there.

"After Nazis invade our country," she said, her English less than perfect, "the Reich Protector of Bohemia was SS Obergruppenführer Reinhard Heydrich. Second in command to Himmler in the SS branch responsible for the Final Solution."

"A worthy target for assassination," said Jack.

"Yes," said Eliška. "The resistance thought same. They organized in London and pulled it off. Then the nightmare comes. Nazis search everywhere for assassins. Finally, Berlin say the assassins were aided by two families in Lidice." Eliška paused, and her gaze drifted toward the passenger's-side window, toward the snow-covered acres of the memorial. "The punishment was decided by Adolf Hitler himself."

She stopped and breathed deeply, and Jack wasn't sure if she wanted to continue or not. When she seemed ready, Jack came around to help Eliška out of the car.

Theirs was the only vehicle in the parking lot. The snow had stopped falling, but the surrounding hills were covered with a fresh white blanket. Eliška walked to the far end of the lot. With Andie at his side, Jack guided Eliška by the arm, but he let her take the last few steps on her own, sensing that she wanted to be alone for a moment. She stopped in front of a large bronze memorial. It was covered with snow, and in the late-afternoon shadows Jack couldn't tell exactly what it was from this distance. But in the cold breeze, he could almost feel the history.

Eliška continued in an old voice that shook.

"Nine June, 1942," she said. "Close to midnight. Nazis close all roads to Lidice. No way in or out of town. The Gestapo go house to house. They search everywhere. They push families out into streets and loot their homes. Men are taken to the Horak family barn. Biggest building in the village. Women and children are herded into the school building. Then, at five o'clock in the morning, the shooting starts."

Eliška lowered her head, as if she'd said as much as she could say. Jack knew the rest from his research. All the men were shot dead by a firing squad. The children were taken from their mothers and, except for those selected for reeducation in German families and babies under one year of age, were poisoned by exhaust gas in specially adapted vehicles in the Nazi extermination camp at Chełmno upon Nerr in Poland. The women were sent to Ravensbrück concentration camp, which usually meant quick or lingering death for the inmates. The town was burned to the ground. Even its cemeteries were destroyed.

"These are the children," said Eliška.

Jack and Andie came to her side, and now he could see through the blanket of snow and shadows. Eighty-nine bronze children were looking back at him. Eliška's hand was shaking as she handed him a card. It was a list of names and dates. Two names were circled for him. *Petrak, Miloslav: 1931. Petrak, Zdenek: 1933.*

"They were nine and eleven when they were gassed," she said.

The thought sent chills down Jack's spine. "Is that the same Petrak that runs in my family?"

"Petrak is common name," said Eliška. "But in 1942, it was very dangerous name."

"Why?" asked Jack. But the moment he said it, he remembered Andie's research on General Petrak, the leader in exile of the Czech resistance.

"Nazis knew General Petrak helped with assassination. No need to prove relations to be guilty."

Jack's gaze swept the memorial. Children of all ages, from one to seventeen. He was drawn to two, in particular, that looked to be the figures of boys aged nine and eleven.

"That way," said Eliška, "about two hundred meters. That is your grandfather's spot."

Jack didn't move. He still didn't understand. "How do you mean, 'his spot'?"

"It was a barn. I met Joseph there. Eight of us, in hiding. Joseph was with his mother."

"Petrak was her maiden name," said Jack.

"Yes. One week before massacre, we all hear it not safe to stay in Lidice. Not safe for Jews. Not safe for a Petrak. We leave in time."

It finally made sense. "My grandfather got confused at the end. He told me he was Jewish."

She smiled sadly. "He was," she said, "and I was a Petrak. Now go. Go and do your grandfather's wishes."

Andie urged him forward with her eyes, as if to say this was his moment.

The sculpture overlooked a valley, and the walk to the spot was entirely downhill. But it didn't make it any easier for Jack. As he trudged through the snow, he was thinking of his grandfather. He was thinking of his friend Neil, too.

He stopped exactly where Eliška had told him to stop. A wisp of wind grabbed the fresh snow and covered his shoes with powder. He dug the canister from his coat pocket and removed the top.

"I'm a Petrak," he said as he released some of the ashes into the wind. Then he remembered Neil's family name before fear of the Nazis had changed it to Goderich.

"And I'm a Goldsmith," he said, watching the remaining ashes scatter.

Acknowledgments

My sincere *thank you* . . .

To my editor, Sally Kim; my agent, Richard Pine; and Sally's editorial assistant, Maya Ziv, who did a great job shepherding my eighteenth novel through production while Sally was on maternity leave. Olive will be in high school by the time I write another eighteen novels, and I guess her mother should hear this now: It will fly.

To Janis Koch (aka "Conan the Grammarian"), who is fighting to save the world from misspellings and bad grammar, one book at a time. (Don't get her started on the impact of texting on the English language.) The errors that remain in *Afraid of the Dark* are all mine.

To Kevin Smith—inventor, scientist, and your basic all-around genius who could write a book on creative solutions for suspense writers who have painted themselves into a technological corner. Who knew what cool things you could do with aluminum foil?

To my sister, Roberta Hall, for the genealogical legwork that led me to our "Petrak" ancestors in Bohemia, and to the Muzeum Památníku Lidice, for the wealth of information on the sad history of Lidice and the Lidice Memorial.

Finally, to my wife, Tiffany. I'd be afraid of much more than the dark without you in my life.

JMG
May 20, 2010